He was a soldier, and he refused to believe in ghosts!

Jeremy placed Alicen in her own bed as Ned stood in the chamber doorway, face blank. The boy clutched his stomach, looking pale and sick himself.

Sensing his difficulty, Jeremy moved closer and grasped Ned's shoulder. "How does she treat head injuries?" he asked quietly.

"I, I'm uncertain." The boy's chin quivered, and his eyes filled with tears.

Jeremy smiled, though his stomach knotted with worry that the apprentice would be useless. "Think, lad. You must have seen her attend such maladies. What does she do?"

Soak a cloth in cold water and place it on the injury.

The voice filled Jeremy's head just as Ned blurted out, "She, uhm, she uses cloths soaked in cold water."

Jeremy blinked, then asked the boy, "Where does she place them?"

"On the injury."

As I said.

Soldiers' lives depended on awareness of everything around them, and Jeremy knew the only woman in the room was insensate. The voice was not Alicen's, yet it wasn't unfamiliar.

You see an enemy where none exists...

Nay! He refused to believe he heard Kaitlyn O'Rourke's voice in his mind. The only thing he knew was that Alicen needed care.

He turned to Ned. "Fetch what we'll need. I'll make her more comfortable."

To my family:
Thanks for helping me become
the person I am. I love you all.

A War of Hearts

***

Laurie Carroll

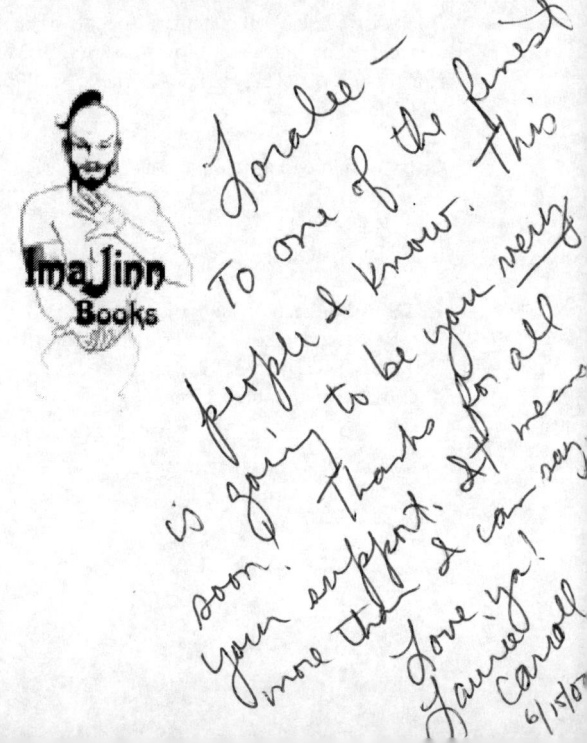

The sale of this book without its cover is unauthorized. If you purchased this book without a cover, you should be aware that it was reported to the publisher as "unsold and destroyed." Neither the author nor the publisher has received payment for the sale of this "stripped book."

A WAR OF HEARTS
Published by ImaJinn Books, a division of ImaJinn

Copyright ©2002 by Laurie Kuna
All rights reserved. No part of this book may be reproduced in any form or by any means (electronic, mechanical, photocopying, recording, or otherwise) without prior written permission of both the copyright holder and the above publisher of this book, except by a reviewer, who may quote brief passages in a review. For information, address: ImaJinn Books, a division of ImaJinn, P.O. Box 162, Hickory Corners, MI 49060-0162; or call toll free 1-877-625-3592.

ISBN: 1-893896-80-3

10 9 8 7 6 5 4 3 2 1

PUBLISHER'S NOTE:
This book is a work of fiction. Names, characters, places and incidents are products of the author's imagination or are used fictitiously. Any resemblance to actual events or locales or persons, living or dead, is entirely coincidental.

Books are available at quantity discounts when used to promote products or services. For information please write to: Marketing Division, ImaJinn Books, P.O. Box 162, Hickory Corners, MI 49060-0162, or call toll free 1-877-625-3592.

Cover design by Patricia Lazarus

ImaJinn Books, a division of ImaJinn
P.O. Box 162, Hickory Corners, MI 49060-0162
Toll Free: 1-877-625-3592
http://www.imajinnbooks.com

One

The north of England, 1425

"Close ranks," shouted Sir Jeremy Blaine. "Surround the duke!"

He could hear little else but the clash of steel on steel as the thunderous din of battle surrounded him. Coupled with the grunt of horses and the cries of cursing men locked in desperate combat, the metallic clang of blades filled his ears like gale force winds. As the battle raged, the volume rose until the gale was primarily comprised of the screams of dying men and their doomed mounts.

The Bastard's men must not escape, Jeremy thought grimly as he hacked his way through the crush of mounted combatants to regain his liege lord's side. No time to lament the butchery taking place all around. Duty demanded he spill enemy blood—and perhaps his own— to defend his lord.

He had reluctantly agreed with Duke William of Tynan that an escort of fourteen men would be sufficient for this trip into disputed land. Now that twenty-five mounted enemy retainers surrounded them and cut off any escape, Jeremy rued that acquiescence.

In his nostrils, the earthy odor of a woods in late summer gave way to brassy smells of sweat and gore.

"Ranks closed," Jeremy roared again, shutting his mind to the grisly image of those who fell to his blade, oblivious to their sounds of agony. William's troops would triumph or perish. There was no alternative. Resolved not to die without taking as many enemies along as possible, he girded his battle-weary heart against despair and let his lethal sword arm perform his will.

Pivoting his mount, he warded off a wicked thrust, then cursed as another foe's blade slashed him just above the steel couter protecting his left elbow. His chain mail stopped the blow, but the impact numbed his arm.

"Jesu," he hissed between tight lips. Pain lent fury to

his strength, and he dispatched both adversaries quickly, then spurred his horse forward to down another and another.

Jeremy had been taught at an early age to lead by example. Thus, he attacked ferociously, relentlessly, knowing the battle-hardened veterans who fought at his back needed but a nudge to respond. His tenacity was quickly rewarded.

"For William!" came their cry.

The bloodlust in his troops' counterattack swayed the fight to Duke William's favor as they broke the enemy's ranks and went on the offensive. Several of their foes rode for the shelter of dusk-darkened woods.

"Stop them! Let none escape." Jeremy motioned with his sword after the fleeing enemy.

He readied to follow, but a pained cry from behind him drew his attention. Turning in his saddle, he saw William topple to the ground, a crossbow bolt deep in his chest.

"Christ's guts!" Jeremy rounded on his second in command. "Taft, inform the pursuit."

As Jeremy slid from his charger and knelt beside the duke, Lieutenant Taft's piercing whistle called a soldier over. Jeremy heard Taft's orders to the man to meet them at the rendezvous point.

"Yes, Lieutenant!" the soldier answered before spurring off after his comrades in pursuit of their enemies.

Jeremy carefully removed William's helmet. "My lord?" Seeing William wished to speak but could barely draw breath, Jeremy leaned down close to him.

"The wound is deep," the duke whispered. "I fear it may be fatal."

Though Jeremy's throat tightened, he kept his voice calm. "Sherford is nigh, milord. 'Tis certain to have a healer."

"He'd best be a man of considerable skills—" Spasms of pain throttled the rest of William's words.

"Speak not," Jeremy cautioned before glancing back at Taft. "Finding a cart will take too long. Help me get him mounted. We'll lash him on."

He did not finish his thought that William would tumble from the saddle otherwise, but his lieutenant's bleak look told him his fears were understood. Of course Taft would understand—only two men knew Jeremy Blaine better than Michael Taft did.

One of the two was dying before them.

"Assist me here."

Three soldiers helped Jeremy lift their now unconscious commander into his saddle, securing him to the high cantle with sword belts and tying his feet to the stirrups. Jeremy surveyed their handiwork. William slumped forward but would not fall off.

"Get the wounded ahorse and form ranks," he directed tersely, grabbing William's reins. He fervently wished it were he instead of his lord who'd taken the ill-fated quarrel. "Light torches."

The moment every man was astride a mount, Jeremy set spurs to his destrier's flanks, and they raced toward the nearby town.

***

Word of the battle must have preceded his company's arrival, Jeremy mused as the troop rode into Sherford a quarter hour later. The soldiers found only abandoned streets and barred doors, effectively keeping them out.

Jeremy had started to rein his destrier toward the houses.

"At Landeyda dwells the best healer in these parts."

Jeremy heard the voice clearly, but a glance at Taft assured him his subordinate was looking away from him.

"The Kent holding. Follow the Great Road south a quarter league. 'Tis twenty rods back. Look for the gate. Hurry!"

Acting purely on instinct, Jeremy wheeled his mount back toward the road and, still leading William's horse, pounded southward. "Follow me!"

His men hesitated only a moment before obeying him.

***

Alicen Kent looked up from sorting herbs at the long counter in the main room of her home. She cocked her head and frowned.

Odd. It sounded as though horses approached from the north. That many horses could only mean...soldiers. Her mouth went dry, her hand automatically reaching for the amulet she never removed from around her neck.

Orrick! Sweet Jesu, have they come for him? What mischief was now afoot?

At the sound of a door closing off the main chamber, she spun from the hearth, hand clutching her throat.

Her eleven-year-old apprentice entered from the infirmary.

By concentrating hard, Alicen kept her fear from her voice. "Ned, bar the door. Riders abroad."

The towheaded boy's forehead wrinkled in concentration. "I hear no—" Just then the troop clattered into the yard. Ned blanched. "Who could it be?"

"We'll know anon," Alicen replied, hoping she sounded at ease so as not to upset Ned. Her heart thundered like a smith's hammer as she opened the square-cut wicket in the heavy door and peered out.

Two blazing torches in the courtyard, aided by a rising full moon, revealed nearly a dozen men. Their steel helmets glinted dully in the meager light, but they wore no discernable insignia on their tunics. One large, powerful-looking rider dismounted and approached her door. As she watched, a searing memory of premonition struck Alicen's mind, stunning her with realization.

'Tis he. The man who will change my life.

She shivered from the force of her certainty and unwittingly stepped back a pace.

"Ned, where is Orrick?" she whispered harshly. "He's not about the grounds, is he?"

The boy blinked. "Nay. I've not seen him in days. He's not due to visit for a fortnight, I imagine."

Alicen nearly slumped in relief, but that moment, the door shuddered from a forceful blow.

"Open in the name of the duke!" a man's powerful baritone demanded, then Alicen heard him mutter, "Pray God this man Kent is home and not away treating some illness." When she opened the door, he said tersely, "We seek the physician by name of Kent. Is he here?"

Alicen found herself looking up to meet the soldier's gaze, something she rarely did owing to her own height. Even in the half-light, she could see his determined expression. Misgivings again assailed her. Did he intend to raze the house?

Nay, he'd have attacked, not knocked, answered her

mother's soothing voice—a voice she knew none other than she could hear. *He seeks a physician. Searching out deserters is not his concern.*

Alicen swallowed hard and forced her voice to belie her fear. "I'm Alicen Kent, the physician."

"Christ's guts," the soldier exclaimed, the dim hope in his expression dying to frustration. "You? You're a wench!"

Alicen knew that in the dim light none could see her flush, but she hoped the soldiers also couldn't see the uptilting of her chin or the tightening of her jaw.

"Observant," she returned stiffly. "What act of war brings you to my home this eventide?" She looked past him to his men.

Whatever fear his size may have instilled in her had melted from the heat of affront, and the knight hesitated, grumbling, "Damn my misbegotten luck. A woman." He pinned her with an intense stare, tone accusing. "A villager claimed you Sherford's best healer. Yet you're not more than eight years and ten."

Such animosity in a stranger immediately replaced Alicen's ire with caution. His presence held danger, of that she had no doubt. She smelled sweat and dirt on the knight's clothing, but the brassy stench of blood that permeated the air around him nearly blotted out those smells.

"One and twenty, in truth," she remarked steadily, "but why should that—"

"We need your aid, though I'm loath to put lives into female hands," he cut in. "I've no time to find another healer."

She gasped, flushing more deeply. "Do you wish my help or no?"

"Bring him in," the knight called over his shoulder. "We were ambushed on the eastern road. The duke—"

Alicen caught sight of two burly soldiers dragging a man between them. Even in the dimness, she saw he bled profusely.

"Jesu be merciful," she cried, slipping past the broad-shouldered warrior blocking her way to help support the victim. "Have a care!"

"Jeremy," William groaned.

"Here, Your Grace," he replied, leaning down to speak into William's ear. "Save your strength." He turned to bark orders. "You four, search this cottage. The rest, the grounds. Detain for questioning anyone you find."

Alicen started, gaping momentarily at the menacing knight before motioning William's bearers forward. "Ned will guide you to the infirmary." She shot the knight another look before adding, "He's the only other person on the estate."

Praying silently that she hadn't lied, she strode to her medicament cupboard. After selecting several jars and loading them onto a tray, she added four steel instruments and bandages, then hurried into the small infirmary just off the main room.

"I'll put the kettle to boil," Ned said, passing her as he moved to the hearth. He cast a fearful glance at the soldiers now overrunning the cottage.

With an effort, Alicen ignored them. "Good. Bring the brazier, candles, rush lamps...I'll need a good deal of light."

Suspicious in spite of her seeming competence, Jeremy followed on the woman's heels. His jaw tightened. A woman healer! Fleeting memories of long ago advice crowded in atop his doubts—"Trust no woman, my son. Lie with her and to her, but never, *never* trust her."

His father had proven a sage in the past. Jeremy's own experience was proof of that.

A darker image assailed him. The memory of a healer's abode with shelves of medicaments much like this one's. And Estelle, *his wife,* lying in an ever-widening pool of her own blood. As much blood as shed in battle, seeping from between her thighs, soaking the linens and the table she lay upon, the floor beneath. Her brown eyes wide and sightless, her mouth a rictus of a tortured smile...

On a shudder of remembered horror, he pulled his mind back to the present. He'd watch this purported healer's every action. If she tried anything amiss, she would regret it.

Apparently unaware of his scrutiny, Alicen Kent set to work. He watched her economically efficient movements as she stripped off William's cloak and cut away his tunic, then severed the buckles holding his steel cuirass in place. She looked at William's face then jerked back, startled.

With a stifled gasp, she looked at Jeremy.

"This isn't Duke Harold." The knight became suddenly very tense and very still as he watched her stiffen. "William."

"Aye. The true duke comes to reclaim his land from the bastard usurper."

His words froze Alicen's soul, and her hand flew to her amulet. Three years before, William's bastard brother, Harold of Stanhope, had routed William's retainers to capture the shire. Sherford had burned, citizens had died...Her friends, her mother.

She shrank from images of remembered horror and tried to concentrate. A patient lay gravely wounded. He needed her. She'd sworn an oath. *Mother, guide me.* It required a deep breath to help her steady her abruptly shaking hands and resume working.

After breaking off the arrow a handsbreadth from the steel breastplate, she began to carefully remove the armor.

Her patient moaned.

"Mind what you do," the knight snapped, stepping close to loom over her. "You bring him pain."

"There's little else he'll feel for a time, I fear," she responded without looking up. She lifted the blood-soaked mail from William's chest. "Ned, more bandages."

The apprentice hurried to bring them while she moved the shaft slightly to test its depth.

William moaned again.

Suddenly, Alicen found her wrist trapped in a powerful grip. "Desist," the knight growled. "'Tis unnecessary torture."

She could feel her eyes blazing as she glared at him. "Get out of my way and allow me to work, or leave with this soon to be corpse! You meddle as he loses precious blood. Trust me, or he has no hope for the morrow." She jerked free from Jeremy's grasp and looked to her assistant, who stood gaping. "Fetch water and put the blades in the coals, Ned." She gave the knight her back while he stood fuming.

Gruesome memories fought with reason, and Jeremy was powerless to overcome his abhorrence of women healers. But he was also desperate. Their surgeon had not accompanied them, and none in his troop had knowledge enough to treat such a grave injury. He silently damned himself for not being between William and that crossbow bolt. Then he silently damned all women. *Good for naught else but to take one's ease upon.*

Of the three narrow beds in the chamber, he chose the one beside William's—near enough to observe all the wench did. He sat, testily fingering his jeweled dagger. If her actions warranted it, he would have to kill her.

No sooner had he entertained this thought then the jewels in the dagger's hilt seemed to burn intensely. With a strangled cry of pain and startlement, Jeremy dropped the weapon from scorched fingers. It skidded across the floor and came to rest under William's cot.

Concentrating on her patient, Alicen was only vaguely aware that the duke's henchman had encountered some sort of difficulty. It would have to wait. William lay pale and silent. Bright red froth bubbled from the wound with his every labored breath; flecks of red clung to lips and nostrils. He'd lost a dangerous amount of blood, and the hard ride might have shocked him beyond recovery. A lump of fear lodged in her heart. It would take all her skill—and vast luck—to see him through.

Remove the bolt from the back, Alicen, her mother's voice instructed.

Glancing at Ned, waiting nearby, she said, "Hold his shoulders down while I push the quarrel through."

"You'll make the wound more deadly," Jeremy cried as he leapt to his feet. "Leave it!"

She gave him a look that would have frozen the sun, then pushed the shaft out the duke's back.

William's groan galvanized his captain. Livid, Jeremy grasped Alicen's shoulder and yanked her around to face him. "I told you to leave it."

His menacing countenance almost made her step back. Instead, she hid her fear with effrontery and snapped, "I thought you a killer, not a healer." Taking advantage of the shock she saw in his eyes, she pushed away from him and bent to resume her task. She stanched the flowing blood, stating in a wintry tone, "Iron barbs poison if left in the body. Especially the lung." Methodically, she exchanged clean bandages for bloody ones. "The more poison, the less hope of recovery. Had I pulled the shaft back and the head detached, removing it would be fatal." She scowled at her nemesis. "Comprehend now, *squire*? If so, get out of my light!"

Alicen's greatest problem was closing the holes she'd just widened in William's lung before it collapsed. Worse, internal hemorrhaging could drown him in his own blood. She packed two wads of bandages into the wounds and checked her instruments.

Then she turned to the soldier. "I could use your assistance. When his brow raised in question, she explained, "'Twill go better for him if he's completely still when I cauterize the wounds. Ned is too small to hold him."

"Tell me what I must do."

Once she had the soldier positioned correctly, Alicen turned to Ned. "When I give the word, remove the bandages." She lifted a red hot blade from the coals. "Now."

As soon as the boy pulled away the wadding, she cauterized the wound. William jerked once, but his powerful captain easily restrained him.

Jeremy clenched his fists as the stench of burning flesh filled the room. The death smells from the most recent carnage assaulted him, bringing suppressed battle visions. The pounding blows on his shield and blade, the sting of sweat in his eyes, the screams of the wounded and dying all around him...

He shuddered, then recalled his circumstance. His current battle involved painful experience with a female healer, and he had to bury the past and think only of the present. This Alicen Kent woman knew well how to treat a grievous wound, but admitting so pained him nearly as much as remembrance of the fight which had led to his being in her home.

Alicen returned the instrument to the brazier before examining her handiwork. The bleeding had stopped, at least temporarily. She daubed the burn with salve and covered it with a fresh dressing.

"Now the back."

Once they'd treated the wounds, they carefully laid William down. Several bolsters assured his head lay higher than his heart. She checked his breathing.

"How is he?" came Jeremy's brusque question. Tension radiated in his tone.

Alicen started, having temporarily forgotten her unwanted guest. "The lung fills, but his heart is far weaker than I would like." She shrugged. "Now we wait and pray for the best."

She knew that, though the duke had survived the worst of this ordeal, his contracting pleurisy still posed a very real danger. The gravity of the wound bespoke the possibility. This thought, and the presence of his henchman, did naught to raise her hopes. She straightened, stretched, and turned to leave.

"Where do you go?" the soldier demanded immediately.

"That's none of your concern, Lieutenant."

Large and foreboding, he took an intimidating step toward her. "It *is* my concern. And I'm *Captain* Sir Jeremy Blaine!"

"Rank notwithstanding, you've no right to detain me." She tossed her head in defiance.

"I'll do what I think best for my lord," Jeremy retorted. "And I think it best you remain to care for him."

"I've done all I am able to. Ned will watch him while I tend the other men's injuries."

Flushing, the captain snarled, "Careful, wench! Your arrogance will cost your life if the duke dies."

Instinctively Alicen recoiled. Her premonition returned, accompanied by intense fear, and breathing turned difficult. But pride intervened. She'd not allow him to browbeat her. She forced herself to stare boldly into his hostile blue eyes.

"It won't be my arrogance that kills him. If he dies, 'twill be part because the wound was too grave and part because you've handled him too carelessly." She straightened her shoulders. "Threaten your men all you wish, *Sir Squire,* but I'm not one of your lackeys." She glanced at her apprentice. "Fetch me if there's any change." With that, she departed.

***

Jeremy stood with fists clenched and jaw tight. "You should be flogged for your impertinence, wench." Glaring at her young assistant, he regained his bedside seat to do what that wretched woman should have done—watch over his duke.

***

Shortly before dawn Alicen finished treating the seriously wounded men and then made her way back to the cottage. Two had died, but the others would survive to kill again. She had determined that the minor wounds, most of them hastily bandaged after the ambush, could wait until daylight for proper treatment.

"How can such cruelty exist?" she asked herself yet again, numbed by the pain men inflicted on each other. The threat of destruction had returned. William would fight to reclaim his lands, and many innocent people would die.

Could she protect those she loved, this time? Memory lashed her—desperation and futility—but she fought off despair. Her duty was to heal, not to bemoan human folly. She would check Duke William, then take refuge in sleep. If her mind allowed, the destruction she'd seen and the destruction she foresaw would momentarily disappear.

Slipping into the infirmary, she found Ned asleep on the bed next to William's. She gently pulled a blanket over the boy, then assessed the duke's condition. He rested quietly, and it pleased her to note his unlabored—though shallow—breathing. No blood appeared on his lips or in his nostrils.

A good sign, her mother assured her. *Seek your own rest. You've need of it.*

"As soon as I finish here," Alicen whispered in response. After adjusting William's pillows, Alicen turned to leave.

And ran right into Jeremy Blaine's hard chest.

Jumping back, she stifled an alarmed cry.

"Now, where do you wander?" Hard eyes glittered in the dim light of two candles.

"To bed."

"William needs you here."

"He sleeps. I can do naught more for him at present." She tried to step past, but the knight caught her arm in a hard grip, effectively halting her departure.

"Stay here," he said, voice flat. "Sleep beside the boy."

"I'll sleep where I please, my lord squire." She gasped when his grip tightened.

"You'll do as I say! I'll not allow you to seduce one of my men and then cry rape."

Enraged beyond good sense, Alicen slapped the knight's face with enough force to numb her palm.

"Despicable cur," she hissed. "You bring carnage to my door, threaten me, then call me whore? Are all William's minions so loathsome?"

"I'm a peer of the realm!"

"You're a cold-hearted mon—"

The last thread of Jeremy's patience snapped. Of its own volition, his hand snaked out to grasp her throat, squeezing slightly. He watched her green eyes go wide with panic. Strands of silky chestnut hair had come loose from her chignon to be trapped beneath his fingers. Her neck felt slender and fragile, the mad racing of her pulse emphasizing her vulnerability. With very little effort he could end her life. But killing a woman held no honor. Despite his earlier vow and the threats he'd made, he could never slay her. Nay, not even hurt her. Yet her fear gave him advantage. For now, he'd use that.

"Concern yourself with William's health, wench, not with what you think me to be."

"Release me this instant," she choked out, pulling ineffectively at his fingers in an effort to loosen his grip.

This show of courage gave him pause. "I'll release you when—"

The hair on the back of his neck prickled as he sensed another presence in the room, though he heard nothing. He had just begun to turn and face whoever it was when motion from the second bed surprised him. Ned, with an angry yelp, abruptly hurled himself at Jeremy. The boy collided with the man's shoulder and managed to cling there like a limpet.

"Stop hurting her," he cried, his youthful voice cracking. He swung at the knight but slipped without landing the blow and started to fall to the floor. "Leave her be!"

Jeremy stumbled only a step, but in trying to ward off the lad he released the mistress. Recovering his balance, he swung his arm and brushed Ned off. But just as he stepped toward the boy, he heard movement behind him. He turned in time to catch two pounding fists full on the chest. Amazed at the woman's daring, Jeremy grabbed her shoulders and held her at arms' length. She fought harder, kicking and struggling until he pulled her tight against his body to still her assault.

They were chest to chest, and beneath the press of her firm breasts he could feel the thunder of her heart as she fought his hold. He felt the amulet she wore grow warm where it was pressed between their bodies. The smell of herbs and mint filled his nostrils, and he was suddenly painfully aware of his reaction to her in the region below his waist.

"Don't harm him," she cried, voice strangled with rage and her efforts to escape. "He's a child! A true knight would never harm a child."

Her statement pricked Jeremy's conscience. This, and the knowledge that he held a spirited woman but could not act on his sudden desire, frustrated him enough to shake her once, hard.

"Cease this!" he ordered.

But worry for Ned's welfare had driven Alicen beyond reason. "Harm him and I—I'll kill the duke."

Her adversary went completely still. "Nay! You'd not dare, if you value living."

Voice shaking, she nevertheless met his stare and retorted, "I've done all I can to save him and his men, yet you've brutalized Ned and me. If my best efforts displease you, why should I rue the consequences of my worst?"

"I know your kind," Jeremy taunted, trying to impel her into a foolish move, to show her true intent. "You kill innocent babes, not grown men whose allies could avenge them."

Alicen's jaw tilted up. "You know me not at all. Life is sacred to me. It means so little to you that you'd force the one person who could save your duke into killing him."

Jeremy glanced to the bed where William lay. A look back at the woman told him she was desperate enough to carry out her threat. He swallowed hard. She spoke true—he knew naught of her. And his actions since the melee that had injured William had bordered on madness. Concern for his duke, distrust of women, and apprehension at leaving men's lives in her hands had unnerved him to such a degree that he'd treated her abominably. His total loss of control disgusted him. 'Twas time to regain command of himself and the situation.

His gaze met her stormy green one as he slowly dropped his aggressive posture and lowered his hands.

"As William's retainer, I am honor-bound to treat women with respect," he stated rigidly, noting that she stiffened slightly at his statement. "I regret I've not done so with you." He nodded toward Ned, still sitting on the floor. "See to the boy," he said quietly. "And stay here for what remains of the night. 'Tis unsafe for a woman to be about among soldiers."

"For the woman, or for the soldiers?" Alicen muttered to his broad back as he strode out.

Her words stung, but Jeremy showed no outward sign that he had heard. Mentally he gave himself a shake, yet he couldn't relinquish the feeling that someone else had been in the chamber with them.

He'd seen no one. But he'd not survived years of battle just relying on his eyes to warn him of danger.

Two

"Thank you, miss." The young soldier blushed and bobbed his head as Alicen finished applying salve and a bandage to his right palm. "Seems almost a waste of your time to tend my hand."

Alicen somehow managed a smile, although she felt numb from fatigue. "Nonsense. Blisters like those can easily become infected." She released his hand and glanced around at the interior of her stable. "The seriously wounded have been tended, so there's no reason to neglect any other wounds."

The man bobbed his head again. "Just the same, I thank you."

"You're most welcome."

She stepped out into the late-August day. Pausing near the stable door, she placed both hands on her lower back and stretched, then glanced quickly around. She'd intentionally avoided the volatile Captain Blaine for most of the day, and he was nowhere in sight at that moment. But now she had to check on her most important patient, and 'twas certain the knight would be by William's side.

What's to come of us with the rightful duke here? she thought bleakly.

Only time could answer that question.

***

Sickened by his show of weakness—his battle weariness and inexcusable brutality toward a woman and a boy—Jeremy mastered his self-rebuke through industry. He'd set up a work schedule for the men and penned missives the rest of the morning.

"Taft, send Tom Fairfax to Tynan with these," he said as he left William's side for the first time that day. "This to Warrick, this to the duchess," he indicated, handing over each dispatch.

"What if Guendolen wishes to join William?" Taft asked about the Duchess of Tynan.

"Impossible! Sherford is disputed land. Until we

determine the shire's loyalty, we dare not reveal ourselves. William is too vulnerable." Taft's solemn look confirmed Jeremy's own fears that the duke would die. He'd not admit such to anyone, however. "I've ordered Warrick to keep Guendolen at Tynan. Her presence here would worsen circumstances, either by revealing our present location or giving Harold an opening to attack the court."

He paused to survey the surroundings. Felt a dull ache behind his eyes. Ignored it. "We need more men, Michael, but fetching them could alert the enemy. I fear we've little time before Harold learns of the skirmish."

"He may suspect William was with us, but he'll not presume he's still near Sherford."

"That's my hope. No enemy escaped, but 'tis certain Harold's loyalists hereabout could discover us." His gaze turned to the cottage. "Mayhap the physician herself is an enemy."

Taft shook his head. "'Twould be odd for a traitor to labor as she has since last eventide. Not to treat a foe."

With a shrug, Jeremy countered, "Pretense perhaps? From birth, women are skilled deceivers."

Taft winced at that statement but said only, "Your palfrey's swiftest. Fairfax could cover the ten leagues by dusk and return with Warrick's reply by morn."

"Tell him to mount up. Then set the watch. I wish to see how our wounded fare."

***

Jeremy soon had Landeyda in military order. Two soldiers patrolled the edge of the woods, and three lookouts were posted. The three remaining able-bodied men repaired equipment and saw to the horses. Such arrangements gave Jeremy a modicum of security, a feeling that stayed with him until he re-entered William's room. Then, sight of the tall, slender physician tending the duke brought him a rush of discomfort. The memory of how she had felt in his arms the previous night tormented him.

He noted Alicen's tension when he approached the bed. His shameful behavior toward her made him flush, yet he refused further contrition. He'd acted on his duty, though he felt certain *she* thought his actions unnecessarily harsh...

Jeremy immediately saw no need for false contrition. Alicen neither looked at nor spoke to him, and he thought fleetingly she'd most likely walk right over his body if he obstructed her, so strong was her force of will. Instead of testing that idea, he sat on a stool well out of her path and studied her.

It irritated him to admit she knew what she was about. His men's wounds had been tended skillfully, and the fact William still lived attested to her talent. She had enough medicaments in the jars on her shelves to do the best-stocked apothecary proud. A dark thought assailed him: How many of those jars contained lethal potions?

He closed his mind to that path by continuing his perusal of the room. A single large volume sat on a small table nearby. Having been schooled in Latin, he knew it to be a medical text. So, the wench appeared learned. Odd that she relied so on herbal remedies, then. As far as he knew, the medical school at Salerno did not teach herb healing. Nor did any school on the Continent, for that matter. Only the ancient monastic orders.

And the even more ancient Druids.

Jeremy shivered at the thought, but shrugged it off as mere fancy. Superstition held no sway with him. Fatigue, worry and guilt had combined to distract his mind from duty and send it astray. He returned to observing his nemesis' home.

'Twas plain she was no peasant. Her cottage rested on the foundation of an old Roman villa and was quite large, with three chambers off the main room and a massive central hearth to provide adequate heat. Wainscotted walls of oak clapboards adorned by rich tapestries surrounded him, and each two-light window was of glass. Rugs softened the chamber floors. A coat of arms, flanked by a lyre and a mandore, graced one wall. Apparently, her family held some minor title, and she enjoyed music.

Yet he couldn't bring himself to trust her, no matter her extensive talent. No woman should be a physician. This one was. Her defiant independence horrified his military sensibility. An aura of power radiated from her in an almost tangible force, and Jeremy regarded it as a threat. Ire rose afresh when he recalled her behavior yestereve. Arrogant wench! She acted as though no man could rule her.

Taft's entrance abruptly dispersed Jeremy's irate musings, and his attention shifted to his subordinate before quickly returning to the woman. Finished with her duties, Alicen slipped quietly past the junior officer and out the infirmary door. Turning his attention back to Taft, he noticed his lieutenant's grin.

"She's a brilliant healer."

Jeremy snorted in disgust. "Last eve she did exactly as she pleased, refusing to take orders from a superior."

Taft's brows rose. "*Women* should obey your every order?"

"William's life is at risk," Jeremy snapped. "I am responsible for protecting him in any manner necessary."

"This Kent woman must feel she's not under your command, not being a soldier and all," the lieutenant retorted wryly.

Jeremy ignored his subordinate's comment. "Her presumption could endanger all our lives."

"And she'd have to work harder to tend the wounded."

"Michael, state your business, then get out."

"All is secure. But I fear the duke is far more at ease than you." A glare brought Taft's hands up in entreaty. "I know you distrust females, but should that taint all Mistress Kent has done for us? She's proven steadfast."

"Nay, she has not," Jeremy stated as he clenched his fists. "Healers have means to kill, and until William is able to ride, I'll trust none but the men I command. Of a certain, I'll not trust some ungoverned virago."

Taft sat down beside the unconscious duke as Blaine departed. "The blind could see that man's misease," he said aloud. "He's more like to ignore a woman, not rail about her. Milord, methinks Sir Jeremy chafes at the debt we all owe Alicen Kent." He leaned over and whispered in William's ear, "Best recover right quick and disabuse him of thinking a debt to a female is worse than death."

***

Though Alicen deeply feared Orrick's unannounced appearance, the next two days passed without incident. William had yet to awaken, but he suffered no fever, and his lungs functioned properly. Rest would build his strength. The soldiers were mending nicely and, while she hated the danger their presence created, they had made Landeyda a well-organized encampment.

Four of the ancient villa's stone outbuildings had fallen into disrepair over the centuries. The men removed the rubble and rethatched the roofs, quickly transforming them into useable structures. As of old, the separate kitchen again smelled of cooking fat and wood smoke. The large stable—which housed just two horses, a dozen chickens, and a cow—became the soldiers' quarters and infirmary. On their captain's orders, men busily repaired the stone wall surrounding the grounds.

Regardless of the restoration of her home, however, Alicen wished them all gone. They posed too dire a threat. How could she explain Landeyda's improvements? And if Orrick discovered their presence, would it push him from the precipice he clung to? She saw no way to prevent his coming there if she did not find him elsewhere. And presently she could not walk ten paces without encountering men-at-arms, their wounds demanding her skill.

Their leader suspecting her loyalty.

One vow, one responsibility she would renounce only at her death—she was honor bound to serve these men regardless of the danger they represented for her. To do any less would be to break the promise sworn to her mother three years prior.

Yet the troop's surly leader made her wish to forsake her vow immediately. In all her life, she'd never been persecuted as she had in the days since Sir Jeremy Blaine arrived. Her skill brought her respect, at times even fear. Blaine seemed obliged to mistrust her for that same talent, and the cause of his hostility escaped her.

Have a care not to provoke his temper, daughter.

Alicen sighed. "I know that well, Mother," she whispered. "Yet I can scarce constrain my temper when he is near...He frightens me nearly witless."

He feels responsible for the duke's injury.

Alicen had no idea how he could believe that, as she'd gathered from the soldiers that the captain had almost single-handedly turned certain defeat into a rout for William's men. *Why punish Ned and me for his guilt? We*

did nothing to cause the battle.
There is more to his ill feelings than mere responsibility for William.

"I gather he resents women healers for some reason," Alicen muttered. "There's little I can do to change that opinion, however. And that's what frightens me."

Are you more frightened of the reaction he causes in you than of the man himself?

Alicen had no answer for that question.

***

The man responsible for Alicen's distress was aware only of the growing list of his men's needs. Having finished inspecting the company's supplies, he and Michael Taft planned strategy.

"Send out hunting and foraging parties today, and purchase provision we can't obtain ourselves. The men will pose as wayfarers. Five horses must be shod. A 'horse peddler' will take them to Sherford's smithy. Now, what about chickens?"

Deep in conversation with his subordinate, Jeremy quickly rounded the corner of the stable.

And met Alicen shoulder to shoulder. The collision sent her sprawling onto her back in the dirt, a basket of freshly gathered herbs flying from her hand.

"Mistress Kent," Taft exclaimed, rushing to her aid.

Completely nonplused by another mishandled encounter with the healer, he stood gaping while Michael helped her up and brushed off her clothes. Then Jeremy broke from his perplexed trance and bent to scoop up the scattered herbs.

"Are you harmed?" he asked gruffly, shoving the basket, now stuffed with broken stems and dirt-covered blossoms, at her.

She contemplated her ruined harvest before giving him a wry smile. "'Twould take more than such a paltry blow to injure me. But your solicitude is touching."

Stung by her scorn, he retorted,"'Twas merely concern you'd be unable to tend the duke."

"Of course." Her eyes glittered. "Naught must interfere with our duties to William."

"Aye." Her boldly defiant gaze irritated him.

"You've been much about his business these past

days." Alicen straightened several of the tangled herbs in the basket.

"There is much to do."

Her smile tightened. "Such as burning all my firewood?"

Jeremy's hard look held hers as he said, "Michael, send men to gather wood. 'Twould not do to have a cold hostess."

He saw the flare of anger in her glinting stare and took satisfaction in knowing he'd put it there.

"Did searching the grounds prove fruitless," she countered, "or do William's enemies lurk hereabouts? Perhaps they lie hidden 'neath straw in the stable?"

"I've checked there," Jeremy retorted, jaw tight.

"Then, as I see no one hanged from a tree, I may assume your effort was wasted." Alicen stared him down, hiding profound relief that Orrick hadn't been found lurking nearby. What had possessed her to mention the stable? Again her temper had overruled her head. *Tread carefully,* she warned herself. *Give him no reason to suspect anything amiss.*

"All in the line of duty."

She watched as his face showed sudden discomfort, but he squared his shoulders as if to shake off the feeling. Doing so made him wince slightly.

This movement drew her gaze to the sleeve of his arming doublet. Noticing a stain, her expression turned to concern. This would distract him from seeking out spies and reaffirm her integrity. She raised both eyebrows.

"Tell me, does duty include suffering, sir?" she asked softly. "Will bearing pain prove your strength and worth?"

He scowled. "What do you mean?"

She nodded toward his arm. "That wound needs tending."

He glanced at his sleeve, then shrugged. "'Tis unimportant. There were and are many more serious wounds to attend." He made to move past her, but she reached out and touched his sleeve.

"'Tis high time your injury was seen to."

"'Tis naught but a bruise, and most likely half healed by now," he growled. "I need none of your infernal concoctions."

She briefly looked heavenward, then touched his sleeve just below the stain, examining it closely. "Your wound is far more serious than you know. It requires immediate care."

"You've not yet seen it," he scoffed, pulling away. "Are you able to discern an injury's severity before viewing it?"

"That stain, and your skin's pallor, indicate infection." She paused before continuing in an indifferent tone. "If 'tis not attended, I fear you'll lack employment, as the duke will likely have little use for a one-armed soldier."

Taft, who had silently observed this exchange, nodded. "The lass is right, Captain. See to yourself."

Jeremy scowled at Taft then glared at Alicen, who continued as if he'd asked her to, "A bruise would have since healed, but it appears this brings you pain. Do I hit the mark?"

His mouth tightened as he gave a slight nod. "Your apprentice may see to this for me."

"'Tis beyond his skills," she replied cooly. "I must tend it myself."

His gaze locked on hers. "Then be quick. I've little desire to be in a woman's company except to taste her charms."

Alicen ignored his deliberate crudeness and motioned toward a nearby oak. "Sit at the table yonder, and we'll begin."

Jeremy stalked to the stone bench beside the indicated table, Alicen at his heels.

"You must remove your doublet and shirt. Even *I* can't heal a completely covered wound."

Jeremy scowled. A quick jerk of his powerful hands drew off the garments.

Corded muscles Alicen couldn't help noticing rippled across his chest. She briefly thought his the most sleekly powerful physique she'd ever seen. And handsome at that. He wore his curly black hair even with his ears on the sides, to his nape in back. High cheekbones, a straight nose, and a strong jaw framed those piercing blue eyes. Black brows and dark lashes emphasized his intense gaze. How could a killer look so perfect?

She contemplated this as Jeremy found his linen shirt

stuck to the wound. He reached to pull the sleeve away, but Alicen placed her hand on his to stop him.

"Don't," she said, quietly emphatic. "You'll tear the flesh by carelessly uncovering the wound."

He sneered, "What difference to you?"

"'Tis needless suffering." She noted his disbelief before she turned to Ned, splitting wood nearby. "Is the water boiling, lad?" He nodded. "Fetch me a panful while I get my instruments and fresh bandages."

Alicen's hand remained atop Jeremy's until she moved to enter the house. In that brief moment, he became acutely aware of her warmth spreading through him, making his skin tingle. Her gentle touch stunned his senses. He didn't realize he'd stopped breathing until she disappeared inside the dwelling, then he inhaled, annoyed. Should the wench charm him from his vigilance, disaster would follow.

He'd never admit to her his arm ached constantly. He'd thought little of the injury since the melee, but now allowed it truly was worse than he pretended. Yet her solicitous manner angered him, made his guilt over William's injuries intensify. God's teeth, he loathed bold women!

In her absence he refortified his defenses against such an event by recalling his seventh summer. His father and eldest brother, Manfred, had returned from campaign with King Henry. Jeremy, out riding that day, saw the soldiers from atop a bluff and went to meet them. Then he raced ahead back to the castle to proclaim their arrival.

Without exception, his father expected his sons to care for their mounts. Eager to give his mother word of Lord Blaine's return, Jeremy thought to ask the stable master to attend his horse. Just this once. He burst without knocking into the man's room at the rear of the livery.

To find his mother abed with the wretch.

Lizbeth Blaine's shock mirrored her son's, but her reaction turned quickly to dread. Jeremy saw the fear in her blue eyes before he turned and raced away...

Remembrance ended there, as he quashed thoughts of the events which followed. Knowing his beloved mother for an adulteress had closed his open, giving heart. Other betrayals had locked the door completely. Now, he had a man's concerns to attend. And no desire to expose his soul to more rending.

Physician and apprentice returned just then carrying an array of supplies. Warily, Jeremy waited. What would this proudly defiant girl do? If she was like the vengeful harpies from his past, he had given her a grand opportunity to harm him. He breathed deeply and clenched his jaw. No matter what torture she inflicted, she'd not enjoy his pain.

***

He expects you to be cruel to him, Alicen. Treat him as you did the wolf you found at the edge of the forest six years back.

I see his reaction, Mother, Alicen thought. *I must needs win the captain's trust, or I'm in danger of being bitten by the beast I seek to help.*

Suspicion glittered in Captain Blaine's eyes. He had proven himself capable of violence, and winning his trust would take great effort. Yet a dark sentiment told her to seek no such thing. She knew what soldiers were about. They did their duty to the exclusion of aught else. This man had power to hurt those she loved, and she'd seen firsthand the consequences of such power. A childhood friend with a shattered mind was only one of those.

Why not repay Blaine in kind for mistreating Ned and her? *Nay! You'll not willingly inflict pain,* Kaitlyn O'Rourke's voice chastened her daughter. *Your talent is healing.*

Alicen briefly closed her eyes. *I'll not betray my calling for vengeance on an arrogant ass, Mother.* She would treat him, as any other patient, with gentle care.

Turning to her task, she soaked a cloth in the steaming water, then removed it with a pair of tongs. After the excess had dripped off, she laid the cloth over Jeremy's sleeve at the point where it adhered to the skin.

His eyes flew wide, but he made no sound. She saw him press his lips into a straight line then suck in a breath and hold it.

"This loosens the fabric and begins to draw the poison," she explained softly. "It won't take long."

Once the cloth cooled, she slowly rolled down the

soiled sleeve. The exposed flesh was a fierce red, hot to the touch. Whitish fluid oozed from a thin cut across the bruise's midline.

She indicated the wound to Ned. "Red portends severe infection that must needs be drained. But first, remove its cause. Hold his arm steady, lad. Then watch and learn."

With a quick, sure motion, she drew her honed steel blade along the path of the cut. Jeremy ground his teeth and locked his jaw while, using a thin probe and forceps, she removed nearly a dozen bits of metal from the gash. By the time she had carefully soaked up the worst of the contagion with a clean bandage, his whole body looked stiff.

Her gaze met his, this time with no hostility. "I must cause more hurt, Captain, but you'll heal better for it."

"Do it, then," Jeremy growled through his teeth. "I'm no stranger to pain."

"'Tis certain you're not."

She squeezed the incision's edges together to force out more fluid. He remained stoic, but his body stayed rigid as she pressed harder, then again cleansed the wound.

"Should I fetch the honey?" Ned asked.

Alicen nodded, smiling at his initiative. "Aye. We must draw the deep infection out."

When Ned returned with the medicament, she poured a goodly amount into the wound, covered the whole with a dressing, and wrapped the arm in a neat bandage.

"This should dry the remaining contagion," she said as she picked up Jeremy's shirt. She paused, momentarily uncertain of how to proceed, then stated, "This garment is too soiled to wear atop an injury. If you have not a clean one, I could wash this."

His brow cocked, but he merely said, "Our cook also tends our clothing. He'll see to it."

She nodded. "Very well. Rest your arm as much as possible today and drink all the water you can manage." With that, she made a sling around his neck, put his arm into it, and turned to gather up her instruments.

The physician's gentle treatment confounded him. He'd expected rancor, yet she'd caused no excessive suffering. Already the poultice was drawing the infection, and his arm felt better. It irked him, though, now to be in her debt for something beyond the duke's life.

Alicen straightened, instruments in hand. "Tonight I'll sew the edges of the incision together."

Jeremy's eyes narrowed. "Sew the wound? Preposterous!"

"Not at all. Persian physicians have done so for centuries. 'Tis like darning a torn garment. Wounds heal faster and with smaller scars when treated thus." The corner of her mouth rose. "Do you fear a little more pain, sir?"

He snorted in contempt. "I fear naught you could do to me, wench."

Amazingly, she chuckled, green eyes twinkling. "'Tis a brave man who can face the unknown so calmly. Very well, tonight I'll finish your treatment."

"Beware of whom you taunt, vixen," he rumbled low as she walked away. "None threaten or make sport of me."

If Alicen Kent heard him, she didn't acknowledge it, and he continued to watch her dignified withdrawal. Rich chestnut hair, held back by a single leather thong at her nape, fell to the middle of her back, covering her plain dress. She was slim but broad shouldered, with a narrow waist and well-rounded hips. And very long legs...

He shook his head to clear his lusty thoughts. Although she obviously disliked him, she'd readily treated his wound, and her careful tending aroused his misgivings. What was her ploy? She defied him. Her hostility cut, then her compassion soothed. More than likely she sought some favor, but he couldn't guess what that could possibly be. He'd have to remain alert to treachery.

***

It was long past dark that night, and the men had settled into their blankets in the stable. Alicen was finishing with the duke's bandages when Jeremy entered the infirmary.

"How does he fare?" the tall captain asked.

She glanced up. "No sign of fever. He should awaken within the next day or so."

A flicker of relief crossed Jeremy's features. "Jesu be

praised."

Staring at his friend and lord, he ran a hand through his hair. William's color was much improved, his breathing shallow yet steady, his bandages unstained. Perhaps he would recover. *Forgive me, my lord, for failing to protect you,* Jeremy silently said. He owed the duke's life to Alicen's considerable skill, and that fact troubled him nearly as much as his guilt over William's wounds. He'd sworn years before never to be beholden to a woman. It rankled to find himself in debt to such as she.

"I'll see to your arm now, Captain."

"What?" He snapped out of his brooding. "Oh, aye."

"Come sit at the table in the main room."

Jeremy removed his tunic while Alicen threaded a needle and set it in a small bowl of steaming water. Then she carefully cleansed away the now sugared honey.

"Here." She offered him a glass of hard cider. "It helps with the pain."

"I'm certain I can bear it."

"Alas, I cannot," she returned, eyes glinting with mischief. She drained the glass in a long swallow. "Shall we finish this?"

The needle's first prick set Jeremy's teeth on edge, but the discomfort was not extreme. He would endure. Soon, he was concentrating on the healer's technique. He studied Alicen's hands setting stitches neatly in his flesh. He recalled how her touch had warmed him that afternoon and, amazed, found himself fascinated. Feminine hands with strong, tapering fingers so dexterous they seemed to possess magic. He studied the dark head bent over her work and smelled the fresh, herbal scent of her hair. His eyes closed, then snapped open.

Ridiculous! He liked naught about her. How could he find her hands of interest, or her scent? Yet he supposed some men would call her a fair-looking wench. Her thick chestnut hair invited his touch, and though he liked women more buxom and rounded, she wasn't an unpleasantly shaped creature.

Bah! She wasn't soft enough. She had a lean muscularity women who aroused his lust lacked. Her body was lithe, her waist narrow. Those he tumbled were soft and fleshy, with bosoms like pillows to nestle his head upon. He doubted this wench's firm breasts would even fill his hands....

He blinked, pulling his thoughts from the path they ranged and returning them to crucial matters. He'd no time to engage in lustful contemplations, especially ones involving Alicen Kent! Duty demanded his complete regard. William lay wounded because of Jeremy's failure. He'd allow himself no further errors.

Within minutes, Alicen had closed the wound with fifteen even stitches and applied a light dressing and bandage. "In a week I'll remove the thread," she stated. "In the meantime, don't o'erstrain yourself by slaughtering too many people." She looked up, concern darkening her eyes. "Is aught amiss, Captain? Didn't I cause enough pain to satisfy you?"

"Where is your husband?" he blurted out.

By her expression he knew the question took her aback, but she didn't falter. Her brows drew together before she responded quietly, "My betrothed died at Harfleur, fighting for King Harry." *At least to me, the battle killed him.* "I'm unwed."

"The boy is not your son?"

"He's a bit old to be mine," she retorted, uncomfortable at the turn of the conversation, afraid she'd have to lie more. "I'm but eight years his senior."

"Is he your brother?"

"Nay. An orphan who has lived with me three years."

"Your father?"

"Dead these five years past."

"No worthy sire allows his daughter to live alone," Jeremy stated bluntly. "With brigands about, 'tis remarkable you've not been attacked."

Recalling Orrick's pitiful vow to guard her, she coldly replied, "I need no man's protection." She started to rise, but Blaine's harsh laugh stopped her.

"Every woman I know depends upon a man. Even those who... trade...need men to survive."

Alicen choked, then planted her fists on the table and leaned toward him. "I am neither whore nor partisan, *Captain*. A fact you seem incapable of believing."

"You are vulnerable living here."

"Nay, I am not!"

"'Tis foolish to think thus. You are isolated, away from the town and at the mercy of any wandering rogue."

"I'm safe here," Alicen insisted, chin tilting up as she straightened. "A freeman works my fields. The town's citizens expect me weekly." She paused, debating whether to continue, then rashly added, "And all who live hereabouts think a powerful spirit protects Landeyda. 'Tis a belief I do naught to dispel."

At her words, Jeremy's jaw dropped. She could almost see his mind working as his eyes scanned the contents of the nearby containers. Almost hear the questions he had about those containers. Poisons? Potions? She suspected he'd seen such before and sensed a prickling fear inside him.

She used his uncertainty. "What troubles you, sir? Afeared of goblins? Dreading I'll turn banshee and suck out your heart as you sleep?" Her chuckle echoed before her mirth faded. "You needn't worry for your safety, or that of your men. 'Tis my mother's spirit said to guard this place." Before she realized, her voice had dropped to a poignant alto. "Every day I seek to fulfill my promises to her."

A silent moment passed, then, mortified at sharing such personal grief with this hostile man, Alicen buried her gloom and raised her gaze to Jeremy's. "I'm pledged to do only good through my healing art. Though some fear my talent, no dark evil dwells here." She sighed. "Mother did much good in the world. A pity few remembered when such memories were needed."

Amazed, Jeremy studied the healer. Alone save for a small boy, she feared no consequence of her vulnerability. Perhaps a spirit truly did protect her...Still, she'd treated his men fairly, and him also. Her actions befuddled him. One minute belligerent, the next solicitous. He saw the familiar mockery once again glinting in her gaze. Her defiance had returned.

"Still suspicious, Captain?"

"I don't claim to understand women," he answered shortly. "When I was very young I thought I did, but I was proven wrong. Since then, I've not bothered to try."

"Life is too short to spend it looking back," she returned with forced lightness as she rose from the bench.

"Some things are better left forgotten."

Her words ring true, he thought as she left. *But sometimes 'tis harder to forget than to bear the pain remembrance brings.*

Three

A tolling bell at dawn the next morning woke Alicen with a sound she'd feared since the soldiers' arrival. Orrick wished to see her. Shaking from far more than a chill, she drew on a cloak against the damp and went out to return his signal. Two tolls, a pause, then two tolls rolled over the countryside. She turned to reenter the cottage but halted when the omnipresent Jeremy Blaine appeared in the doorway. Her breath caught in her chest.

Does that man ever sleep? she wondered, panic rising. She had to brazen this out. The unthinkable could happen if Blaine discovered Orrick.

"What were you doing?" The knight blocked the door with his large frame.

"My services are needed elsewhere," she stated curtly, pushing past him to enter. Before he could respond, she had rushed to her chamber and slammed the door. In moments, she had donned riding clothes from a coffer—sturdy cotton shirt, leather smock and heavy cotton hose preceded thick woolen socks and well-worn boots. Last, she tucked her hair into a chaperon hood and was swiftly back in the main room to gather medicinal supplies in a large leather pouch.

To her relief, Blaine was gone. Bag in hand, she ran to the stable where Ned, also alerted by the bell, had saddled her gelding and stood patiently holding the beast's reins.

The boy looked hopeful. "May I accompany you?"

Reaching out to fondly ruffle his hair, she said gravely, "I think it best you stay here, Ned, as there is much to be done. The duke requires nursing, and I leave you that responsibility."

He beamed. "I'll do my best."

"I know. You always do." She gave him a quick hug, then whispered in his ear, "Not a word to anyone of my destination. 'Tis important this remain a secret. Do you understand?"

He nodded, as serious as she had become. "Yes, Alicen."

Once in her saddle, she saw Blaine leave the two soldiers he'd been speaking to. He strode up to seize her horse's bridle.

"Whence do you ride?"

A shrug conveyed nonchalance she didn't feel. It preceded her terse, "To serve where there's need."

"I want your destination," Jeremy commanded and saw her green eyes flash dark currents of anger.

Brazen it out, Alicen ordered herself. "You've no right to detain me when I must be elsewhere."

"You'll be escorted, then."

Sweet Jesu, no!...Brazen it out. "I'll not bring warriors to Sherford's people," she snapped. "They've known the wanton ruin soldiers perpetrate as amusement." *Orrick in particular.*

By wheeling Hercules, she jerked the reins from the knight's hand, then urged the horse through the gate at a gallop.

"Come back here," he shouted, then rounded on the nearest soldier. "Naismith, follow her no matter where she goes."

"Aye, sir!" The young man leaped into his saddle and thundered out the gate in pursuit of the healer.

Jeremy fisted his hands on his hips. "Impertinent jade," he spat. "You'd have been free had you but told your destination." Nay, not true. She'd have been escorted to keep her from mischief. He glared at another soldier. "How dare she leave with William still abed! Her duty is here. The boy hasn't the skill for this." He stomped inside to check the duke himself.

***

At mid-day, Jeremy beheld a sight that made him burn with bloodlust. Corporal Naismith reined in at the stable. Alone. Incensed, the captain grabbed the hapless man's reins and reached up to yank him from his saddle.

"Where is she?" he snarled, holding Naismith at eye level by a fist grasping the front of the man's doublet.

Naismith's eyes rolled wildly in his head. "I...I lost her, sir," he stammered.

Although his voice was low, the fury in Jeremy's eyes

lanced through his subordinate. "You what?"

"I...lost...her."

"You were to escort a *woman*," Jeremy said tightly, "yet you failed. Explain." To keep from tearing Naismith apart, he clenched his fists.

"She evaded me, Captain," the wretch muttered.

"I can't hear you." Jeremy released the soldier's tunic.

Naismith hung his head at his superior's anger. "She left the road, took a path. I tried to keep sight of her, but...."

"You mean to say that a slip of a wench outrode one of my best men?" Jeremy scoffed. "I cannot fathom it."

"'Tis truth, sir. She rides better than any I've seen, yourself excluded." He kept his gaze lowered. "I searched for her the entire morn."

Jeremy's grip tightened even further on Naismith's tunic. The man was fortunate his clothing and not his throat was beneath Jeremy's hands. He forced his voice to remain level. "You're aware, are you not, of the punishment for disobeying an order?"

"Aye, sir." Naismith's eyes remained focused on the ground and his voice a whisper. "Execution, sir."

"Execution." Tension easing somewhat, Jeremy studied his man. "Knowing what your fate would be, why did you return?"

The young knight swallowed, squared his shoulders, and at last looked directly into Jeremy's eyes. "My duty was to report that Mistress Kent was not under my escort, sir."

Pride in his soldier made Jeremy fight to retain a stern face. Ordering Naismith's death was out of the question—the youngster was far too promising, the situation unusual.

"You understand my position, then," he stated. "By leaving Mistress Kent unescorted, you've given William's enemies the chance to use her as a spy. That lapse must be punished."

"Aye, sir."

"Lieutenant Taft, take this man to the stable and administer fifteen lashes." Before Naismith was led away, Jeremy gave him a look that left no doubt of his captain's respect.

But his ire had not yet abated. As he stoically watched the punishment, simmering rage made him ache with tension. Alicen Kent should be the one whipped. If her skills weren't so badly needed, he'd consider punishing her for such audacity. At the very least, she'd know her exact place while William's troops quartered at Landeyda. He would *not* allow her to do as she pleased.

***

Outwitting the captain's spy raised Alicen's spirits, and she handled Orrick easily. She hated deception, but keeping Orrick safe was paramount. Now, he'd not venture near for a fortnight, giving her time to devise another lie to keep him away. There was no predicting what would happen if he discovered the soldiers. Pray God he remained ignorant of them.

Leaving his hut, she proceeded to Sherford's market. It proved a pleasant day—her first away from Landeyda in a week. Speaking to Orrick allayed some of the fear that he would catch her unaware. And she enjoyed escaping Captain Blaine. His scrutiny of her every action unnerved her.

But her mood darkened when she dismounted at the stable and noted the soldiers standing at attention within. Simultaneously, she saw a man tied to a beam and heard the sound of a lash striking flesh. What devilment was here? When she realized the man she'd eluded was being whipped, fury ignited in her.

She rushed inside, stumbling to a halt in front of Captain Blaine who stood, feet spread and arms crossed over his broad chest, observing the punishment. He motioned Taft to stop the flogging when Alicen rounded on him.

"How dare you do this," she cried. "My property isn't a torture pillory!"

"You're to blame here, woman," Jeremy retorted, glaring.

She gasped, immediately realizing his logic. *Brazen it out.* "I? Whatever did I do?"

He nodded to Naismith. "You evaded your escort this morn."

Alicen's gaze flew to Naismith's blood-striped back. The import of her actions stunned her, but she maintained an air of innocence. "I need no escort. Why provide me one?"

"As a precaution."

"Against what?"

Jeremy stood even straighter. "Word of William's presence here could prove invaluable to his enemies."

Astounded at his conclusion, she laughed in disbelief. "His presence here is still secret."

"Is it?" Jeremy cocked a dark eyebrow. "And do none save we here know his true condition?"

"If others know, 'tis not by my word." That was truth.

"Can that be proven? You've been away all day...alone." He planted his fists on his narrow hips and glared at her.

She refused to fear his intimidating stance. "I'm neutral in this conflict, no matter what you choose to believe."

"Neutral? Why flee my man if you had naught to hide?"

Alicen stared as if he'd gone mad, grinding her teeth to keep from answering his challenge with complete hostility. "Because I could," she stated quietly. "Because I don't betray a trust. Because I cannot work with a guard nearby!" Eyes ablaze, she ground out, "Do my answers satisfy you, *Captain*?"

He gave her his most accusatory scowl. "Your whereabouts remain unaccounted for—I'd hardly call your answers adequate."

"Yet they must suffice, as they're all I'll give." Then outrage overcame wisdom, and she hissed, "Or will you flog me to extract false confession and confirm your errant distrust?"

"I don't flog women," he bit off, ignoring his previous thoughts on that very subject.

"Not even to gain military advantage?"

Her words brought a collective gasp, then the men covered their shock as best they could. Except for some shuffling of feet, the stable was silent.

Jeremy's face flamed. "Understand me well, Mistress. Did I order it, you'd be stripped naked and whipped until you couldn't stand. Perhaps then you'd not question my authority."

Alicen paled but didn't flinch. *You seek quarter I'll*

not give, Captain." She pointed at Naismith. "*That* is barbarity."

Jeremy clenched his jaw until it bulged. "Call me no more. My man bleeds for your insolence."

"A situation I'll remedy anon." Alicen started forward, but Jeremy grabbed her arm.

"You'll not go near him."

She shot him a dark look over her shoulder. "He needs tending."

"He'll have none from you." Hard fingers shackled her arm. "The men will see to him."

Twisting to face him in an attempt at loosening his grip, she cried, "He's suffering."

"And as you caused it, you'll not soothe it."

"Cold-blooded monster!"

"I am a soldier," he grated out, shaking her once. "And discipline is a soldier's credo. No army functions without it."

"Discipline and cruelty are *not* the same things. This is cruelty."

Furious to hear her twist the responsibilities of his position, Jeremy backed Alicen up against a support post, pinning her with his hands curled in the shoulders of her tunic.

Complete silence filled the stable.

Alicen knew instantly her defiance had been a hideous error. Captain Blaine's eyes sparked rage, and his clenched jaw made his neck cords bulge. She felt his white-knuckled hands shaking and thanked God her flesh was not caught beneath the fabric he mangled in each fist. Given his strength and size, he would kill her if he struck her. She had no doubt the blow was coming and could do naught to prevent it. Fear made her knees wobble, and the fight drained from her, just as she knew the color drained from her face.

A sudden chill hit Jeremy, like the bite of falling into a Highland lake in spring. A blast of frigid winter wind that numbed his entire body. Drawing breath grew nigh impossible as the cold pierced him as if a pair of icy arms encircled him, squeezing the air from his lungs. As he struggled to breathe, he saw, before she concealed it, the stark terror on Alicen's ashen face. She appeared ready to faint. Though his hands were stiff and senseless from cold, he felt her legs beginning to buckle.

Christ's guts, what have I done? Appalled, he forced his frozen grip to loosen. He needed to beg forgiveness, but his tight throat choked off speech. Unnerved by Alicen's countenance, he gaped. He had never thought to instill such terror in a female, even one he could not bring himself to trust.

"Fish, Graves," he ordered in a voice on the edge of cracking, "escort Mistress Kent to her cottage."

As the two men moved to flank her, Alicen locked her knees and straightened. Staring straight at Jeremy, voice unwavering, she stated, "I shall thank God on my knees each night that I'm not under your command, sir." Head high, she pushed his hands away, then forced herself not to bolt, instead walking slowly out the door.

Jeremy, still chilled, stood unmoving. He had come within a hairsbreadth of striking Alicen Kent, and his wretched intent sickened him. It had taken every ounce of his strength to keep from hurting her. He felt nauseous.

Ruthlessly clasping his hands behind his back to still their shaking, he throttled his emotions. He would show no doubt. Duty required he maintain discipline. She had defied his command...Yet, she was no soldier. And he'd never menaced a woman, no matter how dark his rage or how just his warrant. He'd not hurt Estelle when she refused his bed after his return from France. Nor his mother or sister-in-law, who took lovers when their husbands were away fighting for the King.

How then to explain his treatment of the healer?

Losing his vaunted self-control horrified him. He owed her William's life! He owed her an apology. Yet in truth, he'd likely have to break down her door to deliver it, and he could ill afford another such breach of propriety. Sweet Jesu, he was weary of strife.

Contemplating his debauchery, he cursed his father's warning against women. And the females in his life who had confirmed the warning. And his office, which dictated he wield authority, no matter who suffered. She'd threatened his power. He'd crushed her resistance.

But knowledge that he'd acted within his right brought him no comfort.

Jeremy's vicious brother Manfred had struck his wife for any imagined offense, thinking that an effective means for governing her. Soon after marrying, his gentle bride became a wraith, cowering in constant fear when he was about. Her terror had disgusted Jeremy. Now he'd caused that same fear in a woman.

All in the line of duty.

Duty without mercy turns men to beasts. What will you be provoked to do next in the name of duty?

He heard the words whispered in his ear, but no one stood close enough to have done so. With that, the chill left him as abruptly as it had come. He stared wildly about, but only his soldiers occupied the stable. This was the second time he'd felt a presence he couldn't see...Bah, 'twas mere fantasy, naught else.

But how could he explain the voice's gender? Alicen was the only woman on the grounds, and she'd not whispered in his ear.

Rounding on his men, who stood staring at him as if he'd grown another head, he snapped, "Cut Naismith down and see to his wounds." He turned to Taft. "I ride to Sherford to seek the lay of things. Double the watch, and don't let that woman touch Naismith or leave the premises. If you need me, send a rider to the inn."

Without another word, Jeremy stalked outside to where his war horse, Charon, stood tethered. He mounted and galloped off toward the village.

He urged Charon to a dead run, trying through sheer speed to outdistance his guilt and frustration. Finally, when Sherford was within sight, he eased his mount back to a walk.

"Good lad," he crooned, patting the stallion's sleek neck. "You've earned your keep for that ride, my friend."

Jeremy had barely noted Sherford on his previous harried visit. Now he observed it closely. Far south of Scotland, its citizens had little to fear from the fierce Douglas clan's raids in Northumberland. Yet Sherford was isolated, and mercenaries and robbers presented constant danger.

The town's plan reflected the need for self-protection. Comprised of burgage plots—thirty feet wide and four hundred feet deep—it had houses at the head and gardens behind. The plot-head houses stood side by side, fronts forming an unbroken wall behind which residents could shelter against danger. The backs of the dwellings opened onto a large, protected commons.

Sherford had approximately fifty houses arranged in a square around the green. Those on the west fronted the market. A flour mill, a bakery and a smithy stood across from the southern frontage. North side residents could view English hills and forests stretching beyond the horizon. The east side faced the Great Road.

Jeremy ruefully thought that under other circumstances he'd appreciate Sherford's beauty. But not today. He'd come to spy and to forget mistreating Alicen Kent. Posing as a wool merchant, he was soon speaking with the citizens and shopkeepers, gathering information on the townsfolk and their loyalties.

***

Alicen hadn't seen Jeremy depart. Once inside her cottage, she leaned weakly against the sturdy door, afraid to walk farther lest she collapse. Only intense effort steadied her breathing and slowed her racing heart. Her hands continued to shake. By forgetting the captain's distrust, she'd nearly gotten injured. Belatedly, she no longer underestimated him. He loathed her, and she abruptly felt helpless and alone. He could have her killed if the whim struck him...

But why? He'd resented her the moment he discovered her to be the physician, and she lived literally at his whim. His authority and suspicion made her position tenuous.

"Alicen?"

Ned's sudden appearance caused her to start in alarm.

"Alicen, what is it?" The boy rushed to her side and seized her hand. "Come sit down. You look faint."

She allowed him to lead her to the table and seat her on the bench, then accepted the mug of tea he thrust into her trembling hands. She managed a few shaky sips.

The boy's dark eyes mirrored his concern. "What happened?" His gaze fixed on her pale face. "Your lips are bloodless."

Seeing the question on his expressive face, she stated, "Captain Blaine threatened me just now."

Ned leaped to his feet. "That whoreson! I'll kill him!"

"You'll do naught of the sort," she said with forced calm, reaching out to restrain him. "Now, sit down."

"But he's *terrified* you." Ned pulled away from her hand.

Her brow arched. "And for that you'd slay him? Even if you succeeded, they'd hang you for murder. Then where would I be?"

"But—"

She sighed. "No arguments, lad. We'll do naught about the incident save put it behind us."

At her grim look, he reluctantly took his seat. "Well...you're likely right," he muttered. "But why did he do it?"

"I'm partially to blame." She gave a brief account of the day's events without articulating her fears.

Ned threw his thin arms around her. "I'll protect you, Alicen. He'll not frighten you again. I give my word."

She hugged him close. "Bless you, lad, but I'll care for myself. And rest more easily if you keep far from his path. Though I'm certain 'tis only I he loathes, I'd rather not try that certainty."

A sudden knock at the door drew both their startled gazes.

"I'll see to that," Ned said, rising. "Perhaps you should attend the duke."

Alicen was warmed by her apprentice's protectiveness but wouldn't endanger him for her sake. "No need. 'Twas my action that caused the trouble, and I'll deal with it." Seeing him start to protest, she quickly added, "I'll not have you involved in this. Now, see if the stew is warm."

With that, she strode to the door and, drawing a deep breath, opened it.

Michael Taft stood there, his felt hat in his hand.

She glared, focusing her animosity on Blaine's subordinate. "What do you want?"

"May I speak with you, Mistress Kent?" The soldier's eyes were kind, and he had a mouth that smiled easily.

"Your captain threatened me," Alicen said bluntly. "What's to stop you from doing the same?"

"I don't threaten women. And until today, Sir Jeremy had never done so, either. He regrets it."

"Forgive me for not believing you."

Taft looked away momentarily. "The captain is honorable, but your eluding Naismith was more than could be borne. Worse yet, you reminded him of how distasteful discipline can be. I know Captain Blaine well. He'll not harry you further."

"As he was so quick to point out, he acts as he sees fit. Now, if you don't mind, I'm busy, Lieutenant."

The soldier blushed. "Please, lass, I mean, the men and I...we...we wish you to know we're sorry for all that happened today."

"Do you speak for your captain, or just for yourselves?"

Taft shook his head. "Captain Blaine speaks for himself. When he's not furious."

"Does that ever occur?"

"I've no words to explain my superior's actions," he replied.

"Make no attempt." Alicen started to turn away.

An upheld hand stopped her. "Duty is all to him, lass, so much so that it obscures even compassion. He regrets frightening you. I saw that regret in his eyes. But to admit to such in front of the men would undermine his command."

Alicen blanched, remembering the flash of pain revealed in Blaine's gaze after he'd attacked her. She must have been mistaken, his look a trick of the light.

"I should think his men would appreciate honesty," she said flatly. Noticing she twisted her apron in her hands as she spoke, she forced herself to stop.

"You don't understand, Mistress. Had you not challenged him, he never would have reacted in such a way."

Her lips thinned. "You believe I've no right to oppose brutality on my own property?"

"The captain never punishes excessively."

"Fifteen lashes isn't excessive?"

"He could've hanged the man," Taft stated. "We men respect him because we know at all times where we stand." He paused, studying her. "He has far more trouble with women."

"So I gathered," Alicen replied dryly.

"I believe he was as shocked as anyone at what

happened." When Alicen shook her head in denial, Taft added, "Yet his men know he but protected his authority."

"I appreciate your candor, sir, but thrashing a man for being outwitted is unconscionable."

"Were you a soldier, you'd understand."

"As I told your captain, I thank God I'll never be such."

Taft smiled. "We thank Him for that, too, Mistress. You're too fine a healer to be aught else. You saved William's life and have treated us well. Captain Blaine will admit his mistake, at least to himself. Whether he'll admit it to you, I know not."

Alicen believed Sir Jeremy Blaine would rather die first, but she said nothing. She shook Taft's proffered hand, then watched silently as he left the cottage.

Her thoughts returned with shuddering clarity to her predicament. She must not force the captain into a corner. Like a wounded wolf, his reaction was to protect himself. She desperately hoped what Taft said about him—that he'd reacted uncharacteristically—was true.

Otherwise, could she continue to protect Orrick, Ned and herself?

On impulse, she plucked her cloak from the peg by the door. A brisk walk through the now repaired garden gate brought her to the woods behind Landeyda. She glanced around to see if she'd been observed, then slipped into the dense underbrush via a well-hidden path. Soon she stood in a small clearing dominated by an ancient oak. At its base was a weathered Celtic cross, a sprig of mistletoe draped over the crosspiece.

Grasping her amulet, Alicen knelt in front of the cross and bowed her head.

"Mother, I'm afraid. The soldier of my vision. He who'll change my life. It's Jeremy Blaine. What am I to do?" She listened carefully but heard only a gentle breeze rustling the oak's leaves. Then the stones in her amulet began to warm. The breeze picked up, swirling around her, pulling at her cloak, tangling her hair.

He has forced you to abandon your neutrality. Kaitlyn O'Rourke's voice filled her daughter's mind.

"I've no intention of betraying my vows, Mother."

But what if those vows don't fit his plan?

"I won't break my oath to you."

You may have no choice, Daughter.
The wind died, her amulet cooled, and Alicen was left to contemplate the meaning of her mother's words.

Four

He was far more intoxicated than he had planned.

Jeremy had patronized all of Sherford's shopkeepers, then taken a room at the inn. Although he had no need of a bed, it gave him an excuse to spend hours in the common room, eavesdropping.

What he'd heard made him guardedly optimistic. No overtly partisan sentiments had been discussed, and no one eyed him with suspicion, as they would have had they feared his intentions. Those who'd come and gone throughout the evening—some alone, others with families or friends—had spoken only of everyday matters in an English village.

Five patrons at a table opposite Jeremy's formed the night's most vocal tipplers. They pinched serving wenches, ate and drank noisily, and sang bawdy songs. But they'd said naught of Harold the Bastard, or of Duke William.

In order to allay suspicions of his presence, Jeremy had imbibed quite steadily for several hours. As the night wore on and the conversations remained common, he found himself thinking more on Alicen Kent and less on plots against William. And each time he recalled how he'd mistreated the healer, he took another drink.

Now, the inn's common room swam before his eyes. He thought to ride back to Landeyda, but feared he'd not be able to mount Charon. Nor could he even be certain of mounting the stairs to the room he'd acquired at the inn. Mayhap a meal would clear his head.

But when he looked up to signal the serving girl, Alicen stood before him, accusation in her emerald eyes. He choked, shamed to see fright still brimming in that lovely gaze. Had she followed him? Brought friends to avenge her? He knew he'd drunk too much to defend himself from a gang intent on thrashing him. Fighting instinct made him sit straight, alert to danger, but his reflexes were so befuddled his body could hardly respond, and he knew the effort was futile. She had him trapped.

Blinking, he looked again. Alicen's tall, lithe figure melted into a short, buxom blonde with uneven teeth. He vaguely recognized her...one of the inn's serving wenches.

She moved closer to slide her small hand up his leg.

"Coo, yer lordship, ye look ta be lonely." Without waiting for an invitation, she sat in his lap. "How'd ye like ta spend some time wi' Sylvia?" She slid her hand higher up his thigh then placed it on his groin, sobering him considerably. The wench leaned against him, her crooked mouth pressing to his neck and cheek. "We could go ta yer room. Get more cozy."

With a grunt, he found himself lurching to his feet and spilling Sylvia from his lap. Had she not had her arms around his neck, she'd have fallen to the floor.

"My, ain't ye the randy buck," she squealed in mock protest, then grabbed his hand to guide him out the tavern's back door and onto the green.

Once outside, Jeremy stopped moving, and Sylvia was forced to either stop also or let go of his hand. She stopped.

"I'm too drunk to please you properly," he lied. Truth to tell, he wasn't drunk enough to overlook her slovenly appearance and odorous breath. Her touch may have somewhat aroused him at the table, but he wasn't about to act on that arousal. He had never rutted indiscriminately, and—sotted or no—had no intention of bedding a woman who sold herself. Though beautiful courtesans clamored for him, since Estelle he'd been discriminating.

With sudden blinding clarity, he imagined Alicen's slender, supple body beneath his hands, moving to the rhythm of his fingers. He saw her face framed in thick chestnut hair. But instead of passion-filled eyes, her expression showed naked terror—like the fear he'd caused that afternoon. With a low curse, he shook his head to clear it of that stark image. Alicen's likeness faded to the reality of the woman before him.

"I'll not pay you for a dalliance," he found himself saying. "I will, however, pay you for information."

Sylvia gaped at him. "Pay me fer infermation?"

"Aye." He fumbled in his cloak and brought out several gold coins. "I'll reward you well for any worthwhile knowledge."

"What do ye wish ta know, yer lordship?"

Jeremy motioned with a jerk of his head. "Upstairs first."

***

A short time before dawn, Jeremy left his room at the inn, never to return. Although Sylvia had made it clear she'd welcome any bedsport he desired, he'd done nothing but interrogate her about Alicen Kent.

The serving wench had visibly trembled when he'd asked about the physician.

"The best healer in the north of England, that one," Sylvia swore. "She cured me of fever once. But..."

At the uneasy look in the girl's eyes, Jeremy had prompted, "But what?"

"There be rumors about her holding." Sylvia's eyes grew wide with fright, but Jeremy's raised brow inspired her to add, "'Tis said the ghost of Kaitlyn O'Rourke protects Landeyda."

"And who is this Kaitlyn O'Rourke?"

"Alicen's mother," Sylvia whispered, as if to raise her voice would call down this vengeful spirit. "'Tweren't no better healer than Kaitlyn. Her daughter takes after her, but even Alicen isn't her equal."

Kaitlyn O'Rourke must have been God's right hand, Jeremy thought, if she was more talented at healing than her daughter. "Did Alicen's mother ever harm you?"

"Nay! Nor her daughter, either. Both of 'em did naught but heal."

"Then why fear her spirit, if it does in fact dwell at Landeyda?"

"Kaitlyn was killed after a battle. While trying to help the wounded." Sylvia's voice became even softer as she added, "Such a skilled healer would know well how to kill. And who but a mother who loves her child would do aught needed to protect that child. Even if it meant comin' back from the grave?"

Still nursing a head muddled by ale, Jeremy rode slowly back to Landeyda, contemplating all the serving wench had said. He recalled the sudden chill he'd felt when he'd threatened Alicen in the stable, and it occurred to him that the voice he'd heard could very well have had the hint of an Irish brogue. Lord, he was addled to partake in such ridiculous fancy! Too much ale and the suggestions of a frightened and ignorant woman had made him contemplate the possibility of a ghost. Loose spirits did not exist. Dead was dead.

***

Sensing Captain Blaine wouldn't return for several hours, Alicen felt compelled to aid his hapless victim. His orders kept well in mind, she took Ned along to the stable, where they found Naismith face down on a straw pallet with Malcolm Fish clumsily tending his lash marks. Fish stood hastily when he saw her.

"Mistress Alicen, ye mustn't be here," the distraught soldier cried. "Cap'n's orders."

"I'll not be insubordinate, Malcolm," Alicen assured as she knelt by Naismith. "Sir knight, I am sorry you suffer for me."

"I'll not doubt a woman's riding skill again," the young man returned with wry humor. His laugh finished on a grunt of pain.

"We'll ease your discomfort."

"Please no, Mistress," was Naismith's hoarse plea. "You'll be punished if you defy the Captain's order."

"I'll not disobey. Ned will see to your back, not I."

"But—"

"Your captain's orders were to me. Ned was not barred from tending you. He'll make you more comfortable in short order."

Fish sighed in gratitude. "I'm much obliged fer yer help, Mistress. I'm far better at causin' wounds than at tendin' 'em, as Johnny here can prob'ly tell ye."

"Aye. He doesn't have your soft hands, either, Mistress."

"Ned's hands must do, but 'tis certain they're far gentler than Malcolm's." She smiled to take the sting from her jest.

Naismith's back was raw, with several deep, oozing gashes. Guilty anger flooded Alicen at causing his pain. But she would aid him. And follow orders. She and Ned worked swiftly, keenly aware that if Blaine heard of this they could be punished for skirting his command.

***

Less than an hour after dawn, Jeremy staggered from

the stable, headed for Landeyda's well. With shaking fingers he grasped the crank on the winch and lifted a bucket of ice cold water from the depths. He stank of smoke and ale, and the combination made his stomach turn.

Jesu be merciful, his head ached! He couldn't remember the ride back from Sherford, and what he could recall was somehow related to Alicen Kent. Of a certain, he'd awakened in her stable—face down in the straw at Charon's feet. It was his good fortune that his well-trained destrier had not trampled him while he slept off the effects of all the ale he'd drunk the previous night.

Blinking didn't immediately clear Jeremy's blurry eyesight, and the vision that flashed into his head was of him kissing away Alicen's fears and making love to her until the dawn.

I've gone completely mad, he thought grimly, forcing from his mind the image of bedding the healer. *Did I even wish to sport with her, she'd not let me near enough to touch her.*

Nor would I.

Jeremy closed his eyes. *Go away. You don't exist.*

A very feminine laugh filled his head, but he ascribed that to excess drink. Or, he truly was mad. But mad or no, he had his duty—protect the duke, then help him regain his lands. Alicen Kent's duty was to follow his orders and to heal William. She'd already gone far in fulfilling the latter. It was her not carrying out the former that had him grinding his teeth.

He groaned low in his throat, his entire body reminding him that excess drink and little sleep came dear. 'Twas miraculous he'd managed to ride Charon back to Landeyda.

A gulp of morning air steadied him, but shame at his excuse for intemperance burned. He'd sought to forget his appalling actions, to forget at least for a time the woman he'd mistreated. He could not undo his deed, yet this truth brought no ease. No amount of ale could drown his memory of Alicen's fear.

Gingerly, he ran both hands through his hair. He must regain his wits. There was much to do, much to set right, and he'd wasted a good deal of the previous eve. With a muted grunt, he thrust his head into the bucket in hopes the icy water would end his suffering. He stood this shock as long as he could before raising his head to inhale deeply.

A pitchfork's wicked tines were mere inches from his face.

Jeremy's senses cleared in an instant, but alcohol yet slowed him. He took a cautious step back and sized up his adversary. Blood red eyes widened in surprise. Ned stood before him, feet planted, the dangerous implement held firmly in small hands. The look on his face indicated he had every intention of using the pitchfork.

"You attacked Alicen," Ned cried, voice rising. "You frightened her." He stabbed at Jeremy, forcing the man to take another step back. "Leave her be!" This statement was emphasized with yet another thrust.

Despite the possibility of being skewered by a lad of three and ten, Jeremy couldn't hold back a smile. 'Twas certain Ned had grit. He stepped back again and straightened to his full height. Then he lifted his hands in a gesture of truce.

"Hold. I'm unarmed."

The boy didn't lower the weapon, so Jeremy kept a wary eye on the threatening tines.

"I thought to kill you, but Alicen wouldn't let me."

"That was wise of her," Jeremy replied softly. "You'd have hanged for murder if you had. 'Twould be a waste of life."

His words brought confusion to Ned's brown eyes. Seeing the boy's expression change from anger to doubt, Jeremy tried diplomacy. "Put down your weapon, and we'll settle this dispute as grown men should." He caught wariness flickering across the young face and added, "You've my word as a knight and an officer I'll not harm you."

Ned lowered the pitchfork with arms that trembled from the effort to keep it aloft. "Why did you touch her?" he demanded.

Flushing at the reminder of his knavery, Jeremy muttered, "She made me lose my temper." *Nay, she made me lose my wits.* "It was poorly done of me. 'Twill not happen again."

"If you don't like her, why not leave?"

Jeremy sighed. "It's not that simple, lad. I must guard Duke William until he's able to return to his court."

"Stay in Sherford."

"Impossible. I must run the duke's affairs while he cannot himself. I must be constantly near should he need me." Jeremy took the pitchfork from Ned's hands, then set it against the well. "On my word, I'll not distress your mistress again."

"If you do, you'll answer to me for it." Ned adopted a belligerent pose, hands fisted on hips.

The boy's solemn statement and determined expression almost made Jeremy smile. "I'm sure the lady is grateful for your protection and feels safer because of it."

"She's my friend," came the emphatic reply. "I must protect her from curs like you. Should you harm her more, I *will* kill you." He strode away, leaving an amused knight in his wake.

That amusement fled with Jeremy's returning headache. And with the admission that he should never have given Ned reason to seek his life. Slowly, he finished washing. When he looked up again, Taft stood beside him.

"Good morn, Michael," he said without enthusiasm. "Last night was peaceful?"

"Aye, sir." Taking in his superior's state, Taft smiled. "I could ask the same of you."

Jeremy grimaced. "Do not! And when next I decide to drink, run me through first. 'Twould be a far less painful end than dying of excessive ale."

"Breaking fast will cure the malady." Taft laughed and clapped Jeremy on the back. "Cook has brandywine, eggs and bread on the way."

"I should promote you, Michael."

"Nay, the challenge of keeping you from roguery is reward enough for my pains. I know I'm doing some good."

"I'll drink to that." Jeremy winced at the image his statement brought to mind and hastily added, "Or mayhap not."

The lieutenant laughed again as he led the way to the kitchen the soldiers had repaired.

"You're certain naught occurred last eve, Michael?" Jeremy asked casually as they dished their food into wooden bowls.

"Aye."

"Strange. I checked Naismith when I awoke, and I'd swear his lashes had been expertly tended."

"If you believe Ned to be such, then you're correct, sir."

Jeremy's casual demeanor vanished with his subordinate's shrug. An intense glare replaced it. "Do you seek to protect the healer?"

"Nay, sir," Taft stated calmly. "As ordered, she didn't touch Naismith."

"Yet she instructed her apprentice in the treatment of his wounds," Jeremy returned with a flash of insight.

"Aye, she did." Silence spun out a minute before Taft added, "I admire her courage. She has strong convictions."

"Aye. And she schemes to undermine my authority."

"I rather think compassion drives her to risk her own welfare for her duty. And I daresay you think the same way."

Jeremy scowled. "Place no wager on that assumption."

The two fell silent as they ate beneath the oak in the courtyard. Ned found them thus. He ignored Jeremy, addressing his lieutenant instead.

"The duke has awakened," the boy stated. "Alicen says you may see him for a few moments if you wish."

Jeremy's misery disappeared with those sweet words. "Praise God and all the saints in Heaven," he exclaimed, ignoring the dizziness caused by leaping to his feet. He grinned and slapped Taft on the back. "William's awake!"

He nearly ran to the infirmary.

A weak smile greeted him when he entered the room. William, propped up with bolsters, looked somehow small and wan amidst the bedding. Jeremy knelt beside him as much in gratitude to God as to show loyalty.

"My lord."

"Jeremy, arise," William softly chastised him. "There is no need for ceremony betwixt us."

"I failed to protect you," the younger man said, voice gone husky. "I thought I'd never speak with you hence."

He rose to his feet to grasp William's hand in both of

his.

"I thought the same. Yet, to my extreme good fortune, you brought me to a gifted physician." Jeremy couldn't meet his gaze. "What troubles you?" William prompted.

Before he knew it, Jeremy had poured out the story of what had ensued since their arrival six days before. William looked grave at word of the whipping and Jeremy's treatment of Alicen Kent.

"Apologize at once. We all owe her a great debt. Anger between the two of you won't serve."

"I'll do my best, my lord," he replied reluctantly. He knew he owed Alicen an apology, but how could he trust her not to betray them all when she contested all Jeremy tried to do?

Noting William's drowsiness, he excused himself. Had his messenger returned from Tynan? He hoped so. With the duke now alert, plans to remove him to his court could progress.

***

At midday, Alicen fed William a bowl of hearty broth. It was far too soon to try him on solid food, but his good appetite and returning strength encouraged her.

When he spoke, his breathy voice held a rich timbre. "Sir Jeremy told me of yesterday's regrettable circumstance."

She stiffened immediately. "'Tis done. No good is served by bringing it to light again."

"I'll not mention it hereafter. But I wish you to know that he regrets—"

"Then why does *he* not say such?" Temper edged Alicen's voice as she cut off the duke's comment. "You all are certain he's contrite, yet I'll not believe he rues his actions in the least 'til I hear such from his own lips." Seeing William's incredulous expression, she lowered her gaze. "I pray you, my lord, please make no excuses for him."

William's jaw dropped. "None save the King use that tone to address me," he stated. Then he smiled. "I admire your forthright manner, lass. But understand, such boldness in females raises Sir Jeremy's ire."

"I've been made painfully aware of that already, my lord."

Wry compassion entered William's eyes. "I'll not command him to beg your pardon."

"Nor would I expect that. I've no want of empty words spoken only to appease a superior."

"I applaud your honesty," William said with a smile.

"'Tis my way." Alicen winced inwardly at the lie.

"Then tell me honestly why you so dislike soldiers."

She shot him a glance, but replied steadily, "My betrothed died at Harfleur serving the King. Father also fought for the Crown. He never protected Mother and me when we needed him. He was always away, fighting in someone else's name, perhaps protecting someone else's family...Or killing them. Others came first. Never his own loved ones."

Her mother's deathbed entered her thoughts. *"Vow n'er to take a side in any conflict, Alicen."*

"But, Mother, Harold's troops did this to you. How can I heal them?"

"You must. 'Tis what you are. Soldiers kill. They fight for love of battle. Like your father. But what they do must not change what you do."

The light of recognition abruptly entered William's eyes. "Your father was Phillip Kent?"

"The same."

"We fought together at Agincourt. King Henry and his peers, myself included, considered him a very fine soldier."

"He was. But I hate the qualities that make a man a fine soldier." Her voice quavered. "Loyalty, obedience, love of combat—all warriors have such traits, do they not? They slaughter on command and pillage for profit, but won't stay home to see their families safe." Swallowing through a tightened throat, she looked away.

"Did your father make provision for you to wed another?" he asked gravely.

The seemingly casual question chilled Alicen. Her gaze sharpened, but she forced a calm reply. "Father died in France. He had no time to make arrangements for me."

"You are alone?"

"I much prefer it that way," she replied with soft emphasis.

"But all women not of the Church should be wed,"

William returned, voice firm despite his pallor. "As your liege, 'tis my duty to see you cared for. You need a man's protection."

"Nay!" Alicen blurted before controlling her sudden panic. "My lord, please. I could never love a man so much as I love healing. How unjust to tie him to a woman who'd care little for him." *None would understand what I do and why,* she thought forlornly. *Orrick once did, but he knew me from a child. No other could accept the power of my healing art.*

A knock at the chamber door interrupted the tense silence.

"'Tis Jeremy, my lord," came a deep voice.

"Come." William cast a sidelong glance at Alicen as she removed the eating utensils. She stiffened and swiftly wiped at her eyes with her fingertips.

Alicen noted how the knight filled the room with his presence. His color had improved since morning, and his walk was again self-assured, but upon seeing her he hesitated.

"If you need aught my lord, alert Ned or me," she said tightly, indicating the handbell on the table. "Ring for us, or send a man."

"Thank you, Mistress," the duke replied sincerely, still studying her. "You've been more than kind."

"You need a good deal of rest. Don't o'ertire yourself."

She averted her eyes as she moved past Jeremy to the door, but he watched her with an intensity she could feel.

Following Alicen's departure, the room fell silent.

William leaned back on the pillows and spoke to the ceiling. "I see you've yet to apologize for being an ass yesterday."

"The proper opportunity has not presented itself," came the clipped reply. Jeremy suddenly realized he still stared at the door Alicen had passed through. He hastily turned to the duke.

William glanced at him. "I try not to give advice concerning women, but now I must. Mend your quarrel with Alicen Kent before matters become untenable."

"She goes out of her way to subvert my command." Jeremy started to sit down, then straightened and began to pace instead.

"Your own actions are partly at fault. Your mistrust has raised her guard."

Jeremy clenched his jaw and, without thinking, fingered the hilt of his dagger. "I've reason not to trust her."

William's brows rose. "Has she betrayed us in any way to anyone?"

"Nay, not yet," was the grimly firm reply.

"Has she mistreated or neglected any of the men?"

"Nay. She's treated every man's wounds...including mine."

"And saved my life. Do traitors act thus?"

A long pause ensued before Jeremy sat down beside the bed. "I presume not."

"You suspect her because she's a woman." At Jeremy's grimace, William's tone softened. "I understand your misgivings. But all women don't favor Estelle Hawk or your female kin. You can't condemn the entire gender for those few."

"I'll strive to remember that, my lord." His jaw tightened. "But only Manfred's Lucinda is faithful, because he keeps her so with his fist. Edward treated Blanche kindly. She sought to cuckold him with me, and succeeded with one of his retainers. And Estelle—" Jeremy swallowed. "But you know all, having been my family's lifelong friend."

"I've offended you." William sighed. "I wish you no hurt. You're as a son to me. But you must stop your rancor. My God, you can't distrust half of all mankind!"

Jeremy moved to the window and braced both hands on the sill. "And why not? Man fell from grace because of woman."

"History cannot be undone. But you need not think that women are good for naught more than tumbling into bed."

Jeremy shot a look over his shoulder. "Of course, my lord. Women cook, clean and sew. My kindly childhood nurse—"

"This situation hardly calls for jocundity, Sir Jeremy."

Despite William's abruptly formal tone, Jeremy didn't relent. He turned to approach the bed, saying as he did so, "If Adam had felt as I do, instead of being seduced by the tree of the knowledge of good and evil, then Man would be in the Garden still."

"Be assured Man would have fallen eventually, my friend," William replied dryly. "Even you can't keep a woman abed all the day 'round."

***

"Hercules, get your nose out of those oats and let me brush your face," Alicen scolded her gelding as she groomed him late that afternoon. "You think of naught but food. Fat swine."

The bay snorted, tossing his head and knocking the brush from her hand. It landed on the opposite side of the stall, leaving her with two options—crawling under his belly or going around to retrieve the tool. Sighing, she moved toward his rump.

"Wretched beast," she grumbled.

"I'll get it."

The deep voice brought her up short. Startled, she turned to see Jeremy Blaine's broad-shouldered figure five steps away. Fear swept through her like a fever. She froze as he bent to retrieve the brush, her first thought that he had come to punish her for her audacity. They were alone. Her gaze darted to the door behind him, and she tensed, ready to fight him if need be or run if the chance presented itself.

With a pang of regret Jeremy noted Alicen's terror. She thought he'd harm her. And based upon his previous conduct, he had to admit her fears had some justification. He must proceed with caution so as not to frighten her more.

Summoning a slight smile, he asked in his most civil manner, "Have you another brush? If I groom this side while you do the other, the work will be done in half the time."

Alicen went weak with relief. Moving swiftly, but not fast enough to betray her anxiety, she put Hercules' comforting bulk between herself and the fearsome soldier. Still, her hands shook when she reached for a second coat brush to resume the grooming.

Moments passed in strained silence as neither spoke. Risking a glance across the horse's back, she saw Blaine intent upon his task. She wasn't comforted. Memory of his intimidating manner remained fresh. Even garbed in a plain tunic, hose and short boots, he looked every bit the warrior.

Jeremy groomed the gelding's coat to a deep gloss. Finishing, he patted the sleek neck and ran his hand across the muscled withers.

"A fine animal," he said appreciatively, catching Alicen's wary look. "You must value him highly."

She rubbed the horse's soft muzzle and returned Blaine's perusal with more courage than she actually possessed. "Indeed I do. Hercules is a good friend."

"Hercules," Jeremy mused aloud. "One possessing great strength. It fits him." At her frankly surprised expression, he added, "Not every soldier is an ignorant lout, Mistress Kent."

She lowered her gaze, embarrassed he'd guessed her thoughts.

"And, not every soldier behaves as despicably as I have toward you." He paused before adding, "Even though your deeds provoked me."

Alicen's cheeks flushed. Her head snapped up. "Mayhap you acted within your authority, Captain," she retorted, "but the punishment was unjustly cruel."

"Citizens have no say in military matters," he returned, stunned at how swiftly their conversation had gone from horses to apologies to argument.

"Landeyda is my *home*. Seeing it turned into an encampment appalls me." She clutched Hercules' mane in her left hand.

"Were the duke able, I'd take him from here. He's not. And no matter how loathsome, we must tolerate the present situation."

"I may tolerate it, but I'll never enjoy it."

"'Twould be more pleasant if you occupied yourself solely with healing." He leveled a cold look at her.

Her narrowed gaze locked on his, and she stood tall. "Then will you *not* occupy yourself with healing, Captain?"

"What do you mean?" His scowl carried through to his tone.

"Will I be able to aid all who need my attention?"

"You circumvented my order concerning Naismith

quite easily, from what I understand."

She paled at that barb but held her ground. "May I perform my tasks with no soldier following?"

Both his look and tone brooked no argument. "For as long as the duke remains here, no."

"Then I am your captive." She took a shuddering breath.

He gaped in surprise at her conclusion. "You'll not be kept here against your will. But you'll be escorted when you leave."

Her right fist strangled the handle of the brush she held. "You think me a traitor! How could you?"

"A soldier's intuition, I suppose."

"Lucifer take your intuition," she cried, hurling the brush to the floor. Hercules jerked his head, but Alicen ignored him. "I take no sides in this—or any—dispute!"

Jeremy eyed her speculatively, carefully gauging her state of mind. He found he preferred her anger over her fear. "You treated the men we captured after the ambush, did you not?"

"Aye." She hesitated, sensing a trap. "But they were well guarded—"

"You'd treat a mercenary, a deserter or a traitor if the scoundrel presented himself at your door, would you not?"

"I've had little occasion to do so." *Except for Orrick.*

"But you'd not hesitate," he accused.

"Nay, I'd not hesitate." At the triumphant glint in his eyes she added, "I'm a physician, Captain. I treat the ill. Social station, political beliefs...have naught to do with the ill needing care."

"And *that* is precisely why I trust you not. If you'd bind a man's wounds regardless of his fealty, you've no loyalty to your liege lord." Crossing his arms over his chest, Jeremy assumed a posture of stubborn pugnacity.

Anger drove Alicen's fear away. "When you see a child or a woman attacked, Captain, do you ask where her loyalties lie before deciding to aid her?" she challenged.

"My allegiance is not in question here."

"Yet mine is, despite my saving William's life."

"You yourself said you'd aid anyone."

She stared at him, noting the stubborn set of his jaw, and knew for certain the futility of argument. She shook her head. "You see what you wish to see, and in your eyes I am untrue."

At this sudden acquiescence, his brow rose. "You could disprove that accusation."

She shrugged. "Yet 'tis truth I've sworn to treat all who need me. Thus, I'll refuse no one. Nor will I betray William or seek out his foes." She paused before saying slowly, "I understand not why you so despise me, sir. I've done little to deserve such animosity except to speak my mind. And if honesty is so intolerable to you, I can only wonder at your rise to favor in the duke's service."

Staring at his face, she caught a play of...what? Sadness? Regret? Startled, she looked again, but the knight's expression had become closely guarded.

Silently, Jeremy hung his brush on a nearby peg and left the stable.

Five

"I tried to apologize, but that wretched woman wouldn't let me," Jeremy seethed as he sat by William's bed the next morning studying a sheaf of messages. "She detests soldiers—"

"As much as you mistrust women," the duke broke in archly.

The knight grunted. "So it seems." He tried to focus on the writing before him, but couldn't get Alicen's image out of his mind. Tension twisted in his belly.

William laughed weakly. "What a pair you make. Forced together and ready to rend each other at the least provocation."

"I see no humor in this," Jeremy muttered, lifting his gaze to the duke. "Were you fit to ride, we'd leave this miserable place."

"I enjoy her, though her unwed state vexes me," William asserted. Then he added slyly, "Mayhap I should invite her back to Tynan to find her a match."

Jeremy's entire body went rigid. "Take her to Tynan? Jesu forbid it! You'd force me to rejoin Bedford in France to get as far away from her as possible."

"Why would her presence plague you? I'll see her wed to some clerk, and you'll be well quit of her."

"What man would willingly marry such a hoyden?" The knight shuddered. "She'd harry him unto his grave."

The older man's dark eyes twinkled. "You don't find her at all attractive?"

"Much too slender," Jeremy scoffed. "I like a woman with flesh on her, not one who's shaped like a lad."

"A curvaceous lad, I'd say. With all that rich chestnut hair, and those eyes—" William's expression turned thoughtful as he covertly studied his captain.

"Her eyes carry only daggers for me. I hardly remarked her hair."

William nodded as if answering his own unvoiced question. "Mayhap you were far too preoccupied with her shape to note any of her other fine features."

Too angry to hear the duke's sudden change in tone, Jeremy stated, "Hell will resemble a Norse winter 'ere I'm preoccupied with *any* of that shrew's features."

Yet even as he swore this declaration, his reaction when Alicen tended his wound—and his visions at the tavern—filled his mind and belied his oath. Sweet Jesu, how could women do such things to rational men?

He was struggling to return to his letters when the infirmary door burst open and Taft rushed in.

"What the devil," Jeremy exclaimed, springing to his feet.

"Come quickly! Our rider approaches at a dead gallop."

Jeremy cast a glance at William.

"Go," the duke ordered.

Taft spun on his heel and left, his captain right behind in a sprint to the courtyard.

"'Tis Fish, sir!" cried the watchman at the gate.

Both officers rushed to where Fish pulled his lathered mount to a halt at the stable.

"Enemy soldiers," Fish gasped, sliding from his saddle. "A league north of Sherford. Search party."

Expression cold, Jeremy sent a look at Taft then turned back to Fish. "How many?"

"Two score at least. Takin' care to check buildings an' such."

"Looking for their missing patrol?" Taft speculated.

"No doubt." Jeremy directed his next question to Fish. "How long before they arrive here?"

"An hour at the least, Cap'n. They don't seem in a hurry, but they're surely after somethin'."

"Nicely done, Malcolm." Jeremy clapped him on the shoulder. "You may have given us time to escape their net."

He turned to the men gathered behind him and began snapping orders. In moments, all were racing to carry out his commands.

Although he schooled his features to show nothing, Jeremy couldn't help turning to stare at Alicen's cottage.

"How will we protect William?" Taft asked soberly, following his commander's gaze.

Expression hard, Jeremy said, "I'll inform our hostess that guests approach." He strode to the cottage, Taft following.

***

"As we cannot retreat, you and the seriously wounded will remain inside," Jeremy explained to Alicen, looking around the circle of men for their affirmation. "The rest of us will deter any of Harold's troop who seek entrance at the gate."

She paled. "You cannot fight here!"

Her intense declaration gave Jeremy momentary pause. Behind him, the men were tautly silent. "'Tis as good a place as any, considering the wall surrounding it."

"Nay! Even did the odds favor you, I'd not allow a battle." A hint of desperation tinged her bold announcement.

Jeremy's jaw tightened. "You threatened to kill the duke just a few nights past."

"To protect Ned," came her terse reply. "You drove me to voice an empty threat."

Jeremy crossed his arms over his chest in his most intimidating pose. "As you said, William cannot be moved, so we'll defend him here. You've no choice in this matter."

She shook her head, her body shaking as well with the force of her emotions. "My home is no killing ground. 'Tis a place of healing. To fight here is to destroy a sacred trust."

Though her voice had faded to a whisper, Jeremy was certain every man heard her words, spoken with such exquisite anguish as to touch all with their poignancy. She lifted her gaze to his, torment clear in the green depths of her eyes.

Something in his chest tightened, but he instantly tamped down his sympathy.

"You'd have us surrender without a fight?" he asked evenly.

"Nay, no fight is necessary. The sign of plague will deter them. They'll not dare risk their lives to enter."

"And if they heed not the warning?"

"Ned and I will burn clothing and bed linen to warn them further of the danger here."

"Aye, there'd be truth to that," Jeremy replied coldly as he rested a hand on his sword hilt. He studied her tense features. "Do you plot a trick to trap us?"

She flinched, but didn't allow her conviction to falter. "There will be no killing here."

"Mayhap we'll keep the boy with us, to assure your loyalty."

Anger flared in Alicen's suddenly narrowed eyes. "I'll allow no killing at Landeyda. That's where my loyalty lies."

Jeremy shrugged as if discounting her statement. "We've the element of surprise to aid us."

"And fewer than a dozen able-bodied men. Against forty." Unbidden images of a massacre assailed her. "'Twould be a bloodbath." She barely succeeded in suppressing a shudder.

Jeremy stared. Beneath Alicen's stubborn defiance he'd caught a glimpse of raw fear. Despite her insubordination, he wanted to touch her, but throttled the notion of comforting her. Mayhap she sought to detain and betray them. He trusted her not, making his base desire for her even more maddening.

And he'd no time to contemplate the derangement of lust. His enemy was nigh. He had to make it appear that what they sought wasn't there.

"Does it come to battle, whose side will you hope prevails?" He saw her pale further at his question.

"You've forced me to take your part in this, Captain," she returned, voice barely above a whisper. "Jesu be merciful, I swore to Mother on her deathbed I'd not be partisan!"

Despite his attempt at indifference, Alicen's bleak features wrenched his heart. "Circumstance undoes you, Mistress," he stated bluntly, again crushing his urge to comfort her.

"I hold you to blame for that," she snapped, burying her trembling hands in her apron pockets. "But though I've no choice whose part I take, you'll not fight here."

Jeremy glowered, leaning toward her. "That is not your decision to make."

"Oh, but it is." Her uptilted chin hid her fear. "Soldiers think only blood resolves conflict. 'Tis foolishness. Peaceful means oft work far better."

"Time grows short. I'll not debate philosophy when we may be besieged momentarily."

As he turned to leave, she caught his arm. "Captain, please. Let me keep them at bay," she pleaded. When his gaze swung back to her, she added, "Those men will surely learn of Landeyda. Once they know a healer dwells here, they'll expect one. I can divert them with a tale of plague."

"Or inform them of our presence," Jeremy answered, fighting to ignore the warmth creeping up his arm from the point where she touched him. "I think not, Mistress Kent."

Anger suffusing her face, she yanked her hand from his arm. "You'd fight when I've a means to avoid it? You *are* mad!"

He shook his head, dreading battle but seeing no other choice. "I'll pose as the healer."

"'Twould never work. All with eyes can see you're no physician. The moment you appear, they'll know aught is amiss."

Taft grunted. "She's right on that count, Captain."

"William will decide," Jeremy stated, then moved Alicen aside and entered the infirmary.

***

An hour later Alicen implemented her plan. William had favored escape, but she'd convinced him 'twould be fatal. Gaining approval of her strategy had proven more difficult. With Jeremy adamantly opposed, they'd wasted precious time arguing. Finally, both men had given in to her logic, William with far more grace than his captain.

Now she and Ned stood in the courtyard, feeding old bandages and garments into a bonfire. The choking smell of burning rags filled the air and stung their noses. Squaring her shoulders, she readjusted the shabby cloak she'd donned. They had dressed in tatters and dirtied their skin with soot. Ned's white-blond locks were streaked with ash, and she had sullied her hair in the same manner. These intruders must have no wish to tarry at Landeyda. She prayed the stench of burning rags and the appearance of the two people wearing clothes similar to those rags would discourage dalliance.

"They'll be here anon." She'd heard the rattle of harnesses and equipment—the troop was nigh. Her chest tightened until it threatened to crush her lungs. Offering a prayer to God, her mother, and any saint or spirit that might have been listening, she gave Ned a reassuring smile.

When the troop was close enough only the deaf wouldn't hear them, she jumped and spun as if startled. With an eerie cry, she dropped the stick she used to tend the fire and rushed toward them. At sight of her, they immediately drew rein, all except the first man.

"Nay, go back," she screeched, heading for the lead rider. "Did ye not heed the signs? Go back, I say!"

When it looked as though he'd continue to the cottage, she stepped in front of his mount. Her every nerve screamed for her to run from the dangerous war horse, but that would be fatal for all. She made no quick movements, just held her place.

The destrier snorted a warning, his rider drawing rein a mere step away. Alicen tensed yet showed no outward sign of awareness of the peril she was in.

"You deny us entry, hag?" the leader asked. "We seek for information."

Inside the stable, Jeremy surveyed his men. They gripped their weapons tightly, so still they looked carved in rock. But rigidity would shatter at the slightest cause. As did he, they foresaw a fight to the death, and so prepared themselves in their own private ways.

He started at the sound of a familiar voice, one that pierced him like a shaft of steel. Peering from behind the stable door, he felt his face pale as recognition dawned.

"Kenrick." He swore beneath his breath.

If Theo Kenrick served Harold, William's shire—including every citizen—was jeopardized. No more ruthless a mercenary lived in the Christian world. Jeremy strained to hear what Alicen said to his most hated enemy, but little of the conversation came to him.

"Enter these grounds at great risk," Alicen keened, voice on the edge of lunacy. "My villein and his lad died last eventide. Neither showed signs of affliction ere three days hence." She lifted a bunch of flowers to her nose, giving the mercenaries time to watch Ned add blankets and linen to the burning heap. He'd tied a nosegay around his neck so both his hands were free. "I fear the signs," she screeched, recalling their attention to her. "Both had lumps in groin and armpits."

This declaration had the desired effect. The soldiers grew restive. Whispers broke out in the ranks, and Alicen heard more than one man mutter "plague." But their leader remained unmoved. His hard eyes and cruel mouth tightened. Alicen's throat went dry.

"We've had no sign of pestilence for years," he sneered.

"And nary a sign at all ere it took so many lives," she returned, injecting just enough drama into her voice to sway them. A broad gesture included the estate. "We seek to hold contagion here. Thus, none in Sherford are privy to our plight." She fixed an intent stare on the mercenaries. "You sought information. You have it. Depart. Most like, you'll be in no danger. Yet, if exposed, expect half your troop to die within the week."

She turned her back on the soldiers to pick up her staff, forcing herself to move to the fire although the hair at her nape stood up. Despite the roaring blaze, it seemed unnaturally cool. After a long, breathless moment, she heard harnesses rattle and leather squeak as the riders wheeled their mounts. The thunder of hooves shook the ground when the mercenaries galloped out the gate.

Alicen and Ned remained in place until the troop had disappeared down the road. Then they threw down their staffs and embraced. William's men streamed from their hiding places to quickly surround them, clapping them on the back and rejoicing at the successful ruse. Tension expelled itself in loud whoops and impromptu dances.

Jeremy skirted the celebration with barely a glance at the participants. He was soon at William's bedside.

"You saw?"

"Aye," William answered gravely. "Kenrick. You should have killed that whoreson years ago when you had the chance."

"Curse my soul for putting honor above prudence," Jeremy swore bitterly. "He'll show no such mercy if he finds us here."

A grin abruptly lit the duke's face. "Methinks he'll ponder long 'ere he darkens these gates again." Worry released itself in a chortle. "Thought of the Black Death chilled his devil's soul! Alicen terrified that blackguard to his stones."

Jeremy's expression hardened. "In truth, she's an apt dissembler," he stated, none too kindly.

William's mirth faded. "What do you suggest?"

"I'm uncertain," Jeremy admitted slowly. "Yet methinks Kenrick retreated too easily."

"Wouldn't you if you thought the plague was nigh?"

Jeremy shrugged. "Most like. But 'tis not the lie that so concerns me, 'tis the woman's talent for deception."

"She acted a part, like any player."

"You're certain? None truly heard her words. Mayhap she's known to Kenrick and warned him away."

"What would be the purpose, since he had the advantage?"

"To keep bloodshed from her allies, perhaps?"

"Jeremy, you mistake the lass—"

"You needn't defend me, my lord," Alicen stated from the threshold. She swallowed hard before adding, "The captain believes I protected his enemies from him." Unable to completely hide her pain, she glared at Jeremy. "Were I he, I'd likely doubt every intention of those around me as well."

"Mistress—"

Both men spoke at once, but Alicen talked right over them. "You'll think what you will of me, Captain, but be honest with yourself at least. If I was loyal to Harold, why not just poison all of you when I found out who William was? Why repel Harold's patrol, when I could have pointed them to the stable and had them easily surround you? And why not contemplate poisoning all of you now?" She tried to glare at Jeremy, but her resolve crumpled, and she suddenly found herself fighting tears.

Turning, she fled the infirmary.

Six

Jeremy winced at hearing the door to Alicen's chamber slam. The woman had saved their lives, and he repaid her with suspicion. He stood staring bleakly at the empty doorway, wishing to revoke his cold words, wishing he'd joined his men in lauding Alicen's cunning. But he could do neither, and this made him even more wretched.

"Jeremy, I never thought you a jackass," William asserted, "but methinks I erred in my assumption."

"I'll have that device added to my coat of arms," the knight muttered before he left the cottage to patrol the grounds.

***

He was penning an urgent missive to Warrick that afternoon when Ned entered. At sight of the towhead's solemn face, Jeremy smiled. An unreturned gesture, but he knew Ned's anger toward him had eased. He'd caught the boy studying him of late, and this interest warmed Jeremy. Ned certainly had courage and loyalty. Perhaps the two of them could fashion a truce.

"I'm to remove your stitches," Ned stated without preamble, brandishing a long-tipped pair of tweezers.

Jeremy's brows shot up. Why didn't Alicen oversee, if not perform, this task? Through the chamber window he glimpsed her—once more freshly scrubbed—striding away, basket in hand. 'Twas obvious she'd not appear, and a baffling disappointment unsettled him. His agitation at her absence upset him more, however. What matter if she'd sent her apprentice to remove his stitches?

She'd spurned him since he'd discredited her to William that morn. And while he couldn't recant his words, he had determined to avoid offending her more. Her pique would cool. However, if he trusted his eyes, her anger might last for some time. He glanced out the window again, but she'd moved from his line of sight.

In truth, he regretted losing this chance to have her close. It shocked him to realize that her gentle touch and subtle fragrance soothed him. Of course, she was a gifted healer, and he appreciated skill. Yet he'd not admit he desired her near for more than his wounds.

"Sir? Could you remove your tunic, please?"

Jeremy's attention snapped back to Ned. The apprentice fidgeted. Clearly, he'd never performed this task but was doggedly determined. He snipped and tugged, and in a few minutes had removed all the thread closing Jeremy's wound.

"My thanks, lad." Jeremy donned his shirt, knowing the procedure wouldn't have stung so much had Alicen done it. But he'd not discourage the boy. "You did well."

Ned's face lit up. "Did I, sir?" At the captain's nod, he exclaimed, "Thank you, sir!" Then he fairly skipped from the room, his expression a study of relieved joy at his feat.

Jeremy ignored his regret that Alicen had not tended him herself, returning to William's correspondence.

'Tis no more than you deserve for playing the cad with her, a voice said inside his mind. *Ye refuse to trust her, yet ye wish her near. Why long for something you've willingly pushed away?* For the life of him he couldn't tell if those were his own thoughts or those of someone else—with an Irish lilt.

***

Dusk had fallen when Alicen returned from herb gathering. Several soldiers lounged in the yard, honing weapons and cleaning tack. They called out greetings as she passed.

"I've an ailment I'm certain you could cure, Mistress Kent," Hitch Stacy said loudly, catching her gaze.

Her emerald eyes darkened in concern. "What is it, Hitch?"

The young man smiled at his mates, then turned his impish look on her. He touched a finger to his lips. "This ache can only be eased by the kiss of a lovely lass." His grin widened when she blushed and ducked her head. "Would you end my suffering, Mistress?"

"Best kiss your horse instead," she returned with a shy smile. "When there's no lass nearby to soothe you, he'll be about. Nor will he complain if he has no pleasure from you."

The men, including Hitch, laughed heartily.

Their mirth pleased her. Oddly enough, she enjoyed this banter with the men-at-arms. They welcomed her company, and each had praised her daring plan more than once. Their captain alone was openly hostile. Worse, Blaine had even questioned her efforts.

This thought effectively dampened her mood. He'd scrutinized her every action since his arrival, and after the incident with Naismith, she'd hardly enough privacy to relieve herself. As usual, the cur stood close by, following her every action. Alicen caught sight of him in the stable door.

Most like, the mistrusting wretch fears I'll poison his men, then ride off to find the mercenaries, she brooded.

She crushed a sudden urge to provoke him. 'Twas unwise to bait the varlet, and sending Ned to remove his stitches in her place was as defiant as she dared be. Swallowing her ire, she strode to the stable—her destination before the captain's presence there had given her pause.

Silent, Jeremy moved aside to let her enter, then studied her as she went stiffly about her chores. Her usually expressive face looked stiff, and though her eyes were shadowed, he didn't need to see them to sense she fought back tears. He felt a curious sadness at realizing he had caused her sorrow.

God's wounds, she has a way about her, he marveled. Her courage this day had strengthened the entire troop's respect, and every villein for ten leagues 'round would likely follow her to Hell. *Pray Jesu she never gets political ambition.*

That idea made him flinch. She could lead a faction down any path she wished, having won William and the men over easily enough. His lips compressed. Despite her besting Kenrick, his mortal enemy, Jeremy refused to trust her.

Yet he admired valor, and she'd endangered herself to spare bloodshed. *You're made of sterner metal than other women,* he thought, still staring at her. Healing, he reluctantly admitted, not power, lured her, and as a healer, she was dedicated and gifted.

His head jerked up. If he'd spoken aloud, anyone

hearing would believe he *liked* Alicen Kent. He shuddered. Bold, arrogant, headstrong, independent—offensive traits in a female. Women should be reserved and modest. But her touch could be so gentle...

Christ's guts, am I mad? Did she discover he respected her—somewhat—he'd forfeit his authority. Yet her guileless dealings with his men captivated him. Plagued him. Her laughter warmed in a way he'd rarely felt. And her smile...His heart had thumped oddly at sight of that infectious look, the first he'd seen from her since his arrival.

Then she'd noticed him nearby and, as if a cloud had passed over, her smile faded. Her sparkling eyes again grew guarded.

He cursed the pain her withdrawal brought him, but his authority could not be challenged. Yet he didn't seek to frighten her. He wanted—what? To have her laugh and jest with him? Despite his disdain of them, women fought to be in his favor. In his bed. Yet this woman plainly loathed him. She could jest freely with common soldiers, even with the duke himself, but with him she wore her contempt like chain mail.

He wished to remove that barrier. As long as doing so didn't jeopardize his position, he reasoned mulishly. Still, she should know he appreciated her effort on the duke's behalf, know he wasn't the insensitive brute she believed him.

Bah, he cared not for her good opinion! William owned his fealty. What Alicen Kent thought of him was unimportant. Bemused, Jeremy left the stable and his unsettling nemesis and went to toast with his men a victory won.

Alicen immediately felt the knight's departure. Relief consumed her. Could he not leave her be, not even to tend chores? And could he not at least admit her plan had worked? As usual, he completely unnerved her. Did he suspect she'd visited Orrick after eluding Naismith? She prayed the man wasn't that wary.

Finished with her tasks, she steeled herself against the captain's rancor, determined never to let him see her cry over his scorn. She dashed away fat tears with the back of her hand. Only great pride kept her from outright weeping.

That she cared a jot for a soldier's regard troubled her nearly as much as Captain Blaine's mistrust. But she found she could do nothing to still that upset.

***

"My wife's missive sheds no light on London's political intrigues, Jeremy. I would know what my enemies at Court have been about lately."

William was sitting, propped up by several pillows, for the first time in almost a fortnight. He studied a roll of parchment.

"Warrick and I are in close communication. Our agents at Court report little change." Jeremy's look darkened. "The Duke of Bedford yet rapes and plunders France. After three years, I'm amazed there's aught of value left."

"An appalling abuse of a regency," William agreed soberly. "John never misses an occasion to fill his coffers. And what of England's own Regent, the Duke of Gloucester?"

"Quarrelsome as usual. Humphrey takes after his brother Bedford in that. Cardinal Beaufort yet opposes him at every turn."

"As Chancellor, Beaufort is wise to do so. Humphrey's whimsy will ruin England should none keep him at heel. When Henry VI reaches his majority, he'll have naught to rule."

"Only England and a little of Normandy," Jeremy remarked dryly. He set aside quill and ink and stood to momentarily stretch.

William shook his head. "He'll lose France, I fear. Burgundy is our ally, but the Dauphin will fight for his titled land. Our English Council and regents should then find pillaging abroad less fruitful." He waved away the topic. "Enough of France. How fares what remains of my duchy?"

Jeremy smiled slightly and resumed his seat on the stool beside the small table. "Dare I say well? Your consort runs Tynan efficiently. And Warrick rode post to Northumberland to speak with Percy concerning Harold's campaign."

William pondered this. "And Percy's thoughts of my

brother the usurper?"

"Should Harold raid Northumberland, Percy would be hard-pressed to halt him. The Douglas clan has of late been active along Percy's northern border, likely honoring Scotland's French alliance. Kenrick could plunder virtually unchecked."

"The Douglas may merely slake his passion for fighting the earl," came William's bland reply. "He has warred against the Percys since God rested on the seventh day."

"That's truth." Jeremy's jaw tensed. "Our plight worsens with Kenrick's troops afield. Harold will likely gain more men, and Percy won't aid us in winning our lands back. He has other concerns."

"With James Stuart confined in London, 'tis doubtful the Scots will venture far south." The duke rubbed his temples with his fingertips, a weary sigh escaping him. "We'll have to rely on York against my brother."

"Aye. And to that end, your wife has been most helpful." Jeremy produced a parchment scroll from inside his tunic. "I'd meant to tell you of this earlier, but I was distracted."

Lifting his hand from his forehead, William looked at Jeremy and grinned. "Has Alicen been about nearby?"

Jeremy ignored the intimation, slapping the parchment into William's hand. "Your lady wife's arranged an audience with York. He's in Burgundy but returns home in a month."

"Guendolen is a marvel." William beamed. "Marry for love, my friend, not for profit."

Jeremy looked away. Love wasn't as simple as William suggested. It stripped a man of pride, left him at a woman's mercy. She twisted his logic, clouded his reason until naught but her love mattered. Then when she betrayed him he died inside. Like a suit of armor hanging in a hall, his outer shell protected naught but the vaporous humors of a former soul.

He was well acquainted with those foul humors.

The duke studied his captain. "I'll not apologize for stirring painful memories, for mere words will not assuage that pain," William stated bluntly. "Therefore, I'll speak only of what presently concerns you. God blessed me much with a man of your ilk, Jeremy, and I thank you for your loyalty. You make my confinement near bearable." He smiled when Alicen entered with her tray of medicaments. "You, and my lovely healer."

"You mentioned us in the same breath?" Alicen raised a quizzical brow, then set the tray down beside William. "You could not have spoken well of either of us, my lord. I fear the good captain wishes me clapped in irons for treason." The look she sent Jeremy dared him to deny her accusation.

Jeremy glowered, but William chuckled. "Forgive him, Mistress. The fairer sex plagues him sorely, and he sulks over his ill luck. I assure you he is a good man."

Alicen's brow quirked again as she glanced at Jeremy. "Too cheerless for my tastes, my lord. He never appears to enjoy himself."

Jeremy's jaw set, as if to hold back a stinging retort.

"Being my right hand is a weighty task," William countered smoothly, glancing between the antagonists. "He regards duty very seriously."

"Mayhap you could order him to smile upon occasion," Alicen returned, eyes glittering. "His countenance could dull the sun."

Jeremy clamped his jaw shut, determined to ignore Alicen. But despite his best efforts to prevent it, the wench tormented him mercilessly. Whenever she was near, potent emotion gripped him—anger or suspicion or...desire.

Nay, I'll not desire the shrew. Never!

William laughed as hard as his weak lung allowed. "She has it aright, lad. You have been gloomy of late."

"I find little of cheer in this place, my lord," Jeremy retorted, "since I must discern if what appears true is not merely illusion." His hands fisted then relaxed. "Sir, is there aught else you need of me? If not, I've business to attend."

William sighed, regret etching his features. "You do naught but work. I'd prefer you—" With a shake of his head and a wave of his hand, he dismissed Jeremy. "Go to your affairs. Alicen will care well for me in your absence."

Jeremy's blue gaze turned icy. "No doubt she's spent much time convincing you she can do just that." He stalked out.

"He's the best man ever to serve me, yet I worry for him," William stated quietly. Alicen continued to arrange her ointments. "His wife's betrayal shattered him. He'd thought Estelle a loyal consort. A woman unlike the faithless jades in his family."

"Perhaps she could not abide a soldier's duties," Alicen replied flatly, unbandaging and re-salving William's wound as she spoke.

"Mayhap. But her killing his unborn child and herself broke Jeremy's heart. Now, it seems his whole concern is serving me."

Stark horror clutched Alicen's soul. What manner of woman married then refused to bear her husband's child? She hid her shock with a casual reply. "His dedication makes him valuable, my lord. With naught else to occupy him, he does his best to please you." *And to plague me.*

"Still, men need diversion. Jeremy's like a tool—useful, but devoid of spirit. A man in that state is ill at heart."

"I've long held the less emotion the better the soldier," Alicen said bitterly. "Feelings can obscure duty, and that would be ruinous." *Like they ruined Orrick.*

William pondered a moment. "Five years ago, Jeremy forsook untold riches by leaving the Duke of Bedford's service. Rather than plunder the Loire Valley, he joined me to make his living in a less barbarous manner.

"Neither of us sought a return to France, but my fealty to the King required it. The slaughter was pitiless. We longed to return to England and peace." William's voice chilled. "My bastard brother had stolen much of my lands, including that which I'd granted Jeremy."

Silent, Alicen contemplated the duke's words. The vexing Captain Blaine was a scourge to women. Yet, based on this account, he had cause. A scheming wife certainly had ruined more than one strong soul. Mayhap Blaine's single-minded pursuit of duty kept his personal pain at bay. But did he truly dislike much of what that duty required?

His wife's perfidy must have scarred him deeply to turn him so against females. And William claimed he'd foresworn great profit to keep his honor. But how could he be merciful one moment, unyielding the next? And how could he dislike soldiering yet be so skilled?

She needed time to reflect upon William's words and decided to ride to Sherford. After saddling Hercules, she left Ned instructions on the duke's care.

"I'll see to everything until you return," he vowed. "You've no need to worry."

"I'll not fret. Expect me by eventide." With a grin and a quick ruffling of his blond hair, she was gone.

Her hopes for a peaceful ride died aborning when she saw who awaited her at the gate astride his own horse.

She smiled sweetly to cover her resignation. "Out to take the air, Captain?"

"If you keep a slow pace."

"You've no pressing responsibilities to attend? Something of more import than escorting me. Some village to burn or peasant to flog?"

One brow rose. "My men favor you too much to watch you closely. As I don't share their sentiment, I'll attend you when you're away from the duke."

Alicen's exaggerated smile turned brittle. "Ah, yes, I might plot treason. Very well, Captain, I'm your captive. Your pardon, however, if I'll not sacrifice a good ride to remain confined in my home." She pulled Hercules around and kept him ahead of Jeremy's charger during their wild dash to the village.

***

Jeremy brooded as they left Sherford an hour later at a far more sedate pace than they'd entered. Having seen Alicen's back the entire way there pricked him. It underscored the superb riding ability Naismith insisted she possessed, and put Jeremy at a loss to understand why that angered him. Were she a man, he'd congratulate her for her skill.

The woman had occupied most all his waking thoughts of late, which was dangerous to his men, himself, and chiefly to William. Yet he couldn't keep her from his mind.

Nor could he refrain from needing her nearby. More than once he thought to apologize for being such a thorn in her heel, but the proper words eluded him. She rendered him speechless.

For her part, Alicen found herself tired and irritable when she'd hoped the excursion would improve her spirits. She blamed Jeremy Blaine. Far more than at any time prior, his nearness frayed her nerves. An overwhelming desire to be alone arose.

"Have my actions assuaged your suspicions, Captain?" she asked archly.

He visibly tensed, then glanced her way. "If you ask whether you may roam freely alone, the answer is 'nay.' With William in residence, you'll not venture from Landeyda unescorted."

"You burn daylight following me."

He fixed her with a hard stare. "Do I?"

"Yes," she hissed, hoping she gave no hint of her lie. "I've done naught to deserve distrust." *Naught you've seen me doing.*

"Your feelings are of no moment to me, Mistress. You'll not ride alone until we're quit of you, so leave be."

"You suspect me of treachery against my liege lord?" Her question was more an indignant gasp.

He shrugged. "Your knowledge of his condition makes you a potential traitor. Thus, I deal with you as I do."

"How would I approach Harold's people? I know of no one in Sherford sympathetic to him."

"Words easily spoken."

"You've searched the town yourself. Have you found citizens disloyal to William?"

Her question alarmed Jeremy. How much did she know of his activities? He'd slowly brought men to the area—in the guise of merchants, carpenters, hirelings. They'd taken up residence, begun to trade....Now, his force in town numbered just over a dozen, with a score extra on outlying land. Could she know that? Had someone discerned this plot and informed Harold's loyalists?

"I've warned you not to concern yourself with military matters," he said harshly. "I'll suspect you until such time as William is safe."

"You have no soul."

He didn't so much as flinch, though her ire pierced deeply. "I have my duty. You have yours."

"You kill and I heal," she scoffed. "We're at cross purposes."

His expression remained unchanged, but fury ignited in his eyes. "You believe I enjoy killing?" he asked, voice tight.

"Don't you?" She knew that query's falseness, but was too stung by his animosity to retract it.

Jeremy ground his teeth a long moment, then said simply, "Killing is a lamentable aspect of my profession."

"You are capable of naught but soldiering?"

"I wished to serve William," he retorted. "I kill when I must, no matter how wretched that is." The spark in his eyes flamed higher, but his voice remained level. "Tis easy for you to judge me. You, the revered guardian of this shire. Yet your duty has no more value than mine, though you'd have it so. I protect William's subjects. Do I spill blood in the process—offensive to you or no—'tis oft expedient."

"Is there pleasure in feeling a man's life drain away upon your sword?" she sneered.

"I do *not* kill men for sport!" Jeremy clenched his reins, body rigid. "I kill only to protect my duke, my soldiers, or myself. Believe me or no, I hate senseless slaughter."

Alicen recalled William's saying much the same of the captain.

"Tell me, then," she asked archly, "if not battle and mayhem, what pleases you? You distrust me merely because of my sex. Follow like my shadow, with as little expression as that apparition, and treat me harshly. Does harrying innocent women amuse you?"

Snarling, he raised his fist, then dropped it immediately back to his side. "Were you a man, by God, I'd have satisfaction for your insults!"

Alicen had goaded the wolf into baring his teeth. 'Twas time to retreat. But not without one last sally. Staring at his fist, she tilted a mocking brow, then half smiled. "I'm glad you still discern between those to kill and those to protect." Her gaze flicked to his furious eyes. "I've wondered whether your hatred of women clouded your soldier's honor."

"I've rarely harmed a woman," he spat. "Though they oft manage to harm me."

At the end of his stamina, he wanted to howl with rage. But just as he contemplated giving in to that wish, a sudden change in Alicen's expression startled his fury away. From antagonism her look melted to a distant, musing gaze, as if she heard far off church bells. The hair on the nape of his neck rose. For that moment, he ceased to exist in her world.

For that moment, he didn't want to.

She shook her head as if to clear it, then turned pensive eyes to him. "I must return to Sherford." She reined Hercules around.

He rode up beside her. "Why?"

"Someone requires my aid," she said quietly.

"You've the power of divination?" he asked half-mockingly, his tone masking sudden wariness. He could not completely dismiss the strange experiences he'd had since his arrival at Landeyda. But he would try. "Mayhap you're a sorceress who conjured Landeyda's benevolent spirit."

Alicen paled visibly and swallowed hard. "Ridiculous fancy. I've oft sensed when others needed me. 'Tis a skill I was born with, not one acquired in unholy ritual." She swallowed again before saying, "Witchcraft is easily misunderstood and thus dangerous to speak of even in jest, Captain."

His mouth twisted into a wry grin. "So, the dauntless healer fears such talk? I scarce can believe it."

"I've no wish to be suspected of evil," she replied somberly. "Thus, I must ask you to cease this discussion."

"I'll give your request all the gravity it deserves." He smiled slyly. "After you've appeased my curiosity."

A chill slid up Alicen's spine. "Regarding what?"

"How you came to the healing craft. 'Tis more than passing strange for a woman to practice medicine."

"Someone had to treat the sick and wounded while the men were off killing for their king," she bit out between her teeth.

"You've not answered my question."

The chill again. Alicen felt like a hare in a huntsman's trap. She could neither flee nor hide from this man. Mayhap the truth would appease him.

"I learned from my mother."

Jeremy's look was openly amazed. "Who taught her?"

"Her mother," Alicen said in a nearly inaudible voice.

"Three generations of women healers in one family? Not all the men hereabouts were off to war. Yet no *man* of your relation was a physician?"

"Nay." She rushed on. "Less than four generations ago plague claimed half the populace. War with France went on over fourscore years. Thousands died. But my great-grandam survived to pass her knowledge of healing to my grandam. And she to my mother."

"Does the local priest approve of your occupation?"

Alicen fought down clawing panic. "He believes illness is the will of God. I, for one, do not agree."

"And so you seek to heal?" At her curt nod, he asked, "But through divination and herbs? Aren't those the ways of—"

"We must hurry!"

Without so much as a glance at her escort, Alicen kicked Hercules into a canter and raced for Sherford, leaving Jeremy's question unasked. He could only follow and await a better opportunity to question her further.

But question her he would.

Seven

The moment Alicen entered town, a heavy woman of untold age accosted her, effectively postponing Jeremy's interrogation.

"Mistress Kent," she puffed, winded from haste, "praise Jesu you've returned! My Jack hurt himself and can't rise from bed."

Jeremy repressed his surprise, yet marveled at Alicen's intuition even as he followed the two women to a large house on the southerly street.

An hour later, once again on their way to Landeyda, Jeremy contemplated the discovery he'd made about Alicen. His actions had mortified her. How else to explain her rush to finish in Sherford and be gone for home? Or her choice of a shortcut?

Had Jeremy known such bawdy deeds would set her off center, he'd have tried them earlier. Alicen's disquiet fascinated him. She wasn't so aloof when flustered and out of her element, and he liked that.

He had instantly known the source of the patient's pain, though the man himself seemed ignorant of the cause. The soldier saw the lustful looks the serving wench had sent the invalid's way and understood. Remembering the scene, he chuckled.

The wife gave no sign she realized her husband's perfidy, but crimson stained Alicen's cheeks. After treating his malady, she had quickly collected her fee and then bolted from the house to leap astride Hercules, an amused Jeremy in pursuit.

She hadn't said a word to him since before their return to Sherford.

They were now well into the woods. Branches interlaced high above them, forming a leafy vaulted ceiling. With autumn's approach, the leaves would soon turn colors and carpet the ground, but for now they dressed the trees in verdant shades.

The path was barely wide enough for two to ride

abreast, but Jeremy deliberately kept Charon beside Hercules. Alicen's discomfort almost made him laugh outright. She shot him an exasperated glance, but the look only caused his smile to broaden. This was the most he'd enjoyed Alicen Kent's company since first they'd met.

"Will the miller's back heal quickly?" he asked innocently.

She stared warily at him before answering, "If he doesn't o'ertax himself, he'll be about in a few days."

"So, he'll ride again soon." Looking over in time to see her gulp, Jeremy forced back a guffaw. "'Tis certain the serving wench will appreciate his quick recovery."

At that, Alicen turned so quickly toward him Hercules danced sideways a few steps. "Lecher! You approve the man's adultery!"

"I said naught of approval," Jeremy stated, grinning. "I merely hinted the wench would laud your healing talents."

"I did not tend him to aid his lewdness. His wife asked me to help him."

"Ah, she excuses her husband's dalliances."

"No woman wishes a faithless man. 'Tis a soldier's notion that his woman be true while he pursues infidelity."

Jeremy's humor vanished instantly. "I honored my marriage vows. My lady broke faith. And robbed me of both my child and herself." He drew several breaths before adding, "At least she did not cuckold me, as Mother and my sister by marriage did their husbands."

"Mayhap she had no wish to raise your child alone." Alicen saw him wince and, noting deep anguish in his eyes, and switched tacks. "When you are about the duke's business, what of your woman at Tynan? Who protects her? Who guarded your mother and your brother's wife whilst their men fought abroad?"

"They found their own comforts," Jeremy responded in a low, resentful tone. "And destroyed two honorable men."

"But what of your lady?" Alicen persisted, unable to fathom why his answer was important to her. "How does she find comfort with you long away?"

Blue eyes turned cold. "I've pledged faith to none since Estelle. She taught me that a lady wins a man's heart, then uses it as a bauble. No woman will ever again do such to me."

"Is that why you are a tyrant?"

"Tyrant?" He laughed mirthlessly. "When Father discovered Mother's indiscretion, he hanged the stable master and beat her. That ended her infidelity. For a time. My eldest brother beats his wife for every imagined treachery. She's never broken faith with him."

Alicen couldn't hide her appalled expression.

"Edward treated his wife with all kindness," Jeremy said matter-of-factly. "She betrayed him with his closest friend."

He didn't add that his mother couldn't leave her bed for a fortnight after the beating. Or that as a seven-year-old boy, he'd despised his father for hurting her. Later, at fourteen, he hated Manfred's turning Agnes into a terrified wraith. And he mourned for Edward, whose kindness had been wretchedly misused.

Let Alicen think what she would. Just as Estelle before her, she could not accept a soldier. He was better off without such women in his life.

This volley between them had turned too painful, and he liked not the feelings it brought him. Thus he sought to regain the upper hand in their latest argument.

"The duke told me your father fought at Agincourt."

Alicen's expression became guarded. "Aye, he was in the King's service for a goodly number of years."

"And your mother was Irish?"

Her affirmation came more warily this time.

At her hesitation, he pressed his advantage. "The Celt's Druid priestesses were herb-healers, were they not?" His hard look challenged her to deny his statement.

"Generations of my foremothers were healers," she answered carefully, growing panic evident behind her steady reply. "They conveyed knowledge from mother to daughter. Naught is amiss in that."

"Did I suggest such a thing?" His smile taunted.

She faced him squarely. "Nay, Captain Blaine, yet you seem convinced my skills are evil. Father thought to blend old ways with new and bought medical texts on a diplomatic mission to Italy. Mother also taught me those methods."

"So you admit the old teachings are Druidic?" Jeremy's intense stare dispelled his tone's indifference.

"I admit Mother was the finest healer in the north, and that I'm honor bound to follow her path as best I can. If such is sinister, then I am condemned already in your eyes."

Her voice had grown steadily more quiet, her manner more guarded, and Jeremy knew he'd completely unnerved her. Oddly enough, that angered him. He'd expected a show of her fine temper, yet he'd only succeeded in cowing her. He wanted the snarling vixen with the flashing eyes. He wanted a fight.

"Condemned but not punished," he replied firmly.

He regretted his cruel jest the moment he spoke. Alicen's face drained of color, and her eyes turned to huge green pools. Such naked vulnerability tore at his conscience.

Be damned, why doesn't she defend herself?

"Alicen—" He reached for Hercules' reins.

"Stay away!" Before Jeremy could react, she had urged her gelding into a headlong run down the forest lane.

"Alicen, wait!" He held Charon to a slow trot, hoping she would realize he didn't pursue her and would thus stop running.

Fleeing in complete terror, she never looked back.

She was still within sight but pulling steadily away when a fox darted from cover directly in front of Hercules. As panicked as his mistress, the gelding shied.

"No!" Jeremy watched helplessly while Alicen catapulted over her mount's head. She somersaulted in mid-air then landed in a crumpled heap at the side of the road.

Within moments he was kneeling beside her still form, his heart lurching.

"Alicen? Can you hear me, lass?" His dry voice cracked.

He cautiously rolled her to her back. A low moan assured him she yet lived, but he feared serious injury. Gently running his hands along her limbs, he felt no broken bones and thanked God she had landed on ground softened by recent rains.

He slipped his arm under her shoulders to lift her,

then pulled back the hood confining her chestnut hair. A lump twice the size of his thumb lay well behind her right ear, but he was heartened to see that his fingers bore none of her blood. He barely noted his shaking hands as he gathered her close then slid his legs beneath her for support. She groaned again, softly.

"Jesu, lass," he said, voice husky with pain. "I never meant for this to happen." He traced her lips with a trembling finger. There was no reaction. "Don't die. Please."

Lord, have I destroyed the finest healer I've ever known?

Guilt burned inside, and he cursed himself and his family. As a man, he hated Estelle, his mother and his sister-in-law for their perfidy. But he hated his father's and brother's brutal reprisals as well. The women in his life were unscrupulous, the men unmerciful. But for Edward, who'd had his heart shredded in return for his boundless love. He had never recovered from that betrayal. Jeremy hated Edward's wife most of all.

And now, his own ruthlessness had injured a woman whose only crime was being female.

A very fine female, he grudgingly admitted. Lord, what power did she wield over him? The urge to touch her silky hair proved strong, coupled with concern he'd missed an injury. He pushed stray locks from her face and combed his fingers through the auburn mass, enjoying the feel as he reassured himself she'd received only the one blow to her head. She was quite lovely when not vexed with him. With his thumb he gently removed a smudge of dirt from her cheek.

She didn't stir, and her lack of response to his ministrations troubled him more than he would readily admit. She was so pale and still, oblivious to her surroundings. Mayhap she'd not recover. This possibility made him swallow through his parched throat, and his lips moved in silent prayer that her stubborn nature would keep her alive. If she died, what would he do?

A sudden chill wind surrounded him, though nothing stirred. The hair at his nape rose just as the voice he'd heard before whispered, "You see an enemy where naught exists. Ignore this warning at your peril."

The wind instantly died. The chill in his soul remained.

***

"Mistress Kent? Can you hear me? Awake, lass."

She recognized the deep, resonant voice. Orrick? No, not that tone for many years. The concern confused her, as did the hand tenderly stroking her cheek. Dull pain throbbed behind her eyes, demanding they remain closed tight. But the voice's gentle insistence drew them open.

It shocked her to realize that she lay in Jeremy Blaine's lap as his fingers lightly traced the planes of her face. His blue eyes, indigo in the dim forest, showed unmistakable concern. This turned to relief when her gaze held his. His smile dazzled.

"Welcome back, lass."

Shaky, but inexplicably determined to move away from him, she sat up with a groan. Dizziness descended. "What happened?"

Jeremy stood and indicated Hercules. "Your gelding shied and threw you. For that, he should be punished."

"Nay!" Alicen surged to her feet to clutch Jeremy's sword arm, then instantly regretted the action as fire roared through her brain. She swayed, but managed to subdue the pain by dint of will. "Don't hurt him," she implored. "Please."

Supporting her by the arms, Jeremy stared at her pale features, his mouth set in a grim line of self-loathing. "I but jested, Alicen. Another ill-conceived jest, I fear. I'd never harm Hercules. And I didn't intend to—" He broke off, then finished silently, *harm you.*

She squinted against more throbbing pain. "Is he injured?"

"I think not. He didn't fall." When she started toward the horse, Jeremy quickly said, "Sit a while, Mistress. I'll see to him."

Though her mind warned to flee, her body could not respond to the urge. Instead, she sank to the ground and cradled her head in her hands to keep from fainting. She started at a touch on her shoulder a few minutes later.

"He'll be sore for a time," Jeremy said, "but he's done himself no serious injury."

"I'm walking back to Landeyda," Alicen declared as firmly as she could manage. That her statement made little sense never crossed her addled mind. She noticed Jeremy tying Hercules' reins to Charon's saddle. There was little else she saw, though, as a shaft of sunlight penetrated the trees and drove daggers into her eyes. She clenched them shut, trembling.

Jeremy's hand on her elbow steadied her. "You'll ride with me." His tone broached no discussion.

Her eyes snapped open and turned to him. "I'm able to ride alone, Captain."

Seeing her terror, her defenselessness, stunned Jeremy. She looked like Manfred's wife, and it galled to think he'd put such intense fear into Alicen's emerald eyes. It also galled that the stubborn wench would never admit she needed aid, at least not his. Controlling his anger—at himself and at her—he untied her reins. Then he silently mounted Charon.

Alicen struggled into her saddle then, leaning to retrieve the reins, immediately felt faint. Swaying, she yet managed to stay mounted and even took the lead. Again, the wild desire to escape the man riding with her sprang up, but she set a slow pace. It suited her reeling senses not to ride quickly. Despite the care she took, however, a stab of pain again made her cringe and bring her hand to the back of her head. She squeezed her eyes shut.

Just for a moment. I'll close them just a moment...

Jeremy caught Alicen around the waist the very instant she began to topple from her saddle. He pulled her across his lap, startled by what this action made him feel. She weighed more than he had suspected. Solid. Strong. And he enjoyed her weight when he drew her close, enjoyed tucking her head 'neath his chin. It somehow seemed right to hold her thus. To smell her fresh scent and feel her warmth against him.

But concern ended sensual pleasure. She was seriously injured, else she'd never allow such contact between them. She needed proper care, and it fell to him to get it for her.

He retrieved Hercules' reins. A dead gallop would be imprudent, but he set as fast a pace for Landeyda as he dared. Alicen would *not* die. Amazed to find his grip on her tightening, he concerned himself with making the ride as smooth as possible. She'd endured enough pain that day.

Remorse clawed at him. Had he not sought to best her in their constant battle of wills, she'd not have fled. Not have been injured. He swallowed bile. His animosity toward Alicen Kent had crumbled—he cared for her much more than wisdom dictated he should.

Jeremy knew the exact moment Alicen awakened. Her body tensed, and she drew in a sharp breath. Half smiling, he tilted his head down to whisper in her ear, "Don't shriek too loudly, Mistress. If you startle Charon, I'll have to drop you to control him."

"Put me back on Hercules, Captain."

"As you wish, although I'll ride with you. We wouldn't want you falling off your saddle again."

Looking up slowly, Alicen caught the soldier's brief smile. This teasing side both attracted and frightened her, and she was uncertain she liked it. However, she distinctly understood her feelings about being in his embrace. That felt entirely too good.

And *that* terrified her.

Why must the cur be so close when she lacked means to protect herself? She was drawn to a man she couldn't love, and she wanted to resist, to make him release her. But her body hurt so, and she had no strength to push his comforting arms away. Slowly, she lowered her head back to his chest. The world spun less when her cheek rested against his doublet. Her eyes closed.

"I didn't fall off," she grumbled. "I was thrown."

"You'll not be thrown again," Jeremy whispered back. "I'll not allow it."

He wasn't certain she heard. She'd fainted once more.

***

Ned panicked when Jeremy dismounted, Alicen in his arms.

"You blackguard, I'll kill you for hurting her!"

"Hercules shied and threw her, lad," Jeremy said with calm firmness as he carried Alicen swiftly into the cottage. "Now come with me. You may kill me after you help me tend her."

He placed Alicen in her own bed as Ned stood in the chamber doorway, face blank. The boy clutched his stomach, looking pale and sick himself.

Sensing his difficulty, Jeremy moved close and grasped Ned's shoulder. "How does she treat head injuries?" he asked quietly.

"I, I'm uncertain." The boy's chin quivered, and his eyes filled with tears.

Jeremy smiled, though his stomach knotted with worry that the apprentice would be useless. "Think, lad. You must have seen her attend such maladies. What does she do?"

Soak a cloth in cold water and place it on the injury.

The voice filled Jeremy's head just as Ned blurted out, "She, uhm, she uses cloths soaked in cold water."

Jeremy blinked, then asked the boy, "Where does she place them?"

"On the injury."

As I said.

Soldiers' lives depended on awareness of everything around them, and Jeremy knew the only woman in the room was insensate. The voice was not Alicen's, yet it wasn't unfamiliar. "You see an enemy where none exists..." Nay! He refused to believe he heard Kaitlyn O'Rourke's voice in his mind. The only thing he knew was that Alicen needed care.

He turned to Ned. "Fetch what we'll need. I'll make her more comfortable."

Words easily spoken. But the moment he began removing Alicen's clothes, keeping his mind on his task grew nigh impossible. Boots and chaperon afforded no trouble, but he suffered a racing heart and unsteady hands as he stripped off her muddy tunic, followed by her torn and sodden hose.

Though he refrained from looking at what he uncovered, he could feel smooth thighs and shapely calves beneath his palms. Firm muscles and satiny skin wreaked havoc on his senses—but before he ruined them both, rationality prevailed.

What in Jesu's name was he thinking? He'd caused her injury—he had no right to entertain such desires.

Steady, man, he warned himself. *'Tis neither time nor place for such folly. You're no better than the brute she thinks you if you cannot refrain from lusting for a defenseless woman.*

That stark fact brought him control.

Alicen lay helpless. He could ill afford to compromise her, could ill discern why he had to subdue his body, his base instinct. He clenched his jaw. As much as he desired Landeyda's mistress, she wanted naught of his attention. And he could not take her and claim himself honorable afterward.

"My apologies for bringing you such misery, lass," he murmured. Raising her hand to his lips, he softly kissed it.

Then he caught his breath, loosened the ties of her shirt, and drew the blanket above her breasts. By careful maneuvering, he managed to remove the garment without baring her to his gaze. With a sigh of relief, he adjusted the blanket around her.

A glitter at Alicen's throat caught his eye, and he found himself automatically reaching for the source. He turned the silver Celtic cross over in his fingers. Embedded in the wire frame were five distinct stones. Where had he seen gems set in that pattern before?

Alicen's apprentice burst into the infirmary, pulling Jeremy from his thoughts. Ned handed him the wet cloths, and he placed one against Alicen's injury. Then he ordered the boy from the room.

"I'll take the first watch, lad," he said when Ned protested. "You've other chores to see to, and the Duke to check. Replace me at mealtime, then I'll return at dusk. Thus, she'll be tended at all times, but we'll not fatigue from our efforts."

"Can I trust her with you, sir?" Ned asked candidly.

"I swear it."

"See that you keep your word," the boy stated as he headed for the door. "Else I'll keep mine."

And 'tis certain I'll help him do so, said that distinctly Irish voice.

Jeremy spun around, but there was no one behind him. A fact that didn't even surprise him.

***

"What happened," William asked as he stood in the chamber doorway.

Jeremy motioned him to a stool without looking up

from changing the cloth on Alicen's injury. Instead, he explained in a few terse words.

"Is there aught I can do?"

"Nay, my lord. She broke no bones. And stood by herself momentarily just after her fall." He used ministering to Alicen as an excuse not to meet William's gaze. "I understand I must wake her every few hours through the night." He was not about to tell William how he'd gained that knowledge—that a very feminine Irish voice had given it to him.

"And how much of this is your responsibility?"

Jeremy finally looked up, meeting his lord's intense stare. He shrugged helplessly. "All of it." He closed his eyes. "I frightened her so badly she fled from me. And then Hercules was startled..." Looking down, he realized he was crushing the damp cloth in his hand. "She could have been killed," he whispered, barely able to suppress the shudder that thought gave him. "And I would have been to blame."

Eight

"You know Sherford residents have little love for Harold. Do you yet suspect Alicen of treachery?" William's voice held an edge.

Jeremy shrugged at the question. "I've not located any supporters, yet they may exist."

"You've not answered my question regarding Alicen."

Sighing, Jeremy returned the used cloth to the basin and stretched his back. "She could certainly influence most of the shire's residents."

"Against me? To what purpose."

"I know not." Jeremy intently eyed his duke. "Should Kenrick learn you're here, he could destroy us all. Landeyda'd not withstand his attack."

"You've yet to convince me Alicen is a foe," William insisted.

"And yet I don't know that she's not."

"Enough!" Glaring, the duke approached Jeremy. Though his voice was quiet, there was no mistaking his feelings. "I needn't remind you of our debt to our hostess. Speak no more of her supposed disloyalty."

Jeremy nodded to indicate the point had been made. Only privately did he admit pure stubbornness kept his doubts alive. He wished for Alicen to be untrue, thus giving him reason to despise her...instead of what he'd recently begun to feel.

***

"Have you struck a truce with Mistress Kent?" William asked four days later.

He sat in a chair by the window, reading one of the seemingly endless communications they'd been receiving of late. A thick woolen blanket was draped across his lap, but he'd insisted the window be open to let in fresh air and light.

Jeremy set aside the diagram he was working on. "We're warily civil." At his lord's questioning look, he added, "And she's not left the grounds since her accident."

He'd sought absolution from the guilt of causing her injury by circulating a rumor that she had taken to bed with a serious illness. He reasoned that, if no one sought the healer's aid, she'd have time to mend. Yet the stubborn wench was up and about after two days' rest! He knew she wasn't entirely healed, as she retired earlier than at any time since they'd met. Guilt squeezed his heart.

That and remembering the feelings holding her had brought. They posed incredible dangers, especially to his weary soul. Only distance from her could help him. Which was nigh impossible to achieve.

With William yet weak, I cannot quit myself of her, he brooded. That meant resisting the desire to kiss away the trepidation in her eyes. His mouth twisted into an ironic smile. She would never stand for comfort from a soldier.

"I like not that she'll be alone after we depart," William said into the strained silence. "'Tis dangerous for a woman."

Jeremy shrugged and turned back to his diagram. "Solitary ventures suit her. She could chronicle this shire, having spent a dozen years at sickbeds. By escorting her about, I now know of all the residents, too."

William nodded in approval. "Ever the strategist."

"Knowledge prepares me for any event."

"I'm charging you with her safety until she is properly wed."

Jeremy's head snapped up and around. "You truly wish to see her matched, my lord? I thought you but jested."

"Since this latest mishap, I feel most strongly about this."

"Who would pledge troth to her?" Jeremy wondered aloud. "The woman is, by any standard, unusual."

William cocked his head. "*Unusual?* She is completely unique! I've ne'er met a woman like her." He frowned. "Singularity aside, however, she needs a husband, else we'll leave her defenseless."

Jeremy stared out the window, heart beating dully at the portent of such words. *She's been alone for years. Why should aught be different now?* Lost to his own musings, he didn't see William studying him.

"'Tis fascinating Alicen shares her learning with you."

Jeremy missed William's smooth tone. "She's recorded effective remedies for every malady she's treated. A reference for the boy, does he choose to follow her calling..." His voice faded as he caught William's amused expression. "My lord?"

"In the past three years, you've noted little of any woman. Are you, perhaps, somewhat taken with the physician?"

Jeremy knew his cheeks blazed, and used anger to cover his riotous emotions. "Taken by surprise or fever, taken by Death to the land beyond, but *never* taken by that woman!"

He thought to leave, but Alicen's entry cut off retreat. To hide his telling expression, he moved to the window. A few slow breaths steadied him. Knowing what this audience would entail and curious to see Alicen's response, he turned, leaned back against the window casing and crossed his arms over his chest.

"You sent for me, my lord?" Alicen glanced in Jeremy's direction, looked back at the duke, then glanced at Jeremy again.

William indicated a stool near the bed. "Please be seated, Mistress," he said affably. "I trust you're feeling better?"

"Aye, my lord." Another glance at Captain Blaine offered Alicen little enlightenment. He was staring into space.

The duke spared her further conjecture.

"Your unwed state troubles me." His upheld hand stopped her immediate protest. "Hear me, Mistress Kent. Your lack of a husband puts you in grave danger—"

"I'd faced little peril until your arrival, my lord," she broke in tartly. William might be her liege, but she'd not meekly submit to his marriage decree!

"And you'll be in even more danger when we leave," William continued, no change in his expression. "Therefore, 'tis my wish to see you wed before I depart Landeyda."

Unable to remain seated, Alicen rose. No refuge at the window with the captain there. She gathered her courage and extended a hand to William in supplication.

"My lord, please let me speak." She dropped her hand to her side only when he nodded. Voice low, she stated, "I'll not long endure a match to a man who cannot love me."

William's eyebrow rose. "Think you no man would wed you?"

"I know it in my soul. Orrick, my betrothed, has been dead to me these five years past. In all that time, no other has paid me court." She bit her lip. "Most who know me fear me."

She caught Jeremy's surprised look before William's next words drew her attention.

"I can scarce believe they'd dread taking you to wife," the duke stated. "You are a gifted, selfless healer."

"Thus they've no desire for me." At his blank stare, she asked, "Who would share me with my healing call? Allow me to go where needed, when needed?" Hands clenched in front of her, she paced. When she stopped, her eyes met the duke's. "God's truth, my lord, I'd not abide a man who chained me to him. I vowed to serve any in pain. I'll not break that vow to please a husband."

"But 'tis a man's duty to protect his wife," William replied. "Your wanderings place you in danger."

Alicen stared pointedly at Jeremy. "Before you and your soldiers arrived at my door, little of true danger occurred."

"Your concerns have not fallen on deaf ears, Mistress," the duke said gently. "Nonetheless, you'll wed within a month."

A visible shiver racked Alicen's body. "If that should come to pass, my lord," she returned evenly, unable to mask her rising despair, "there's no telling what will come of it."

Jeremy chanced a look at William and saw that his duke was as discomfited as he at Alicen's statement.

***

Riding north with Fish in search of enemy encampments had proven a boon. Jeremy had been waiting and watching too long, which didn't appease his desire for action. Now, after being abroad for three days, he again felt in command of himself. Their search, though futile, had distracted him from irksome thoughts—

William's plan for Alicen to wed. Her reaction to that edict. His own response to the woman herself.

He resented that his feelings nettled so intensely. Holding her the day she'd fallen had rekindled a long lost dream, one he'd shut his heart to after Estelle's death. He'd resigned himself to an existence without wife or children. Without love. Yet the feel of Alicen in his arms had made thoughts of hearth and home return in a painful rush.

Hating those needs, he cursed her for evoking them. She had made him savor her nearness, her womanliness. It irked that she didn't acknowledge his manliness in return.

He'd leave. Go to York and Tynan, then to the field to win back his lands. Alicen's memory would fade to naught. After his victory, mayhap he'd take a mistress. But he'd never marry her. Wives were unfaithful unless coerced.

His thoughts returned to the healer and his despicable conduct toward her. He'd bullied her, terrified her into flight and injury. Desired her. She made indifference and discipline evaporate. Neither William's health nor Kenrick's threat had unseated her from his mind. 'Twas maddening.

But having her could never be.

With men's lives hanging upon her whim, he could not allow himself to care for her. 'Twould compromise his duty. A quick tumble was not worth risking lives, and his feelings would never go beyond lust. He told himself such. William wished her a good match. As a despised soldier, Jeremy would not be considered. Not that he desired such consideration...

"Why is the wench so difficult to blink?"

In reaction to this abrupt outburst, Fish grabbed his sword. "What?"

Coloring, Jeremy glanced sharply at his subordinate, but vowed to brazen out his chagrin. "I spoke of Landeyda's mistress! A holy terror, she is. She plays endless flint to my tinder. To hear her, I grow fangs and horns at a mere hint of battle."

Fish shrugged and released his sword hilt. "You must admit Cap'n, whene'er Kenrick's name is spoken, Sweet Jesu, your teeth grow long!"

Jeremy's jaw hardened when his glare brought outright laughter to his subordinate's weathered features. "You see jests where none live, Malcolm. The Duke obeys her like a trained hound. Christ's guts, he's a peer of the realm!"

"He desires a sure recovery from his injuries."

Jeremy snorted.

"She's comely," Fish stated. "Likely the duke misses his duchess, and Alicen's pleasant aspect eases his loneliness."

The notion that his soldiers saw Alicen as pretty unleashed a startling, raging jealousy Jeremy had to fight down. "'Tis foolhardy of William to blindly follow a wench's orders."

"With respect, sir, the landed *lady* of whom you speak is the shire's finest physician. I'd not think poorly of any who heed her remedies. In truth, the duke trusts her."

Jeremy grunted. 'Twas obvious Fish thought Alicen a saint. A comely saint. Nor was Jeremy himself unaffected. Despite obstinate denial, his want of her had shaken him. He wished to do far more than just hold her.

In contemplation, he massaged the bridge of his nose with forefinger and thumb. Celibacy disagreed with him, he decided. He'd not been with a woman in months. When given the opportunity to touch a female, he'd reacted to base need, naught else.

He smothered a sigh.

They rode into Landeyda's empty yard half an hour later, and he recalled Taft organizing men to repair more of the estate's wall. Most likely the bulk of the troop was there. Oddly enough, the stable door was closed. Jeremy opened it quietly.

Make haste! Alicen needs you! Just as the woman's voice filled his head, he heard screams.

***

"You've been gathering herbs for three days," Ned commented as Alicen unloaded yet another basketful of plants. He eyed the heaps of thyme, purslane, acorns, yew root, lemon grass, sweet flag, mallow, and juniper berries occupying every flat surface and bare floor. "These will yield a year's medicinals, I trow."

"They'll not last a month," Alicen said curtly, sorting

her acquisitions. "Not with soldiers about intent upon war."

How to explain that she'd worked so hard in part to feel she still governed herself? William's insistence that she marry had at first shocked her. Now it frightened her witless. Whom would he think suitable? And would that man allow her to practice her healing art? If not, how could she live? She shuddered.

"Lay these aside for a little, Ned," she said more gently. "I'll feed the animals and then start boiling the acorns."

"I could help you with the horses," the boy offered.

"You've worked as hard as I of late. Take some respite." So saying, Alicen went about her chores.

Cleaning stalls gave her time to examine the abrupt change in her life. Could she make William abandon his plans without revealing the lie of Orrick's death? Gladly would she wed a man who loved her, but who could that man be? None in Sherford, certainly.

Deeply distressed, she failed to hear the stable door close. But, linked with an unnatural quiet, a sudden prickling sensation along her skin caused her to turn.

Her tension did not abate when she recognized her visitor.

"You lied to me, Alicen!" The accusation came in a child's tone from an adult mouth.

"However did I lie, Orrick," she asked quietly. His mien said he'd be difficult to placate.

"You told me not of the s-soldiers." Stepping closer, the lanky man jutted out his lower lip in a pout. "I saw. Then I...—I heard you took ill. You're well."

"I fell and hit my head," she stated levelly. Showing no emotion was imperative. "I've been abed near a week."

"Not hit head!" Orrick gestured wildly, then paused and closed his eyes as if in contemplation. "He said you bad ill!"

She went cold. "Who?"

"The smith." Sudden cunning lit his near-vacuous eyes. "He made me knife. See?" He reached to his hip, but found no blade or scabbard. Enraged, he tore at his clothes looking for them. "No! No!" He spun wildly around before staring again at Alicen. "Left in hut! Want it *now!*"

She lowered the pitchfork and plucked at Orrick's

sleeve. "I'll ride to your hut tomorrow and see it then."

He slapped her hand away, snarling, "Liar! You not come. S-soldiers here. Orrick hates s-soldiers. You said hate them, too. You lie."

"Orrick, how can you say—"

She had no time to defend herself before he grasped her by the tunic and slammed her into the stall partition. Her breath escaped in an agonized whoosh as his weight crushed the pitchfork handle into her chest. Knees buckling, she slid down the wall to kneel in front of him.

"Devil spawn," he hissed. Grabbing a fistful of her hair, he pulled her to her feet. "S-soldier's whore. S-Satan's whore."

Pain sharpened Alicen's senses. He would kill her without knowing he had. Crying out, she swung hard, breaking the fork shaft against his knee. He shrieked as he fell, then lurched up to slap her. The blow turned her head, making her ears ring, but she managed to scramble back a step. In hopes of forcing his retreat, she feinted with the pitchfork's tines.

Slowed by his injured leg, he nonetheless dodged her counterfeit thrust then ripped the weapon from her grasp and sent her tumbling into the aisle between the stalls.

"Liars die!" he vowed, face mottled with insane fury.

He raised the fork to impale her, but Ned, rushing down from the loft, threw himself at the madman. Both went down, Ned beneath. The sickening snap of a breaking bone could be heard as the boy's arm gave way under their combined weight.

Alicen and Ned screamed as one. Staggering to her feet, she tried to drag Orrick from Ned's inert body but was flung off with inhuman power. Her senses dimmed when she hit the floor.

***

Jeremy and Fish were racing toward the scuffle as Alicen landed hard on her back. They heard the stranger swear, saw him untangle himself from Ned and start for her. With a snarl, Jeremy leapt at him and bore him to the flagstones. He rose, dragging the stranger upright by the front of his tunic.

"Whoreson!" He hurled his adversary against the nearest stall, then slammed him into it repeatedly.

Fish had dragged Ned to safety before Jeremy became aware of Alicen clutching at his arm.

"Captain, stop!" She labored to sound assertive, but fear pervaded her voice. "Please. Let him go."

He glanced at her stricken face.

"Please."

The moment Jeremy's grip relaxed, Orrick fled. He moved to pursue.

Alicen's grip tightened. "I implore you—let him go."

Jeremy's muscles bulged from rage, and fear coursed through him. He could do naught but shudder at what had nearly occurred. He realized Alicen had released his arm and, turning, saw her leaning weakly against a stall.

"Who was that man?" he asked her, tone fierce with turmoil.

She turned away to focus her attention on Ned.

Jeremy saw confusion and terror behind her bold front, and this tortured emotional struggle startled him. Whom did she wish to protect? What feelings to control? And why should her cares be his concern?

"'Twas Orrick," the boy moaned softly.

Jeremy saw Alicen flinch, and a sudden thought riveted him. "Orrick? You called your betrothed Orrick."

The bleakness in her eyes confirmed his suspicions.

Nine

"He is my betrothed," Alicen said, weary resignation in her voice.

Jeremy glowered. "I thought him dead in battle."

She closed her eyes a moment before gesturing weakly with her hand. "You saw him, saw his actions. Battle killed his mind. He deserted. He's been like a child since."

"A very dangerous child," Malcolm muttered. He brushed straw from Ned's hair and helped the boy to sit up.

Jeremy silently agreed. At Alicen's defeated look, he reached out to her. "Mistress Kent—"

"Offer no solace, Captain." She pulled away, then said on a shaky laugh, "William will have you hunt Orrick down and hang him for desertion, then use this incident to force me into a loveless marriage." She lowered her head into both hands.

Jeremy felt himself flushing. "If we'd not arrived—"

Her head snapped up. "Your arrival incited the attack! Had you never *arrived* at Landeyda, I'd not now fear attack from a man who once loved me. What danger I've endured has been begotten by soldiers."

Jeremy fisted his hands on his hips and scowled down at her. "If we bring only danger, mayhap we should have left you to your fate just now."

Alicen's green gaze was watery with unshed tears. "I thank you for helping us, Captain. But I'll not recant my statement. Ere soldiers arrived here, Orrick posed no threat. Now, he believes I lied and, in his madness, could seek to harm either Ned or me."

"He'll never get close enough," Jeremy countered.

"So long as William remains here. But he is healing quickly." Alicen thought she saw Jeremy flinch, then cover his reaction with a glare.

The man could be daunting in the extreme, but she knew he wasn't as ruthless as she'd first feared. He cared for his duke, his men, and his horse—a villain cared for naught but himself. And although he had little use for her beyond her healing skills, he was no true villain. For some reason, he sought to intimidate her, but she refused to show vulnerability to him. With new composure, she turned her head and glared at him.

"If you think to terrify me, sir, have done. I prefer to die standing than to live kneeling." Chin high, she limped to Ned's side, bending to gather him in her arms as he whimpered in pain and fright.

Malcolm rose and moved to stand next to his captain.

Jeremy shook his head. *Be damned, vixen, you've more gall than any female I know. What you fear you'll not reveal. A bold man would be well matched to such as you.*

Such sentiments made his scowl deepen. He moved to the stable door, saying quietly to Fish as he went, "See Taft doubles the watch tonight." He paused a moment. "And, Malcolm, no word to anyone as to the man's identity."

"Yes, sir." The soldier dropped his gaze. "She had it aright 'bout our bringing trouble, didn't she, Cap'n?"

"I fear so."

Jeremy stared back at Alicen as she held the still crying Ned. Though too distant to hear, he knew her words comforted. The sight riveted him, and when she struggled to rise with Ned in her arms, he moved to help her.

"Let's get you to bed, lad," he said, squatting down to carefully tousle the boy's hair.

Alicen began to protest, but his eyes dared her to stop him. She surrendered Ned without a word.

"My thanks for saving us, sir." Esteem lit Ned's gaze.

"'Twas naught, lad," Jeremy murmured.

Alicen flushed, then cursed her sudden stab of envy. She could understand Ned's feelings. Orphaned at eight, the boy had soon after come to live with her. He'd no father or brothers to emulate, and Orrick's madness repelled him. Jeremy Blaine was, by all accounts, an accomplished knight. And not everyone deplored soldiers as she did.

Pushing aside her animosity, she hurried on still-unsteady legs to open the cottage door for them. Then she moved to pull back a bench from the table and motion

Jeremy to place Ned on it.

"You're injured." Jeremy noted, looking pointedly at her leg.

She stood tall and avoided favoring the leg. "'Tis naught."

"You limp for naught?"

Without reply, she started to turn away, but Jeremy's irritated statement made her glance back at him.

"My question was civil. I deserve a civil answer."

Her instinct was to flee, yet she replied levelly, "I scraped my knee just now in the stable."

Setting Ned carefully down, Jeremy straightened to his full height. "It requires attention. Let me look at it."

"I must needs attend to Ned."

Jeremy grunted. "After he's settled, I'll examine your injury."

At this bold declaration, she cocked a brow. "You have healing skills, Captain?"

Jeremy clenched his jaw hard. In four strides he had reached the infirmary. "I'll speak to William, then I'll see to you," he stated. "Though why I'd aid such an obstinate shrew bemuses me." He closed the door firmly behind him.

Alicen stared at that door for several moments. Why should her injury concern him? It would not prevent her treating William or his men. Though the duke still could not travel, he required merely rest and nourishment. Was the captain even now disclosing the night's events? She shuddered at the possible consequences of such a report, but forced away her fears and concentrated on Ned.

From a small crock she brought out a brown, thumb-sized cake of narcotic made from dried lettuce leaves. "Eat this," she said, handing it to him. "The pain will ease presently."

While waiting for the drug to take hold, she removed Ned's sleeve, then wrapped him in a warm blanket. Her next task was to set his arm.

"The extract won't numb this entirely," she warned as she arrayed splints and cloths on the table.

"It must be set, Alicen," Ned stated, trust in his dark eyes. "I won't shame you."

She smiled at his resolve. "I'll be quick." Grasping his

wrist, she ordered, "Brace yourself with your other arm, and don't resist with this one." When she felt him relax, she gave a swift jerk and straightened the bone.

The boy's eyes widened then watered, but he did not cry out. Only his tense features betrayed pain. Alicen tested the break, splinted the arm, then secured it in a sling.

"You were very brave." She kissed his temple. "I know how much it hurt."

"You'd have been brave in my place." He trembled suddenly, whispering, "Why did Orrick attack you?"

The question brought dreadful images, but she buried them.

"He claimed I'd lied to him. And, in a way, I did." At Ned's questioning look, she said, "I convinced him to stay away but told him nothing of William's troops." Her pounding head made her pause and rub her temples. "He heard I'd fallen ill and thought I'd lied of that, too."

"What will he do now?"

Alicen saw Ned's fear and desperately wished to reassure him. She could not. Up until this eve, she'd never imagined Orrick would hurt her. Now madness overpowered his prior love. A chill made her shiver.

"I'm uncertain," was all she could say.

Ned squared his thin shoulders and stilled his quivering chin. "I'll protect you, Alicen."

Tears abruptly filled her eyes, but she smiled and gave him a careful hug. "I know. Now eat. And then to bed."

Ned had swallowed the last of his porridge when Jeremy returned.

"Time for sleep, lad." He carried the boy to bed, returning quickly to approach Alicen where she stood by her medicinals cupboard. "I'll tend your leg now, Mistress."

She bristled. "You give me no orders in my home, Captain."

"When I'm in the right, *you* must listen." Before she could protest, he had steered her to a seat on the bench. "Don't consider moving even a finger," he commanded.

He brought hot water, candles and clean cloths to the table. Thus armed, he drew up a stool and sat.

"Let me see your leg."

The husky compassion in his voice struck Alicen like a revelation. Ignoring the comfort she found in that tone, she shot him a withering look, yet made no move to leave. Neither did she show him the injury.

Sighing, Jeremy grumbled, "Such stubborn pride, Mistress. Have you forgotten pride is a sin?"

"Who would know that better than you?" she retorted.

To her complete astonishment, he chuckled, seized her ankle and carefully bent the leg. With a knife, he enlarged the hole in her hose, exposing the gash. Dried blood clogged deep furrows in the skin, but no bone or tendon showed.

She ground her teeth and remained silent while he gently probed the broken skin in search of embedded objects.

"It appears you'll live, Mistress," he stated drolly as he daubed away the blood with a damp cloth. He seemed to unconsciously knead her cramped calf muscle as he worked.

"How disappointing for you," she returned through her clenched jaw, fighting the languor his ministrations brought her.

A grin too brief to be more than a trick of the light softened his hard features. Alicen blinked.

"I must needs endure, I suppose." He had everything cleaned in short order. "Which ointment do you use?"

Still bemused, she answered slowly, "In the saffron jar."

"Don't flee while I'm gone." Upon his return, he dressed the wound then sat back to survey his handiwork. "Laudable for one whose skills lie in inflicting injury, don't you think?"

His comment goaded, and the fact he'd treated her injury as she herself would have chafed. He was the picture of considerate kindness, and she disliked seeing him as aught but hard.

"You needn't reward me for my services, Mistress," he said, abruptly somber. "'Twas little, in return for all you've done for us."

He rose to collect her supplies.

"Had I known where treating the Duke would lead,"

Alicen said peevishly, "I'd have slammed the door in your face the night you brought him here."

"No doubt you would have." A slight smile tugged at Jeremy's mouth. "Then you'd never have had occasion to punish me for being a soldier. Make the best of it."

"'Tis certain I will!" Alicen lurched to her feet. "I'll dance with mirth the day you depart and leave me in peace."

In her rush to leave, she caught a toe on the bench leg and lost her balance. Her stiff knee could not bend to catch her and, with a yelp, she pitched headlong.

Only Jeremy's quickness prevented her fall. She went just so far as his broad chest as he stepped forward, grasping her under the arms. Impact robbed Alicen of breath and strength.

"Easy, lass!" Jeremy said, voice husky. "I have you."

Reflexively his arms circled her waist, and he gently pulled her closer. A flood of possessiveness, the like of which he'd never felt, assaulted him. She was in his arms, and he wasn't of a mind to let her go.

He was mad! She was betrothed, albeit to a man no longer capable of wedding her. Defiantly, his embrace tightened.

In the time it took to collect both wits and breath, Alicen felt a comforting warmth course through her. With a start, she realized it radiated from the hard body pressed to hers. Memory returned her to the forest after her fall, and Captain Blaine's comforting embrace. Then, as now, this soldier's body—his scent, his heat—held too much allure.

Shocked at the path her thoughts raced, she pulled back. And saw deep turmoil in Jeremy's eyes. He was clearly as stunned by their proximity—and equally as unprepared for it—as she.

He held her gaze for a moment before his eyes darkened and he lowered his mouth to hers. The kiss began softly—a tentative exploration—but soon deepened, became seductively demanding, insistent. His tongue traced her lips, then plumbed deeper. Startled at this invasion, she tried to push it from her mouth with her own. But the sensation of their tongues meeting sent a thrill down all her nerve endings, and she gave up the effort. Her lips parted further, allowing him better access.

Her arms slowly encircled his neck.

Jeremy raised one hand to tangle Alicen's hair in shaking fingers. The other trailed down her back and rose again to tease her nape. A groan rumbled from deep in his chest.

She felt more than heard the sound. And though she burned at every point their bodies touched, she welcomed the fire. Had he not drawn her close, she'd have leaned into him herself. She felt safe in his embrace. And more alive than ever before.

All the trembling weakness in her legs moved upward. She molded to him, offering her body to be seared by his.

A soldier had brought about her surrender...A soldier...As this thought exploded inside her head, Alicen's mind cleared. On a strangled cry, she tore her mouth free from Jeremy's. A hard push against his chest broke his embrace, and she bolted to her chamber.

Transfixed, he stood slack-jawed. Sweet Jesu! Alicen had responded to his kiss, then retreated like an outmaneuvered general. What in Christ's name afflicted him, to engage in such folly? And why her heated reaction? Could animosity so easily kindle to passion? His logical mind found no rationality.

But his body burned. He closed his eyes and filled his lungs with her lingering scent, his tingling fingertips recalling her silken hair and heated skin. It seemed he stood there an eternity before wrenching his thoughts away from Landeyda's exasperating mistress.

He never guessed that, once safely inside her room, Alicen sank to the floor, head in hands, and wept bitter tears.

***

"You oppose this course, Jeremy?" William watched closely as Jeremy paced the chamber. "It seems last night's attack only supports my position."

Jeremy stopped, gave William a baleful look, then resumed pacing. "Beg pardon, my lord, but as it came despite our presence, I fear wedding the woman to some clerk won't afford her more protection."

"Thus, you choose to ignore my wisdom?"

"Nay." Jeremy would die of mortification if the truth of yesternight were known.

He'd not slept, using wakefulness to bank his rage at the assault. By her betrothed! He wanted to kill the man. And he'd fought to exorcise intimate memories of Alicen's soft lips and firm limbs. Furtively, he raised a hand to his brow, finding it cool to his touch.

"Mayhap I long to return to court and be quit of this place and its occupants." A glance at the duke revealed a disbelieving pair of dark eyes trained upon him.

"Have you taken ill? You're never on tenterhooks to return to Tynan. Not since every woman there—save my lady wife—seeks dalliance with you." William smiled. "Campaigns suit you better than court intrigue."

"Ere I regain my land, Tynan is my home. And home brings welcome respite from battle." Jeremy hoped his words appeased, else William would badger him to say why he so wished to leave Landeyda.

"Should I enlist Mistress Kent to treat your malady?"

"Nay!" At William's odd look, Jeremy composed his voice but knew his cheeks flamed. "Pardon, my lord. 'Tis only that—"

William sighed. "I know your nature, and I fear my injury has been more a trial for you than—"

Alicen's entry halted further comment. Jeremy looked away, gathering his writing tools.

"Good morrow, Mistress," William greeted her warmly, but his eyes were on Jeremy. "I'm pleased you're hale despite last night's attack."

Alicen shot Jeremy a wary look. "'Tis what I wish to speak to you of," she responded, voice tense, cheeks suddenly burning.

William frowned. "You've not taken ill from the ordeal?"

"Nay, my lord." She paused, and Jeremy saw her take a deep breath. "Please, sir, if I may speak. Don't use last night to force me to wed. As I was unharmed, what happened is of little import."

"Sweet Jesu, woman," William cried, "a man attacked you and is still at large. I wish you to be safe when we depart."

Alicen's tone stiffened. "I'd no need of protection 'ere you arrived. I'll need none after you go."

"You disparage the gravity of this situation," William

returned. "As my subject you are under my protection."

"But I have no wish for a husband to protect me," Alicen whispered wretchedly. Her head bowed as she fought tears.

Both William and Jeremy studied her closely. At sight of her vulnerable, beaten look, Jeremy's rage over the assault returned full force. He knew the pain of a loved one's betrayal. And the cur's attack had forced William's hand. Mayhap bringing this Orrick to justice would change the duke's mind about a nuptial. He rose hastily.

"I plan to lead a search party immediately, my lord," he stated. "We'll catch the knave if he's in the shire."

Alicen winced, her face pale. "Don't o'erset the recently wounded on my account, sir," she said weakly, trying for mockery and failing. "I'm quite certain the man will not return."

William straightened. "How are you certain? Is he known to you?"

Alicen's gaze flew to Jeremy's. *Christ be merciful! If Blaine tells all, Orrick will die!* Striving to quell her alarm, she set her jaw and raised her chin a notch.

"I've little recollection of last night," she stated baldly, unblinking. "It ensued so quickly. But intuition tells me he'll not come here again." Her look defied Jeremy to respond.

Uncomfortable silence lengthened as he stared back at her.

"Then we'll not squander time in pursuit, but mend the rest of the walls...To keep out other intruders," Jeremy stated as he left the room.

"Sweet Jesu," Alicen whispered, forgetting William reclined close enough to hear her epithet. She wrung her hands in her apron.

"What troubles you, Mistress? Even dismissing last night's attack, you've been pensive of late."

Relief over Jeremy's unanticipated aid didn't stop her from saying, "I've little more than a fortnight to forestall marrying an as yet unknown suitor, my lord. Perhaps that colors my mood."

William sighed. "I know the danger we have brought you. The fear. Though I'll not regret Jeremy's bringing me here. Had he not done so, I'd now be among my ancestors' spirits."

Alicen shrugged off the compliment. "Fortune was with me."

"Fortune and peerless skill." He paused before adding quietly, "Your pardon for bringing you such disquiet."

Startled, she shook her head in refutation.

"Deny it not, lass. You and Jeremy barely abide each other. Yet as I convalesce you must. I'd not willfully cause you pain, but I fear we're victims of fate."

She dared not meet the duke's eyes as she murmured, "You may change my fate by rescinding your marriage decree. As for the captain..." She gave a wry laugh. "I'll not pledge an end to our hostilities, but I'll not search him out to fight."

Inwardly, she grimaced. Captain Blaine, for whatever reason, had concealed Orrick's identity. Now she owed the knight a debt. Along with that knowledge came the insight that, if she ever did seek him out, 'twould not be for sake of argument.

***

Jeremy's quick retreat had concealed emotions he knew surged across his face. No kiss had ever kindled a flame in him as had theirs of the previous night. And experience with women told him Alicen had reacted in kind. Ere she came to her senses. Yet her wish to see a villain go free incensed him more than her retreat from him. Did she still love Orrick, though he was a lunatic?

Alicen Kent vexed him, now for reasons far different from his initial mistrust. Aye, she'd deceived them from the first, but not to betray William. To protect a lover. That thought brought amazing pain. Had Alicen and Orrick been lovers? Jeremy didn't want it to be so.

His common sense had fled, leaving him to wade through endless streams of riddles without solutions. And he could speak of this dilemma to no one.

In a black mood, he vowed to find respite from his cares. Yet he could not justify riding to Sherford. By all accounts, the citizens supported William, not Harold. Lookouts watched every approach to Sherford and Landeyda. The threat of spies discovering William's hideout still existed but had weakened considerably.

Jeremy's immediate concern was now distancing

himself from Alicen. The rest of the day, he avoided her.

***

Alicen worked herself to near exhaustion to forget Orrick's attack and the contradictory man who'd held her so intimately afterward. But weariness could not drive from her mind the feel of Jeremy's body. His mouth. His blue gaze darkening as he lowered his lips to hers. She smelled the wet wool of his tunic, heard his ragged breathing. And felt her response.

She yearned to kiss him again.

No! He seeks only to wage war. I cannot desire such a man. I swore an oath to never forsake my duty. He'll catch and hang Orrick.

Will he? Her mother's voice filled her head. *He could have easily revealed your deceit to William.*

Yes, and his reasons for not doing so escaped Alicen.

Think harder, daughter, and you'll discover the captain's reasoning.

Alicen dismissed her mother's words. She had other things to worry about, not the least of which was a deep fear of Orrick. He would have killed her had help not arrived.

Then after...She *wanted* Jeremy's caresses, wanted to feel safe in his arms as she had last night and after her fall. Sweet Jesu, how could a soldier make her feel such exhilaration? Soldiers were fickle. They always left to pursue glory in battle.

Her premonition on the night of Duke William's arrival had proven true. Soldiers—particularly Sir Jeremy Blaine—had changed her life forever.

Ten

Nine days after Orrick's assault, Alicen knew she'd have to start creating chores to keep her mind off her troubles.

"We'll have to build shelves in the stable to store our extra salves and medicaments," she told Ned as they hung the cottage's linen to dry in the sun.

"Fish and a Naismith built shelves for you in the tack room," Ned reminded her.

"I'd forgotten." In truth, she'd had other things to occupy her thoughts.

She'd seen naught of Jeremy in nine days, and that, she tried convincing herself, was good, as it kept her from thinking about his kiss. She stifled a bitter laugh at her own expense. She'd thought of little else but that! And her growing desire for Jeremy. Knowing she could never have his love, she worked until exhausted, seeking escape from herself.

She soon had no more projects to distract her.

And unforseen dangers were about to engulf her.

***

Jeremy and Michael Taft raced a storm the last league to Landeyda and had barely pounded into the courtyard before the brunt of the wind-lashed rain fell. Taft grabbed Charon's reins, shouting that he'd care for both horses. Jeremy roared his thanks into the wind, dismounted, and struggled head down to reach safety in Alicen's snug cottage.

Although shutting the sturdy oak door muffled some of the tempest's fury, he could still hear the wind. The room felt empty. He hung his sodden cloak on a nearby peg before glancing around. His guess was correct; he was alone.

Vague disappointment at receiving no welcome nagged his heart, but he realized the horrid weather had most likely driven everyone to their beds. Still, the illusion of having someone to come home to had been nice. A cheery fire beckoned, yet he didn't wish to enjoy it alone. And this wasn't his home. He had none.

Calling himself a fool for wanting what wasn't, he shook off his weary melancholy and went to report to William.

When he left the infirmary a little later, he was just in time to intercept Alicen, dressed for travel, readying to leave.

"Where are you going?" He tried to hide his concern, but didn't quite manage as he stepped up beside her.

Startled, she spun on her heel to face him. "Out," she retorted, mutiny in her eyes.

He moved to block her departure. "Need I remark that you've been sorely abused of late, and a storm is raging outside?"

She yanked the hood of her cloak up over her chaperon. "I'm neither blind nor deaf, Captain. But the weather isn't my concern. Get out of my way."

"Why such haste to rush into this hellish night?"

"I'll not waste time or breath explaining." She tried to push past him. He refused to move.

He frowned. She looked pale, from pain or fear he couldn't tell. "Don't be foolish, woman. 'Tis folly to go abroad on such a night."

"Then stay here where 'tis safe and dry!" She ducked past him, then shot him a withering look when he braced his arm against the door to hold it shut.

"You could be injured again." He saw her chin lift and sighed in resignation. "What is wrong? No signal bell can be heard through the wind."

"'Tis none of your concern," she snapped, pushing his arm away from the portal.

"Aye, it is," he returned silkily as he again barred the door with his body. "William has charged me with your safety."

Her shiver at his words, the vulnerable look in her eyes, told him she was not as indifferent to his nearness as she protested. And he was certainly not indifferent to hers. However, when she raised artless eyes to his, he lost the novel sensation of having gained some understanding of her. Wariness smothered his fleeting insight when she smiled sweetly.

"Very well, Captain. The duke's enemies meet in the forest this eventide. I go to reveal his secrets to them."

With an oath, Jeremy grabbed her firmly by the shoulders to prevent her turning away. "Christ's guts, woman, what's wrong?"

Glaring, she remained silent.

His hands loosened and slid slowly down her arms. He felt her body lurch beneath his touch, saw the building wrath in her eyes. He stopped his caress to await her reaction.

Alicen sniffed haughtily. "I've no need of your help in this instance."

"Just as I wasn't needed after your fall? Or a se'nnight ago in the stable?" Jeremy cocked a dark brow.

The wretch would flaunt her follies now, Alicen thought hotly. In truth, until tonight he'd not mentioned her nearly disastrous tumble from Hercules. And he'd stayed particularly aloof since Orrick's attack...Since their kiss.

Unlike the overbearing cad he'd been upon his arrival, Jeremy was now subdued. Had she known naught of their mutual dislike, she'd think he felt guilty for causing her troubles, and especially for kissing her so ardently. She swallowed hard, then gave herself a mental shake. 'Twas no time to try understanding Jeremy Blaine's mind. Who would ever have that much leisure?

Perhaps the truth would persuade him to let her go.

"I'm needed, Captain," she said with quiet assurance. "A birthing."

Jeremy's expression stiffened, but the light was too poor for her to read his eyes.

"You've had another portent?" he asked a bit hoarsely.

She eyed him warily, answered softly, "In a manner of speaking. I know Liza's near her time, and I'm certain things aren't as they should be."

"She chose a poor time to drop her get." Jeremy glanced over his shoulder at the window just as a particularly violent crack of thunder shook the ground nearby.

Alicen jumped at the sound, then silently quelled her anxiety. If Blaine saw her fright, he'd never allow her to leave. She had to go now, while she still had some semblance of courage to sustain her.

"Sir Jeremy, please," she began, appalled at the quaver in her voice. "I must go. Let me by."

He studied her intently, then seemed to relent. "You're not going alone."

She ground her teeth at his stubbornness. "I've no wish to burden anyone, especially on a night like this."

"You're not going alone," Jeremy repeated as he crossed his arms and leaned back against the door.

"Sir Jeremy is correct, Mistress. You'll not travel into this night unescorted."

Alicen turned to see William standing in the infirmary door, a blanket wrapped securely around him.

She gasped, then started toward him. "My lord duke! You should be abed."

"Not until you accept my captain's aid."

She halted, her gaze cutting quickly from one man to the other. Knowing she had no choice, she swallowed her ire and said tartly, "As you wish, my lord. I thought to expose only myself to the storm's hazards, but I'll suffer an escort."

"Mayhap the captain should go alone," the duke countered.

"There's sense in that," Jeremy agreed, giving her a pointed stare. "You tire easily of late. I can discover for you the knowledge you seek."

"Nay," Alicen replied with quiet force. "Liza needs *me*. I know it." To end the debate, she adjusted her cloak more tightly around her and turned to Jeremy. "Are you ready, then, Captain?"

"Aye," he murmured, shaking his head at her lingering anger. He leaned away from the door.

Alicen darted out, racing for the stable. The wind tore at her chaperon, rain quickly soaked her hose, but this discomfited her not at all. Her certainty of Liza's peril built to urgency, and she silently berated the men for delaying her. Jeremy ran hard on her heels and had Charon ready even before she finished with Hercules. He led his mount from the stall and approached her.

"Keep to your bed," he stated quietly. "I'll discover if you're needed."

She pursed her lips, then replied, "I am. I'll not stay

behind."

"Stubborn wench," he accused with little rancor.

"Aye, sir. I am that."

"This shire's citizens are fortunate to have such a dauntless champion."

Alicen was uncertain she'd clearly heard Jeremy's comment, coming as it did as he led Charon away. She stood staring for a moment, shocked he might have complimented her, equally shocked that his words thrilled her. Then, scolding herself for engaging in fanciful thoughts about a man who was purposely unnerving, she led Hercules to the stable door.

They both mounted, bending into the wind to travel as quickly as possible.

They were halfway to their destination when the storm's fury mounted even higher.

"Dismount," Jeremy shouted to be heard. He wiped water from his eyes with a leather-gloved hand. "We'll have to lead the horses."

Alicen hated to concede the wisdom of his suggestion, but realized they couldn't ride safely any farther. She could barely see the road. Sliding to the ground, she strained to peer through the driving rain.

Jeremy contemplated their mad quest as they stumbled along toward Sherford. He thought to turn back, but he knew the stubborn woman at his elbow would concede the field only if tied across her saddle. And he could never do that and escape unscathed.

Inexplicably concerned, particularly since Alicen's recent mishaps, he had remained aloof in hopes of dulling his perplexing desire. But he'd lost only sleep. Even now, with a storm battering them, he felt his body quicken at her nearness. He was glad to be alone with her, though it meant escorting her into this torrent.

The gusting wind threw a curtain of water in their faces, forcing them to stop and protect their eyes with their sodden cloaks. By stepping in front of Alicen and turning his back to the blast, Jeremy shielded her from the brunt of it. The sudden partial calm brought her head up, and she tipped forward from the lack of resistance.

He caught her by the waist to steady her, drawing her near. Through her cloak he felt her rapid breathing and shaking limbs.

"You're trembling."

"'Tis cold," she ground out between her teeth. *And you're far too close.* "'Tis little wonder I tremble."

He smiled, seeming to take no offense, holding her tighter until she gently disengaged herself from the warm press of his body. She tingled where he'd touched her, and a moment passed before she could release her pent up breath. Gaze unwavering on his face, she quirked a brow at him. He shrugged, then turned away as the wind lessened somewhat.

They had struggled another half league when the storm began to subside, and the wind died enough that they could remount. They galloped to the edge of the forest north of Sherford, stopping at a small hut which stood in view of the town.

The door opened a handsbreadth at Alicen's rap. A single candle in a gnarled hand illuminated an old woman's wrinkled face. Seeing the healer, she opened the door wide, then placed the candle on a small table. Turning slowly under the burden of time, she seized Alicen's hands in hers.

"Good eventide, Rhea," Alicen said with little irony.

"I knew you'd come." The old woman smiled. "Praise God the storm abated."

Alicen suppressed a shudder. "How fares Liza?"

The young woman lay on a rough-hewn bed by the far wall, her distended belly indicating the advanced stages of pregnancy.

"Her trial began at dusk." Rheumy eyes peered into the shadows behind Alicen. The midwife's look flicked to Alicen, then she cocked her head toward Jeremy. "A rather old apprentice."

"Rhea, may I present Jeremy Downe. He's assisting me while Ned's arm heals." Alicen grinned at his disgusted grunt.

Rhea's thin lips pulled up into a smile. "Then he's skilled at delivering babes?"

He's doubtless more skilled at creating them, Alicen thought a bit maliciously. She kept her counsel, however, and shrugged. "We'll know anon."

Rhea's tone turned grave as she whispered to Alicen,

"Liza's lying-in will not be easy."

Alicen nodded and crossed to sit on the low stool beside the bed. Grasping the expectant woman's shoulder, she bent and said quietly, "Liza, 'tis Alicen. How is the pain?"

Dark eyes flickered open, the circles beneath showing deep exhaustion. Liza started to speak, but flashing cramps gripped her, twisting her mouth into an agonized grimace. "Breathe deeply." Alicen probed Liza's abdomen, then turned to Rhea. "'Twill be hours yet. Return to your own bed."

Rhea snorted. "I may be old, child, but I'm not yet ready to be laid to rest."

"None would say you should be, dear friend," Alicen replied, smiling. "Still, the babe won't appear soon. We can only give Liza a draught for pain and seek sleep for ourselves." She rose to embrace the midwife, then moved with her to the door. "You're her steadfast friend, Rhea. Why exhaust yourself when your help is not yet needed?"

"You've the wisdom of one my age, lass. Perhaps more. I'll return on the morrow." She glanced up at Jeremy as she asked Alicen, "Would your apprentice see me home?"

"Escorting women is his specialty."

Jeremy rolled his eyes, but politely draped Rhea's cloak over her stooped shoulders.

The midwife turned to Alicen. "'Twas very brave of you to come out in such a tumult."

Suddenly nervous, Alicen muttered, "I knew something was amiss."

"Did Alicen tell you she's terrified of storms?" Rhea asked Jeremy. "She gets nigh ill with dread."

Jeremy cast his nemesis a sharp glance. She choked.

"Nay, she did not," he replied evenly, eyes narrowing.

"I... I've gotten over it, Rhea," Alicen insisted weakly. "I've not had such fear for a long while."

"But, the last time it thundered so you—"

"You've had a terrible time with Liza," Alicen cut her off. "You should rest rather than talk."

Rhea gave her friend an assessing look. "But, lass, I—"

"Not now, Rhea." Her tone brooked no protest.

Jeremy scowled. Disregarding the others present, he

stated tersely, "You did not make your fears known to me!"

"You didn't ask."

"I asked of your certainty to go out in this weather," he retorted.

She gave him a look that said she thought him mad. "I *was* certain! Liza and Rhea needed me."

"So, you hid your fear? 'Twas ill-advised."

"Nay, not at all. Healing is my trust. I acted on that trust."

With a small step, Rhea placed herself slightly between the two combatants.

"You purposely deceived me," Jeremy coldly stated. His hand clenched his sword hilt.

The gesture didn't go unnoticed. Alicen swallowed through a suddenly parched throat. "I—"

"'Twas completely foolhardy," he broke in, voice still icy. "You should have stayed behind."

"And left you to deliver Liza's baby?" Alicen retorted. "I'm perfectly capable of doing without your aid or advice."

Jeremy shot a frustrated look at Rhea that was a glare when he turned it on Alicen. "What if you'd panicked and Hercules bolted? You could have fallen and broken your foolish neck."

"I didn't panic." Alicen refused to admit to terror so intense panic would have been a controlled emotion. "And I ride well."

Jeremy no longer clutched the hilt of his sword, instead fisting his hands on his hips. He glowered. "You just said the babe won't arrive tonight!"

Alicen threw her most defiant look at him. Then she turned away, ignoring his glare as she moved to the small hearth which housed a kettle of boiling water. After pouring some into a wooden mug and adding herbs, she cooled the brew with water from a crude wooden pitcher.

Rhea spoke at last. "Shall we go now, Master Downe?" she inquired drolly. "'Tis late."

He snapped his head around to momentarily stare at the old woman. "My pardon, Dame Rhea."

Without another word, he escorted the midwife out.

Alicen slowly recovered from her embarrassment at Rhea's revelation and the anger Jeremy's reaction had caused, reasoning that what he thought of her made not a whit of difference.

Still, she'd concealed her fear so well she hated to have the facade of courage destroyed. For a short time she'd mastered her terror and was reluctant to forfeit that mastery. A quiet sigh escaped her lips. The incident would merely reinforce William's assertion that she needed a husband.

Jeremy returned just as Alicen was administering a draught of painkiller to Liza. Once she'd determined Liza was nearly asleep, she gathered her courage and turned to him.

"Captain, take the counsel I imparted to Rhea. Seek your own bed. The babe won't arrive for several hours, perhaps not before tomorrow eve. You're of little use here."

"I'll remain." He struck his most unyielding pose, arms across his chest. "If you think to be rid of me so easily, you're mistaken."

His stubbornness exasperated Alicen enough to add an edge to her voice. "This woman will soon bear a child! She's no spy, nor is she able to carry knowledge to Harold. Think you she'll slip away while you sleep and disclose secrets I've given her?"

"You forget I've been ordered by William to see you safe," Jeremy rumbled.

"And you have. We're here, are we not?" She glanced down at her fisted hands and sighed heavily. "I'll say yet again—I've no care who rules this shire. I'm sworn to heal all, not to aid either camp against the other."

Jeremy shifted his stance to stand even taller. "I stay."

She gasped, outraged. "Your mistrust insults me!"

"Then wallow in your distemper. I'll not leave you to your own devices." So saying, he turned and barred the door. When he once again faced Alicen, he added, "Think you your physician's skills are protection from mercenaries? The jackals would crawl between your legs in a trice and ask for neither your name nor your vocation." Voice cold, he continued, "If Kenrick suspected you harbored his enemy, he'd torture you until you'd broken. You'd admit to performing the Crucifixion by the time he finished. Yet death would not bring escape from the pain. You'd live until he and his men tired of you."

"You lie," Alicen whispered shakily, hoping he did.

He laughed bitterly. "I've seen just such. In France... Here...Atrocities exist wherever men lust for power." He stared into the hearth's glowing embers, seeing raging fires, hearing piteous cries, feeling impotent rage.

Alicen observed as the pain of frightful memories pinched his handsome features into careworn planes. Before she could stop herself, she reached out and touched his arm.

"Why seek to protect me?" she asked quietly. "My eyes have seen much the same as yours...My mother fatally wounded while aiding a soldier's brutalized victim...Death, destruction. I've reaped war's bloody wages. Yet I strive to sow peace. I'm a woman who despises warfare and the men who make it. Do you not detest me for that reason alone?"

He met her troubled gaze but held his tongue. How could tell her he hated war as much as she? That he respected the fidelity she gave her vow to her dying mother? That even now he ached to hold her close, safe and warm, against him?

She'd not believe him. He himself could scarce credit his solicitous thoughts of her. Reason warned him to have a care lest he begin wanting something he'd vowed never to seek again. But his respect for Alicen's fortitude grew. She put another's welfare before her own, which said much of her character. He wished to ignore her courageous selflessness, but could not. And that as much as anything else irritated him.

"You serve a purpose," he replied at last, wincing inwardly at his cold tone. "I'm to protect you until that service ends and the duke has seen you wed."

His statement had the desired effect. Alicen went rigid, then yanked her hand from his arm as if the contact burned. In silent rage she spun away, pulled her cloak around her, and practically threw herself down on the floor beside Liza's bed.

Jeremy sighed. Soon, he was wrapped in his cloak and lying, sword unsheathed beside him, across the threshold. Guilt stalked him for willfully baiting Alicen. He'd had no cause. Guilt made sleep dream-filled, restless, empty of his greatest desire—her in his arms.

***

At sunrise Rhea arrived. Concern creased in her face's innumerable lines, she crossed the hut in five strides to kneel beside the still sleeping Liza. After pushing tumbled hair off the patient's face, Rhea looked up at Alicen.

"How does she?"

"Little different." Alicen rose slowly from her pallet. "She rested yestereve, but I fear today will bode much struggle."

Rhea nodded. "I thought as much. The babe will not enter this world willingly—." She caught Alicen's warning glance at Jeremy and stopped speaking.

Abrupt silence followed, and the soldier sensed he was, for whatever reason, the cause. Added to that discomfort, he felt the urge to heed nature's call. Not wishing to endure these women's bold assessments should he use the chamber pot, he excused himself for the woods. His absence would give them leave to wag their tongues.

"He watches you closely," Rhea commented after Jeremy's departure. "He must set a very high store by you."

Alicen's laugh was almost a snort. "He trusts me not, so he shadows my steps. 'Tis fear I'll betray his duke, naught else."

Rhea made the sign of the cross. "Then my suspicion was true. He's no merchant."

Alicen nodded gravely. "He's Jeremy Blaine, Duke William's right hand."

Dark brown eyes glanced quickly around the hut, and Rhea's voice dropped to a harsh whisper. "William's near Sherford?"

"He's been at Landeyda since the battle."

"Jesu be merciful! You and Ned have endured much danger!"

"Aye, but not by choice." Alicen shrugged. "Blaine brought him to me, and I was oath-bound to help. He's been unable to travel these weeks past, so he's sheltered in my home."

"What if Harold's troops return?"

"I suppose William has plans for that eventuality. I really care not to know of any military stratagems."

"But why, if you've kept silent about the duke's presence this long, does the captain yet follow you?"

Alicen's gaze unwittingly went to the door. "William has sworn to see me wed and has set Sir Jeremy to escorting me. Yet he would do so even if not ordered, due to his base suspicions."

She felt herself blushing and prayed the weak light from the small window beguiled her friend's vision.

"Yestereve, he assured me aught would go well," Rhea said slowly. "'Mistress Kent is a fine healer, grandam,' said he. 'Put your mind to rest for the lass and her babe.'"

Alicen shrugged. "It cost him naught to make such comment. Most likely he thought I'd never hear of it."

Rhea awkwardly rose from her knees and drew a stool up beside the bed. Placing a small basin of water and a clean cloth next to Liza's head, she sat down. "Mayhap 'tis as you say," she commented. "Yet, he speaks of you with respect."

Now Alicen did laugh. "No doubt he sought to charm you and thought the straightest path to your heart was through complimenting me. You've been gulled."

"Nay, I know the tone of high regard when I hear it. There is more substance to Jeremy Blaine than these old eyes can see."

Alicen thought to challenge that belief, but the door opened and the object of their dispute ducked to enter. His broad-shouldered frame filled the doorway, blocking the light. As her gaze locked on his imposing figure, cast in silhouette, her scathing comment died on her lips. Knowing full well she stared, she was yet unable to stop.

Liza's low moan pulled Alicen's gaze away from Jeremy and back to the task at hand. Now fully awake, Liza twisted and stiffened as pain clawed at her. Her groans deepened, and she grew pale.

"Rest easy, child, and save your strength," Rhea crooned. She wiped Liza's face with a cool, damp cloth. "The babe will take his sweet time arriving."

Alicen moved close, a mug of tea in hand. "Drink this, Liza. 'Twill help."

"I'll see to breakfast." Rhea rose and bustled about the small hut, producing a cooking pot and stoking the fire.

Jeremy glanced around, feeling stiflingly confined in the tiny hut. The scene playing out before him dredged up memories of a similar scene he'd long ago quelled. Worse yet, Alicen's proximity played havoc with his self-control. Alternately he found himself angry with and desirous of her. Neither emotion would serve in this situation.

Upon surveying the room again, he noted a lack of firewood.

"Is there an axe?" he asked as he removed his sword and placed it on the table.

The rich sound of his deep voice startled Alicen and Rhea, who'd both been deeply engaged in aiding the expectant mother.

Alicen recovered first. "Under the ell."

Jeremy nodded and left. He leaped astride a bareback Charon and headed into the woods. Half an hour later he returned, Charon dragging a fallen log as big around as Jeremy's thigh. He stripped off his tunic and shirt, seized the axe, and set about chopping and splitting the wood.

He'd been told his skill with an axe was nearly as formidable as his skill with a sword, and within an hour he had returned to the forest for another log.

"The meal is ready, Sir Jeremy," Rhea called to him as he rode up with the second tree trunk.

He dismounted, an odd look on his face. "Why do you address me thus?" he asked carefully.

Rhea smiled. "'Tis obvious you're no merchant. You've a knight's bearing, and the well-honed sword to back that claim." When she saw him glance at the hut, Rhea's smile died. "She told me naught of you, sir, until I asked."

"She should lose her wretched tongue," he muttered angrily.

Eyes widening, Rhea grasped his hand. "Nay, sir! Alicen knew her confidence was safe, or she'd ne'er have confessed you're not what you claim."

Jeremy made a disgruntled sound deep in his throat. "Did she consider the danger knowing the truth may mean for you?" When Rhea paled at his words, he gently laid his free hand atop hers. He smiled. "All you know is that I'm Jeremy Downe, a merchant."

"Aye, sir, that's all I know."

Giving Rhea's hand a reassuring pat, he turned to the well. "I'll be in presently." Quickly, he washed his face, hands, and arms, then splashed cold water on his sweaty chest. After donning his shirt and gathering an armful of kindling, he entered the hut.

Alicen, seated at the table, smiled tightly at his entrance. "There are no military coils to ponder, nor enemy spies to root out, sir, that you now chop wood to pass time?"

"The nights are grown colder of late. The woman has little firewood," he retorted. "If I must await her child, I prefer to do so in comfort."

Alicen glared. Was he such a miserable wretch that his own welfare came before someone else's sorrow? He now acted callous, though she could almost swear he blushed...His inconstant nature had her close to screaming with frustration.

He looked ready to speak, but kept his council, turning instead to Rhea's huge repast. There were eggs and ham, biscuits and gravy.

"Cooking is a task women are well suited to," he stated between mouthsful as he devoured the meal.

After that, time passed wordlessly, the quiet broken only by Liza's occasional moans. Closely watching her patient helped Alicen control the desire to throw a pot at the arrogant knight's head. She noted Liza's delivery had not progressed. There was yet more for the young woman to endure.

Jeremy finished eating, gave Rhea a charming smile, and rose. "'Twas excellent fare, grandam," he said earnestly. "Food somehow tastes better with a woman's touch. I get precious few well-cooked meals in the field."

"Mayhap you should hire a wench as your cook, Captain," Alicen stated archly. "Though you'd likely have to concern yourself with poisoning."

Jeremy's expression darkened. "Camp followers abound near any army," he retorted. "But the women's skills in other areas surpass their ability to prepare food." He slammed out the door.

"Damned contrary woman!" Jeremy raged beneath his breath. "Why in sweet Jesu's name do I permit her to goad me so? She has me raving faster than anyone I know!" He yanked off his shirt, flung it under a tree, grabbed the axe, and started splitting wood with a vengeance. His tirade continued unabated while he vented his feelings on the kindling. "She knows just how to raise my ire, and does so dawn to dusk."

Women! God created them expressly to plague men. And *that* woman made vexing him an avocation.

Yet more disturbing than her antagonism was his response. He wanted to prove he wasn't what she thought him, that he valued life and sought—as did she—to preserve it.

But he *had* to fight, to regain property stolen by Harold of Stanhope. Then, mayhap he could live as he longed to—watch his lands and villeins prosper, know the love of a faithful woman, raise happy children. If he left the campaign before defeating Harold, he had naught to return to. That knowledge drove him on.

That knowledge was all that kept him going. He'd become a warrior bereft of the battle lust which sustained men at arms. Somewhere between the dazzling court of London and the blood-soaked fields of France, he'd lost his zeal to wreak havoc for king and country.

After he won back his lands, he'd fight no longer.

He struck the log with sustained vigor, so hard his hands tingled from the reverberations of the axe handle.

***

Rhea looked toward the bed where Liza lay before turning to Alicen to whisper, "You and the captain favor antagonists in a bear baiting."

Alicen, sitting across the table from Rhea, leaned closer to say quietly but succinctly, "He's an overbearing lout." Then she raised her voice to call out, "Liza, if the pain mounts, don't hold your tongue. Call out."

"I will," came the hoarse reply.

"He appears a gentleman to me." Rhea kept her voice low, for Alicen's ears only.

Alicen scowled. "You truly know him not. He *abhors* women. To him, we're good only to take his ease upon, little else. Once we've assuaged his lust—or his stomach's hunger—we may as well be dirt on the floor."

Rhea's face blanched. "Did he force himself upon you?"

Heat shot up Alicen's cheeks as she realized what she'd implied. "Nay, of course not! 'Tis just that..."

She'd worked herself to near exhaustion, hoping to forget their intimacy. But not even exhaustion could drive from her mind the memory of Jeremy's embrace.

Could she explain the chaos he caused in her? Though the soldier repelled, the man attracted. He was churl and charmer—infuriating one moment, bemusing the next. She conceded to being out of her depth with him.

"He's spoken plain that he dislikes me because I'm female," she stated carefully, trying to gather her thoughts and control her feelings. "Yet, he visited the inn just before William awoke..."

Alicen knew she was blushing. Rhea's keen stare didn't help her discomfort, either.

The old midwife nodded. "He's the one! That slut Sylvia bragged to all of her night beneath a handsome stranger. She claimed him a magnificent lover."

"He's likely a rutting beast," Alicen huffed, ignoring the twinge in her chest brought on by images of the knight in a whore's arms. "Though 'tis certain Sylvia's had enough variety to make a sage judgment."

Rhea frowned. "Methinks Sylvia lied. I sensed she had no carnal knowledge of him at all. 'Twas something in the way she spoke of him...Still, you chafe the captain o'ermuch. If he truly doubts you as deeply as you say, 'twould be wise to walk softly around him."

Alicen recalled Jeremy's recent gallantry and felt her legs grow weak. "I doubt he'll harm me. After all, I've a use." She stifled abrupt melancholy. "But you speak true that I vex him apurpose. He raises my ire like none I've ever known."

"He has an air of sadness about him that bespeaks a great hurt. Mayhap he can only vent that hurt in anger."

"And I'm the target of his wrath."

Rhea covered her friend's hand with her own gnarled one. "You've the healing gift, lass. Methinks the captain is drawn to that, yet dares not voice his need for it."

"I can do naught for his soul," Alicen scoffed. "Fate drew him to me—his duke near death and I the closest healer." Alicen's heart and mind were filled with untold turmoil when she looked up from Rhea's hand to the woman's aged face.

Her feelings must have shown in her expression, because the old midwife's look went from wistful to wry in a breath. "I daresay you've little understanding of men, lass."

"Nor do I desire to improve my knowledge. Sir Jeremy Blaine is a nettle I'll happily soon be rid of."

"If that is as you say." Rhea rose to clear the table.

Alicen pondered Rhea's words until the ring of the axe penetrated her musings. Jeremy was not obliged to chop kindling for Liza, and he'd already split enough to accommodate the length of his stay. Did he continue out of kindness? The man certainly was capable of chivalry for its own sake.

She loathed admitting that on more than one occasion he had attempted civility toward her. Yet her pride demanded she not reciprocate. Except when he held her...

She closed her mind to that memory. What had passed between them was a mistake. It would never occur again. But mistake or no, she'd deliberately angered him and now owed him an apology.

'Twas her turn to fashion a truce between them, as he'd tried to do several weeks before.

Eleven

The third log was quickly succumbing, and Jeremy's anger with it.

"Alicen Kent be damned," he cursed low at the wood he hacked to pieces. *She has my escort at William's command, not at her wish...or mine...Falling into enemy hands would serve her, the way she courts misfortune riding about alone.* He struck the wood again. *Abduction would teach her a lesson in humility she'd not soon forget.*

Intent upon his dark thoughts and the task at hand, he kept to his grueling tempo without breaking rhythm, his body racing to keep pace with his ire.

With appreciation, Alicen stood in the doorway of the cottage and watched him work. Broad shoulders tapered to slim hips, and long, hard muscles undulated along arms and chest. Only a narrow line of dark hair around his navel marred his sleekness. He put her in mind of a fine race horse, lean yet powerful, with endurance beyond the ordinary. Strong thighs hinted at hours of riding. The man was an image of splendid, graceful lines.

Alicen started from her musings. She had come to make amends for her shrewish actions, not to admire his physique. Yet, how to proceed? She bit her lip and worried the problem.

Circumstance provided her an opportunity as, in the next moment, Jeremy's grip on the axe slipped as he struck the log. He cursed roundly and dropped the tool to grasp his left hand.

"Christ's guts!" He turned as Alicen moved toward him.

"What happened?"

Holding up the injured hand, he said calmly, "A splinter."

Alicen almost gasped when she saw the inch-long splinter driven under the skin up the side of his thumb. She seized his wrist and examined the injury. "You do naught in small portions, Captain." Leading him by the hand, she sat him down beside the well then left to get her instruments.

Once she'd set a blade near him, she again took his hand. His skin's warmth made her pulse race. Lowering her head, ostensibly to look more closely at the splinter, she hastily gathered her scattered wits. The patient's need saved her.

"Fortunately, this didn't go straight in," she commented when her voice returned. "You'd have lost your thumb. It may be discomfiting for a time, but you'll not forfeit use of the hand." She slit the skin atop the splinter and pulled the piece out. In a trice, the wound was cleaned, salved and bandaged.

"There. 'Twill be like new a few days hence." She paused, still holding his hand as if inspecting her work. "You needn't have cut so much wood, Captain, though it will be put to good use. That was very kind of you."

She looked openly into his eyes a moment, seeing wariness in his guarded blue stare. Embarrassed, she released him and rose, imagining he thought her a fool. Avoiding his intense look, she quickly gathered her things, escape dominating her thoughts. How she controlled her impulse to dash back into Liza's hut, she didn't know.

Gaze riveted on Alicen, Jeremy sat motionless while his mind raced. At her simplest touch his entire body tingled. His senses quite simply hummed with her about. Each was filled with this woman—with her feel, her smell, her essence—and he could not prevent their assault on his reason. He found himself reaching out to touch her sleeve.

"Will the injury worsen should I continue?" he asked, then dropped his gaze sheepishly. He sensed her discomfort at his nearness, but need overpowered honor. She must remain. "Inside, I'm of little use. It suits me to work out here."

Amazement flashed in Alicen's eyes, but her tone indicated only efficiency when she replied, "If the pain is bearable, Captain, do as you wish. Should your thumb begin bleeding, though, 'twould be wise to rest."

He gave her a brief smile. "My thanks."

A knot grew in his throat as he watched her walk away. Alicen could soothe his hurts merely by asking to see the wound. Her compassion comforted him as nothing else could.

A powerful image besieged him, that of a woman terrified of storms braving a tempest to aid a babe's birth, risking her life to bring new life into the world. He quelled the memory of their kiss. With any other, such an occurrence might have led to something he could ill afford between Alicen and himself. He had to keep his distance.

Duty demanded aloofness.

With lacerating certainty he knew he'd erred in accompanying her here. Instinct warned him to keep a wall of indifference between them. He couldn't. Not when her welfare concerned him, when he'd insisted on staying. Now, the sight of Liza Wick's labor scoured his emotions raw until Estelle's betrayal and death shrieked down the corridors of his past.

He tried to convince himself his presentiment was unfounded, that recent desires had combined with memory to unbalance him. Yet, he knew for certain his presence would have grave results. A sudden chill up his spine and a cold breeze seemingly rising from nowhere reinforced his certainty.

Let her go, he thought he heard a woman whisper. *You can't change what's past.*

He straightened, shaking his head to clear it. His preoccupation with Alicen Kent had caused him to give in to fancy. Enough was enough. He'd not dishonor himself by disobeying William's orders. And he knew firsthand that avoiding Alicen didn't purge her from his thoughts. With a sigh, he returned to work.

By dusk he had chopped half a cord of wood, and he ached from fatigue. When Rhea called him to eat, he gratefully put down the axe and washed at the well. A bucket of cold water poured over his head brought a welcome shock.

Suddenly, Alicen stood beside him, towel in hand.

"Here, Captain, dry yourself with this."

He nodded and put the cloth to good use. Yet while she drew a bucket of water and hastened back inside, he stood bemused, wondering if she'd intended the kindness or if Rhea had suggested it. He hoped Alicen had come of her own will.

After shaking water from his hair, he wiped his face then donned his shirt, all the time pondering Alicen's motives. Her complete unpredictability matched his own reaction to her at any given time. One moment he wished to throttle her, the next...He forced himself to discontinue his line of thought.

***

"Rhea, oppose me not, I pray," Alicen said patiently as they sat finishing the meal. "You've toiled all day and deserve your rest. Is the foundling, Pearl, not at your home? See to her. I'll send Captain Blaine when you're needed."

"Whelp, I can work as hard as you," Rhea retorted with feigned affront.

Alicen laughed. "You speak truth. Thus my resolve that you should return home. 'Twould be too humbling to admit someone thrice my age has more endurance."

At this, Rhea cackled. "I'm yet young enough to take you o'er my knee to teach you reverence for your elders. Keep that well in mind, lassie."

Alicen laughed. "Advancing age makes you more than a trifle vain. I'll never see you turn me over your knee."

"I could, though I might have to seek aid." Rhea shot a sly look at Jeremy.

"You've no need for reinforcements, friend," Alicen responded smoothly and saw relief in Jeremy's eyes when he looked up at her. "I concede the field. Now, get you home to rest."

"Since you concede, I'll retire." Smiling, Rhea moved to pick up her cloak.

Jeremy already held it. "May I see you home, grandam?" he asked gallantly.

"Nay, sir. You could see me to the inn for several cups of ale, though."

Jeremy looked startled, and both Rhea and Alicen laughed.

"Lock her in her home if you must, Sir Jeremy," Alicen stated dryly. "Else no young swain will be safe tonight."

"I'll leave such sport to Sylvia," Rhea retorted. "She's far better suited to that than I."

Alicen covertly studied Jeremy, but he did not react at mention of the whore.

Jeremy remained stoic, but their talk reminded him of his drunkenness at the tavern, of buying information from Sylvia, and of his aching head the next morn. He winced inwardly. No force on Earth could make him repeat that lamentable performance.

Rhea's suddenly grave tone broke into Jeremy's thoughts.

"Send for me when the time comes, Alicen," the old midwife stated.

"Rest assured I shall." Alicen stood in the doorway watching Jeremy mount his horse then easily lift Rhea up behind him. She found Liza's temperature elevated when she checked her, carefully probing the girl's swollen belly. "How do you feel?"

"The pain grows," Liza gasped. Her eyes widened with agonized fear. "My mother died in childbed," she whispered. "Will I, also?"

Alicen swallowed hard, but managed a calm answer. "You're not your mother. With your help, I'll bring you through." She firmly grasped Liza's hand. "We've yet several hours. The babe's not in position. Stay with me!"

***

Just after midnight, a woman's agonized scream wrenched Jeremy from sleep. *Estelle!* Disoriented, he had gained his feet, sword in hand, before recalling himself. His heart thundered as he saw Liza writhing on the cot, and the vision of his dying wife faded from his mind's eye. Alicen pressed wet cloths to Liza's forehead and spoke soothingly.

"Please fetch Rhea, Captain. And tell her 'tis best Pearl not attend this lying in." Alicen glanced up and met Jeremy's gaze. "The child attempts to arrive soon."

Her calm tone pleased Alicen, as it belied her inner turmoil. Liza had been in labor for two days and now bordered on complete collapse. She'd not hold up under much more strain.

When Jeremy arrived with the midwife, Alicen had everything in readiness. She hurried to the old woman's side and drew her into the corner farthest from Liza's bed.

"The child is breech," she murmured for Rhea's ears only.

Rhea grimaced. "I suspected such. The labor's been too long for a common birth."

Jeremy noted the women's worried expressions and hushed tones. His stomach tightened, and instinct warned of danger. He moved closer. "Is there aught you wish me to do?" he asked, voice as low as theirs.

"Do you pray, Captain?" Rhea questioned solemnly. "If so, we could use aid from Saint Anne. And Saint Gerard."

Jeremy raised inquiring eyes to Alicen.

"The circumstances are dire," she explained. "We may—"

Liza's scream brought them all to her bedside. Delirious, she thrashed in an effort to free herself from the agony.

The soldier's mouth went dry. "Is there naught to help her pain?"

"Very little," was Alicen's terse reply. "Less than an hour ago I gave her a draught of mithridate and treacle to speed the labor. But I can give her no more." It took great effort for Alicen not to wring her hands in her apron. Fear closed a vice around her heart.

Rhea wiped sweat from Liza's forehead and murmured words of encouragement. Then she turned, quietly saying, "She's failing quickly and won't live out the night." Old, black eyes met young, emerald ones. "You'll have to kill the infant."

Rhea's words seared Jeremy. He inexplicably started to shake, staring hard at Alicen until Liza's next chilling cry made him jump. Instinctively, he stepped back.

Alicen bit her lip, mind roiling. Could she save both mother and child? Without question, she had to try. *Mother, what should I do?* She closed her eyes a moment, listening. Then her eyes flew open.

"I'll turn the babe around."

Jeremy started, ready to swear he'd heard a voice say those very words in an Irish brogue that was becoming familiar to him. He felt something brush his shoulder, as if someone had moved past him, but there was no one else in the hut. He was about to ask if the others had felt the same thing, but Rhea's reaction to Alicen's proposal saved him.

The midwife gasped. "Are you able to do such?"

"If I'm unable, I'll lose either Liza or the baby. Or both. 'Tis a hazard I must face."

"You've the courage of a lioness, my friend," Rhea stated, shaking her head.

"Courage is simple for me," Alicen responded through a tight throat. "My life will not be lost should I fail." She breathed deeply. *Guide me, Mother.* "Captain, sit at Liza's head and raise her upright when I tell you to. You'll have to support her until she delivers."

"Shouldn't I go tend the horses?"

Alicen looked into Jeremy's stricken face and knew he'd rather be anywhere than in that hut. "We need you here," she stated. "Rhea and I can't do this ourselves."

Jeremy swallowed and moved to sit at Liza's head. With a shaking hand, he grasped one of hers. When she squeezed back, his eyes flew wide at her grip.

Alicen stroked the laboring woman's cheek and spoke clearly. "Hold back on the next contraction. No matter how you wish to bear down, you must not. Do you understand?"

"I cannot hold back," Liza sobbed. "I cannot!"

"You must. Breathe deep between pains. Pant when they come. And don't crush the captain's hand." When another shudder began to wrack Liza, Alicen moved swiftly to the foot of the cot. "Rhea, hold her legs. Captain, keep her lying flat for now. Liza, hold back!"

Liza screamed again. "I must push!"

"Do not," Alicen commanded. The baby's rump was between its mother's legs. "Hold back." When the contraction eased, Alicen said a silent prayer, slid her hand in next to the infant, and pushed it back up the birth canal. Liza wailed. "Just a bit longer!" Alicen encouraged. "In a moment, push all you wish."

"I'm going to die," the woman moaned. "Sweet Jesu, I'm going to die!"

This hopeless cry raised the hair on Jeremy's nape. Bile burned his throat, and he struggled to hold back his stomach. A battlefield had more appeal than this. Such intense suffering threatened to suffocate him. Sweat trickled down his back and from under his arms, and his body went rigid with tension. *Dear Lord, small wonder*

Estelle feared this!

"You'll not die." Alicen's voice held steady. "Hold back until I tell you to push. We're nearly finished."

"God's blood, but you've a cool head," Rhea whispered.

Another pain hit, but with encouragement from Rhea and Jeremy, Liza kept from straining down.

As soon as the spasm passed, Alicen turned the baby and positioned its head correctly. Guided by an inner vision, her fingers probed to find the umbilical cord and assure it didn't encircle the child's neck. Satisfied, she looked at Jeremy.

"Please sit her up, Captain." When this was accomplished and the next contraction overcame Liza, Alicen caught the woman's gaze and held it. "Now, Liza! Push!"

Liza needed little encouragement to do so. Grunting, she bore down, and the baby's head appeared.

"Again. The babe is almost here!"

Rhea placed her hand on Liza's swollen abdomen and gently assisted. Liza screamed another agonized cry. On the fifth push, the child, amid the fluids and blood of the caul, lay in Alicen's waiting hands.

"You've a son," Rhea exulted.

Her lined face broke into a smile as Alicen handed her the tiny boy. She tickled the infant's feet, eliciting a gasping cry. Once the cord was tied and cut, the old woman went to the basin to cleanse the baby then swaddle him in linen.

Speechless, Jeremy laid Liza gently back onto the bed then slumped against the wall and stared at the hut's other occupants, emotions chaotic. He could not honestly say he'd relished witnessing the beginning of life.

Liza's suffering resulted not from battle but from an act he had heretofore performed with little thought to more than pleasure. He'd certainly never considered the anguish of the woman who bore the fruits of that act. Were other men as ignorant of their culpability as he? He could almost understand the fear that had driven Estelle to purge herself of his child.

He nearly retched. His head spun, and he realized how close and hot it had grown. He needed fresh air.

"Not as pretty as a battlefield, eh, Captain?" Alicen

laughed, but the sound was hollow and shaky. "I'm surprised the sight of blood so affects such a brave soldier."

He clenched his teeth, fearing if he opened his mouth to reply he'd vomit instead. The wretched vixen took advantage of his misery, and naught could be done to stop her. He'd have gladly choked her if he thought he had the strength for it.

But her attention was already back to Liza.

"Rhea, assist me," she murmured. "There's much bleeding, and I would set some stitches to stop it. Hold Liza's legs."

Rhea glanced around, the child in her arms, then placed him beside his mother.

"Nay, not there," Alicen said, picking up the infant. "Does she lash out in pain, he could be injured." She turned to Jeremy, who had risen and was sidling toward the door, looking like he'd just lost a major dispute with his stomach. "Hold the babe while we attend Liza."

If possible, he paled even more. Complete shock registered in his horrified expression. "I? I cannot!"

With a slight smile, Alicen offered him the boy. "You're fearless in the face of death, sir, yet terrified in the face of life. I assure you, the lad won't hurt you."

"I might drop him." Jeremy's deep voice rose in pitch. His hands shook.

"Just hold him as I show you, and all will be well." She laid the baby in the crook of Jeremy's elbow, along his forearm. "Use your other hand alongside for support. Not too tight, now. There."

The baby gave a hearty yowl. Unnerved, Jeremy tried to pull back.

Alicen restrained him by grabbing his elbows. "Steady, Captain. The lad is fine."

"But he's crying!" Stricken blue eyes pleaded with Alicen not to abandon him to this child's custody.

She patted his arm encouragingly. "He's tired, naught else. I must see to his mother, or his sleep will be delayed longer."

With Rhea's help, Alicen quickly sewed Liza's torn flesh, then disposed of the bloody linen. The midwife cleansed the young mother, resettled her, and gave her a drink of water.

"He's a fine boy, Liza," Rhea said as Alicen returned.

"Thank you," Liza hoarsely whispered. "Thank you both."

Another yowl obscured any reply, and the three women gazed as one at the man holding the protesting infant. Jeremy Blaine was misery incarnate. Dazed, he stared at the child squirming in his arms. Sweat beaded his upper lip, and his face was taut with concentration. He stood stiffly, as if afraid to move lest he drop his precious burden. He dared a desperate glance at Alicen as she went to his side. "I'm hurting him!"

"Nay, you're not. Be firm but gentle." Again she repositioned his hand. "You only need hold him a few moments more, then he'll sleep beside his mother." She chuckled as Jeremy gaped at the boy in wonderment.

"He's a wee thing," he said, voice hushed with awe.

"Aye, but he'll grow to be a man." Seeing the captain clumsily trying to soothe the fussing babe made Alicen smile. "Mayhap you could become a midwife when your warring days are done, sir knight," she lightly teased.

Intent on the child, Jeremy made no reply. Instead, he placed his blunt-tipped finger in the boy's hand. A delighted grin lit his face when tiny fingers curled around his.

"He has a mighty grip for one so small," he whispered. "His is a fierce desire for life."

A fierce desire for life.

Suddenly, the impact of what had transpired hit Alicen. Her brazen gamble almost overwhelmed her, and her knees began to tremble. She sank weakly onto a stool as Rhea took the infant from Jeremy's shaky arms and placed him upon his mother's breast.

"The babe needs your touch, lass." Rhea guided Liza's weakened hands around the child. After the new mother had settled her boy comfortably, the midwife moved to Alicen's side. "My friend, 'twas the most incredible feat I've yet seen. You've a dead man's fear."

Too shaken even to smile at the compliment, Alicen quietly replied, "I did what I could."

"And saved them both! I've brought two hundred children into the world in near threescore years, but of the dozen breech births I've seen, this is the first where both babe and mother survived." Rhea's dark eyes glowed in the candlelight. She clasped Alicen's shoulder. "You did well, lass."

"'Twas good fortune." *And help from a far better healer than I. Thank you, Mother.*

'Twas you who saved them, Alicen. I can do no more than advise.

My thanks just the same.

Alicen felt a warm breath brush her cheek as she crossed on still wobbly legs to the basin to wash. She ran a cold, damp cloth over her face and across her neck. When she turned, she caught Jeremy staring at her, an unreadable expression in his eyes. Too preoccupied to wonder at it, she let a tremulous laugh betray her condition. "Rhea, is there any ale? I've ne'er before needed a drink so much."

"The cask hangs in the well. Fetch it, and pour draughts for the captain and me, also."

Soon, they raised their mugs in three unsteady hands to salute the miracle of birth.

Jeremy drank silently, unable to tear his gaze from the boy who now slept upon his mother's breast. Liza fairly glowed, plain features transformed to true beauty. It astounded him that, after her ordeal, she yet had strength to hold the child against her.

"I'll spend the next several nights here," Rhea stated, breaking the silence. She met Alicen's weary eyes. "Best you return home. You look spent."

Jeremy noticed that Alicen barely managed a nod.

"Get yourself to your bed, lass." Rising, the old midwife hugged her. "If aught goes amiss, I'll send word with Pearl."

"Do not delay in doing so." Alicen briefly grasped Liza's hand, stroked the baby's dark head, then left, Jeremy at her heels.

They rode without speaking. The eastern sky showed faint lightening as they followed the Great North Road toward Landeyda. At this hour, the highway was deserted. A cool breeze blew at their backs, forcing them to a more purposeful gait, and thus they continued for several moments.

Charon's easy canter lulled Jeremy deeper into his musings on the two days past. He'd witnessed life's beginning. Held a newborn infant! Respect for women's resiliency and strength grew within him. And while Estelle's betrayal still seared, Liza's incredible effort to bring forth a babe awed him. He'd seen warriors unable to endure far less pain, far less effort.

He shook his head and cast a glance at the woman riding beside him. For someone who'd just delivered a child—and saved the mother's life as well—Alicen showed amazing restraint. Perhaps exhaustion tempered her happiness.

"You never let your doubts hinder your actions," he stated abruptly.

Alicen started up from her own thoughts and shot a wary glance at him. "And if I said I never have doubts?"

Jeremy smiled. "I'd say you lied. You questioned yourself last eve, but like a good general you weighed the outcomes, took your chance, and triumphed."

She straightened in her saddle. "Never compare me to a soldier," she snapped. "I've naught in common with killers."

Her heated response crackled in the cool air.

"Forgive me my clumsy attempt at praise," Jeremy retorted. "But, loutish warrior that I am, I admire courage and decisiveness. All great leaders have those traits."

Alicen suddenly felt like a petulant child. Indeed, she'd acted as such. Her defiance crumbled. "Have a care, Captain," she said softly, "else I'll begin thinking I have your regard."

Still stung, he growled, "I respect the ability to perform well in a crisis. Naught else."

He knew his words had galled her when she straightened in her saddle, but he felt no triumph. Honesty forced him to admit Alicen Kent possessed many admirable qualities.

Still, 'twas passing strange she showed little pleasure in her most recent triumph. Had he been in her place, he'd have felt like cock of the roost. His thoughts returned to Liza, and the question lurking in his mind suddenly found voice.

"Is the child's father dead?"

"If God is just, the man no longer lives."

Although quietly spoken, Alicen's reply chilled him. Though he suspected he knew the answer, he asked, "What happened?"

"She was raped."

Inexplicable pain shot through his chest. "A local man?"

"Nay." Alicen turned fierce eyes on him. "The *father* is Harold's retainer. They stormed through Sherford, killing whom they wished, taking what they wished..."

A tight throat made the next question even more difficult to ask. "Did the soldiers reach Landeyda?"

"Aye."

His guts twisted, body tensed like a bow at full draw. "Did they—Were you—?"

"Ned, Rhea, Pearl and I hid in the woods a fortnight. We were gathering herbs when we heard them. They broke crockery, destroyed some furniture, but in the main left the place intact."

His pent up breath hissed slowly through his teeth. Finding his hands fisted on the reins, Jeremy deliberately loosened his grip. "Could they have known Landeyda is a healer's home?"

"Aye. They did."

Her declaration brought him around in his saddle to stare at her. Although the horizon had brightened to pink and blue, shadows still hid much of Alicen's expression. "How?"

"After Harold's victory over William's retainers, I treated several of Harold's wounded."

A tumble into icy water couldn't have shocked Jeremy more.

"Your mother died because of such as those men! How could you aid the whoresons?" He regretted his vehemence the moment he saw pain ravage Alicen's face. Clearly, memory lashed her. And he had just opened the dam of that memory.

She swallowed twice before saying, "I've told you, Captain, I swore an oath to my mother on her deathbed. When a life is at stake, I question not what banner a man follows."

"You cannot serve both sides," he said with firm

conviction.

"I am bound to do so." Her chin raised. "Only a barbarian would deny his enemy a physician's care."

Jeremy flushed. "I'd never deprive a foe of such. But no one can attend two masters, especially not in combat."

"I have no masters but the casualties that armies spawn."

"Then 'tis well I've accompanied you these weeks," he bit out, "lest you saw fit to serve William's enemies and gave them knowledge of his whereabouts."

Glaring, Alicen picked up her reins to kick Hercules into a gallop, but Jeremy reached across the short space between their mounts to grasp her arm.

"Nay, Mistress, do not bolt." He shook his head. His gaze softened, as did his tone. "I pray you, accept my apology for my harsh words. I am a man of war, not of poetry, and oft have no skill at tempering my speech." He offered a crooked smile and slowly released his grip on her. "Liza and the babe live because of you. Is that not reason enough for gladness?"

"Gladness for a ruined woman and her bastard son?"

"The boy could have been an orphaned bastard, yet he is not. Liza could have lost the child, yet he lives. From what I saw of them together, there is hope for a better day to come. They owe that to you."

"I find cold comfort in such thoughts, Captain."

Jeremy sighed quietly. Clearly, Alicen's vow warred with the understanding that, in preserving life, she might be sentencing mother and child to poverty and derision. Small wonder her bitterness. Still, he was unprepared for her next outburst.

"'Tis simple for a man! He takes what he wants. No matter a woman is unwilling, he lies with her, assuages his lust, and is gone within the hour. What concern if he's gotten a bastard on her? He'll ne'er have to claim it. After all, the world is populated with bastards." Her loathing took form in a murderous glare at him, the only man available to see it.

Jeremy reddened, shame for his gender's barbarity making him avert his gaze. Though he'd dallied with little concern before he'd wed, after Estelle's death he'd been certain no issue had resulted from his few liaisons. Now he was fiercely glad there had been none.

No woman who had struggled as Liza had to bring forth new life deserved having her babe left a bastard. He suddenly decided to ease her burden somehow. Still clinging to his belief that women were inherently fickle, he nonetheless admitted Liza deserved better than she'd gotten. He would see her and her child properly cared for.

But he'd not reveal his plans to Alicen, lest she think his view of females, including her, had changed.

For a mile they rode again in silence, both with their own thoughts. Then Alicen reined in and cocked her head.

"Someone cries out in pain."

"I hear naught."

Alicen shot Jeremy an exasperated glance, then concentrated. "To the west." Her heart suddenly thundered. The sound had come from the direction of Orrick's hut. *Sweet Jesu, what will Captain Blaine do if Orrick needs help? And what if Orrick sees me with Blaine?* She shuddered involuntarily but made up her mind. No matter the source of the cry, she was bound to give aid.

However, when she moved to turn Hercules off the road, Jeremy used Charon's body to block the way.

"You're exhausted, woman," he said gruffly. "See to yourself for once."

In a blink, fear turned to anger. "I could ignore a call for help as well as you could live without aiding William," she snapped. "I must go."

Before her escort could protest further, she had maneuvered Hercules around Charon and kicked the gelding into a trot along an overgrown path. But the destrier was quicker. The big stallion muscled the smaller horse aside and took the lead.

"Stay behind me," Jeremy ordered over his shoulder as his mount moved past. "You're too reckless to be left to your own devices."

Alicen swallowed her ire and followed. She truly must be exhausted, since, despite her fear of what he would find, she didn't argue with her nemesis.

The hut they sought sat less than a hundred rods into the dense forest, at the edge of a small clearing. As they broke from the trees, Jeremy stiffened and reined in. Making sure Charon blocked most of Alicen's view, he glanced quickly over his shoulder.

"Wait here. I don't wish you to see this." He rode to the hut, then dismounted, drew his sword and knelt beside the still figure of a man.

A scream built in Alicen's heart and burned in her throat. Her mind tried to deny what her heart knew to be the truth, and she found herself fighting to remain sensate. She had dismounted from Hercules and was running toward the source of her terror before she even knew what she was doing.

Twelve

"Orrick! Sweet Jesu, no," Alicen cried, rushing to kneel beside his battered form. He lay in a pool of slowly spreading blood. 'Twas obvious to any who looked that he was dead.

She raised her tear-filled eyes to Jeremy's, and he saw a grief so deep it pierced his soul. Not understanding his reaction, he suddenly needed desperately to know what Orrick meant to her.

"Do you still love him?" The question made his throat raw. "You'll answer before we..."

His utterance died as he mentally counted a dozen riders emerging from the forest into the clearing. Instinctively, his grip tightened on his sword. Resistance would be fatal, but from the look of them he had no reason to expect a long life.

A glance at Alicen revealed complete calm. Her self-control stunned him. No one who hadn't just seen her could ever detect in her eyes a grief too profound to name. While he understood her composure in the face of Liza's crisis—babies were women's business—he knew the most stout-hearted man would fear these odds. Was mischief afoot here?

"Jeremy Blaine! 'Twas rumored you'd tired of France and returned to England. And now we meet again."

That much-hated voice brought Jeremy's eyes to focus on the mercenary leader. His every muscle tightened, and his tone grew equally hard as he retorted, "I thought you'd been hanged long ere now, Kenrick."

"If you'd had your way, 'twould have been a foregone event." Kenrick grinned, showing a predatory beast's teeth. He sat his horse with the arrogance of one accustomed to riding. "But I was fortunate enough to escape you. And now 'tis your turn."

Alicen went completely still as recognition of their assailant dawned. The search party! The hatred between Kenrick and Blaine fairly crackled in the air.

A muscle twitched in Jeremy's jaw. "You used the woman to lure me here?"

"In truth, I had no knowledge you were nearby. Spying for William, I presume. We'd heard he was near Sherford some time back. And wounded in a skirmish with Harold's troops." Jeremy's expression didn't change, and Kenrick scrutinized Alicen. "I'm glad you escaped the plague, Mistress Kent," he said mockingly. Alicen nodded, remaining silent. "Duke Harold sings hosannahs to your healing skills, and I've need of them. I'd planned to ride to Landeyda, and encountered this man upon the way. He proved very informative."

Alicen quaked at the evil in Kenrick's tone and his implication that he'd discovered her secret, but she clung to her tranquil demeanor with a will. This man had murdered Orrick and was capable of untold horrors.

"You slew a harmless madman," she stated blandly. "There was no need to do so."

Kenrick's eyes narrowed. "He claimed you as his betrothed. Said he protected you." He laughed heartily. "He couldn't even protect himself. Pathetic creature."

Sweet, mad Orrick, poor fool, Alicen mourned silently. "As I said, a madman." Pleased her voice did not betray her agony, she feared she'd not hold to the pretense long. Grief and anger battered her soul. She must release them soon or go mad herself.

Then, just as she felt her resolve wavering, Jeremy Blaine rose to his feet, shifting Kenrick's regard away from her.

"You still work best under clouds of deception, Kenrick," he said with contempt.

Shrugging, the mercenary leaned forward to rest his crossed arms on his saddle pommel. "I prefer shadows, thus I remain a difficult target. My strategy rarely fails."

Jeremy's cold expression gave no hint of a mind scrabbling for a way to alert William of Kenrick's location. The mercenary apparently knew naught of the duke's whereabouts, God be praised. Mayhap the bastard truly had come to seek Alicen's aid. But that made little sense, as there were bound to be healers closer to Harold's camp.

His chest tightened painfully. What if she *had* betrayed William? Equal parts of anger and misery shot through him, but another thought immediately crowded out such bitterness. If Kenrick rode to Landeyda, a skirmish would ensue. And, regardless of what had brought him here, the mercenary would know William's location.

This truth pulled Jeremy back to his senses. Should Alicen accompany Kenrick anywhere, he would quickly know William's location. If she didn't give such information willingly, she'd tell him under duress. Kenrick would kill him, but what the knave would do to Alicen when he was finished with her services would be far more horrifying. Regardless of his suspicions, Jeremy could not leave her to the cutthroat bastard. Not without a fight.

"Let the wench go free," he said quietly, sword at the ready. "She's naught to you."

"On the contrary, she's all to me." The sneer widened to a smile. "She's served Harold before. She'll serve him again."

"You'll pay for her services in blood," Jeremy stated, contempt in the gaze he swept over Kenrick. "Get off that horse and fight me. Or are you yet a coward?"

Glistening teeth bared in a snarl. "Doubtless you still are superior in combat, Blaine. I value my life too much to forfeit it. Besides, why fight for what is freely given? The healer has come to me, you with her. Indeed a fortunate day."

"I'm ready to depart," Alicen said calmly. She turned and mounted Hercules. "If you need me so desperately, there's no sense remaining here longer."

Jeremy stared at her. Her lack of alarm told him she thought herself safe. She'd learn the error of that assumption soon enough. No visible sign betrayed his feelings, though he knew he could not warn William of Kenrick's whereabouts, could not escape his own death. Regret gripped him. Regret and...what? Bitterness. A wrenching bitterness that his suspicions might be correct about Alicen's duplicity. Yet, though he die this day, he'd not die like a dog. His stare bored into his foe as the latter addressed Alicen.

"How came you to be in this knight's attendance, Mistress?" Kenrick asked coldly. "He's a well-known enemy of Duke Harold."

Alarms clamored in Alicen's mind, urging extreme caution. She moved Hercules forward. This evil man played a game she had little knowledge of—one of intrigue and deception. Yet she must join the fray or face consequences she instinctively knew would be dire. Gathering her wit, she prepared a deception of her own.

Injecting just enough innocence into her voice to sound convincing, she replied, "In truth, I'd ne'er set eyes upon him until a fortnight ago, sir." She gave Jeremy a tolerant look, then sighed and shook her head. "Alas, I've had little peace since. Follows me about like a lovesick swain, he does. Hardly an hour passes but he protests his regard for me." She smiled coyly. "I share not his feelings and have repeatedly told him so. Yet he refuses to believe me."

Kenrick smirked. "The man loves only duty. He has used you, the better to spy for his duke."

With a gasp, Alicen turned hurt-filled eyes upon Jeremy. "Fie on you, sir, if you've sported with me. I insist you leave me be. I wish to see you no more."

By the blessed Virgin, make this Kenrick believe me and release Jeremy, Alicen prayed. *He'll return to Landeyda and warn William. Mayhap even avenge Orrick's death...*

She gave the lout Kenrick her most charming smile. "Shall we to your camp, sir, and leave this faithless man behind?"

"I had planned just such." His look seethed with malice before he grinned. "Is that to your liking, Sir Jeremy?"

Jeremy's pulse pounded like a galloping stallion's hooves. Both his and Alicen's lives rested in this monster's hands. Knowing his own death was inevitable, he sought to spare her the same fate. He had to warn her to escape these killers.

"You understand the thoughts of a man in love, Kenrick," he said dryly, one brow cocked up in mockery. "Therefore, allow me to bid the woman a proper farewell."

"Love, Blaine?" Kenrick snorted. "This bears witnessing, I think...You know well I'd never come between love and a soldier's heart." He crossed his arms over his chest, face an impassive mask. "Get on with it."

Jeremy sheathed his sword and stepped up to Alicen's stirrup. He extended his hands toward her. "Come down and bid me farewell, lady."

His intense expression made Alicen's protest die unvoiced. Though unable to fathom his purpose, she allowed him to lift her to the ground. The moment her feet hit solid earth, she was engulfed in his strong embrace.

He pulled her to him, his head bent, mouth next to her ear. "Do you go with him, he'll kill me, then force you to tell him about William."

"His wounded men—"

"Alicen, I know him. He'll hurt you when he no longer needs you. I can occupy them long enough for you to escape. They'd never expect you to outride them."

"I'm sworn to help any in need," she returned with quiet conviction, stilling her own fears. "I must go."

"Think of those who'll die. William, Taft...perhaps even Ned." His embrace tightened until there was not a breath of space between them. "The lives you may save will never balance those lost. Think of that." He lifted his head to stare at her. "You can't serve both sides," he whispered urgently, lips nearly touching hers. "Too many will suffer if you try."

Without another word, his mouth sealed hers with a hungry, possessive kiss. His lips moved with seductive insinuation, coaxing a response. Unchecked virility surrounded her, swamping all her senses. Her knees started to buckle. She had never felt so wanton, so aware of the powerful sensations this man's body stirred inside her. Helpless to resist, she wrapped her arms around his neck and returned his ardor.

Jeremy pulled his mouth from Alicen's when Kenrick's shouts of laughter penetrated his mind. His hands subtly squeezed her shoulders before he murmured beneath his breath, "Think of those who will die, woman. You can't serve both sides." Slowly drawing back, he gazed into her stunned eyes and gave her a tender, unguarded look. That look darkened to hatred when Kenrick laughed again.

"Very convincing, Blaine," the mercenary jeered. "And touching. Had I not known better, I'd think you actually cared for the wench. And she for you."

Jeremy stiffened, then gave Alicen another long look before turning to stare at his enemy. "Ah, yes, I feign passion very well," he replied archly. "Of course, Estelle cured my romantic bent long ago." He pushed Alicen firmly back and stepped away, leaving her to mount Hercules without aid.

Kenrick's cold eyes glinted malice. "And, sweet, sweet Estelle. Such a tender morsel. I enjoyed her while you were in France." He paused. "Did she ever scream for you? She screamed for me when I had her in your stable all night. She screamed every time I took her."

Alicen saw rage and stark despair flame in Jeremy's eyes. Horror filled her. Kenrick, his most hated enemy, had violated Jeremy's wife! Did the cur's treachery ever end? Pity for the captain wrung her heart. Although his face showed no expression, Alicen knew he'd surmised the truth she'd instantly come to understand herself: Estelle had aborted the child because it wasn't her husband's.

Kenrick sighed mockingly. "'Twould please me to recount more of Estelle, but my wounded await." Giving a slight nod to his men, he said, "Therefore, old friend, *adieu*." At these words, relief engulfed Alicen. They'd leave, and the captain would be safe. She had started to pull Hercules around to go with the mercenaries when the attack came.

Jeremy, red with fury, fought like one possessed. His keen blade deflected a swinging pikestaff hurtling at him, and instead of taking the blow on his head, he took it across the ribs. Though he was without chain mail, his arming doublet absorbed the brunt of the attack. Still, the breath fled his body and he fell. Pain burst in him, but he struggled up, pivoting to face the ever tightening circle of attackers.

One man charged alone. His life ended on the point of Jeremy's sword. As the circle closed, he yanked his blade free and spun, managing to wound two more men. But he couldn't turn fast enough to guard his back, and the jackals closed in.

The butt of a pike crashed into the base of his skull, laying him in the dirt. Kenrick's lieutenant raised his pike, ready to pierce Jeremy's chest.

With Captain Blaine struck down, his foe poised to make the killing thrust, Alicen burst into action. Recklessly, she drove Hercules forward, wedging him against the mercenary's mount, preventing the fatal lunge.

"Stop!" She grabbed the man's upraised arm and attempted to wrest his weapon away. "You mustn't kill him! *Don't kill him!*"

He shook off her tenaciously clinging hands, raising a fist to strike her.

"Enough!" Kenrick's command brooked no argument. His small, dark eyes turned toward Alicen. "You intrude where unwelcome, Mistress. Blaine will die."

Alicen's eyes grew cold and her voice low. "Then slay me. For if you slay him, I'll not go with you for any reason."

Kenrick's thick brow rose. "What is the man to you?"

"A man."

"And such a one as holds you in contempt. Be not fooled by his show of gallantry on your behalf. He has no love for you."

She drew a breath and steadied her voice. Only her strong will kept her from glancing over at Orrick's body. "No man deserves to be murdered."

"Murdered? More like excised. As you would remove a boil."

Realizing Kenrick's determination to see Blaine dead, Alicen fought to maintain courage. Pray God her skills were dear enough to this murderer for him to indulge her.

"I tell you true," she stated, "kill him, and I'll help you not at all. I care not for causes, only for the ill. But I'll not see another man die needlessly." Anger ignited in her eyes. "And do not think to force me to your will. I know as well how to take a life as save one."

Her brazen declaration seemed to impress Kenrick. He turned his look upon Jeremy, who lay bleeding in the dirt at his horse's feet.

"This wench is well worth having, Blaine," he taunted. "Pity I can't goad you by taking her as you watch, but, unlike Estelle, you don't seem to care enough to be angered should I ravish her." He nodded to the man with the pike. "Tie him over his saddle." Turning then, he gave back Alicen's intense look. "You temporarily prolong his life, wench. I'll not free him to return to William. He'll die by my hand ere long."

But not at this moment, Alicen thought with wild relief. When realization dawned that Kenrick had spared Jeremy, she slowly unclenched her fists. Captain Blaine would live. Not that he'd be grateful, she reasoned morosely. His feelings were clear—and she abruptly realized he was right. She could not serve both sides without endangering Duke William and his men, men she'd grown to respect. For once, she understood Jeremy's reasoning.

She stared down at his prostrate form. Why had he kissed her with such passion, then turned coldly away? Her mouth was tender from his ardor. There had been naught of indifference in that embrace. Yet the uneasy feeling persisted that he'd never understand her need to heal.

Her contemplations halted when the brigands, laughing and shouting, began to viciously batter Jeremy. Bile rose in her throat when one landed several kicks to his ribs.

"Merciful Christ, he's helpless," she cried. "Have you no honor?"

Her concern drew a nasty laugh from the henchman. He and a confederate bound the captain's wrists behind him before tossing him over Charon's saddle. Soon a rope secured to Jeremy's feet ran beneath the horse's belly. The hireling tied it in a loose loop around Jeremy's neck. Laughing again, he gave the rope a sharp tug.

Alicen felt a sudden chill. She could see blood in Jeremy's black hair. He needed attention, but would she be allowed to tend him? Had positions been reversed, he would not have balked at her treating an enemy. But evidently Kenrick's idea of honor differed vastly from that of the man who now lay battered and bleeding across Charon's saddle. Alicen felt her breath catch. Might he bleed to death before she had the chance to help him?

She thought to insist upon assessing his injuries, but her request went unvoiced as the party immediately formed ranks around her and spurred their horses away from the hut. Alicen prayed for Orrick's departed soul, and added to that prayer a plea that someone find his body and afford it a Christian burial. Now, at long last, he could be at peace.

***

Awaken!

The whispered command buzzed in Jeremy's ears just before Charon's gait jostled him awake. Wishing to draw no attention to his lucidity, he carefully turned his head. By the lengthening shadows he knew they'd traveled several hours. The sun's position indicated westward movement. Toward the Pennine Mountains. The terrain had become rugged, heath and moor, and the horses traveled in single file, climbing a gradual slope.

He closed his eyes to ease the pain behind them. How long would he ride face down across his saddle like a butchered hart? His ribs burned. Breathing was an effort he had little strength to accomplish.

You must remain alert. Take shallow breaths and keep your wits about you.

Although he'd taken a severe blow to the head, Jeremy knew he didn't imagine the lilting Irish brogue. He was actually glad to hear it. If Kaitlyn O'Rourke did indeed speak to him, she issued sound advice. He had to avoid lapsing back into senselessness, ascertain the situation, and plan an escape.

Kenrick would no doubt kill him at the first opportunity. Jeremy wondered that he'd been spared this long, but suspected Alicen's intervention was the reason. His former comrade-at-arms likely would plan some special diversion, with Jeremy as the entertainment.

Of a certain, I'll give them a diversion they'll not soon forget. And if I'm able, I'll kill that whoreson Kenrick.

His heart's pain mirrored his body's when he recalled Kenrick's taunt. Had he truly raped Estelle? Jeremy forced his thoughts back to his marriage. All had been well for the first few months, then he'd left on campaign, returning to find Estelle distantly reticent. She barely tolerated his lovemaking and never sought it from him as she had before he left. She'd told him nothing of the babe. He'd discovered her betrayal in the midwife's hut the day Estelle died. To keep from roaring his grief at that memory, he bit his tongue until he tasted blood. For years he'd thought she hated him too much to bear his child.

In fact, she'd loved him too much to bear Kenrick's bastard.

Estelle, forgive me, he prayed. *I never knew.*

Hot tears stung his eyes and he let them fall, knowing no one would notice or care. Except perhaps Alicen Kent. His moist eyes dried as he considered her perfidy. She'd claimed her betrothed had died in battle in France, when in fact he'd been less than a league away from Landeyda, very much alive. Yet she had saved William's life and treated his men with all her skill. If she was guilty of anything, it was of believing she could, unmolested, serve any and all in a conflict.

This thought led to a stark realization. If Kenrick learned she'd helped William, Alicen would pay for it. The monster enjoyed brutalizing women. Rage replaced Jeremy's headache. No matter her deceit, he'd not see Alicen raped and abused. She did not deserve that for seeking to protect her betrothed.

He went cold. Had he committed a grave error in trying to prevent the mercenaries from taking her? If Kenrick thought him in the least concerned, Alicen would certainly be hurt. Making both captives suffer would double Kenrick's pleasure.

Still, she was not a cowering victim, the type Kenrick preyed upon. Perhaps her defiance, or her healing skills and apparent standing with Harold, would deter any abuse. He could only pray this would prove true. Yet Kenrick might decide to take sport with her merely because she was a woman....

Fury came to no good, so Jeremy subdued it. Better to hoard strength rather than spend it in fruitless emotion. Anger would aid him, but not at present. He'd bide his time and await a chance to gain advantage. Closing his eyes, he concentrated, willing away pain and hurtful memories. Presently, he slept.

***

They rode until nightfall, when they reached a hidden camp high in the hills. The chill night air hung around them like a vengeful wraith, sucking parasitically at their strength, and the rising full moon shed only cold light.

Exhausted, Alicen practically fell from her saddle

when they at last stopped near the mouth of a cave.

But fear—for what might happen to Jeremy and to herself—had built steadily and now consumed all thought. She struggled to keep her wits, to find a solution to this dilemma. Convinced that solution lay with Jeremy, she was determined to speak to him. If she could. At a glance she saw that Kenrick's men had tossed him under a nearby oak, bound hand and foot. He appeared unconscious, but the light was too dim to see him clearly.

Her boldness had kept him alive until now, but Kenrick would not allow him to live much longer. She would have to be very clever indeed to stay one step ahead of this cruel adversary.

If she could not, doubtless both she and Jeremy would rue her failure.

After several unsteady moments on shaking legs, she found she could walk, and turned to attend Hercules. The gelding nickered as she mechanically removed his saddle and bridle, then rubbed him down with fistsful of dried grass.

Kenrick stepped from the cave, looked around, then stalked forward. He reached Alicen in a few quick strides and, grabbing her by the shoulder, spun her around to face him.

The attack caught her off guard. Exhaustion sealed her fate. Reeling, limbs weak, she collapsed against his dirty tunic. Reflexively, she clutched the garment to keep from falling. But when she looked up and saw his eyes, her grip relaxed. His gaze told her she'd learn firsthand what forms his evil could take. She slid to the ground at his feet. Now trembling like a willow in a wind storm, she lowered her head to hide her terror.

Show him nothing. Fear doubtless pleasures him...Mother give me courage.

Kenrick leered as he bent to grasp a handful of Alicen's hair. Pulling, he drew her to her unsteady feet. She knew he could sense a victim's dread, so she did not reveal it. Instead, she gave him defiance. Her lips thinned and her chin rose.

Surprise lit his face, and he paused a moment. "Beg me to spare you," he growled. "Grovel at my feet."

His grip tightened, and he bent her head back. Hard

lips crushed down on her slack mouth.

She didn't resist his assault in part because she could barely stand. Only his hands kept her upright. The lust in his eyes died instantly.

"'Tis folly to break you ere I've had good use of you," he sneered. "There's time enough to enjoy your charms. Sleep in the cave." He pushed her toward the entrance. "Tomorrow you see to the wounded." He moistened his lips, as if in anticipation, before stomping to the campfire.

In the half light beyond the fire's illumination, Jeremy's pent up breath escaped in a low hiss. His inability to stop Kenrick's assault on Alicen lashed him. He could feel blood trickling from his wrists where he'd futilely struggled to free his hands, and his muscles were bunched and cramped.

Although shaking with frustrated rage, he bowed his head and thanked God for whatever circumstance had kept Kenrick from raping Alicen. Perhaps the villain realized his victim was no ordinary woman, but one whose value made abusing her extremely dangerous.

Or perhaps Kenrick had decided a larger audience to witness his conquest would be more fitting.

Jeremy lurched against his bonds again. That beast would die for what he'd just attempted. For what he'd done to Estelle. But how? Trussed like a swine fit for slaughter, he had no means to carry out his vow. He had to free himself and spirit Alicen away before these whoresons harmed her. Only when she was safe would he return and kill Kenrick. He might even find satisfaction in such a killing.

A long time later, he fell into a fitful sleep.

***

Dawn found him stiff with cold and aching everywhere. He lay quietly, listening to the camp rouse itself to wakefulness. His struggles the previous night had taught him the impossibility of breaking his bonds, and despair rose with the new sun. He'd be little help to Alicen if he couldn't even move.

Take one of her blades.

The voice filled his mind. Getting one of Alicen's instruments was a feasible idea, and he was slightly annoyed he'd not thought of that himself. But even if he did get a weapon, other problems existed. Though Kenrick appeared to believe Jeremy had no affection for Alicen, she had insisted he pursued her, and their kiss had been anything but dispassionate. He would have to be careful to act the spurned lover when Kenrick was about.

He realized that Alicen had never planned to betray William and his men. She'd lied only about the madman, Orrick. He stared hard as the woman in question straightened from one of the wounded and turned to walk toward him.

Her gaze met his momentarily before, apparently uncomfortable under his scrutiny, she looked away. Her smile was wry, forced, when she knelt beside him. "Did you sleep at all last night, Captain?" She reached to push his hair away from the cut on his head.

Before her hand reached him, he shied away, feigning anger. "Don't touch me, you traitorous bitch," he hissed.

His harsh words made her recoil, then pale. "But you're injured," she whispered, the words coming out a mixture of wounded hurt and confusion. Her lips trembled slightly. She bit them to stop it.

"Was that your intent?" Jeremy's jaw set in a hard line, and he glowered at her. No enjoyment came from the pain he inflicted on her, but he remained mindful that Kenrick watched them.

Alicen flinched, then her eyes flashed in anger. A hard swallow brought her voice under control. "I'll protest my innocence but once, Captain, then your mistrusting soul may think what it will. I'd never seen Kenrick before he came to Landeyda. I treated Harold's soldiers three years ago, but none of these mercenaries were there."

"Yet you were willing enough to accompany them."

"In exchange for your life," she whispered.

He laughed. "Think you to prevent my death at Kenrick's hand? He's killed more men than you have teeth."

"I knew naught of this."

Jeremy's mouth twisted. "Yet, you came with him. You're no better than a whore who goes with any who bid her, aren't you?" The naked agony in her eyes cut him deeply, but the danger they faced steadied him. He had to keep up his pretense of contempt.

Eyes bleak, she looked away. "Many here need care," she murmured, then raised abruptly fierce eyes to his. "You see me as base, so be it. You know of my healer's oath. Why can't you accept it?"

Before the tears that welled in her eyes fell, she rose and fled to the relative safety of the other injured men.

Jeremy silently cursed himself. He'd carried his facade of outrage too far. Alicen offered the only kindness he could expect in this place, and he'd driven her away. He studied her as she treated the mercenaries. Her posture conveyed anger, her glistening eyes hurt. But how could he ease her discomfort without revealing his feelings to Kenrick?

Perhaps he couldn't even comfort her because he himself suffered. He'd borne enough wounds to know the amount of physical pain he could endure. But this emotional pain nearly overwhelmed him. The torment of finding Estelle near death in a greedy midwife's hut had driven him to the brink of madness. Now, knowing the true reason for her death, he mourned the years he'd let hatred of her and distrust of all women consume him.

But the torment of hurting Alicen Kent cut even deeper.

When had he come to care for her so much? Perhaps that very first night at Landeyda when she'd not let him cow her. He had denied his feelings, hiding them behind suspicion. Until Liza's baby had arrived just yesterday. Then, the old yearning to father a child by a woman who'd be his wife, who'd pledge her life to him, returned. Alicen Kent was the woman he wanted.

His mouth twisted into a bitter grimace. Such would never be. He had no land to call his own, might even die in the next few days. And soldiers were abhorrent to her.

Unable to watch her any longer, he closed his eyes to will away thoughts of life with the brilliant, maddening healer. Even under the best of circumstances, he was not the man she'd choose to marry.

Thirteen

After a few moments, Jeremy opened his eyes, this time to study the activities of the able-bodied mercenaries and to plot escape. The camp lay in a clearing halfway up a mountainside, just off a main road which ran around the southern side of the peak. He heard horses coming down through the woods and, soon, two of Kenrick's men rounded an outcropping of rock nearby. Apparently, a secondary trail rose to the summit above the camp. It could provide an easily defended escape route.

Off to the southwest he observed what appeared to be Cross Fell, the highest peak in the area. That meant the river running just below them was the South Tynan, and they were northwest of Stanhope. Kenrick must have been pushing Harold's growing holdings into Cumbria. He thought of the lords and landed knights in the area. 'Twas certain many would resist Harold's intrusion onto their demesnes. Help was not far off.

But getting to that help might prove impossible. He had no weapon, no means to free himself from his bonds. And he'd just alienated the one person who might think to aid him. While pondering the obstacles to his freedom, he heard an Irish lilt, *Lure her back to you,* the voice suggested.

A ruse, then. Knowing Alicen couldn't bear suffering, he rolled to his side, knees to chest. Though she could not hear the sounds from where she knelt tending the others, he moaned low through clenched lips. The groans made his expression more realistic, more able to prick her kind heart. She *had* to approach him again.

***

The sun stood at its zenith when Alicen at last rested from her work. Hungry and tired, she stretched, hand to the small of her back. Then fear stabbed her. Where was Kenrick? If he'd seen she ceased working, would he come for her? Panic held her a moment, then she stood tall, hands fisted. In the dark of the previous night, she'd sworn not to be the brute's victim. If he attacked, she'd retaliate. Reaching into an apron pocket, she touched the sharp tools of her profession. They would serve equally well as weapons should the need arise.

Moving toward the fire, she found herself unable to ignore the figure lying beneath the nearby oak. She'd managed, through fervent concentration, to resist looking at Jeremy Blaine since his earlier abusiveness. Now, however, she couldn't prevent a glance his way.

What she saw shocked her. He lay curled nearly in a ball, his face a mask of intense pain. Alarmed, she had taken two strides toward him before remembering his order not to touch him. But he needed attention...And he needed nourishment.

Jeremy watched Alicen as she moved to the cooking pot and dished up a plate of thick stew. Then she was moving toward him, and he dared to hope she'd overcome her hurt. When she knelt in front of him, he'd plucked her heartstrings. She set the plate of thick stew on the ground, then gently touched his shoulder.

"Go away," he ordered in a tone that deliberately lacked conviction.

Alicen duly ignored his order. "Please, Captain, you must eat." She helped him to a sitting position, then extended the plate so he could see the fare. "You need your strength."

"So I'll be more entertainment when they come for my life?"

Her finger flew to his lips before she thought to stop herself. "Do not speak such words! 'Tis wrong to tempt fate." Realizing what she'd done, she jerked back, and felt her face reddening. Her gaze dropped to her hands, now both clutching the plate, before she again met Jeremy's eyes. "Should Kenrick kill you, I would consider myself your executioner."

He gave her an odd look before whispering, "Then help me to escape."

Alicen glanced around the camp. "I—Eat first." She spooned the stew into his mouth.

"We must flee tonight," he said quietly, talking around the food in case anyone watched. "Before Kenrick tires of me." *And desires you again.*

"Will anyone be killed?"

Her question caught him off guard. "What?"

The spoon returned to his mouth as she asked, "Will you kill anyone?"

He didn't like where her reasoning was leading. "Perhaps. But without weapons, t'would be difficult." Her expression made his heart sink. "I'll not promise none will die, Alicen. Yet if we don't escape, they could well slay William and all his men."

"I cannot go with you."

"But—" Another spoonful of stew temporarily silenced him.

"Let me speak." Though her voice was low, hurried, he easily heard her determination. "I'm pledged to heal, not harm. If I escaped with you and you killed someone, I'd be a party to that death."

His expression hardened, his tone caustic. "And yet you'll also consider yourself my executioner should Kenrick kill me. What a dilemma for you."

She flushed, eyes filling with tears. "The wounded need me here."

"I'm wounded." Jeremy knew his tone bordered on desperate, but couldn't control his surging emotions. Glancing up, he saw two men approaching and hastily made his last argument. "You'd remain to tend murderers and rapists rather than leave with me? 'Tis folly to put yourself in such danger."

"I'll see to your wounds now, Captain," she stated flatly. Her bright green eyes suddenly dulled, she turned to retrieve her bag, which lay beside a dying man.

Kenrick intercepted her just as she grasped her supplies.

"How goes the healing, Mistress?" he asked with dry politeness.

His affable question didn't deceive her—lust shone plain in his eyes. *I'll not be your prey*, she swore silently, staring back at him as boldly as a warrior. "One man has died. Two more will likely pass this eventide. The other eight should live, though three will never murder again."

Kenrick laughed mirthlessly at her insolence. "You've done well by them. Harold spoke true when he praised your talents."

"And 'tis certain Harold would wish continued use of those talents." Her gaze speared Kenrick and saw what she'd sought. He recognized her threat. Yet would he control his lust or take the threat as a challenge? She could not fathom him. Any concession she gained by clever wits would be temporary at best.

"Harold's endeavors are so far-flung he cannot attend to them all," he sneered. "Thus he leaves his captains to conduct affairs as they see fit." He stepped closer to hiss, "Wisdom dictates compliance, wench."

Panic threatened to undo her, but she schooled her features to hide it and tilted her chin a notch. "All that can be done for your wounded is being done, sir. Thus do I cooperate." She moved past him in two long strides, returning to Jeremy.

Kenrick followed, a smile playing about his hard lips.

Jeremy tensed at their approach. If Kenrick had somehow tricked Alicen into revealing his plot, his life would end in moments. But Kenrick looked amused, not angry. And lust burned in his jackal eyes. Jeremy knew he again thought to force Alicen. Hatred flared inside him. And despair. He needed her close enough to touch so he could secure a weapon. With Kenrick near, his chance of success lowered considerably. Desire to kill the man already ran too strong to ignore. If Kenrick touched Alicen, Jeremy's rage would not be contained. He steeled himself to remain calm. Their lives depended on his being coolheaded.

"I'm going to treat the captain's injuries," Alicen stated without turning. "To do so, I must unbind him."

The devil's black eyes examined his captive. "He'll not go far should he attempt to flee."

Jeremy glared at Kenrick but held his tongue.

Alicen quickly removed his bonds, arming doublet and linen shirt. Then she was on her knees at his right side, gently cleansing away the dried blood in his hair. That done, she turned her attention to cleaning his many scrapes and bruises. He noticed that her hands shook slightly as she touched his chest, that her cheeks were flushed. Most likely fear caused her tremors, but he wanted to think she reacted to him. Mayhap she recalled, as he did, their ardent kisses. Her touch was certainly far closer to a caress than to a mere healing contact, and, under less perilous circumstances, he'd be hard-pressed not to touch her, too.

But seduction had no place in his plot. He needed a weapon. Flinching, he muttered that she hurt him.

Kenrick laughed aloud. "Count yourself fortunate I allow her to treat you at all, Blaine," he stated darkly, his humor fleeing as quickly as it burst forth. "I'd leave you to rot."

"I think not," Jeremy replied matter-of-factly. "We were friends once, Kenrick. Before France. Before greed and cruelty twisted your soul. Mayhap in remembrance of those days you wish to ease my suffering."

"Bah!" Kenrick spat on the ground by Jeremy's feet. "The past means nothing. You were an idealistic fool, Blaine. But Estelle cured you, did she not?"

"You'll die for what you did to her," Jeremy replied with cold conviction. He turned hard eyes on Alicen. "I've loved no one since. And never will...We've both changed since our fellowship ended, Kenrick."

"You more than I, *old friend*."

Jeremy ignored him, watching instead as the compassion in Alicen's eyes melted to anger. Her pain racked him, but his cruel facade took precedence until they were safe. He strove to drive all tenderness from his gaze, to think only of her lie about Orrick. Of the lie he'd lived since Estelle's death. He had to dupe Kenrick.

Anger, he noted, drove Alicen's gentleness away, and she finished dressing his wounds in rough haste. Once done, she picked up a roll of bandage more than a handsbreadth wide. He assumed that was for his cracked ribs.

"Sit up straight, Captain," she ordered curtly.

Certain of the reason for her pique, he silently complied. Doing so brought their bodies closer, and her knees brushed his thigh. She was as near as she'd get. When she reached across to bring the bandage around his ribs, he reacted.

"God's wounds!" he bellowed, lurching. He hooked his arm beneath hers and levered her hands away from him. Startled, she dropped the bandage. It rolled across his lap and away from both of them. "Your touch is as gentle as a death blow, woman," he ranted.

As Kenrick roared with glee, Alicen shot a fuming look at Jeremy. "You addle-headed dolt, I barely touched you!"

With a snort of pure disgust, she reached over his legs to retrieve the unraveled bandage.

It was all the opportunity Jeremy needed. As Alicen leaned forward, he slipped his right hand into her large apron pocket. Long fingers quickly curled around a handle and withdrew the instrument without alerting her that it was gone. The cleverest cutpurse would have been envious.

Before Alicen had resumed her previous position, her blade lay flat beneath Jeremy's thigh. Even with his hands rebound, he'd be able to use it.

He had his weapon. Now, he needed darkness.

***

As the sun lowered to the western horizon, Jeremy plotted. Apparently, only two men guarded the horses, just out of sight of the encampment, in another clearing. He'd seen a small fire the previous night and assumed the guards used it. With any luck, they'd be so content with their lot they'd not know he was upon them until far too late. Despite the blade, he was nearly weaponless, and injuries would slow him. A hard fight would be disastrous. Yet if he let the odds against success daunt him, he'd never attempt to reach freedom.

Alicen presented another problem. She insisted she'd not aid him, that duty compelled her to remain to treat dying killers rather than leave such threatening circumstances. To his mind, honor sat uncomfortably on a woman's shoulders.

Nay, he'd not deny that devotion to duty was one of her strengths, though it be foolish to cling to in this situation.

Glancing toward the wounded, he saw her sitting beside a badly injured man. She held his hand, offering comfort against his severe pain. Jeremy's chest tightened. Such compassion was too valuable to be abused. Kenrick would never restrain himself from hurting her, perhaps destroying the charity that made the woman so unique.

Jeremy made his decision. Alicen Kent was leaving with him that night—in her saddle or across it.

***

By the light of a single torch, Alicen changed blood-soaked bandages and watched over her charges, feeling like a lioness guarding her cubs. It approached midnight, and she was the only fit person in camp yet awake. One man, delirious, had torn the stitches she'd so recently sewn. No one had been inclined to help her restrain him, forcing her to use a draught of her precious lettuce narcotic to sedate him. Now, he slept like a corpse.

She herself felt sedated. Her back ached and her eyes were gritty from lack of sleep. For over four days she'd had almost no rest. Now, her body told her emphatically to stop her frantic pace. Still, her mind fought her physical weakness. Much remained to be done. She could not rest yet.

But exhaustion won out over will. She rose and moved a little apart to make up her pallet, telling herself she'd rest but a few moments. 'Twas quiet; she could steal a short respite.

The next she knew, a man's hand had clamped tightly over her mouth.

Kenrick! She clawed at her attacker's arm, seeking to dislodge his hand, attempting at the same time to bite him.

"Hush, lass!" came a deep, familiar voice beside her ear. "Cease ere you alert someone." The moment she relaxed, Jeremy released his grip. He drew her to a sitting position, then leaned close again to whisper into her ear. "Silence now. Gather your things quietly. You're coming with me."

"But how did you—"

His finger came out of the darkness to press against her lips. "Shhh. All in due time. I need your aid." When she tensed, he quickly pressed his argument. "I cannot escape alone, Alicen. Come with me."

"I won't—"

He pulled her to her feet and into the great oak's shadow. "You've done all you can. Once Kenrick realizes this, he'll not refrain from raping you." Even in the near blackness, he saw this point hit its mark. "And what of his plan to kill me? You *must* come, Alicen. Help me. It's our only chance."

"I cannot kill—"

"You'll not have to. You only need to distract the guards long enough for me to disarm them. Then we'll take our horses and ride for help."

At that point she realized how tightly he held her upper arms. His urgency came through that grip as certainly as if he'd spoken. She also knew his determination to take her along, willingly or not.

"Tell me what to do," she said quietly.

***

She had never felt so vulnerable. What Jeremy required of her was simplicity itself—she would approach the men guarding the horses and ask to see to Hercules' welfare. Her argument was to be that, in the frantic activity of the past two days, he had lacked proper tending.

Her shaking knees threatened to undo her, but she steeled herself to her task. Thoughts of Kenrick's reaction should this escape attempt fail strengthened her resolve. She stepped boldly toward the fire, noting as she did so that Jeremy was creeping into position behind the two guards.

The thundering of her heart eased somewhat when she observed that only one of the pair was awake. The other slumped against the trunk of a small tree, chin on chest.

"I—" Her voice faltered, forcing her to swallow before trying to speak again. "A favor, kind sir." In the flickering firelight, she saw the man smile. The expression chilled rather than heartened her. "I wish to see to my horse. The bay gelding. I've been so busy of late—"

There was no need to continue. Jeremy, striking with the silent speed of a jungle cat, brought a club as large around as his wrist down across the back of the man's skull, felling him soundlessly. He pivoted and struck the sleeping guard across the head, too, knocking him to a supine position.

"Find Hercules and saddle him," Jeremy ordered Alicen in an urgent whisper. "Quickly!"

Working purposefully, he bound the mercenaries' hands and feet with the rope that had lately bound him. He gagged them with pieces of their tunics and dragged them behind the tree, then stripped both men of their daggers and swords, strapping the longest blade to his hip. Just as he finished, Alicen approached, leading Hercules and a still unsaddled Charon.

"Good lass." He grabbed the nearest saddle and blanket and threw them onto his destrier. "Beyond the lightning-struck oak is the trail," he said to her as he worked. "When the horses begin running, ride as quickly as is prudent. Hide if you hear pursuit."

Taking a short sword from his belt, he offered it to her hilt first.

She stared at the weapon gleaming dully in the moonlight, and shook her head. "I've no use for such as that."

"You may." He pressed it into her hand. "Please, lass."

Wordlessly, she took the sword and stuck the scabbard through her belt.

"Wait for me at the summit. I'll signal you when I arrive. Go, Mistress. Go with God."

As soon as Alicen and Hercules disappeared around the oak, Jeremy drew his newly acquired sword and severed the hobbles restraining each of the mercenary's mounts. Then he seized the unburned end of a log from the watch fire and swung the flaming brand at the animals. The flat of the sword across the rump of the nearest horse made it shy against its closest compatriot. Their alarm, coupled with the waving fire in Jeremy's hand, spread panic. Ears pinned back, the horses screamed their terror and surged down the trail, through the camp, into the trees.

Jeremy hurled several small, half-burned logs at the fleeing animals. Sparks flew when the brands hit trees, rocks, or the hard ground, igniting several small blazes.

"The horses are loose," he shouted. "The horses!"

Hearing the confused cries of the awakening camp and the thunder of trampling hooves, he mounted Charon and, without looking back to see the results of his efforts, urged his steed up the trail after Hercules.

"C'mon lad, we've moonglow to guide us," he murmured, spurring Charon to a trot. Periodic glances over his shoulder told him he was not yet being pursued. But he couldn't be sure for how long.

The tumult from the camp increased as the alarm

spread and men, jarred from sleep, rose in disoriented confusion to fight spreading fires and pursue fleeing horses.

Confusion would mask their escape. The longer his endeavor remained undiscovered, the better his chances of getting Alicen and himself to safety.

He turned his attention to the trail, peering ahead into the dimness for signs of her. Riding hard until some distance from the camp eased fear of pursuit, he reined Charon to a walk.

Alicen could not be seen on the trail before him.

Abrupt fear twisted his heart and made his breath congeal in his throat. Could she possibly be so far ahead? He'd told her to ride hard to the summit, and she was fearless in the saddle. Or had Kenrick placed guards on the trail? His blood chilled at the thought that she could be recaptured.

Charon stopped on his signal, and Jeremy sat listening. Only night sounds reached his ears. A bend in the trail effectively cut off additional sounds from the camp.

He drew his sword.

"Alicen?" he called softly but clearly.

Silence.

Apprehension tinged his voice with sharpness. "Alicen? Where are you?"

He let Charon proceed at a walk. Every sense attuned to his surroundings, he searched with all his faculties for the woman who'd saved his life.

What could only have been moments stretched seemingly into hours. The trail ahead remained empty. Icy sweat trickled down his sides to soak the bandages wrapped tightly about his ribcage. He discovered he was holding his breath.

"Alicen?"

What could have happened? A dozen answers to that question assaulted him, increased his apprehension. It took great effort to refrain from roaring in frustration.

Then suddenly she was there, riding Hercules out from behind a concealing stand of trees a few yards ahead.

Jeremy's relief found expression in vexation, in the harsh expulsion of his breath. "Why did you not answer, woman?"

The half-light could not conceal her abrupt indignation. "I was unsure 'twas you."

"We've lived under the same roof nearly three months, and yet you don't recognize me?"

"'Tis dark, if you haven't noticed," she shot back. "And you didn't signal as you'd said you would."

His reply was a grunt of disgust. He checked down the trail once again before turning back to her. "Ride ahead. I'll guard our backs."

Though it was wide enough for two to ride abreast, he didn't want to be near her at that moment. He had no desire to be reminded he'd just played the fool. Silently, he cursed his ineptitude. He, who rarely erred in dealing with others—friend or foe—became a bumbling idiot around Alicen Kent. The fact she completely befuddled him gouged his pride.

Her stiff posture indicated that his gruff treatment angered her. And, in truth, how could he blame her for doing as he'd said? He *had* forgotten to signal, after saying he would. She rarely followed orders, then when she did, he snapped at her. His inconsistencies most likely were driving her to madness.

They traveled in silence until the moon had passed its zenith and they approached the mountain's summit.

At the apex they heard it. From below them, muffled at first, barely distinguishable from the night sounds of the forest. But the din built quickly—a keening that raised the hackles on Jeremy's neck and caused Alicen to whirl in her saddle.

Jeremy, prepared for the worst, crowded Charon in beside Hercules on the trail.

"That sounds like—" She paused, and he saw her eyes widen. "Screaming."

Fourteen

Frantically she sought to pierce the dimness and clearly view his expression, but he kept his eyes averted.

"What's happening down there?" Her whisper was raw, the tone indicating she meant only to confirm her suspicion.

"Kenrick's killing the wounded."

"Jesu be merciful! *Why*?"

"They'd slow his progress, possibly fall behind and turn informants for his enemies." Despite his revulsion, Jeremy remained calm in an attempt to stem her growing hysteria. "He did the same in France."

The scream that burst from Alicen's throat echoed the rising scream from below. "Noooo!"

She tried to rein Hercules around, but Charon's bulk prevented that. Jeremy guessed her next move and, leaning across his saddle, grabbed her about the waist before she dismounted. With a tug and a grunt of pain, he hauled her onto his lap.

Rage ignited like a flaming brand to tinder, and she fought to free herself even as Jeremy's arms closed around her.

"Put me down! Those men are dying! I must go to them!"

Freeing her right hand, she flailed at him, landing blows to his head, chest and shoulder. Every strike doubled the pain in his ribs, but his grip tightened as he tried to control her and keep them both in the saddle. It took tremendous effort.

"Alicen, they're dead!" His chest heaved with each breath he drew. "You cannot help them."

"I must," she screamed. She wrenched her other hand free and struck with both fists. "Let me go!"

In agony, Jeremy tried to readjust his hold but lost his grip. Like a wraith, she slid from the saddle and ran down the trail.

Toward the slaughter.

"Alicen!" He was equally as swift dismounting, but

the jolt sent pain radiating through him. He had to catch her quickly or his strength would fail and she'd escape. Gathering himself for one supreme effort, he burst into a dead run. His long strides soon closed the distance between them.

Sensing his approach, Alicen increased her pace, but even though injuries slowed him, he was still faster than she. Ten rods into her flight, he caught her and brought her to ground, rolling beneath her falling body to soften the landing.

Their momentum carried Alicen to her back, and Jeremy's chest pressed her to the ground, effectively ending her escape. She struggled but was pinned, helpless, beneath him.

"Let me up!" she pleaded, wriggling fiercely. "The wounded need me."

The impact of their fall nearly made him faint, and he thanked God he'd overtaken her just then. He could not have gone much farther. Panting, Jeremy said as gently as his burning ribs allowed, "They've need of a priest now, not a healer."

The screams had stopped. At this realization, Alicen went limp. "No...Jesus, Mary and Joseph, no."

She pressed a fist to her mouth in a futile effort to stem the cry that built in her lungs and could not be contained. It burst forth, a wail of mortal anguish. The tears began then, seeming to flow from deep inside her, from the very well of life that sustained her. All the horror and anger and futility of the last three years surfaced in a surge of raw emotion.

Unaware that Jeremy had gathered her close, sitting up to better hold her, she buried her head against his wide chest and sobbed. He murmured soothingly and rocked her like a child, caressing her back in an effort to comfort her tattered soul.

Several long, agonized moments passed before Alicen's wrenching sobs began to subside. When they had quieted to intermittent hiccups, Jeremy gently pulled the hair back from her face and stroked her cheek.

"Why?"

Her one-word question pierced his heart. Bile choked him as he contemplated an answer.

"Soldiers," he said, bitterness tingeing his voice, "are expendable."

"He murdered them!"

"Because of me."

Raising her head from his chest, she stared in silent question.

"Kenrick knows I'll hunt him to the ends of the world," he said, resigned. "He'd not have confessed about Estelle had he thought I'd live. Our escape sealed the wounded men's fate because transporting the injured takes time. He killed them rather than risk my catching up to him."

Shocked horror registered on Alicen's face, but her tone held no accusation as she stated, "You knew it would happen."

"I surmised as much." His jaw tensed. "This adds to my need to run that whoreson to ground. He'll pay for his crimes."

"For your wife and all the rest." Her voice caught. "Those men were killed, not in battle, but as they lay helpless. By comrades in arms. Do soldiers expect to die thus?"

No answer existed for that. Jeremy felt the burden of his military service pressing upon him. How many men had died at his hand? In the name of what great cause? Despair threatened to crush him. He'd returned disillusioned from France, determined to put up his sword forever. But Harold's coup had forced him to keep fighting, to keep inflicting death and destruction upon his foes. When would it end?

"I'm sorry, lass," he whispered, voice choked. "Sorry we barbarians exist. We kill, rape, plunder—in the name of glory and honor. Yet neither will be found in our endeavors. Forgive me." He looked away. When he'd secured his lands, he'd honor his vow to never war again.

"'Tis folly," Alicen said quietly after a long pause. "You are injured, yet I add to that pain, then seek comfort from you."

"You once told me the spirit oft requires the same care as does the body," was his subdued reply.

She lifted her head and looked into his night-veiled eyes, then raised her hand to a jaw roughened by three days' growth of beard. At her touch, Jeremy turned his face and placed a tender kiss on her palm.

With a sigh, she slipped her arms around his lean waist and once again lowered her cheek to his chest. Knowing he shared her pain eased her aching soul, but still she needed comfort. The steady heartbeat beneath her ear assured that, despite the valley of death they'd come through, life continued. Such assurance was the most she could hope for just then.

"We must move on," he said after several minutes. "Come."

She rose with his help, then slid her arm gingerly around his waist. He didn't hesitate to drape his arm over her shoulder and draw her close to his side.

"Ride with me, lass, and I'll be able to warm you," he said when they reached the horses.

She didn't immediately comment, had, in fact, barely been aware that he'd spoken. "What?"

He leaned down to speak into her ear. "Do you wish to ride with me?"

At this, her head came up. "I...Nay."

"You're trembling from cold," he pointed out. "Twould be wise to share our warmth."

She paused a moment, then nodded. "Tis a cold night."

He mounted Charon and reached down to lift Alicen onto his lap. Gritting his teeth against the pain in his ribs, he positioned her in front of him on the saddle, then drew his dirty, travel-worn cloak around her and tucked it beneath her leg. His arms tightened, pulling her close. "Better?"

Silent, she nodded against his doublet.

"Try to rest, lass." He gave her waist a gentle squeeze before securing Hercules' reins to Charon's saddle. "You're safe now."

Not from my memories, Captain. I'll never again be safe from those.

***

Jeremy could feel Alicen's tension and knew she didn't sleep. Her muscles remained taut, as though she expected at any moment to have to fight for her life. Her head rested against his shoulder, her arms firmly clasped his waist.

He had to admit her hold comforted him, though. His

arms and heart had been empty for five lonely years. Now both were filled with a woman who didn't want a soldier. Perhaps God punished him for his sins, for doubting his own wife's loyalty and condemning all females for her perceived betrayal. He prayed to Sebastian, patron saint of warriors, that this was not so. Soldiering had always meant physical suffering. Spiritual suffering he could scarcely bear any longer.

They rode thus for nearly half a league before Alicen succumbed to exhaustion. Her grip relaxed, and she snuggled close in Jeremy's embrace and slept.

He tightened his hold, securing her against him. A rush of tenderness assailed his heart, and he gently kissed the top of her head before tucking it beneath his chin. He couldn't hold back a long, melancholy sigh.

Why has she complicated my life so? he asked himself as he rode through the night, cradling his oft-time nemesis. Life had been far simpler with their feelings clear—he disliking her and she him. Now, he worried over her, concerned where he had no reason or right to be. Pure foolishness! He could offer her naught at present. And if his cause was lost, he could offer her even less.

These thoughts startled him. There could be no more between them than what they had—a union born of necessity and dissolved the moment necessity ended. In a fortnight he'd return to Tynan to plan the assault on Harold, while William sought a proper husband for Alicen, and she remained at Landeyda tending her people. That was as it should be. As it must be.

Jeremy scowled in a fierce effort to banish such musings and contemplate what had to be done. They had to find help quickly, enlist the aid of the closest lord, and run Kenrick to ground. Then, Jeremy knew, he would have to kill the mercenary.

He dreaded the deed.

***

Kirkoswald Castle rose from the early morning mist like a giant's crown, and hope rose at sight of the huge edifice. Jeremy kicked Charon into a canter. At the increased pace, Alicen started from her sleep. Crying out, thrashing furiously, she nearly unhorsed them both. Only Jeremy's riding skill kept them mounted. He cursed roundly as he reined his destrier to a prancing halt.

Hearing the epithet, Alicen leaned back away from him to observe his stormy features.

"What possessed you to do such a foolish thing, woman?" he demanded, not hiding his annoyance. "Had we fallen, we'd have both been injured, mayhap killed."

She bridled at his hostility. "Charon's pace startled me from sleep. I did not mean to unnerve you."

He snorted in disgust. "Unnerve me! You practically leaped from my saddle. If I hadn't—"

"Enough, Captain." Glaring, Alicen leaned as far away from Jeremy as she could. "My deed was unintended, and naught came of it. Therefore, spare me your venom." Noting his anger had cooled to a stubborn set in his jaw, she thought fleetingly they were not in danger, or they'd not be sitting there arguing. "Do you tell me why your abrupt haste?"

"Look over your shoulder."

Alicen did so, gasped, then swung her gaze back around to ask, "What keep is that?"

"Kirkoswald, I trust." His exasperation faded, and he smiled. "The lord is Edward, Earl of Cumbria. He fought with William and your father at Agincourt."

Without a word, Alicen slid from Charon's saddle, untied Hercules' reins, and mounted the gelding. Jeremy watched as she brushed tangled chestnut tresses back from her face. Catching his look, she frowned.

"Is aught amiss?"

"Nay," he responded, then grinned. "You've no need of vanity. The earl will welcome us despite our careworn look."

Alicen felt herself blush but managed a half smile. "I must appear wretched," she muttered, then sighed. There was naught she could do for it. "Let's to the castle."

Jeremy urged Charon into a canter, and Alicen followed with Hercules. Their pace carried them quickly to the outer wall via a long causeway. Positioned in the middle of the river, Kirkoswald posed a difficult target to attack. Its massive outer wall was penetrated by a single gate. Although the drawbridge was down, the heavy iron portcullis prevented unwanted entry.

Jeremy hailed the guards on the battlement, identified

himself and his companion, and requested entry. They waited only a few moments before the portcullis was raised and they were escorted into the bailey.

At the steps of the keep they dismounted, their horses led away to the stable. A squat, balding man dressed in Cumbria's livery came to usher them into a corridor to the great hall.

"I am John Waite, Steward of Kirkoswald," he stated in a voice that put Alicen in mind of a gristmill grinding flour. "My lady Rebecca will attend you anon. While you await her pleasure, will you take refreshment?"

"Most gratefully," Jeremy replied. "We've not eaten since yestereve." He tucked Alicen's arm into the crook of his elbow and escorted her inside.

Alicen unconsciously moved closer to him, somewhat unnerved by the immensity of the castle. It had been ten years since she'd seen such an edifice. With her father serving King Hal, she had lived in London and oft attended ceremonies at the Tower or the various palaces to which the King retreated. The pomp of such occasions never pleased her, nor had she liked the implacable buildings in which the celebrations were held. A child's misgivings of dark corners, mysterious corridors and hidden crannies came back with a shiver.

When her grip on Jeremy's arm tightened, he leaned down to her. "Are you ill, Mistress?" he whispered.

She shook her head without reply, concentrating instead on suppressing her apprehension. As they passed Oriental tapestries hung from the walls flanked by coats of arms and ancient battle weapons, she studied the sumptuous patterns closely and tried to lose her trepidation through appreciation of their workmanship. The ploy worked until they arrived at the hall.

Once there, her tension eased even more. Gay banners of crimson and yellow, the livery of the Earl of Cumbria, decorated the walls. Rushes covered stone flooring, and Alicen detected the smell of lavender and violets spread among them to freshen the air. Torches, burning in wall sconces set every ten feet, chased away the gloom. Yet the hall was not oppressively smoke-filled. Just beneath the high ceiling were vent holes the size of battle shields, six to each wall, to provide air flow and allow smoke to escape.

"Come this way," John instructed.

He led them to a cozy chamber off the great hall. Far more intimate and comfortable than the larger room, it was obviously meant for family meals and private audiences. Four high-backed leather chairs were drawn in a semi-circle in front of a hearth. Huge Persian tapestries softened the cold flagstone walls, while tallow candles burned in tall candelabrum, softly illuminating the chamber. A long trestle table dominated its center. Two high-backed chairs sat at either end, and benches on each side completed the dining accommodations.

The steward motioned them toward the table just as the door opened and a pair of scullions entered, the first bearing two ewers of water and the second carrying two basins and several towels. These they placed on either side of the table.

"I thought perhaps you'd wish to freshen up before breaking your fast," John remarked.

Alicen blushed. "That's very kind of you, Master Waite. I fear we're the worse for wear."

Jeremy added his agreement, then put the towel and water to good use. He'd have preferred stripping to the waist and washing away the grime of several days in soiled clothes, but decided such actions would be unseemly. He did manage to clean his face, neck, and as much of his chest as he could reach with dignity. Drying his hands, he placed the towel by the basin and sat down on the bench opposite Alicen.

He noticed that, having regained some of her accustomed cleanliness, she looked far more confident than upon arrival at Kirkoswald. She sat down just as more servants entered, this time bearing food-laden trays. Placing these on the table between the guests, they left to fetch flagons of brandywine.

The steward produced platters, knives and forks from the cupboard opposite the hearth. Setting these in place, he added bronze goblets which he promptly filled with wine. Then he heaped their platters high with venison; a dish containing peas, onions and beans; and fresh-baked bread. He smiled at their rather dazed expressions.

"Should you require aught else, I'll be in the hall."

With that, he bowed and left them to their repast.

Looking somewhat askance, Alicen stared at the food a long moment, wondering if she could eat everything the steward had set before her. Jeremy obviously had no such doubts of doing justice to the cook's efforts, as he straightaway set about proving such. Seeing him savoring every bite of food, Alicen shook off her bemusement and tried a succulent piece of venison.

Both were engaged in consuming their share of the repast when the chamber door opened once again. A portly woman of average height entered practically unnoticed by her two famished guests. A smile touched her weathered face.

"John has surpassed his usual fine board, I see," she said in a high, tinkling voice as she approached the table. "I am Lady Rebecca, wife to the Earl of Cumbria."

Just then noting that this person was in no way a servant, Alicen gasped. Jeremy, flushing hotly, shot to his feet.

"Forgive our rudeness, my lady," he stammered as he hastily moved to draw back the chair at the table's head. "We were not expecting you as yet. Your steward told us—"

Lady Rebecca waved him to silence and allowed him to seat her. "No need for contrition, Sir Jeremy. 'Tis apparent you needed good viands. Don't interrupt your meal on my behalf."

"May I pour you some wine, my lady?" he asked, still standing beside her chair.

Rebecca's smile broadened. Nodding, she turned her pale blue eyes toward her other guest. "You are Alicen?" At Alicen's nod, Rebecca added, "John tells me you come from Sherford. 'Tis leagues away! What brings you so far west?"

"'Twas not by choice, my lady," Alicen replied quietly.

She recounted their recent ordeal, omitting only the slaughter. Just the thought of that barbarity made words lodge in her throat and tears threaten.

Rebecca's expression told Alicen the older woman knew an incomplete account when she heard it. But the lady asked no questions.

"You both are near to collapse," she stated kindly.

"We'll converse more once you've rested."

"I must speak to the earl of the mercenary who abducted us," Jeremy stated with sudden intensity. He had regained his seat as the women talked. "I believe he raids in Cumbria to expand Harold of Stanhope's ill-gotten holdings."

Rebecca's expression turned grim. "Your belief is correct. My husband rode to Penrith three days ago to discuss that very problem with Brougham's castellan. He's due back at eventide." When Jeremy sighed in disappointment, she added, "If I may be frank, neither of you is fit to abandon my hospitality too soon. You must rest and regain strength before pursuing a madman."

Jeremy had straightened in his seat as Rebecca spoke. "I fear the jackal will escape me if I lie idle too long. If he is not quickly checked, much of the country will bleed."

The lady gave a brief nod. "Yet, you can do naught until my husband returns. Therefore, it pleases me to offer you the comforts of my home. When you finish your meal, John will show you to the baths, where you may cleanse away the remains of your privations."

"Baths?" Alicen inquired.

Rebecca nodded. "The second Earl of Cumbria built this castle five generations ago. He patterned its amenities after Henry the Third's palace at Westminster. Hence, the bath room has hot and cold running water. I'm certain you'll find it much to your liking."

"You're too kind, Lady Rebecca," Alicen remarked as she studied the older woman. The latter exuded amiable gentility, and Alicen found herself warming to her. "I'd very much like to speak to your physician after I've bathed, if that is possible."

"There'll be time enough for such at the evening meal," Rebecca responded. "You should slumber rather than tire yourself with the business of healing."

Though the statement was couched as a suggestion, Alicen detected the command of a concerned parent in it. She was for bed, regardless of whether or not she wished it.

"I for one could use the rest," Jeremy interjected. He smiled wryly. "Since I got naught of it last eventide."

Alicen shot him look. "If you seek to stir my guilt for

sleeping on our ride, save your breath. As I recall, 'twas at your insistence."

Turning a roguish smile toward Lady Rebecca, Jeremy said drolly, "What man wouldn't leap at the chance to hold a slumbering woman in his arms?"

Heat scorched Alicen's cheeks, and she gripped her knife and fork so tightly her knuckles whitened. Fleetingly, she considered using the utensils as weapons.

"You are the most despicable—" With supreme effort, she choked back the rest of the malediction.

Jeremy raised his hands in a gesture of capitulation. "Truce, woman, truce! I merely intended to point out that some of us gained more sleep last night than others."

Alicen drew breath to chide Jeremy, but the sight of Lady Rebecca's amusement effectively stifled any retort. Alicen was a guest at Kirkoswald, after all, and had no right to behave like a vengeful harpy. 'Twould be a poor way to show gratitude. As for Sir Jeremy Blaine, she'd have revenge for his ill-conceived jest at some other time.

Swallowing her ire, she smote Jeremy with a look that would have devastated a less confident man. He repaid her glare with a wink, then returned to eating while she pondered her wish to employ her platter to the side of his head. Mayhap *that* would put the jackal in a more sober mood!

The meal ended quietly, although the atmosphere was charged. The steward, upon Rebecca's summons, returned to escort her guests to their baths.

The large, airy chamber was on the same level as the earl's apartments. It boasted two high, arched windows with wooden shutters that could be closed to keep out drafts. Since the day was sunny, they were open to allow sunlight to warm the room. Four wooden tubs sat in a row in the center of the floor. Hot water for the baths was supplied by tanks filled from pots heated in a furnace built specially for that purpose. John motioned Jeremy toward the first tub and Alicen toward the second.

"Charlotte and Agatha will see to your needs," the portly steward remarked, indicating with a nod of his head the two servants who stood next to the respective tubs.

Alicen froze, mortified at the prospect of disrobing in front of two complete strangers *and* Jeremy Blaine. She felt the heat stealing back into her cheeks and knew she had to leave the chamber immediately or flatly refuse to bathe.

Charlotte saved her from retreating. The buxom servant moved to the far wall beneath the windows to draw a heavy damask curtain along a rod positioned above and between the two tubs. This effectively partitioned the chamber into two bathing areas.

Alicen barely had time to breathe her relief before Agatha was removing the soiled, tattered hose, tunic and shirt Alicen had worn constantly for close to a week. The matronly attendant placed them on a low bench, then turned to her charge.

"I'll have these cleaned and mended, my lady," she said kindly as she helped her step into the brimming tub.

"They're nearly beyond repair, I fear," Alicen replied ruefully before sinking to her chin in the hot water.

"'Twill be no trouble," Agatha assured her, patting Alicen's arm. "Now ye just rest yerself and let ol' Aggie see to ye."

"Thank you." She closed her eyes, having all she could do not to groan in pleasure as more water poured over her head. When strong fingers began to wash her hair, she did moan softly. She'd never been so pampered. Giving over to the maid's kind ministrations, she soon found herself on the edge of sleep.

A very feminine giggle from Jeremy's side of the curtain snapped Alicen's eyes open. Her ears attuned to his deep voice and the maid's answering titters, though they spoke too low to distinguish words. The heat in Alicen's cheeks could not be blamed on the bath water. She pictured the maid bathing the man who, mere hours before, had held Alicen in his arms. Her mouth went dry. Having seen most of his body, she knew the temptation to touch him. Charlotte was *expected* to touch the very flesh that so unnerved Alicen.

She envied the servant her opportunity.

Chastising herself for such wanton thoughts, she tried to attend to Agatha's efforts. But her mind kept picturing the activities on the other side of the curtain, and she found even Agatha's personal attentions less than diverting.

For his part, Jeremy enjoyed Charlotte's care, but did not intend to partake of the services she offered beyond his bath. With teasing hands she'd removed the bandages from his aching ribs, stroking his body, wordlessly admiring his physique. Her next touch was blatantly to the issue. Pushing her firmly away, he shook his head and stepped into the tub.

The heat of the water combined with Charlotte's now less than enthusiastic massage, eased his knotted muscles and lessened his aches. He knew his ribs required rebinding, but decided against asking Alicen to do it. He'd taxed her sorely earlier and thought it unwise to request favors after enjoying a jest at her expense. Remembering her expression when he'd remarked on holding her, he smiled. Then he chuckled.

The woman was a vision to savor with her hackles up. The emerald fire that leaped into her eyes made risking her fury a worthwhile challenge. And Jeremy never ran from a challenge. He couldn't explain why he'd made such a bold insinuation to Lady Rebecca, yet he didn't regret it. After all, Alicen *had* spent the night in his arms. That unique circumstances had led her to it was a minor point. And holding her had brought him pleasure.

The sounds of her bath progressing only a few feet away fired his thoughts. He imagined her naked, her body caressed by heated water. And then by his own heated hands. This vision enticed him, making him shift to ease an increasing discomfort. The water felt far hotter than it had moments before. His tight throat forced him to swallow several times. Blessedly, this calmed him somewhat.

But his disquieting thoughts took the smile from his mouth.

Careful, lad, he warned himself. *You think to tread on territory best left unexplored. Far better to dally with this servant and forget Alicen. William will wed her to a steward.*

There could be no gain in seeking pleasure with Alicen Kent. He must remain her nemesis, most definitely not her lover.

His jaw set. Recent events had unbalanced him. He

had to regain his feet, stop Kenrick and see William safely to York. Vital tasks. Nothing—no one—could interfere with those duties. Not even the woman who had bedeviled him for weeks, so much so he wondered how his life would progress when he left her behind.

Fifteen

They slept the afternoon away, she in an airy chamber near Lady Rebecca's apartments, he in the guardhouse. When Alicen awoke near dusk, she found Agatha bustling about the chamber, lighting candles and laying out garments on the bed.

"Yer clothes will be ready when ye depart, my lady," the matronly servant stated. "Lady Rebecca said to give ye these for while ye remain."

Alicen stared, momentarily stunned, at the lovely garments Agatha had brought.

"Surely the lady has no wish for me to wear these," she gasped, consternation bringing her brows together. "They are far too fine."

"Nay, Mistress, the lady chose these herself. They're her daughter's things. Yer meant to wear them."

Without another word, Agatha set about dressing Alicen in a delicate linen chemise. She then slipped a long-sleeved tunic of green sendal over Alicen's head, fastening it at the neck with a bronze brooch. A sleeveless surcoat of light yellow topped the tunic, and a leather belt with a bronze wolf's head buckle circled Alicen's waist and drew the garments close. Short hose, held by garters below her knees, and house slippers completed the outfit.

"Ye look beautiful, my lady," Agatha breathed. "I'll dress yer hair now, if ye'd like."

"Please, just leave it," Alicen begged, unaccustomed to such a fuss over appearances. "I'd prefer you to simply tie it back."

"As ye wish, Mistress." The servant pursed generous lips, then added, "But if I meself were blessed with such rich chestnut tresses, I'd style them to attract a handsome swain."

Alicen swallowed. "A simple style will do."

Obedient, the chambermaid brushed Alicen's hair until it shone, then tied it back with a braided band. Giving a final pat, she stepped back to view the effect and nodded.

"Lovely."

"Thank you," Alicen said with heartfelt sincerity. "I've never enjoyed such care."

"'Tis an honor to serve ye, my lady. Of a certain ye'll turn yer gallant knight's head."

The servant's comment puzzled Alicen. Then realization dawned, and her heart sank. Jeremy! He'd be joining her at supper and would likely laugh at her pretentious manner of dress. After all, she was but a simple country healer. He'd likely delight in watching her play the fool. Determined not to provide him such entertainment, she set her features and prepared to ignore all his caustic barbs.

She need not have bothered.

Silence fell as she entered the hall. It seemed every man in the room, from lordly retainers to young pages, stared at her, and she soon found herself surrounded by admirers. Unused to such attention, Alicen struggled to keep her wits and not bolt in panic. There was no time to worry about Jeremy's reaction to her.

Her appearance had stunned that particular knight to utter speechlessness. In the midst of an intense discussion with the just-returned Earl of Cumbria, Jeremy stuttered to silence, staring toward the hall's main entrance.

"Your lady is a lovely woman," Edward remarked.

Jeremy's gaze snapped back to his host. "She is not my lady, Your Grace." He noted how Alicen's entrance had stirred the men, but didn't look at her again. "She treated William's wounds and has harbored him since his injury."

"Ah." Edward's smile was sly. "A business alliance."

Jeremy shrugged. "Naught else, my lord. Now, as to the plans for pursuing Kenrick..."

***

The hall was nearly empty when Edward and Jeremy finished their stratagems. Satisfied, he bid the old man good night and made for his bed in the guard room. He halted when Alicen rose from her seat in a window embrasure and stepped down to him.

"You've decided upon a course?" she asked promptly.

It was impossible not to enjoy seeing her in courtly

attire. She wore such fashion well. Forcing down an appreciative smile, he answered, "Aye, we ride on the morrow."

"Then best we both retire." She moved past him toward the gallery. "The chase will be hard. Most likely this will be the last good rest we'll enjoy in many days."

Her use of "we" did not escape him, but he had no intention of allowing her to accompany him. It was too dangerous.

"You're staying here."

At this, she spun to face him, eyes narrowed. "Nay, I ride with you. Someone may need me."

Her words made his muscles go rigid, as if to resist a blow. "You'll only slow us down," he ground out. "You're not coming."

Alicen's flush warned of a temper about to explode. "And *your* injuries will pose no hindrance? You should remain behind, since you're too reckless to properly care for yourself."

"I'll not allow my injuries to hinder me," he snapped. "Just as I'll not allow *you* to hinder me."

"I ride as well as any man! I'll no more slow the pursuit than you will. And you'll need a physician if there's fighting."

"Edward's man accompanies us."

Alicen's chin tilted up. "I'll not stay behind, no matter that you wish it so. You cannot detain me here."

"Aye, I can," he growled, determined to have the final word. He stepped closer. "There'll be danger, and I'll *not* risk men to put your safety ahead of their own."

She went completely still, then retorted in a quiet voice tempered with steel, "My will is my own, and that's to my liking. I go where I choose."

She looked as though she were ready to strike something, and Jeremy wisely chose not to test her anger. He took a slow breath to temper his vexation. "Woman, you're a sore trial for me."

"A trial of your own making, sir. By your choice you escort me. Yet you've no claim upon me, none of any kind."

He laughed in pure exasperation. "And does Orrick still lay claim to your attentions?"

All the color drained from Alicen's face.

"I loved him," she whispered. "Before the horrors of battle stole his mind, and he returned to me a child. I lied to protect him from you." Lowering her gaze, she asked, "Will you use my deception to leave me here on the morrow?"

"Most likely."

His deliberate statement got the reaction he sought. Building anger replaced her despair. Again, their gazes locked. They stood toe to toe, no quarter given. She appeared like to scream, and he considered locking her in her room until his return. But reason tempered ire. Force would not accomplish his goal, so he changed tactics.

Lifting a hand in supplication, he said calmly, "I only wish to protect you from harm, lass. 'Tis safer for you here. We pursue dangerous killers."

"Why so concerned now?" Her composure broke, and she spun away. But not before he again saw tears. Her voice, too, betrayed her. "As recently as a few days ago, you thought my sympathies lay with them, that I plotted with a madman against you."

Pressing her knuckles to her lips to suppress a sob, she fled to the window alcove and slumped down onto its bench to bury her face in her hands.

Her desolation rent Jeremy's soul to tatters, and words eluded him. He tried to speak, but only managed a strangled whisper. "You wished to remain with the wounded. Said you'd not assist me in escaping."

"I said I'd have no part in murder." Her hands trembled as she raised her head to look at him. "I had a part in it after all. And now you give me no chance to make amends."

Make amends? Insight cleared his confusion with a jolt. She blamed herself for the deaths of Kenrick's soldiers and Orrick. And now, he insisted on denying her a way to heal herself. He stepped closer, reaching out to touch her cheek.

She shied from his hand, and the gesture lanced into him.

"Alicen, forgive me." He ached to gather her close, but dared not attempt it. "I thought—"

"You thought I'd betray you." Affront straightened her spine, steeled her voice. "You've mistrusted me from the first."

"You lied about Orrick."

"You knew naught of him 'til that night in the stable, yet you'd doubted me long ere that."

He felt himself flush with guilt. "I had to protect William—"

"From *me?* I saved his life!" She leaped up, dashing away tears with shaking fingers. "Do you think me so base I would save a man's life only to surrender him to his enemy?"

"I knew not your mind then. I—"

"You know it now, yet still insist I dance to your tune. What is your excuse tonight, Sir Jeremy Blaine?"

I fear losing you! I love you. But he bit his tongue and silenced the truth.

He'd never before met a woman of such courage. None other would risk her life for strangers, no matter the circumstance. None other thought every human equally deserving.

Merciful Christ, he wanted to make her his alone. To protect her from the world's evils and make love with her until the mountains crumbled. To help her raise their children.

But he could not. She would ever risk herself for her duty, and naught could change that. He was a soldier; she'd never return his love. Mayhap she had seen too many soldiers to see a flesh-and-blood man beneath this warrior's hard armor.

"There will be more fighting, more death," he murmured. "Why willingly subject yourself to such as that?"

"Mayhap he didn't kill them all."

He stared at her bowed head for a long moment.

"We ride at dawn," he said finally. "If you plan to accompany us, be ready. We'll not wait for you."

So saying, he turned on his heel and strode from the hall.

***

Sir Jeremy Blaine contemplated a very unchivalrous act—throttling a member of his troop. If a certain one delayed them again, he swore he'd perform the deed and damn the consequences.

Four days of riding, and they were no closer to Kenrick. Jeremy rued the reason for this futility. They could not press the pace because of one rider's inability to keep up. Complaint would avail naught, as the offender would most vehemently resist being sent back to Kirkoswald. Impotent anger roiling, Jeremy glared toward the source of his most recent trouble.

Lord Edward, having just relieved himself in the woods, limped slowly to his horse and mounted with a stiff-jointed lurch. The old knight stifled a groan.

Jeremy clenched his jaw tight to keep from cursing. Edward was, after all, a legendary warrior who'd bravely defended King and country. But those days had passed, and the Earl of Cumbria had far o'erreached his prime. Too many battles, too many scars had reduced him to frailty. Yet, pride dictated he still fight.

Could soldiers ever become common men, or were they doomed to be naught more than ancient, useless shells of the warriors they once were? Jeremy mentally shook his head.

"We should press on," he said, not unkindly. "If Kenrick is still in the Pennines, I believe he's near Alston."

Edward's mood brightened. "Cumbria is his likely target. He'll strive to annex it for Harold. Mayhap we should—"

Just then the pounding of hooves on the trail behind them brought the forty-man troop to battle readiness. Helmets were quickly donned, swords drawn, pikes brandished.

"Defensive positions!" Jeremy waited with arm raised as the sound grew closer, closer still. In a moment the unknown force would round the bend in the trail. *Steady. Steady.* His body ached with tension. Then the horses pounded into sight.

"Alicen!" His arm lowered as she and two escorts, surprise on their faces, drew rein so quickly their mounts reared in protest. Pent up anger found a vent. "Christ's guts, woman! You could have galloped headlong into the enemy camp!" Striding forward, he seized Hercules' bridle and calmed the gelding. The look he gave her ignited her temper.

"What are *you* doing here?" Alicen shot back with equal ire. "You should be leagues ahead of us by now."

Her remark brought Jeremy such a look of thwarted purpose Alicen thought he would tear something—or someone—to bits. She and her escort had ridden hard for two days and most of the night to catch the troop's main body; therefore, she could not be the source of his rage. At least not this time. That left only...

"Lord Edward, how fares your knee?" she asked politely, turning to the earl and ignoring Jeremy who, fuming, still held her horse's bridle.

"As good as can be expected, Mistress Kent," Edward replied. "Levi tends me well."

Alicen smiled and nodded to the earl's small physician. "He does indeed." Almost all of Levi's time was devoted to easing Edward's numerous pains. *That fact alone must have Jeremy wroth,* Alicen thought with wry amusement. Turning her attention back to the latter, she smiled. "We're ready to continue on immediately if 'tis necessary to do so."

"Excellent," Jeremy returned curtly, hiding his true gladness at her arrival. It seemed she'd been gone a fortnight in search of survivors from the mercenary camp. He'd missed her. Nonsense, he chided his heart. She was the lone woman in the company, how could he not miss her?

You care for her, whispered the voice he'd last heard when Kenrick's captive.

He refused to acknowledge it, thinking only of the task at hand. "Let's away, then."

Jeremy swung in on Edward's left at the head of the troop. Alicen flanked him; Levi flanked the old knight. He set as fast a pace as he dared, not wanting to cause Edward more suffering than necessary, yet knowing the longer they delayed the less chance to take Kenrick. Trying to ignore Edward's low grunts of pain, he turned to Alicen.

"Is it done, then?" He spoke up to be heard over the clank of mounted men, but knew his voice carried only to her ears.

Her mouth hardened into a thin line. She nodded. "Kenrick rarely makes errors. Not to assure all were dead would have cost him dearly." She nodded again, but he noted her glistening eyes as she looked away. "You performed a Christian act, lass. Not every mercenary finds his end in a proper grave."

"Thank you," she said so quietly he could barely hear her. "Thank you for allowing me to do that."

He resisted the urge to reach across the small distance between them and touch her. Not with a troop of men at his back and a cunning enemy before him. Perhaps there would be time later to console her, but he could not now.

***

Jeremy's opportunity came far sooner than he wanted, and this added to his already considerable frustration. Lord Edward insisted on stopping long before dark. 'Twas obvious he could ride no farther, and Jeremy ground his teeth to keep quiet. If he continued thus, he'd soon have naught with which to chew his food. Added to his vexation was their scout's report: Kenrick was, indeed, in Alston, hiring men to swell his depleted ranks.

Pacing would not suit. He had to suppress his rage, reason with Edward, and convince him to go home. But how? His patience was at an end, his negotiating skills buried beneath anger. And none but the King himself gave orders to an earl. Unless the earl thought it was his own idea...

"Have your bindings been attended to of late, Captain?"

Jeremy started from his dark thoughts. He'd been unaware of Alicen's approach, unaware that he massaged his aching ribs.

"Not since before we left Kirkoswald," he grumbled, dropping his hand away. "But have no concern for me. I'm fit."

She had the temerity to laugh. "Then why do you attempt to ease your pain? Or do you merely scratch an itch?"

"I often massage my side when I'm thinking," he baldly lied. "It helps clear my mind of vapors."

She laughed louder. "'Tis a remedy I've heard naught of. But I'll keep it well in mind should I ever need to clear away any vapors." She grinned.

He ignored her good humor. "Do you have aught else

to do besides plague me, wench? It seems someone, somewhere, would enjoy your harpy's company this eventide."

She shook her head, still grinning. "Nay, Captain, only you require my talents—besides Lord Edward, but Levi sees to him." Instantly, Alicen sobered. "'Tis difficult to tell a man he's no longer of use, is it not?"

Jeremy quirked a brow at her. "Are my thoughts so open?"

"Nay, but I know what finding Kenrick means to you. We'd be near to Alston had Edward not slowed us."

Jeremy chose not to berate her for continually using "we." In truth, it soothed him. She had in no way hindered him, as she was reliable almost to a fault. When she left to bury the slain mercenaries, he knew she'd rejoin them quickly. His hand again lifted to his ribs.

"More vapors to dispel, Captain?"

He shook his head, yet fidgeted. A long moment passed as he struggled with his pride. At last, he met her gaze. "Perhaps you—I thought—I mean—" His jaw set, he took a slow breath, then said in a rush, "If you've naught of importance to do, could you see to my damned bandages? They've been wrong since Levi wrapped them at Kirkoswald."

With a short nod, Alicen hid her smile at his roundabout praise. She found his sudden indecisiveness oddly endearing. "I could do so now, if you wish." She summoned a nearby squire, saying as the lad approached, "Sir Jeremy requires assistance with his mail and doublet. Have a care for his ribs when you remove those items."

She ignored Jeremy's annoyed glare, turning toward the pack horses carrying the troop's supplies. When she returned, he sat on a stump, bare-chested. Her gaze trained on his broad shoulders and muscled torso. Lord, he was magnificent. Suddenly, she wished to run her hands over that expanse. To touch him as a woman, not as a healer.

When she finally met his eyes, she caught an odd expression on his chiseled face, but took no time to ponder it. She had to complete this task before losing what little nerve she now clung to. Through sheer will, she ignored his tempting flesh and simply removed his bandages. Her lungs were laboring for air by the time she laid the cloth aside.

To determine the extent of his healing, she pressed her palms against his sides. He flinched, sucking in a quick breath.

"Is your pain that great?" Now intensely concerned, she fixed him with a stare.

"Nay," he replied instantly. "Your hands are cold." Jeremy's inner tension eased when she appeared to accept his lie. Truth to tell, he'd responded to the warmth of her touch, and his reaction had him on edge. Try as he might, he could not remain indifferent. Alicen knotted his innards without even knowing she did. And she could easily do the same to his heart. After discovering the truth about Estelle, he doubted his judgement of women. He had no wish to gain more scars. Or to cause any.

Alicen quickly reapplied his swathing.

"You won't heal properly until you stop all this riding and get some needed rest," she chided softly. "Binding can only help so much. The rest depends on you."

"There's time enough for that," he replied gruffly, quelling his desire to pull her into his arms and kiss her. "I must find Kenrick before he increases his troop."

Hearing the hard edge that crept into his voice with that statement, Alicen searched Jeremy's face for the kindness she had learned he possessed. He'd buried it beneath his warrior's mien. She saw him tense, watched his gaze shift to a point beyond her. Without looking, she knew who approached.

"A soldier's wounds never quite heal, do they, Sir Jeremy," Edward stated.

"Indeed, my lord, they do not," he replied with the barest trace of civility. He gave over to the squire's aid and had soon donned his doublet and mail, ignoring his audience.

Alicen saw Jeremy's agitation. Yet, he could not help that Edward's pride prevented him from admitting weakness. "I fear the captain directs his dark look at me, my lord." When Edward's gaze shifted to her, she continued, "I've just informed him I'll keep to his cruel pace no longer."

Alicen saw Jeremy start, then study her through

slitted eyes.

"Have you found the ride that taxing, Mistress Kent?" Edward asked, his expression hopeful. "'Twould hurt my heart to think we've been too demanding of you."

From the corner of her eye, she clearly read the menace in Jeremy's gaze. His expression told her he not only wondered at her scheme but that he'd like to hurt more than the earl's heart. 'Twas obvious the captain had lost all tolerance for the battered old knight. It fell to her to keep the two men allies.

"I suggested he split his force," she blithely lied. "He'd ride ahead with two-thirds of the men to meet Kenrick at Alston, while we prevented our quarry from escaping to the south."

Edward slanted his look back to Jeremy, who now wore an inscrutable expression. "Do you seriously contemplate her plan?"

Jeremy shrugged before saying blandly, "It may have merit, but I've had no time to think it through, since Mistress Kent has only now stated her wish to slow the pace."

Alicen shot him an exasperated look before she turned to Edward, eyes wide with supplication. "My lord, I crave a favor. Sir Jeremy would fain be rid of me." When Edward began to protest, she cried, "Nay, do not deny it, sir. Well we both know he finds me bothersome." She turned injured eyes to the object of her barb. "He says I hinder this campaign." Gaze downcast, she paused. "I must admit it's been difficult to keep up...Would you divide your troop and stay with me, sir? Sir Jeremy can sate his penchant for haste, and we'd follow at a more reasonable pace."

Edward's eyes glinted, and Alicen thought for a moment he would leap for joy. Mayhap he would have had he been able to rely on his knee to support his landing. She had offered a compromise that satisfied both parties. Now, she only hoped she'd baited her hook well enough to snare him.

With regal chivalry, Edward brought her hand to his lips. Raising his head from the kiss, he clasped her curled fingers to his breast and held them there. "I would be honored to escort you. That is, if Sir Jeremy agrees I should."

Jeremy rose, stony expression hiding relief and masking his appreciation. The clever minx had manipulated the earl and solved their problem. And Edward would never know.

"My lord, let us speak of this more thoroughly. I'll not follow a healer's half-witted whims until I've examined the advantages of her strategy." He clapped Edward firmly on the back as he steered the earl toward the latter's large tent.

As he and Edward left, Jeremy turned and gave Alicen such a look of gratitude that it warmed her the rest of the afternoon.

Sixteen

The smell of rich black dirt cloyed in Jeremy's nostrils as he lay on a forested ridge directly above Kenrick's encampment. Dropping off sharply to the plain below, the site gave him an excellent view of his quarry's activities. Kenrick's sentry lay bound and gagged five rods back from this vantage point, unable to alert anyone to the presence of the Earl of Cumbria's soldiers.

With his hand, Jeremy signaled those hidden troops. He'd deployed the twenty-five men in a semi-circle north of the mercenary encampment. Normally, he would have chafed at being outnumbered, but his Cumbrians carried deadly long bows, a distinct advantage over mail-clad men wielding swords and pikes. And their purpose was to prevent Kenrick's escape from the Edward of Cumbria's advancing force, not engage in battle. If luck was with them, Kenrick would give himself up without bloodshed.

Yet Jeremy felt Dame Fortune did not smile on him this day. Kenrick would fight—letting men bleed and die—rather than surrender. And he was the man Kenrick most wished dead.

He, in turn, had sworn to kill Kenrick for raping Estelle. His heart ached. Once friends, they now sought each other's demise. 'Twas certain one would spill his life onto the ground before day's end. Jeremy was grimly determined it would not be he who did so.

He shifted. The dew seeped through his arming doublet into his shirt, bringing damp discomfort. The earl and his force should have arrived, but it wasn't surprising they hadn't, given Edward's infirmities. Jeremy as yet had little reason for concern, however, since he could hold Kenrick as well as cut off his retreat. If the cur ran, his only route would take him straight into Edward's troop. He fervently hoped their number didn't include Alicen. Pray God she had sense enough to stay well away from the battlefield.

Sunlight glinting off steel caught his attention at the

same time a commotion stirred below. Looking south, he saw Edward's force break from the forest. They aligned in battle formation—stirrup to stirrup across the road—and with lowered lances and closed helms, advanced slowly toward the encampment. In his quick perusal of the troop, he didn't see Alicen.

Jeremy watched the mercenaries scramble to retrieve weapons and gear. Edward's approach had caught them unprepared. Their doom was imminent should the approaching host wish it.

It was time.

Standing, Jeremy cupped his hands to his mouth and shouted to the camp, "Kenrick, you're surrounded. Surrender, and spare your lives. Flee, and you'll all be cut down."

Kenrick emerged from his tent and glared up at Jeremy.

"Come down and fight, Blaine," he roared, drawing his sword to brandish in the air. "Die like a dog. Or have you grown cowardly upon your return from France?"

"Naught will be proven when I take your life except that I could do so. And in the course of battle, men will needlessly perish. Surrender instead. Live to fight another day."

Kenrick's laugh rang bitterly. "You think I trust you? Even you aren't fool enough to spare me. We've too much between us. I'll fight you until one of us dies."

That settled the matter. There would be bloodshed. But perhaps the destruction could be minimized.

"I challenge you to a trial at arms," Jeremy offered. "If I win, you surrender. If you win, you go free."

"Ever the idealistic dolt, Blaine," Kenrick sneered. "You seek to spare lives, when a soldier's only duty is to spend others' as well as his own. What manner of warrior are you?"

"One who is weary of death," Jeremy murmured to himself before calling down, "The warrior who will end this conflict."

He mounted Charon and rode south along the ridge toward the earl's men, rejoining Edward just long enough to summon the squire tending his borrowed armor and weapons. The young man leaped to do his bidding as

Jeremy quickly listed his needs.

"I left a man trussed on the ridge, my lord earl," he stated tersely. "Send someone to fetch him."

Edward nodded. "Dawkins, see to it." The earl turned back to Jeremy, his look grave. "Is this your wish? You're not at full strength."

"Wounds have never stopped me before," Jeremy responded flatly. "Kenrick owes me a debt of honor. It must be paid."

Edward saluted. "May God watch over you, Sir Jeremy."

While Jeremy prepared, two squires equipped Charon with his own armor. Soon, a peytral and crupper covered the horse's chest and rump, and a steel shaffron guarded his head. His field saddle was replaced by a larger war saddle. Sensing the fight about to ensue, he tossed his head and pawed the ground with steel-shod hooves, ready to engage.

Jeremy regretted Charon's lack of proper armor. All his battle gear was at Tynan. He'd never guessed he'd have need of it for what had begun weeks before as a diplomatic mission. He smothered a sigh. What Edward provided would have to do.

Over his own hose Jeremy pulled chain mail chausses. Attached steel greaves shielded his shins, and cuisses protected his thighs. Keeping his arming doublet, he donned a mail hauberk and a steel cuirass atop it, then stood patiently as the squire buckled the chest and back pieces together. Jeremy himself pulled at his coif until the mail hood covered his entire head except his face. Ill-fitting, hourglass-shaped gauntlets would suffice for his hands. Pride kept him from borrowing any better equipage.

"Your helmet, sir?" The squire offered a serviceable barbut.

"Thank you, lad." Jeremy tucked it under his arm as he chose several long lances and the sturdiest battle shield he saw.

The squire strapped these to the pack horse and mounted his own animal to await the next command. It was not long in coming, as Jeremy promptly donned his helmet and mounted Charon. He turned his elegant destrier's head toward the field.

Then his gaze fell upon Alicen's pale face, and he paused. How had he missed seeing her before? She sat astride Hercules, perfectly erect and still. But her tight mouth indicated this calm visage came at a price. When she met his look, he saw terror in her eyes. He touched his gauntlet-clad hand to his helm in salute. Then he kicked Charon into a canter that quickly closed the distance between him and his mortal enemy.

He reined to a stop a few rods from his hated foe. "This will be our last meeting, Kenrick."

"Nay, we'll meet in hell, Blaine. But you'll arrive 'ere I." Kenrick slammed his visor down with a clang.

"I think not," Jeremy replied calmly. "Thanks to you, I've walked those streets for quite some time." *Ever since I forgot how to love. Forgot how to trust my heart to a woman.* "Yet, I've left hell behind. You'll walk there alone after today."

Wheeling Charon, he trotted him back several rods, accepted the shield from his squire, then grasped a lance. Adjusting his helmet so the t-shaped face opening was exactly centered, he waved the boy aside.

"Ready my second lance, lad. I've a feeling I'll need it."

The onlookers tensed while the moments before the joust seemed to slow to hours. The wind died, as if the Earth, too, held her breath.

Jeremy steadied his breathing with a concentration of will as he regarded his foe. Kenrick was far better with lance than sword. Jeremy sought to unhorse him and fight on the ground. A difficult task, that. But not impossible. He'd never lost a joust and did not think to lose this one. This time he fought for more than prizes and honor—he fought for his duke, and his own past and future.

He uttered a quick prayer to St. Sebastian, then charged.

***

Alicen's grip on Hercules' reins tightened until the leather bit into her palms. Her heart pounded in exact rhythm with the hooves of the two horses now racing headlong toward each other.

Please God, come to Jeremy's aid, she prayed silently. *He's injured, exhausted. Give him strength to persevere.*

In dawning horror she realized that by praying for Jeremy's victory she had prayed for Kenrick's death. Everyone there knew only one man would leave the field this day. She wanted that man to be Jeremy Blaine.

Nausea swept her as the riders closed, and she squeezed her eyes shut. The impact of lances on shields drowned out the sound of hoofbeats. Eyes still tightly closed, Alicen flinched as if she'd taken the blow herself. Her nausea increased tenfold.

A collective groan from Edward's men snapped her eyes open.

"What happened?" She frantically searched for Jeremy. Was he down? Injured? She saw him turning Charon.

"Both lances splintered," Edward explained calmly. "Neither man was unhorsed, so they'll make a second pass."

The riders had reversed positions. Jeremy now faced Edward's troop, and Kenrick his own. The squires raced to bring new lances and, when both were again armed, the knights charged.

Alicen's breath caught as she watched the second pass.

At impact, Jeremy's lance broke off three feet from the hand grip. Kenrick's lance held, and Jeremy took the blow directly on his shield. The force nearly toppled him backward from his seat, but Charon veered away from the other war horse, his high-cantled saddle keeping Jeremy mounted.

Cheers resounded from the mercenaries as Jeremy struggled to right himself. Though difficult to do with no breath in him, necessity proved a strong motivator. If Kenrick chose not to follow the knightly code, he'd attack while Jeremy was helpless.

The mercenary leader merely returned to his end of the field, and Jeremy said a quick prayer of thanks that some scrap of decency remained in the man.

"Are you injured, Sir Jeremy?" The squire was pale as death when he voiced his concern. "That was quite a blow."

"Aye, lad, mayhap his best." Jeremy assessed his injuries. "My ribs ache, but no further damage was done." He added, "Let that be a lesson to you. Buy the best shield you can find. It could save your life, like mine just did."

The squire's mouth dropped open. "I'll remember that, sir."

"Good. Now give me another lance."

Although Alicen could not hear this exchange, clearly Jeremy had sustained no serious injury. She saw him clap the squire on the shoulder before selecting another lance for a third pass.

Keep him safe, Lord. I beg you.

With horrified fascination, Alicen found she now could not take her eyes from the scene playing out in deadly earnest before her. She wanted to escape from the inevitable end, but was rooted to her place beside the Earl of Cumbria.

Take Kenrick. He is evil. He killed Orrick, slaughtered his own men. Raped Estelle Blaine. Spare Jeremy's life.

Alicen's heart twisted. She'd prayed for a man's death! Set herself up as judge and sentenced him to die. Forsaken a deathbed oath to a gentle woman. Alicen hoped Kenrick ended his life on Jeremy's lance.

What manner of creature had she become?

The final charge began.

At the last possible moment, Jeremy guided Charon to pass on Kenrick's right, opposite the normal passage on the left.

"By God, he's trying Marshall's maneuver," Edward gasped, watching intently.

Raising his lance high enough to clear Charon's head, Jeremy switched it to his left side and urged a burst of speed. The destrier responded, giving Kenrick no chance to counter or avoid Blaine's lance, which sailed neatly over his own and through his breastplate, burying itself deep in his chest.

As the mercenary tumbled screaming from his saddle, the lance broke, half of it projecting from his body. He landed on his back, the fall knocking his helmet from his head.

Reining in hard, Jeremy threw what remained of his lance to the ground and dismounted. He approached, sword drawn. Kenrick had taken a fatal blow, but experience dictated caution.

"You were ever the better soldier," the mercenary whispered through frothy bubbles of blood when his enemy stood over him. "And the better man." He glanced down at the wood impaling him, then looked up at his conqueror. "Remove it. Please."

Jeremy blanched. Kenrick's pain would be twice as great. "You're certain you wish this?"

"Aye. No man should die spitted like a hog. Even such as I would not do that to a foe."

"You could have attacked when I was nearly unseated," Jeremy said quietly. "Yet you did not."

Kenrick's smile was pinched. "Honor is hard to completely exorcize." A tortured groan escaped him when Jeremy pulled the lance free. His eyes fluttered closed. "Thank you, friend."

Just then, Jeremy sensed Alicen standing beside him. He felt her presence before looking, but when he glanced over, the agony in her eyes made him ache. She had seen him kill a man and now suffered for sight of the deed.

Kneeling by Kenrick's side, she gently lifted his head and brought a small flask to his lips. "For the pain," she murmured.

Anguished eyes again opened, this time to fix on her. "You are too kind, Mistress. I deserve no such consideration."

Alicen went cold at his words. *Kind? I prayed for your death! And my prayer was answered.*

Half blinded by tears, she rose and fled to where Hercules stood. She wanted to leap into the saddle and bolt, but feared she'd ride him to death without realizing it. With a tormented moan, she buried her head against his strong neck and fought to control her sobs.

Jeremy could not leave the field to offer Alicen comfort, not while his fallen enemy still lived. He stood helplessly by, watching her. Her pain momentarily obscured the fact a man lay dying at his feet. His only thought was that he himself had caused her suffering.

"That one holds your heart, Blaine," Kenrick said, voice breathy and labored. "Keep her at your side, or one such as I will have her."

The mercenary's eyes then fixed in a sightless stare, and he expelled his last breath.

"Go to her, man," Edward ordered Jeremy from where he sat his destrier nearby. "She needs you."

"Not dressed as a killer," Jeremy returned evenly. "She's seen enough killing." He turned to the squire, desperation heavy in his chest. "Rid me of this armor."

Before the boy could even move, Jeremy was stripping away the steel plates, haphazardly throwing them to the ground.

"Take your time with her, Blaine," Edward offered. "We'll secure things here and prepare to start south by this afternoon."

Jeremy's expression was his thanks to Edward. Now clad in only arming doublet and hose, he pulled on his boots and ran toward the tethered horses. Suddenly unsure of how to proceed, he slowed as he neared Alicen. Had Kenrick's death appalled her? Did she despise him for killing the man? Reaching out, he touched her shoulder and gently squeezed.

"I had to do it, lass," he rasped through a tight throat. "It saved much bloodshed."

He tensed, anticipating anger. But Alicen stood silently, face pressed against Hercules' neck, left hand absently stroking the horse's mane.

Jeremy covered her slender fingers with his large hand. "I regret you had to witness that."

He swallowed a gasp when she turned and raised her gaze to meet his. The sparkling emerald lights within them had died, leaving a dull, lifeless void.

"I'm glad you killed him," she whispered. "I prayed for his death." Her voice broke on her despair, "God, what have I done?"

With a soft denial, Jeremy gathered her to him. "You've done naught, Alicen. I killed him, not you."

"But I wanted you to!" She pushed away, then stared through tear-veiled eyes at his intense expression. "Don't you see, I chose a side. I swore to my mother I'd never do such. I've betrayed her, myself...everything I ever believed in."

When she started to turn away, he caught her arm and stopped her. Then he slid his hand up to caress her cheek. "You chose the right side, lass."

Eyes closed, she leaned into his touch for a brief moment. But when her eyes again opened, they were as lifeless as before.

"I must return to Landeyda," she stated blankly. "I've been away too long."

Her abrupt remoteness gave him pause. Anger he could deal with, rage at his barbarity, even fear of him. But this? Her soul seemed to have left her body, abandoning her physical being to its own devices. Could he coax her spirit back? Or was he the cause of this withdrawal?

"We'll leave as soon as Charon has been stripped of battle gear," was his calm reply. "But he'll not hold up under a hard pace until he's had a chance to rest a while."

At these words, Alicen winced. The image of Jeremy and Charon engaged in mortal combat with Kenrick would never leave her. Nor would her joy at his triumph or her shame at wishing Kenrick's death. She mentally shook herself. Of course the beast would need rest! As would the man, who even now swayed on his feet, pale from exertion.

"On the morrow, then?"

He nodded, surprise in his eyes. "At dawn if you wish it."

She looked him up and down. "Did you sustain any injuries?"

Pressing his hand against his ribs, he said wryly, "Only more bruises, I fear. I'll be fit come morn."

Jeremy turned to go.

"Captain, I—" When he stopped and glanced back at her, her courage failed. Unable to meet his keen look, she stared at the ground. "I thank God you weren't grievously wounded."

"I thank Him, too, Mistress." He touched her cheek with the back of his hand, then he was gone.

***

Jeremy and Alicen were mounted and ready to ride at dawn.

Edward rose stiffly and limped out to speak to them. "Tell William my troops and I are at his disposal against Harold." He handed Jeremy a sealed parchment scroll.

"This is an accounting of the knights who owe me service, and the number of their retainers."

"My thanks, lord earl," Jeremy stated, bowing slightly. "William will need all the allies he can rally to defeat Harold."

"I've no doubt he'll win if he has more men of your prowess in his employ." Edward smiled, then turned to Alicen and raised her hand to his lips. "Mistress Kent, godspeed. 'Twas fortunate indeed when I met you. You've restored my faith in mankind."

Alicen gave Edward an empty smile. *Your faith has been sorely abused, my lord. I'm no saint.* "Please convey my thanks to Lady Rebecca for all her kindness. And attend closely to yourself, my lord earl."

"Levi grows old," Edward remarked, brown eyes alight. "He could use an assistant should you wish to leave Sherford."

"Nay, my lord," Alicen replied softly. "Your hospitality is renowned, but I must return home."

"I understand." Edward kissed her hand once again before releasing her. "God ride with you both."

"And with you," Jeremy responded.

"God speed us all," Alicen stated with quiet conviction.

***

"Alston lies east of the Pennine Mountains," Jeremy pointed out to Alicen, although she didn't indicate she'd heard him. "We've few natural barriers between us and Landeyda."

"Let's take advantage of the gentle terrain, then." She set Hercules to a canter.

Jeremy's concern centered completely on Alicen. Her determination to return home was evident in the hard, straight line of her mouth, and he let her set the relentless pace they'd kept to. Hour upon hour, league upon league, she remained withdrawn and remote, resisting all his efforts to draw her out. He even tried to start an argument, to no avail. He wondered if falling from his horse and breaking his neck would shatter her indifference, but decided it likely would not. Her single-minded goal obscured fatigue and discomfort, even awareness of her surroundings and her companion. This detachment worried him. She was not at all the saucy terror whose sharp tongue and defiant manner had goaded him every day of William's convalescence at Landeyda. Her spirit had fled. He much preferred her combativeness to the dispassionate woman who now rode beside him.

They kept to the hard pace all day, stopping only briefly to water the horses and eat some of the supplies Edward had provided them. During one such respite, Jeremy managed to fell two fat hares with a borrowed crossbow. They'd make a tasty evening meal, he decided.

At dusk, he called a halt to their ride.

"We'll camp there." He pointed to a thick stand of trees well back from off the road. "'Tis good shelter from inclement weather and any prying eyes."

They found a natural bower in the center of the stand and made camp. She tended the horses while he started a fire and gathered pine boughs for sleeping pallets. When the fire burned hot, he spitted the rabbits on sticks and roasted them.

Alicen sat staring into the depths of the woods, lost to her melancholy. She didn't notice Jeremy's presence until he touched her shoulder, then she started, distraction fleeing when her eyes focused on him as he bent toward her.

"You should eat." He offered her a still-spitted hare.

"I'm not hungry."

"Try to eat anyway."

She looked at him with veiled eyes. "I'd rather not."

He gave her an assessing look. "Given your healing skills, 'tis certain you know best. Yet, I've always believed a body needs the sustenance food provides."

She couldn't muster a response.

"You told me yourself eating well would heal my wounds more quickly."

"I'm not wounded, Captain Blaine."

A dark brow shot up. "And you claim yourself a physician?" he teased before his tone softened. "You're wounded at heart, lass, if naught else. You must help yourself recover."

A moment passed, then a fleeting smile touched her mouth. "You are keen-eyed, sir." Accepting the rabbit, she managed to eat a few bites.

Jeremy was not to be put off. "You insult me if that is

all of my repast you see fit to consume. I labored hard at this meal and, indeed, 'tis my finest effort yet." He tore a piece of flesh from his own rabbit, popped it into his mouth, and chewed heartily. "Tis a poor cook who'll not partake of his toil."

"I daresay you'll eat your share and more." She managed a few more bites while he continued to attack his portion, tossing the bones into the trees.

Encouraged by her slight show of appetite, he urged, "Wash it down with some cider. This should take away the chill."

Without comment, she accepted the skin he offered, and drank.

"Cider won't warm my soul," she murmured dully. "'Twill take far more than cider for that."

Jeremy privately noted her melancholy, and her sad look pained him. Regret at his inability to cheer her added to his discomfort. That, and his certainty he'd caused her grief.

What could he do? His very presence reminded her of Kenrick's death, yet he couldn't ride off and leave her. He'd rarely attempted to soothe a woman's feelings, reasoning that the many betrayals he'd suffered justified his cold-hearted attitude. Just two months prior he'd not have pondered Alicen's difficulty. He'd have dismissed her plight as something all females deserved. After all, wasn't every woman a scheming bitch who sought to destroy each man she encountered?

He'd believed such folly! Bitterness had twisted his soul and made him indifferent to another's suffering. Now he had a chance to amend his misdeeds, and he couldn't think how to do so.

Glancing at Alicen in the fire's glow, he noted her pale and desolate look. Could he tease her from her gloom?

On an exaggerated sigh, he complained, "I've never prepared a meal for such an ungrateful soul. Cooking is a woman's work, not a soldier's. From this day hence, you cook our food. Then if you don't want to eat it, I'll not care."

Her head snapped around. A flicker of anger lit her eyes, reflecting the nearby fire. "We'll only be traveling another day and perhaps half the night. Why stop to prepare a meal when Edward's provisions are sufficient?"

"Then you admit you cannot cook any better than I?" he challenged. "I never thought to hear such words from you."

Instead of the argument he'd hoped to provoke, Jeremy was sorely disappointed.

Alicen looked back into the fire and said so softly he could barely hear, "My thanks for seeking to coax me from my distemper, Captain. I regret my humor cannot be so persuaded."

Ignoring the urge to gather her to him, he instead clasped her right hand gently in both of his and brought it to his lips.

"Forgive me," he whispered, "for my part in your sorrow."

Seventeen

She started, then slanted her green gaze at him. "And what part is that?"

"I challenged Kenrick, did I not? I killed him." He paused, fearing his voice would break if he spoke hastily. "You recognized me for a brute, and I gave you ample evidence of that brutality. Now you're alone with a man you despise but cannot be rid of. 'Tis little wonder you grieve."

Astonishment lit her eyes. "You mistake me, Captain. I quite understand your actions. Kenrick was a fiend. Though I be damned for thinking it, I'm glad he's dead." Her voice cracked. "Nay, I grieve for lost innocence, for my foolish belief that I could serve all without choosing one cause over another."

The sadness in her voice drew him to sit by her side. "A pity such a noble ideal must end," he stated solemnly.

She shrugged, staring at the fire. "'Tis the world's way."

"Yet that doesn't make the loss any more palatable."

"Nay, it does not."

He studied her profile, then, before he could stop himself, asked, "Why didn't Orrick live at Landeyda?"

"He risked discovery there."

"'Tis no wonder you hate war and warriors so much."

Silent, Alicen glanced at Jeremy, then returned to staring into the fire.

Darkness had fallen, the campfire providing the only light within the bower. To give her privacy, Jeremy went to check the horses. Then he followed the sound of running water to a small stream nearby and proceeded to strip and bathe. The icy water hastened his ablutions and left him clear headed. And shaking. He pulled on hose and boots and scooped up his other garments. With the campfire as a beacon, he quickly returned. When he stopped beside it and shook his head like a mongrel dog, water droplets flew to the winds. Several hissed at meeting the flames between the two travelers.

His antics pulled Alicen from her musings. Following his lead, she rose and made her way to the stream to bathe. She refrained from wetting her hair, knowing it would take hours to dry, chilling her. She also refrained from reentering camp in the same state of undress Jeremy had moments before. She reluctantly had to admit the sight of so much male flesh made thinking clearly nigh impossible.

Upon her return, she saw that he had prepared a large pallet of pine boughs and dry leaves. His blanket lay atop it.

He straightened at her approach. "With your permission, Mistress, 'tis time we retire. I must put out the fire, else we risk discovery."

Thinking to ready her own bed, Alicen indicated the pallet. "Where shall I find such boughs as these?"

Jeremy stopped on his way to his saddle. "We'll both be warmer if we share blankets." He shook out his garment and brought it to the pallet.

"You're not cold without your tunic?" she asked dubiously, sight of his bare chest disquieting.

"'Twill be our pillow." He handed her her cloak. "Wrap up in this. We'll use my cloak and your blanket over both of us."

He folded his tunic and placed it at the head of the pallet. Spreading out his blanket, he indicated the spot where she was to lie. Then he put out the fire and lay down.

Unsure of the wisdom of lying beside the half-clad soldier, Alicen hesitated, memories of touching him making her throat dry. Reason warred with emotion. Certainly this arrangement was best. Caution decreed dousing the fire. Besides, she wouldn't touch him; she'd just lie beside him. What harm could come of that? Wrapping her cloak around her like woolen armor, she lay down with her back to him.

Jeremy covered them both with his cloak and pulled Alicen's blanket up over that. He hesitated only a moment before moving in close behind her and enfolding her in his arms.

"For warmth," he murmured into her thick hair when her body stiffened.

Her answer was a slight nod, but she didn't relax against him. Instead, she subtly leaned away, maintaining some distance.

Sleep evaded him as he contemplated the woman he held. He knew she also remained awake. Did she secretly fear ravishment? Sleeping in his arms as they rode was one thing. This night's arrangement was an entirely different matter.

Yet, she hadn't refused to share the pallet. After several minutes of contemplation, he realized she resisted sleep not because she feared him but because she feared her dreams.

Leaning in so that his mouth brushed her ear, he whispered, "You have my word naught will harm you tonight, lass. Rest now." He felt her tremble slightly, but she made no reply. Tightening his arms around her, he drew her carefully back against his chest.

The heat of Jeremy's body seeped into Alicen's senses, gradually relaxing her. She believed his vow that he'd protect her from anything. Even her heart? He could well defend her body. Could he shelter her from passion as well? She recalled his distrust of women and let it reinforce her resistance to him. Until he came to terms with Estelle's death, he'd want little to do with any woman. She was safe—from herself and from him. Her tension steadily slipped away. Moments later she slept in peace.

Jeremy smiled when Alicen at last slumped back against him. Her fragile strength, the vulnerability she masked behind a bold front, amazed him. Protecting this headstrong woman brought him joy. Would that he could see to her welfare forever.

Aye, he *would* see to it. That thought jolted him to his soul. He had to win her, to have her in his life. William would agree that wedding her to his best knight would benefit them all....

But first he had to reclaim his lands. Then convince her to love a soldier. Both difficult goals, but his courage didn't falter. The prize would be having this lady as his wife.

Lying in the dark forest, he pledged his entire being to the woman he now held. All he did from that night on would direct him toward his goal of wedding her and seeing her happy. God willing, naught would deter his fulfilling this vow.

Toward dawn, Jeremy slept, feeling a sense of purpose and hope he'd not felt for many years.

***

"Alicen! Captain Blaine!"

Ned fairly flew from the cottage as the riders dismounted in Landeyda's yard. He ran into Alicen's arms and held to her with astounding tenacity. When he pulled away, tears filled his brown eyes.

"We thought you both dead," he choked out.

Alicen caught him close again. "Nay, lad. Captain Blaine yet lives to plague me, and I to plague him."

The target of her dart made no comment. Instead, he ruffled Ned's hair before turning to greet the duke, who walked gingerly toward the prodigals, Michael Taft at his elbow.

"We've been worried near to death." William gripped Jeremy's hand. "Old Rhea apprised us of your disappearance. She's been here since." He indicated the midwife, who even then embraced Alicen. "What happened?"

"The tale will be long in the telling, my lord," Jeremy replied, smiling his pleasure at William's improved condition. "Shall we go inside and recount it over a jug of wine?"

"Aye." The duke turned to embrace Alicen. "Welcome home, Mistress. 'Tis good to see you're safe."

"'Tis good to be in such a state, my lord." She wrapped one arm around Ned's shoulders and the other around Rhea's and led them to the house. The men followed.

***

Much to his frustrated disappointment, Jeremy saw precious little of Alicen in the week following their return to Landeyda. Arranging William's impending journey to York to seal his alliance with the duke governed Jeremy's time. He corresponded daily with their allies, reinforced his contingent with more troops, and questioned his spies.

When he wasn't planning, he was in the saddle—checking routes, anticipating problems, seeing to the myriad details needed to assure William's safety. He personally rode to Tynan to secret William's carriage to

Landeyda.

And all the time, his growing love for Alicen crowded into his mind and crept into his heart.

"Taft, take the carriage to Sherford's carpenter and then to the smith." Jeremy handed his lieutenant several rolled sheets of vellum. "Have him make these improvements to the frame and wheels. They should provide William more protection."

Taft poured over the sketches and nodded. "Very good."

"We'll tether William's mount to the coach. If we're attacked, he must flee quickly."

"You've anticipated everything."

"There will be no mistakes this time," Jeremy stated grimly.

Michael clapped Jeremy's shoulder. "Each detail has been reviewed thrice o'er. We're prepared."

"Almost."

"The men respect you for working harder than anyone. But you'll be of no good to William if you drive yourself to ground."

Jeremy waved off Taft's concern. "Too much remains to be done to rest just now."

"You'll do as you will, I know," Taft replied with a shake of his head. "But think, man, and save some strength. Strength will be needed for the coming days."

"That's the truth of it," Jeremy agreed soberly. "I'll be fine, Michael. Truly." He grinned. "Now, get you to Sherford with the coach. There are details yet to be attended!"

***

"Jeremy, you must rest." William set down the dispatches he held when his captain entered the chamber. "All is readied for tomorrow night's departure." He frowned. "Good Lord, man, you're soaked through. Shed those wet garments. And eat!"

"I've no stomach for food, my lord." Jeremy lifted the steaming mug he held. "This pot of cider will do me wonders."

"Get food and rest." William turned to the door. "Ned!"

The boy appeared almost instantly. "Yes, my lord duke?"

"Fetch Captain Blaine some stew, lad. And put his cloak to dry on the hearth."

"'Tis unnecessary," Jeremy protested, holding more tightly to his sodden garment. "I'm well. Besides, I've no time. I meet Taft on the Great Road within the quarter hour."

William ran a hand through his graying hair. "You shake with chill. All is readied. You need a good night's sleep."

"I'll rest tomorrow. I've much yet to see to tonight."

William rose from the bed, moving toward Jeremy. His commanding voice held nothing but authority when he stated, "Someone else can tend them."

Jeremy stiffened. "Your safety is my responsibility, sir."

"I regret to inform you that I'm ordering you to bed." The duke reached for the wet cloak. "You've done all that I expect from my best captain. Now, rest on your laurels."

"But, my lord—"

William's upraised hand stopped the protest. "Enough! Strip off those clothes and retire." He pulled the cloak from Jeremy's shoulders then bore it to the chamber door. Ned reentered at that moment.

Jeremy started to object, but was abruptly too weak to do so. He blinked, trying to focus his eyes. William's council was sound—a brief respite would do him good.

"Perhaps I..." He tried handing his empty mug to Ned, but it slipped from his fingers and crashed to the floor.

"Captain?" Ned reached out to steady Jeremy. "You look ill, sir."

"Nay," Jeremy objected, even as his mind grew fuzzy, his eyes more unfocused. "I must meet Taft..."

His knees buckled.

"Fetch Alicen." As Ned raced to do the duke's bidding, William knelt at his friend's side. "Jeremy, can you stand?"

"I think yes," he replied slowly, tongue thick and unwieldy. He felt himself shuddering but couldn't stop.

William helped him to his feet and to a bed, then was pulling off Jeremy's boots when Alicen hurried in.

"Ned said—" Understanding struck. "Allow me, my lord." She waved the duke away. "Please tell Ned to bring more firewood and put the kettle on."

Tension radiated through William's question. "The fever?"

Alicen nodded without looking away from Jeremy. The silence in the room stretched, and she realized William stared at her. She raised her head, her calm gaze meeting his worried one.

"Will he recover?"

"I'll not deny the severity of his ailment," she answered as she stripped off Jeremy's mail. His wet tunic soon lay atop the discarded armor, then she toweled off his body. "Fever is always dangerous, and he's fatigued. Yet there's hope he has enough strength in reserve." She paused. "Much depends upon his will."

William's face paled. "I should not have allowed him to work so hard! Should he die, I'll ne'er forgive myself."

Alicen covered Jeremy with a blanket, then toweled his wet hair. "You know him well, sir. He n'er takes an easy route and would have changed naught even had you asked."

"Though you're right, lass, I feel no better." He helped Alicen place his own blanket over his captain.

Drawn by the lord's mournful tone, she turned and lightly touched his arm. "Captain Blaine is a warrior, sir. He'll not succumb to this siege without fierce battle."

"I pray God is just," William said tightly, crossing himself, "and grants Jeremy the victory."

***

The hours stretched long, and Alicen did not leave Jeremy's side for even a moment. He looked so helpless lying there—the invincible knight now vulnerable—she couldn't turn away.

"You'll not die, Captain," she murmured, impulsively caressing his fevered cheek. "I'll not allow it."

She swallowed a sigh and bathed Jeremy with cool cloths. Did any other man possess such a form? She thought not. Life was a series of ironies. Common fever could bring all Jeremy's muscle and sinew low. Shifting back, she flexed her shoulders to ease them, then wet the cloth again and began retracing the planes of Jeremy's sculpted chest.

***

He felt a cool hand on his burning forehead, moving

lightly across his brow. Who ministered to him? Estelle! She smiled and laughed, so happy to be carrying his child....

"Estelle?" The name slurred on cracked lips. "Estelle?"

A soothing draught of water was pressed to his mouth, and a firm hand held his head as he drank thirstily. Next, he was given a warm tea tasting strongly of calamint.

"Estelle?"

"Hush. All is well. Try to rest."

That comforting voice belonged not to Estelle. 'Twas lower pitched, melodic. He could not remember where he'd heard it...

"Estelle?"

"Sleep now, Captain. You need rest."

The woman's soothing tones caused his eyes to close. Her light hand caressing his temple lulled him back to sleep.

It was later—how much later he knew not—when coolness again washed across his face. It passed slowly down his neck, to his chest and across his belly, only to be replaced by the fire consuming him. Groaning, he opened his eyes to see Alicen leaning over him, brow furrowed. She ran the cloth along his skin, but the trail of relief from the hell he endured left when she withdrew her hand to re-wet the cloth.

He blinked. Her image seemed disjointed, unfocused and out of place. He tried bringing her into sharper relief but failed.

"What—?"

"Drink." A strong hand again raised and held his head as a draught was administered. "Good. Now save your strength."

"Where is Estelle?" he rasped out. "She was here a moment hence. Our child will arrive soon...."

Alicen bent closer. "I cannot understand you."

He tried again to frame his thoughts, but failed to force coherent sounds from his tortured throat.

Placing a hand on his cheek, Alicen whispered, "Please, Captain, sleep. Think of naught but recovery. William and the others are well." She brushed a lock from his brow and eased him back onto the pillow. "Rest."

He could not. Concentrating, he willed his vision to

clear. Vivid green eyes mesmerized him. Expressive. Beautiful. Dark when angered, sparkling when amused. No other had eyes more lovely. Now, worry painted them an emerald he'd never seen.

Yet, why sat she beside him? His mind skipped about, seeking explanation for her presence. Who caused her such worry? Some desperately ill child, mayhap? He tried raising his head to see, but could not control his muscles. The situation must be grave indeed. Alicen looked drawn and tired, had obviously gone without sleep for some time. She must care deeply for this youngster if she fought so hard to save his life.

When I'm able, I'll ask her about the child. But first, I must rest a moment....

Slumped on the stool beside the bed, Alicen leaned against the wall and dozed fitfully. Though she'd not told William how ill his favored captain was, it had taken firm insistence to banish the duke to her chamber for the night.

Jeremy's fever and delirium raged. He cried out, repeatedly muttering Estelle's name. He pleaded with her, implored. Clearly, he had loved her with his whole heart. Did he love her still?

For a moment, she envied Estelle. Only profound love would suffer so from such perceived betrayal, and Alicen craved the love Jeremy bore his wife. This admission stunned her like a cudgel blow to the head. Her feelings for him went far beyond a healer's concern for a patient—they came from her heart.

"No," she whispered fearfully, but her soul answered, "Yes." Her heart drummed a terrifying beat. "No!" her mind screamed, even as her heart admitted the truth. Denial did not change it.

She loved Jeremy Blaine.

But she'd not tell him. The paths they walked could never converge, their lives opposed and destined to remain so. The influx of wounded to her door could not be controlled, but emotions could be. She'd broken her vow of neutrality once and was determined never to do so again. If Jeremy recovered from this, he would ride away, return to his own world and forget her.

And Duke William would wed her to another.

Mother, what should I do? she silently pleaded, then

hung her head, ashamed at seeking Kaitlyn's council after betraying a sacred oath. Alicen knew the truth—healers should never love soldiers. She and Jeremy did not belong in each other's lives.

She would never know his love. To her dismay, she felt her eyes fill with tears. Then she felt a warmth wrap around her shoulders like a pair of arms. Warm air brushed her cheek, and she closed her eyes to enhance the sensation.

You are a healer, Alicen. Come what will. Find your destiny and follow it, but never forsake your healing gift. To do so will kill you.

"I'll remember, Mother," she whispered. "Always." The warm embrace left her as abruptly as it had come, but although brief it proved a balm to her soul.

Jeremy's groan pulled Alicen's attention to back to him.

Though determined not to voice her feelings, she could not prevent her touch from showing her love. Her caresses soothed his restiveness, her murmured endearments challenged him to fight the fever with all his spirit.

She forced him to drink cup after cup of liquid. Dried lettuce leaves in calamint tea calmed him, but the fever still raged. If it did not break soon, he would not recover.

Well after midnight, Alicen knew her efforts had failed. Jeremy burned from within. He was dying.

Use the horse trough.

Alicen rose instantly from the stool and roused Ned, sleeping in William's bed.

"Fetch Lieutenant Taft and three of the men," she said quietly. "I've need of them."

Ned glanced at Jeremy, then hurried out. Within minutes, Taft and the soldiers were crowded into the infirmary.

"Lieutenant, your captain will die if his fever doesn't break very soon. Carry him outside immediately."

Every man in the room gaped at her.

"This is a desperate stratagem," she stated, "but it's the only one I have left. Please, help me."

"Aye, my lady," Taft answered.

The men carried Jeremy outside, following Alicen as she preceded them to stand at the end of the trough.

"Lower him in gently," she instructed.

She grasped Jeremy under the arms, keeping his head dry. Submersion in the trough of icy cold well water, brought searing pain to her hands, and she ground her teeth to keep from gasping. In moments, her fingers were numb. If the fever didn't break quickly, Taft would have to hold Jeremy while she returned some sensation to her arms and hands.

The moments dragged. Alicen clenched her jaw and grimly hung on. Then just when she felt her grip loosen, Jeremy cried out, thrashing like a bear in a trap. Her nerveless fingers lost their hold, and he slipped under water.

"Help me," she shouted.

The men instantly plunged elbow deep into the trough, pulling Jeremy to the surface.

"Back to the infirmary," she ordered. "He must be warmed immediately."

"Will he recover, Alicen?" Ned asked anxiously as the men carried their captain inside.

"I'm praying as hard as I can, lad," she replied. "It's in God's hands now."

EIGHTEEN

"Jesu, this is a welcome sight," William proclaimed when Jeremy, lucid for the first time in two days, awakened at mid-morning. "Now I'll ride to York with an untroubled mind."

"I'm riding along." Jeremy moved to sit up, but his superior's hand restrained him.

"Nay. Mistress Kent didn't trouble herself to save you only to see you kill yourself within a day. Remain abed and mend."

"But, William—"

"Cease!" the duke commanded. "You worked yourself near to death. I'll not risk that again. Rest here. I regret leaving for York without you, but the alliance must be sealed anon. Harold grows stronger by the day."

"Not since Kenrick's demise," Jeremy retorted sourly.

"I'll reward you well for that service." Jeremy knew his eyes widened in hope, until the look William gave him crushed it. "But not this eventide."

"You repay me with confinement?" Jeremy made no attempt to conceal his anger. "I'll not regain my land while lying abed."

William shook his head. "Two nights ago I nearly lost you, and that I cannot endure. Curb your rashness and follow Alicen's bidding."

Jeremy thought to argue, but the worry in William's eyes stopped him. And Alicen's entry shifted his attention. She held a tray with steaming broth and a thick slice of bread.

"If you command it, my lord," he grumbled, glaring at her instead of at William.

"Consider it so, Captain." William smiled. "Take the woman's advice."

Alicen smiled, also. "I fear you condemn him to a fate worse than death, my lord. For certain, he'd rather risk his life riding with you than stay here with me."

Did I think the wench amiable? Jeremy silently

groused. *Fever must have destroyed my mind.* "You're keen-witted today," he snapped. He'd never admit her apparent eagerness to see him off buffeted his pride.

"I'll consider that high praise, though not intended to be," she retorted saucily.

"Mayhap the captain *would* be safer on the road." Before Jeremy could even meet William's gaze, the duke added, "Nay, I think not. Three days of rest will do you good." His voice grew husky. "You'll not kill yourself on my behalf."

Jeremy's jaw clenched. Confined to bed when the game was afoot! The alliance with York made regaining his lands that much closer to fruition. And he'd not be there.

Moreover, naught could be worse than wanting Alicen and having none near to keep him from her. The woman's mere presence turned his every honorable intention to dust.

Did he have the patience to woo her gently? That question remained to be answered. And if he wooed and won her, would the Duke of Tynan see them married?

"*Three* days?" he asked, bleakly.

"Not a moment earlier without your physician's consent."

"She'll keep me here a week just to provoke me."

Alicen arched a brow. "And put myself through such misery? I think nay." Her next words dripped with good cheer. "Best begin healing now, Captain, by eating like a good lad." She laid a cloth on his lap and drew up a stool.

"I can feed myself," he growled.

"Sir Jeremy!" William's tone was stern, but his eyes twinkled.

"She'll likely strangle me in my sleep."

Alicen slammed the spoon down on the tray so hard soup splashed from the bowl. "You arrogant, ungrateful wretch! I'll not wait until you sleep—I'll strangle you this instant."

"Children, children," William scolded, his hands raised for peace. "Must I ask Ned to keep you from each other's throats?" Silence. He sighed. "Captain, you are ordered. Three days' rest." He turned to Alicen, clasped her hand and kissed it. "We've sorely abused your largesse,

Mistress, yet I appeal to you—indulge this last patient a few days more." He grinned. "Though surly and difficult to abide, he is my finest soldier. I'm loath to lose him."

"I'll strive to see he returns safely, sir."

"I'll hold you to that. And thank you for all, Mistress. Were I not a happily married man, I would make you my duchess!"

Alicen smiled wryly. "I'm honored you think me so worthy."

"Worthy of far more than I can ever repay." William bent and kissed her cheek. "Worth more than gold."

He turned back to Jeremy. "Rest, Captain. We'll talk ere I depart."

Jeremy fought sudden jealousy at William's exchange with Alicen, but he masked his irritation. "Send Taft in, my lord. There are several details he must know."

Chuckling, William shook his head. "Stubborn man, obstinate to a fault. But 'tis a minor fault. Until tonight, Jeremy."

"The soup grows cold, Captain," Alicen stated after William left.

Jeremy smothered his restlessness and let her feed him. They passed the time silently, and he soon caught himself watching with unsettling intensity her hands. Her eyes. Her lips. Lord, their nearness decimated his will. The clean smell of her hair made him want to release it from its ribbon and riffle it with his hands. Memories of holding her brought an ache to his arms that only she could ease. The ache moved lower.

This was torture, plain and simple.

At last she finished and prepared to remove tray and dishes.

"Do you require aught else? If not, I must to my chores."

He had to tear his gaze from exquisite green eyes and focus rebellious thoughts on his distaste of inactivity. "I'm fine," he said, voice oddly rasping. "Perhaps somewhat tired."

"Then I'll leave you to your sleep." She pulled the blanket higher around his shoulders, smoothed it, then left.

His body tingled where she'd touched him. Openly

studying the graceful lines of her slender form, he decided that, for an uncommonly tall woman, she pleased the eye.

***

A light touch on his forehead woke Jeremy from sleep. He opened his eyes to see Alicen bending over him.

"Captain," she exclaimed, pulling away with a startled jerk. "I..., I didn't mean to wake you. I thought to check for fever...before I retired."

Feeling her flush spread, Alicen silently cursed that half-truth. When she'd looked in on him and noted a lock of black hair had fallen into his eyes, she'd smoothed it back. Mortified at being caught in such a bold act, she struggled for composure. Mayhap the candlelight would not provide him a good view of her features.

Jeremy tensed. "Am I yet ill?" he asked tightly.

A snarl of thwarted purpose threatened to burst from Jeremy's throat. Should aught delay his departure, he feared madness, as Alicen's nearness tortured him. He needed distance to retain his honor and not abuse hers.

She smiled a bit shyly. "The rest has done you much good."

"Then naught shall prevent my leaving in the morn?" He couldn't keep the desperate tone completely from his voice.

She shrugged, but her nonchalance wasn't reflected in the emotion that flashed in her eyes. Sadness? "Another fever could hinder you, but 'tis doubtful that will happen."

He fell back on the pillow in relief. "Jesus be praised."

"Amen," came her dry response.

Jeremy's grin faded. Suddenly, he wanted to rail at her indifference. Could she not know of his regard? Know he left only to win back his lands in order to win her?

Suddenly, a violent fit of coughing stopped his brooding and brought Alicen's brows together. Seeing her deep concern made him stifle the next spasm.

Without hesitation she placed her hand over his heart. "Is there pain?"

"Nay." He coughed again and, at her dubious look admitted, "Aye. But only when I cough." Her frown remained, dismaying him. "'Twill not detain me, will it?" *If I cannot depart soon, I'll not be able to keep myself from you.*

She fussed with the blanket before meeting his gaze. "I know not. Pleurisy will require your remaining here."

"More idleness will kill me," he grumbled, feeling his heart thud dully. "I can't abide lying abed," *without you here in my arms.*

"Let me see." Folding the covers back to his waist, she put her ear to his chest. "Breathe deeply." He complied. "Again."

He took another deep breath and let it out slowly.

Her hair brushing his body inflamed him. Craving a kiss, he labored to voice only concern for his condition. Yet his tight throat gave the question an abnormal huskiness. "Is aught amiss?"

Alicen glanced up. "I'll know by morn."

He choked. "I *must* leave for York in the morn."

"I'll not promise you'll be able." Plucking a jar from her nearby tray of medicaments, she added, "Yet, this balm should clear the congestion and make you fit on the morrow."

"But—"

She cocked a brow at him, scooped out a generous amount of the substance and began rubbing it along his throat. "Lie still, Captain. Vexation but worsens matters."

He jumped at her touch, then quickly quelled his reaction. "What if this doesn't—"

"Shhh," she scolded softly, intent on her task. "Worry won't aid you."

Smothering his fears and needs, Jeremy gave in. Spicy smells filled his nostrils as she spread balm down his throat and across his shoulders, chest and torso, kneading with infinite care. Her touch brought no pain to still tender ribs, providing a soothing caress instead.

His skin grew warm, tingling. Surrendering to sensation, he relaxed and let his heavy eyelids drop. He began to drift to sleep.

Then a wave of pleasure hit him.

With a start, his eyes flew open. Sweet Jesus! Leaping pulse, quickened breath, fire everywhere—he'd rarely been so aroused. Praying this internal heat burned not on his face, he tried to throttle his raging thoughts, to concentrate on the import of the coming days. He could not think of pleasuring Landeyda's healer!

Alicen pulled back. "Is the liniment too strong?"

"N..., nay...But I..." He stared at her. "I'm...That's sufficient." His every vision of her combined in a rush of desire so strong it nearly overwhelmed him.

Alicen looked askance but made no comment. Instead, she recapped the balm, assisted him into a nightshirt, then adjusted his blanket. "Don't concern yourself with this. Oft the condition worsens with apprehension."

"I'll keep that well in mind," he affirmed, staunchly avoiding her bewitching eyes or thinking of her maddening touch.

He thanked his Maker the blanket covered his loins. Flexing a knee, he lifted his leg to further mask his condition. He'd always believed lust indicated good health, but this was an inopportune moment to experience such recovery. Pitilessly, he crushed his impulse to pull this woman into bed and love her until neither of them could move.

Jesu be merciful, he silently pleaded. *Give me strength.*

He wanted more than a mere tumble with Alicen, more than brief physical release. He wanted to offer her a lifetime.

This thought brought no comfort. Until Harold's defeat, Jeremy could give Alicen naught except his heart. He knew from experience that was rarely enough.

A curious look suffused her face as she studied him. "Should I fetch a sleeping draught for you, Captain?"

"I need naught to help me rest," he stated. *Aught I need is you here beside me. Beneath me.*

"Nay, you're taut as a drawn bow. Worry o'ertaxes you."

Trapped. He couldn't tell her that her mere presence set his senses spinning. That he wanted her—his hands in her thick tresses, his lips on hers, his body deep inside her. He'd endured serious battle wounds that brought him less pain than want of her did.

Either he left in the morning or arrived in York too late to do William service. It was his last night at Landeyda, perhaps for months. Honor warred with need. To slake his desire was to take advantage of Alicen in the basest manner. Yet, he reasoned, marrying her would purge the sin he contemplated. And how could making love to the woman he cherished above all others be sinful?

Thoughts of honor fled when he looked at her. Her nearness pushed him to the edge of chivalry.

"The drink will make you slumber like a babe," she said in her most reassuring tone.

He'd be a misbegotten blackguard to use her, his conscience taunted.

"Will this potion help my dreams?" he asked, not quite successfully putting a caustic edge on his voice.

She smiled slightly. "Undoubtedly."

"I don't engage in dreaming," he lied without a twinge of conscience. "My dreams won't let me rest."

With a sigh, she shook her head, moving to the door. "Trust me without question for once. This will certainly aid you. By morn your lungs should be clear."

In her absence, Jeremy battled both mind and body. He shook from want but chided himself for lacking honor. Yet he loved her! Must he not express his love intimately?

Upon her return, his decision was made. She offered him the cup, but he refused.

"Leave it. I've no need just now."

Alicen stared. His anxiety had grown more palpable—he appeared coiled to strike. Yet, he insisted naught was amiss. Setting the cup on the stand between the beds, she fussed a moment with his pillows. She had no reason to remain, except that she wanted...

"Good night, Captain." Her voice sounded hollow in her ears. "Rest well."

But as she turned to leave, Jeremy seized her arm, his hand sliding to her wrist when she turned back to him.

"What?" Her whisper was breathy.

Their gazes locked, exchanged heated promises. Then Jeremy looked away and released her.

"God rest you, Mistress," he replied through clenched teeth, not meeting her eyes.

She left as he ignored with ruthless will his pounding body. He could not follow. Instead, though it was madness, he lay admiring her graceful carriage. While many women practiced seductive gaits, Alicen knew naught of her sensuality. He found such innocence alluring. The flame simmering inside him ignited into an inferno. Christ's guts, just looking at her drove his senses wild!

"No," he said, with fierce determination tempering his desire. "Not yet."

***

Jeremy lost his battle. Common sense had flown the moment he touched Alicen. Now raw need battered him, and he was too weak to resist. Rising, he yanked on his hose and scrubbed the liniment from his chest. He crossed the main room, paused briefly at her door, then pushed it open on noiseless hinges.

Her back to him, she stood before her washstand clad only in her linen chemise. Seeing her thus, he hesitated. She looked so vulnerable, so oblivious to danger. So desirable. He cleared his throat.

Alicen flinched at the sound and spun to face him, eyes wide with startlement. Holding the wet cloth to her breast, she gasped, "Captain Blaine! You frightened me."

"Forgive me, lass," he said, voice gone low with desire. "But I must speak with you."

Alicen could hardly breathe for the pulse pounding in her throat. Achingly aware that the cloth was scant covering, she set it in the basin and reached for the robe lying on the bed. Jeremy intercepted her before she could retrieve it, gently grasping her wrist. He brought her hand to his lips.

"I need your healing skill, Mistress." He cleared his throat. "Please help me."

Riotous sensation nearly buckled Alicen's knees, but concern fortified her resolve. To her, Jeremy looked undeniably handsome in her candlelit chamber.

"What is amiss, sir?"

"Much," he replied, stepping close enough for her to feel his warmth. "I burn with a fever only you can cool. My heart and soul ache with pain only you can ease." His eyes glowed a blue flame. "Heal my heart, Alicen," came his urgent plea. He gently pulled her close. "'Tis my heart needs healing."

She could only stare, knowing there would be no retreat for either of them this time. Her breath fluttered in her chest. Yet she wanted no retreat, only surrender.

Seizing both her hands, Jeremy raised them to his lips for a soft kiss. Then he flattened them, palms open, against his bare chest, spreading her fingers with his.

"I love your hands," he murmured, rubbing the backs of them lightly with his thumbs.

Silent, she absorbed his heart's steady rhythm with her palms, the feel of silky skin over hard muscles. A hint of liniment scent reached her nostrils. Her nerves jangled. If they hadn't been pressed to Jeremy's chest, her hands would be shaking. Somehow, touching him steadied her.

She ducked her head. "My hands are not soft like a gentlewoman's."

"But they are strong and skilled and infinitely tender." When she looked into his eyes, he whispered, "Your touch excites me, Alicen. Touch me more."

Jeremy moved her arms to encircle his waist, captured her hands behind his back, drew her tight against him and held her along his length.

Feeling her heartbeat bound, he sought to calm her by lightly caressing her lips. He kissed cheeks, forehead, eyelids. Rubbed his cheek against hers and nuzzled her throat, all the while murmuring, "Heal me, lass. Touch me and heal me."

He grew harder, but curbed his eagerness, seeking instead to pleasure her by combing his fingers through her hair, rubbing her neck and shoulders, trailing his hands down her back to her hips.

"I want you," he stated in a low rumble. "Do you know what that means?"

"Yes." Uncertain of what course to take now it had come to this, Alicen could only stare. Jeremy's powerful body pressed to hers made breathing difficult. His mouth on her skin clouded reason. She vaguely thought to resist his tender seduction, but admitted she had no wish to do so.

She trembled and leaned against him. "I, I've never..." Her voice trailed off.

Her admission touched a tender spot in Jeremy's heart he'd thought long since scarred over. He would be the man to unlock her passion, the one to show her ecstasy. Trembling expectation seized him. This woman had insinuated herself into his soul, and he wanted to pleasure her so well she'd always be with him.

"Don't fear me," he told her, as much by the way he held her as through his spoken words. "I'll not hurt you."

His mouth again sought hers, sought to draw a response equal to his own. He caressed her back and buttocks until just touching her could not quench the searing inferno. His fingers shook as he grasped her chemise to lift it over her head.

Her shudder of uneasiness gave him pause.

"I wish to please you," he stated with quiet sincerity.

Alicen's tension burst forth in a ragged gasp. "I'd rather you'd just get this over with!"

He smiled wryly. "But we've 'til dawn to enjoy each other."

Alicen felt the blood drain from her face. Until dawn. What then? Long ago, she had resolved to give herself only to the man who held her heart. Orrick had stood to be that man. Now Jeremy Blaine made his claim. But on the morrow he'd be gone. Would this soldier leave behind any part of her unrazed, even her soul?

Jeremy cradled her face in one hand and tilted her chin up. "Love me," he ordered gruffly before his mouth came down on hers.

The kiss devastated her defenses, buffeting her with desire so strong it left her weak-kneed. Nothing she knew compared to such wildness. Her mind warned of the trap Jeremy set for her heart, but that same heart sought to open to him. Sighing, she made a feeble attempt to rein it in.

"I cannot do this," she murmured, raising her gaze to meet his. Her attempt to back away failed, as he refused to relinquish his hold.

A warm, crooked smile lit his face, then he chuckled. "I have few such reservations about you, sweetling."

With unsteady hands he undid the tie of her chemise and lifted it over her head. He tossed the garment to the floor behind her, and she stood before him wearing only her amulet on a silver chain. It rested just above her breasts.

Such bodily perfection dazed him, and for a moment he could only stare. Then, gently cupping her firm breasts, he was rewarded by her startled gasp. He caressed her nipples to hardened peaks, enjoying the change in their texture, their satiny heat.

"Exquisite," he murmured.

Her lavender scent filled his nostrils as his mouth claimed hers and his hands roamed her quivering body. He watched her eyes flare with awakening desire, and he continued his caresses until she rewarded his patience by slowly raising her arms to encircle his neck. A moan of joyful surrender came from deep in her throat. It mirrored his own.

His pulse raced at her response, joy flaming in his heart. He released her long enough to untie his hose and step out of them. Then, he lifted her and laid her on the bed. With his soul as naked as his body, he squeezed his eyes shut a moment so the woman beneath him could not discern his true need.

Fear leapt into Alicen's eyes when he moved against her, and she tried to avoid him. "Captain, I—"

"Hush," he soothed. "All will be well."

Determined to prepare her fully for his claiming, he resumed his caresses. Mouth suckled, tongue laved, hands caressed. He tasted and touched and penetrated areas calculated to drive her out of herself. Her pulse pounded at the base of her throat. It quickened even more when his lips covered her breast. As her resistance gave way to passion, his doubts died.

When his tongue circled her ear, Alicen squirmed.

"Please—" She panted. "I cannot...bear...this."

Jeremy lifted his head, looking deeply into her eyes.

"Trust me, lass." His kiss demanded, tongue thrusting deep, then he felt her breath catch when he again suckled a straining nipple. Her body jerked.

"Please, Captain, stop," she begged. "I cannot think."

"'Tis no time for thought," he said, mouth still against her breast. "Just feelings."

He stroked her belly and thighs, and she started when he touched her intimately and began a gentle possession.

On a gasp, she cried, "What are you doing?"

He continued the explicit caress. "Pleasuring you, sweetling."

Concentrating on Alicen's sensitive body, he let his

fingers play. He could feel her burning from within as he sought to drive her beyond herself to an unexplored realm.

When she finally succumbed to passion, he felt the change immediately. Having defeated whatever doubts she'd battled, she responded fully to his lovemaking. Elation enveloped him. She arched, crying out softly as he built her yearning. Finally, when he had brought her to the fevered edge of climax, he slowly entered her.

Alicen's eyes flew wide as he slipped deep within her, then momentarily darkened with pain at his invasion. Her breath caught, and her wild gaze locked on his.

"Don't resist, lass," he whispered on a groan. "The pain will lessen quickly, and only delight will follow."

He held still as long as he could, watching her face while their bodies melded, enjoying the passion in her eyes and the tight passageway that held him a willing captive. "Jesu, you feel wonderful," he whispered as he brushed a tumbled lock of chestnut hair from her face and kissed the spot revealed. "Come with me, Alicen. To paradise."

His mouth slanted across hers, sweeping her into his rhythm. Enthralled by her heat, he thrust slowly, prolonging contact, feeling her response. He wanted to please her for all time, to bind her to him forever.

They joined in an earthy cadence, blissful moments passing as they partnered each other in the ancient dance. Speech became murmurs, sighs, moans—communicating by touch not voice, each learning the other's body. There was no coming dawn, no leave taking. They had eternity.

Jeremy increased his pace, and soon Alicen arched against him, crying out her climax. At her release, he sought as intense a culmination as hers. He drove strongly into her—once, twice, again—then blanketed her with his body, pressing her into the bed while their ragged breathing slowed. They lay entwined, the wild beating of their hearts gradually calming.

Nineteen

"Did I hurt you?" Jeremy murmured into Alicen's ear before carefully withdrawing.

She stared at him, too overwhelmed to reply, then shook her head mutely.

"I'm glad." He grinned and kissed the tip of her nose. "Don't move."

Feeling certain she'd never stir again, through slitted eyes she watched him leave the bed and walk, casual in his nudity, to the washstand. He soaked a cloth in the basin, then brought both to the bed.

When she raised a brow in question, he stated, "This will make you more comfortable."

Confounded, she lay still as he tenderly cleansed her body. Other women had spoken of atrocities enacted upon them by men in the throes of lust, yet Jeremy had treated her gently, taking her virginity with little pain. His concern for her pleasure penetrated straight to the heart she'd believed would never know passion, and she saw the absurdity of physical intimacy without emotional surrender. She could not elude the ardor Jeremy had inspired, the joy and hope, the longing. Such feelings astonished her every bit as much as her physical reaction to his lovemaking.

But had he acted thus simply because they were lovers for a night, not man and wife forever? That disheartening thought painfully twisted her emotions.

With reverent care, Jeremy bathed away all traces of sweat from Alicen's body and sponged the evidence of their loving from between her thighs. Done with his ministrations, he returned the cloth to the basin.

His brow raised as he lay back down beside her. "Better?"

"Yes," she whispered, knowing no other possible reply.

His attentions comforted, but she had no experience to compare them to. Emotions and sensations jumbled in her mind, not to be untangled. What she had just done with Jeremy Blaine overwhelmed her—her passion shocked her. He had reached her in a way no other ever had, terrifying her. How could she have made love with him, knowing he'd leave to follow his duke?

She ignored the true answer and caught her breath as he slid closer. His blue eyes shone, his nearness putting lucid thought to flight. A relieved smile made his strong face look boyish.

He cupped her chin. "I'd hoped you'd enjoy it. First times needn't be horrifying."

Embarrassment at her inexperience made Alicen snap, "You truly believe this my first time?"

"So knowledgeable in the ways of healing yet so unlearned in the ways of loving," he teased, then winked and added, "You said as much."

She knew her cheeks were flaming and couldn't meet his eyes. "No doubt your many other conquests were not so simple," she muttered.

He gently smoothed back a lock of her hair. "Simple you are not, my sweet."

Realizing he'd seen her vulnerability, she sought to rebuild a defense. "I'll not compare myself to others," she retorted.

Jeremy laughed. "You're beyond compare." His fingers lightly traced her skin from collarbone to shoulder. "Know you how splendid you feel? How glad I am to be with you?" *How much I love you?*

She kept silent, but her wary gaze softened.

Still smiling, he drew her close for a soft kiss, nuzzling her ear and throat as his fingers played upon her skin, eliciting a throaty sigh. But when his finger traced the stones of her amulet, she tensed.

Wondering at her reaction, he sought to put her at ease. "Your necklace is so unique. Wherever did you come by it?"

Her tension lessened slightly when she replied, "My mother gave it to me."

"A family heirloom." He smiled. "'Tis exquisite. Do you ever take it off?"

"Never." Seeming to come to a decision, she added, "My mother feels close when I wear it."

Far closer than you might suspect, he thought, then,

upon reflection, concluded that Alicen not only felt her mother's presence, but heard her voice. Much the same as he had begun to think he heard it.

But other more pressing issues brought themselves to Jeremy's attention, and he bent to kiss Alicen's amulet and the breasts it rested above. He chuckled when her breath caught in her throat.

"Ah, sweetling," he murmured. "This time 'twill be even better between us."

Green eyes widened. "This time?"

He wiggled his brows. "Of course. What came before was mere prelude. We'll enjoy each other the entire night."

Jeremy's words burned deep into Alicen's heart, haunting her..."The entire night..." But come the dawn? He moved her more than she'd thought possible, so much that she feared her soul would not survive their lovemaking. And when he left?

She made a decision. If they had only this night, then she would live it to the fullest, enjoy him for the fleeting time he lay with her. She buried her face against his neck and gave over to the passion he inspired. Taking a deep breath filled with the musky smell of her knight, she gave herself over into his care.

"Show me," she whispered.

Joy flooded Jeremy at Alicen's response. Relieved he'd not hurt her unduly when claiming her virginity, he clasped her hand and held it flat over his pounding heart. "Feel what you do to me, lass." He pressed his hips intimately against her and saw her eyes darken in response. "I need you."

The flaming passion in Alicen's eyes was all the encouragement he needed to continue. Slipping his hand down her back, he stroked her hip and thigh. Then from behind, he slowly slid a finger into her moist womanhood.

She jerked as if burned. "Captain Blaine!"

"Under the circumstances, shouldn't you call me Jeremy?" he asked wryly before deepening the intimate caress. He kissed her again, more confidently, stroking Alicen until she cried out.

"What are you doing to me?"

"Giving you pleasure," he growled low in her ear.

Lifting her leg over his hip and holding her on her

side, he entered her then brought her quickly to climax.

***

"Have I pleased you, my lady?" Jeremy nuzzled Alicen's hair, cradling her to his chest. He lay on his back with her half atop him.

"I am not your lady," she replied, unable to keep bitterness from her tone.

"Do you wish to be?"

Her pulse leapt at his words, but she covered her reaction with a half-laugh. "For but a night? Nay. 'Tis a soldier's way of thinking, not mine."

"Prideful wench. You'd endure torture before confessing you might enjoy me."

His words touched the core of her despair, and she swallowed the tears burning in her throat. She fought a terror that warned against revealing more of her emotions to this man who would depart, taking her heart away.

But, ignoring that stubborn warning voice, she ventured all on honesty. "Don't leave." She emphasized her soft plea by tightening her arm around Jeremy's waist.

Jeremy sighed and pulled her closer still. "I'm bound to, lass. William needs me in the campaign against Harold. To reclaim all the bastard stole."

She raised her head from his shoulder to fix him with a measuring look. "Why? Aught we might require is here at Landeyda."

"But I have naught to give you," he protested, twining a lock of her hair in his fingers.

Her smile was bittersweet. "Not even yourself?"

Her implication made Jeremy's breath catch. Then reason returned, and he set his jaw. "You don't understand."

"Aye, you have that aright." Propping herself on an elbow, she stared down at him, and he saw fear in her eyes. "Must you fight, Jeremy? You could be injured." Her voice dropped to a whisper, "Or killed."

He shrugged. "I owe service to William."

She looked ready to scream. "William of Tynan has hundreds of retainers, and the Duke of York for an ally," she retorted. "I daresay he'd not lament your absence."

"Alicen—" Jeremy reached up to cradle her face in both hands, fingers spreading through her hair. "I am a knight. I have my duty. And I must go to help William."

Tears made her eyes glisten like emeralds. "You're just like my father, like Orrick, like every other soldier! You'll leave your comfort behind to follow some banner."

Jeremy gathered his courage and risked his heart. "I need you. I'll return for you when I'm able. Trust me, sweetling."

"You speak of something you're unwilling to give me in return," she replied grimly. "You trust me not."

She pushed away and made to leave the bed, but he caught her arms and pulled her down onto her side, her back tight against him. She went rigid in his arms, shoulders back and set.

"I wish to give you your due," he whispered. "A lady's life. Your life thus far has not been easy."

She twisted around to face him. "Yet it has suited me these eight years past."

"But you deserve to live as a gentlewoman," he insisted. "I cannot give you that until I win back my lands."

"All I need is you, Jeremy. Naught else is necessary."

"It is for me. How long will I hold your heart if I cannot provide for you? How long can any woman love a man who has naught?"

"I am not like other women," she said with quiet firmness.

"And I am not like other soldiers."

They stared into each other's eyes then, seeing doubts, needs, yearnings to trust...and past experiences that prevented them from doing so. He looked away first.

"Hold me, Jeremy," she whispered. "'Twill suffice."

He crushed her to him. If only passion were enough, he'd not venture a step from this woman who permeated his being.

He would return to claim the peace that was his when he held Alicen close. No other—not even Estelle—had felt so right beside him. Perhaps the spirit of Alicen's mother had guided him there so many weeks before to find his mate, the one woman who would cherish and heal his battered spirit.

Yet duty dictated he leave. How to make her understand that going wasn't abandonment? She didn't trust him to return. He understood that, as his own mistrust had kept his feelings at bay to spare himself more pain. Now Alicen had won his heart, and in return he had to win her trust.

While he contemplated his problem, he stroked her soft skin, enjoying the lean muscles beneath it. Her sensitivity enflamed him, and fervent pleasure drove away dark thoughts. Physically, Alicen was ardent for his lovemaking. Her heart would fall eventually.

She gasped when he bent to suckle her breast. "Are you insatiable?" came her hoarse question as she broke away from him. "Leave me be."

"In truth, I cannot, Mistress." He leaned over her to whisper, "You've enslaved me. I've never pleasured a woman so in my life. And I'm willing to do so as oft as I can this eve."

"Why so solicitous toward me?"

The challenge in her voice warned him to tread carefully. He'd intended to declare himself that very night, but realized she'd no wish to hear such confession. His heart clenched. Why love this slender, infuriating vixen when any number of experienced women boldly sought his notice?

You are destined to love each other.

Hearing the voice in his mind didn't surprise him, but love might not mean he and Alicen could be together. She dreaded his departure, and he could not shirk his obligation to William. Guilt seized him. If only he could stay! Once he'd fulfilled his obligation, he would return to Landeyda. With land and a title, he'd set about reclaiming Alicen's trust.

In the meantime, he hesitated to reveal his innermost emotions. Declaring his love wouldn't change the fact that he had to leave.

"You give comfort and healing," he told Alicen after a moment's silence. "All I know is destruction, death.... Oft I must retreat from those pursuits and seek gentler ones."

Bemused, she stared at Jeremy. Rhea's observation had been correct, yet Alicen herself had not acknowledged this side of him—the sensitive, unshielded side she loved.

Love. That was the unnamed emotion hiding in her heart, keeping to the shadows, afraid to step into the light. She loved him, but he would leave to ride with the

Duke of Tynan in spite of that. She could never speak her love to Jeremy and have it ignored.

But she could show the depth of her feelings. Gathering her nerve, she gently pushed him onto his back. She felt a slight smile draw up the corners of her mouth.

Her hand stroked across his massive chest and over his taut stomach as she whispered, "What gentler pursuits did you think to find, sir knight?"

Growling, Jeremy pulled her atop him.

***

He awoke alone.

Stifling disappointment that he could not wake Alicen with a kiss, he left the bed, donned his hose and went in search of his intoxicating healer. The cottage stood empty, but he heard voices outside so returned to the infirmary for proper attire.

When he emerged a few moments later, both Ned and Alicen occupied the main room—she at the hearth, preparing eggs and thick slices of ham for breakfast, her back to the room.

"Captain Blaine," Ned greeted him enthusiastically. "'Tis good to see you looking well."

"Thank you, lad." Jeremy did not take his gaze from Alicen. "Did the foal arrive?"

Ned beamed. "Aye, a fine colt. I assisted the mare in her delivery."

Jeremy at last turned to smile at the apprentice. "I knew you'd do a splendid job."

Pride's crimson flush stained the boy's fair cheeks. "Alicen said I could accompany her on her next birthing. Of a baby, that is."

A baby. Poignant memories of Liza's delivery caught Jeremy off guard. 'Twas one of many experiences he'd shared with Alicen which had profoundly changed him. Holding Liza's babe had brought such a feeling of awe.

He glanced back at Alicen, mind racing. Could they have conceived their own child last night? A little daughter with her emerald eyes, or a son who'd grow tall and strong? And would she wish to bear this child? He'd not think of Estelle's utmost sacrifice. Alicen valued life far too much to ever consider taking his wife's desperate course.

The possibility of a babe reinforced his vow to return. Surely, Alicen must know that. He ached to hold her and kiss away her fears, but knew he could not. Nothing could change the truth of his leaving.

"Would you saddle my horse for me, lad?" Jeremy asked Ned.

"Certainly, sir!" The boy was on his feet and out the cottage door almost before Jeremy could draw another breath.

Alicen had just removed the pot from the fire. She ladled food into the trenchers, ignoring him as he stepped up behind to gently trap her against the table with his body.

"I would speak with you, lass."

Slamming the ladle onto the table with a bang, she momentarily hung her head. "There's naught to say."

He grasped her shoulders, turning her to face him. "Aye, there is much to say."

Chin raised, she gave him her most indifferent look. "If you're leaving, then be quick about it."

He saw her hurt expression, felt it shoot straight into his heart. "I'll return to you."

"Every soldier who ever took up arms says just such," she scoffed in a husky voice. "'Tis a lie."

He tried to embrace her, but she pushed away, and he had the wisdom to let her go. She stormed back to the hearth.

"I love you, Alicen."

Her head snapped up at his quiet declaration, but she kept her back turned to him. "Do you love me enough to trust me?"

The words seared Jeremy's already vulnerable soul. "Lass, I—"

She spun to face him. "Don't lie! You've not trusted me from the beginning. I must know now whether you still believe me capable of deceit and treachery."

Could he conquer years of pain, layers of betrayal that had thickened into a callus around his heart, keeping tender thoughts out? He knew she'd not betray him. Yet his mind warned that she still could hurt him.

"Until I have land and a title to offer you, how could you ever truly love me?"

At his change of subject, Alicen abandoned convincing him of her loyalty. His painful memories prevented him from believing her. Better to let him resume his life—the life of action he lived so well—than to reveal her heart, shattering from losing his affection.

"I don't require the finery you seem convinced I need," she said sadly. "But without trust, love can never flourish between us." *And without your love, I shall perish.* "Don't return, Jeremy," she whispered, unable to meet his intense gaze. "You'll bring soldiers of death riding at your back. Stay away. I never want you coming here again."

His voice cracked when he replied, "I'm bound to, lass. You know that."

"And I'm bound to mend the havoc wrought by your kind," she retorted. "You'll return with blood on your hands and killing in your soul. Then the blood on my hands will follow." She raised trembling fingers to her temples. "I'm so weary. Weary of war. Of death. Soldiers leave. They never stay to right their wrongs. 'Tis left to their victims to do so."

"I mean to stay."

"For what reason? You'll lay this shire bare. What would compel you to dwell here afterward?"

"You!" He clenched his fists. "You'll scarce believe such a promise, but I'll have my land and with it freedom from war."

"Think you to keep that land without a struggle?" Alicen cried. "You'll fight until they bury you."

He ground his teeth. "Then 'twill be *my* land I fight for, not some godforsaken piece of earth my king's regent covets!"

"Fighting is fighting, regardless of the object. Men die, and the ground drinks blood. It will never cease." She visibly trembled. "I cannot condone what you do."

"I'm not asking you to."

Staring, they fell silent. The time for parting had come, and Jeremy knew they could not break away without inflicting more pain.

He moved first.. Jaw set, he strode to the infirmary to pack his saddlebags. That done, he crossed the main room, pausing with his hand on the door latch, aware of Alicen aimlessly rearranging medicament jars. He retrieved a heavy pouch from his cloak.

"William left money to pay for my care," he growled, turning to hold it out.

Her brows drew together. "I must refuse, Captain. What services I performed were done as fealty to my duke."

Jeremy's heart sank at her caustic use of his title, at her coldness. He had laid his soul bare, yet she spurned his love. He knew the heartless cruelty of his words, but her rejection was riding him hard, and he couldn't govern his tongue. "Would you have left me to my fate had William not pleaded for my life?"

"Nay," she replied levelly, glaring at him. "I've never left *any* man to die."

He gestured to the bag, then sneered, "These coins could go a long way to maintaining your beloved estate." He saw Alicen's composure nearly break, but she raised her chin proudly.

"Leave here. Never return."

Her raw pain almost made him relent. Instead, he tossed the pouch containing William's money onto the table.

Eyeing it with distaste, she scoffed, "To purchase care for those you intend to maim? How charitable."

Silent, he stalked out, slamming the door behind him. Charon stood waiting, and Jeremy leaped astride. Horse and rider were beyond the stable when Alicen appeared on her doorstep.

Raising the pouch, she flung it at the retreating knight. Her aim proved true. It struck him between the shoulders, the coins scattering across the courtyard in a silver-gold spray.

"You said you wouldn't hurt me," she choked out as he rode away. "Then why does my heart feel like a lump of iron beaten by a blacksmith? Why is pain all I know?"

Strangled by tears, she fled to her bedchamber.

***

Jeremy didn't look back, didn't flinch when the coins struck. Just sat taller in his saddle.

You each have a duty, Kaitlyn O' Rourke's voice whispered inside his head. *Have you the courage necessary to prevent those duties from destroying your love?*

He shook his head to clear it of the ghost's words, but was not successful.

Cursing himself for a heartless villain, Jeremy urged Charon into a gallop and hastily put as much distance between himself and his broken dreams as he could.

Twenty

The very air seemed to press down upon him.

Jeremy felt it like a tangible thing, a smothering blanket of oppression which befit his despair. Since leaving Landeyda, he had trained endlessly, ignoring with grim silence all warnings that he risked another fever by driving himself so hard.

Like the wolf who had lost his mate, he nursed his wounded heart and longed for her. His bed became a torture chamber where thoughts of making love to Alicen made his life hell. Without her beside him, shadows taunted from the darkness, mocking his inability to win and keep a woman's love...his inability to trust without reservation.

Driven from his bed, he took to the forest despite the air's frosty nip. He ached from cold. No matter how high he built his fire or how many blankets he wrapped about himself, the chill pierced. Fueling his misery, he dreamed of Alicen's warmth but awoke alone. He cursed memories of her supple body against him, of loving her. 'Twas all his fault. He'd ignored her pleas and ridden away without so much as a glance back.

The hurtful words he'd thrown at her tortured him most deeply. She feared abandonment, yet he'd departed without her. Now he lay alone each night, chilled and wounded in spirit, unable to ward off the cold or ease his body's aching. He fell into restless sleep, aware that the hurt in his chest was the pain of his empty heart.

After a week of self-inflicted isolation, he returned to Tynan. It was the eve of the Duke of York's arrival, and Jeremy, determined not to sped another night alone in his room, went to the guard room to spend it drinking.

The next morning, he regretted that he couldn't remember much of the night. And the single event he could remember made his head ache worse than excessive ale had ever done. He'd fought with another officer who had mocked his drunkenness. Last night, Jeremy had been of a mind to prove that, even sotted, he could subdue that particular varlet. And so he had. But at what price?

***

There was nothing of Jeremy's good friend in the tone William used to address him when he arrived at the duke's summons that morning. "Captain Blaine, await my pleasure in the antechamber while I speak with Captain Richards."

Jeremy bowed stiffly and left, going directly to the nearest window casement. There, he stared dull-eyed at the courtyard below and contemplated his crumbling life. What had possessed him of late? For the past month, to be exact. Never had he been so ungoverned... so haunted...so helpless to end his suffering. He could scarcely believe he'd brawled with another knight on the eve before the most important campaign of his life.

He needed Alicen. His soulmate. His balance. With her near, the world seemed less hostile. The peace he found in her arms was worth fighting twenty of Harold to win. He sighed. Once he gained his land and his lady, he'd never again fight for another. He'd sworn the vow as she slept in his arms on their return from Kirksowald. The night he'd privately admitted his love. No one would prevent him from keeping it.

Except, perhaps, Alicen herself. She'd not responded in kind to his declaration of love. After his battles ended, would she give him her heart? If not, his life would become a void.

Her wish that he not return, the fact she wanted no part of the carnage he would bring, plagued him. But he was bound to go back to Landeyda, to the woman he hoped awaited with caring in her heart for this battle-weary knight.

The door to William's private chamber opened just then, and Jeremy turned in time to see Richards stride out.

"The duke will see you now, Blaine," Richards snapped as he made his departure.

Venturing no comment, Jeremy quietly entered the privy room. His duke stared out the window for several long moments. Then, hands clasped behind him, William slowly turned to face him.

"Despite the warnings of nearly all who know you, you've done little else in the past month but train and prepare for battle," William began. "You've risked a return of the fever that nearly killed you."

This statement startled Jeremy. He thought he'd been summoned for a reprimand. "This campaign is crucial," he said carefully. "I wish to be as prepared as I can."

William nodded, but his expression remained solemn. "I've never known you to be foolhardy, Jeremy. But what I saw last night after Jason Warrick summoned me makes me think common sense had abandoned you." He plucked a knight from the chess table beside him and idly turned the piece in his hands. "My officers are too dear to be wasted over drunken insults. Any who choose pride before duty have no place with me."

"I understand, my lord."

William carefully set the chess piece back on the board before he looked up to meet Jeremy's gaze. "Do you? I know you despise Conrad Richards."

"He fights with his tongue not his sword," Jeremy ground out through a tight jaw. "Lacking the skill to win his rank, he purchased it with his wealth."

"I am well aware of how Richards came to be a knight, yet I cannot afford to have him killed by another of my officers. He may be a cockscomb, but he brings twenty retainers to my cause. Every one a skilled warrior."

Jeremy locked his hands behind his back to keep William from seeing his clenched fists. "My actions were foolish and indefensible. I was drunk. It won't happen again."

Jeremy saw a glint of sympathy in William's eyes and wished he'd not looked up at that very moment. He didn't deserve pity.

"I've not seen you so drunk since the night Estelle died."

That stark memory burned into his mind's eye. "As I said, 'twill not happen again."

"Jason was actually worried about you."

Jeremy vaguely recalled his conversation with Jason Warrick. Something about urging his friend to drink with him and Warrick's saying Jeremy had drunk enough for them both.

And he clearly remembered the brawl with Conrad Richards. Richards' challenge. His own acceptance. He also recalled William's arrival in the guard room. His duke had informed all present that, should any of them duel amongst themselves, he'd execute the victor.

"If you kill Richards, I'll have you hanged," William stated, interrupting Jeremy's morose recollections. The duke's gaze shifted to hold his. "What a waste that would be."

Leaden-hearted, Jeremy remained silent. He'd incurred his lord's wrath, for what? Over a fool's drunken insults? Because he couldn't have a woman? Nay, not just any woman, he reminded himself, the only one he loved. The woman who wouldn't love a soldier because she had sworn to protect the lives duty compelled him to destroy.

"Don't allow your feelings to blind you to what must be done," William warned softly. "You know as well as I that a man on the verge of battle needs a clear head."

"My feelings never interfere with my duty."

"You've not been in love in years," came the wry retort. "Your recollection of past experience is murky."

"I love no one."

William's brow rose. "My wife tells me you've ignored every female at court since your return from Landeyda a month ago. It intrigues her, as you've never completely scorned a lady's advances ere now."

Inwardly, Jeremy shuddered to think the duchess had observed his behavior and then informed William. Likely she knew the reason for it, but he'd not admit she was right.

"With respect, my lord," he began slowly, "Lady Guendolyn is a kind-hearted and romantic soul. But in this instance she sees what does not exist."

"My wife claims you've lost your heart, and I believe her."

"My lord—"

William cut him off with an upraised hand. "Alicen Kent is a fine woman. One worth losing both head and heart over."

Jeremy stared, jaw momentarily slack, then dropped all pretense. "How did you know 'twas Alicen?"

William smiled. "You're like a son to me. A father recognizes his son's suffering. Since your return, you've been a walking ghost. The only thing that could cause such a change in you is a woman."

"Am I that easily revealed?" Jeremy crossed to the hearth and stared into the dying embers.

"Nay. Yet I've known you seventeen years. Since your family sent their eight-year-old son to me to foster. I read your moods well." Jeremy kept silent vigil at the hearth, and William moved to clap him on the shoulder. "Alicen is as fine a lady as any in England. Don't fear surrender to her."

"You have promised to wed her to one of your subjects." He raised his gaze to the duke's. "But, you've not mentioned me as a possible husband."

William squeezed Jeremy's shoulder. "In truth, lad, I said nothing for I was unsure where the wind lay. Now I know you love her, and I'll gladly give her to you in marriage."

"She doesn't love me." His words sounded desolate even to his own ears.

"Have faith!" William emphasized his words by giving Jeremy a gentle shake. "Alicen is completely without guile. She'll be a loyal companion for the rest of your days."

Jeremy's mouth tightened, and he had to swallow hard before speaking. "She cannot love a soldier, nor does she believe I'll return to her after Harold's defeat."

"I see." William nodded slowly. "Then you must convince her you intend to remain with her."

"How shall I do that? Within a fortnight we ride against Harold." Looking down, he noted dispassionately that his hands had again fisted into white-knuckled balls. "I cannot go to her until this war ends."

"You'll see her within two days." Without meeting Jeremy's eyes, William turned to the map of Sherford lying on the table. "We need every available healer for this campaign. York proposes we make his castle our base camp, and I proposed we establish a hospital there." William raised his gaze to Jeremy's. "Ride to Landeyda and fetch Alicen, Ned and Rhea to Durham. Tell them it is at my command. I'm in desperate need of their skills."

"Alicen won't treat just our wounded," Jeremy stated,

pride in his love's integrity a fierce ache in his chest.

"She may tend any she pleases." William's look turned intense. "Will you fetch her?"

"I'll do my best to persuade her, my lord. Though I'm uncertain she can be tempted from her home."

"She'll have your welfare to attend, man. What more could she need to follow you to Durham?"

"Trust, mayhap?" Jeremy countered with a sardonic smile. "I've not given her that."

***

Four days before Duke William of Tynan's army marched north to meet the Duke of York's at Durham, Jeremy rode to Landeyda with Michael Taft and two soldiers. Hoping to influence Alicen's decision to his favor, he first stopped in Sherford and found Rhea. The old midwife readily agreed to aid William, provided they brought along the foundling, Pearl, and Liza Wick and her baby.

Jeremy smiled fondly as he scooped up Liza's two-month old son and held him high in the air. His smile widened at the baby's gurgled laughter. Then his mirth faded. Did Alicen even now carry his child? If so, would she welcome such a burden?

"We'll need all the aid we can procure," he stated to Rhea as he returned the boy to Liza. "Pearl is old enough to assist you, and Liza is also welcome." He turned to Taft, who stood staring at the young mother. "Michael, help them with their supplies. Michael?" He nudged his lieutenant. "Duty calls."

Taft flushed deeply. "My apologies, Captain." He bowed to the women. "Ladies. If you'll show me what needs be loaded..."

"This way, sir," Liza said shyly, gazing up through her lashes at the lieutenant's weathered features.

Jeremy watched, bemused, as Taft followed Liza to her hut.

"Methinks the good man has found a love," Rhea observed.

"So easily?" Jeremy countered with soft irony, turning to the old midwife. "'Tis not possible."

Rhea drew her woolen cloak around her and straightened her bent frame. "Mayhap for you, falling in love is not simple," she said kindly, "but 'tis uncomplicated for those who trust."

Trust. That word had mocked him since he'd left Landeyda a month earlier. Even knowing Estelle hadn't betrayed him—knowing all women weren't faithless—he refused to trust Alicen with his heart. He had told her of his love, and she'd thrown him out of her home. Yet honesty prompted him to admit that her rejection came from fear rather than enmity. Fear he'd not return. That he loved fighting more than he could ever love her. He shut his eyes. 'Twas time to prove his love. And time to trust her integrity and honor.

"Tell Taft I'll meet you at Landeyda," Jeremy said to Rhea. "I must speak to Alicen alone."

***

An unusually warm November sun lit the clearing where Alicen sat at midday beside her mother's grave. After a morning spent cleaning cottage and stable, she'd seized a chance to rest. Ned had tended the animals—naught remained to do that couldn't wait an hour. She escaped to the isolated clearing, intent upon letting her mind rest along with her body.

But thoughts of a handsome knight who'd awakened her passion and won her heart intruded. Not a day had passed since Jeremy's departure that she did not think of him. And every night. Especially at night.

She shivered despite the warm sun. As a healer, she was well aware of the physical aspects of coupling. But she'd never suspected the emotions involved in such intimacy. Jeremy's desire, his tenderness, his love had penetrated her heart. They lodged there, unimpeachable. She ached from missing him.

"Why did you leave?" she asked the slight breeze. "Why ride to York to be with William instead of remaining with me?"

She knew the futility of such questions, just as she knew his reasons for going. But accepting them proved difficult. She had never known a man's love, thus she had no wellspring from which to draw strength for this emotional struggle.

And it truly had been a struggle. At first, she feared she'd been left with child. Yet when her normal cycle resumed soon after his departure, she'd been saddened to think memories were all she had of him. Her despondency had grown so deep Ned became openly concerned. She did not reveal the true reasons for her despair, saying instead she missed life as it had been before William and his soldiers had plunged them into subterfuge.

The breeze picked up slightly to swirl around her, tugging gently at her hair. Her head came up, and she smiled wryly.

"You always said life continues despite us, Mother," she murmured, voice directed to the Celtic cross at the base of the large oak. "And I must, too."

You are first and foremost a healer, Alicen.

"Yes." If she pined away for a soldier, her vow would go unserved. She'd waste away to naught while aiding no one. The memories had to be locked up, her duties continued...

But don't forget you have a heart that must be cared for as well.

A horse's nicker from behind made Alicen's every nerve burn. Lost to her musings, she'd heard no one approach. Dread's chill raced up her spine. Ned would have been on foot. Choked with terror, Alicen rose and turned slowly to face the intruder.

Her breath left her lungs in a gasp. "Jeremy!"

Though she thought she'd shouted, she'd merely whispered. Unable to move or even speak again, she gaped at him astride Charon. He looked thinner, more chiseled than when she'd seen him last. Wild hair tumbled in his eyes, and she saw evidence of several days' growth of beard. His tunic and doublet were dusty, as was his mail.

No one had ever looked so wonderful to her.

Observing the flash of fear in Alicen's eyes the moment she turned, Jeremy instantly regretted stealing up on her. Although the fear died when recognition dawned, it boded ill that their meeting should begin on such unstable ground. And by a gravesite at that. A breeze abruptly whirled around him, and cold spread through him. Again, he heard a lilting Irish brogue in his mind.

Have you the courage, Captain?

He nervously cleared his throat.

"Ned told me you'd be here," he stated a bit roughly. "We must needs talk."

Alicen looked wan to him, and more slender. His gaze moved to her belly. Could his babe be growing there? He'd little recollection of when a woman began to show pregnancy, and equally little idea of how to broach the subject. His felt himself flush at the thought—he'd always held it the woman's duty to tell the man if she was enceinte.

"Will you return to the cottage with me?" he asked, baffled at the formality of his tone but helpless to correct it.

When she nodded, his breathing resumed. He dismounted at her approach and stood holding Charon's reins in shaking hands until she stopped beside him. Lavender scent immediately filled his nostrils, and his heart melted. All those lonely nights without her mocked him. Would he live the rest of his life with such desperate loneliness?

"What brings you here, Captain Blaine," she queried with startling coolness. "I've heard tell of no battles nearby."

Her bitterness told the price of his leaving. He looked away, muttering, "We meet York's army at Durham in two days."

"Saint Clement's Day," Alicen responded flatly. "A holiday before the killing begins?"

"William bade me fetch you. We'll need good healers in the days ahead, and he wishes for you to join us."

Bristling, she faced him squarely. "I'll not attend an army in the field! There's too much senseless slaughter."

"You'll treat casualties at Durham Castle," he ground out, reminding himself that her anger was justified. After all, he'd said he loved her yet had left her and returned to Tynan. He resisted the burning urge to crush her to him and kiss her senseless. Instead, he said tightly, "Rhea and Liza have agreed to go. They'll arrive at Landeyda presently."

At these words, Alicen's face paled then flushed with anger. "Why, you foot licking knave!" She gathered up her skirt and started for home at a run.

"Alicen, wait!" Jeremy yanked Charon's reins to pull

the horse around as he set off after his quarry. His mount resisted, so he abandoned it and broke into a dead run. Catching Alicen at the woods' edge, he seized her arm and pulled her to a halt. "Listen to me!"

She wrenched from his grasp, then aimed a slap at his face. He managed to stop the blow and hold onto her wrist as she stood glaring at him. "Son of a misbegotten swine! You dare use my friends against me?"

Guilt made him lower his head. "How else could I approach you, knowing I'd hurt and abandoned you?" She went completely still, and he cursed himself for hurting her more. He released her, but had to use his vaunted self-discipline to not cradle her face in his palms. "Alicen, William has need of you. He's agreed to let you treat any prisoners we may take."

Losing his battle to keep from touching her, Jeremy cupped her chin in his hand and tilted her head up. Green eyes filled with pain met his look. His fingers lingered a moment on her cheek before he dropped his hand to his side.

"Please come, lass. You'll be safe at Durham. I know you wish to go where you're most needed. Good physicians are always in demand." He swallowed nervously and found his fists clenched. "And consider this. Sherford may not be spared from the fighting. If you cannot accept my love, at least accept my protection."

"Speak not of love 'til you can speak of trust, Jeremy," Alicen stated, voice husky with tears. She turned her back.

Not about to allow her withdrawal, he gently seized her shoulders, then turned her back toward him. With one strong finger, he brushed away the glistening drops wetting her cheeks. "Good men will die without you," he said, voice nearly a whisper.

Her look was grim. "Good men will die in spite of me."

Gathering her into his arms, he held her so tightly he knew she could barely breathe. She belonged with him—his mate, his heart. Her warmth penetrated even his mail, a warmth he'd not felt since their last embrace. He lowered his head to her hair and breathed deeply. She did not resist, which heartened him.

"Come with us, lass," he murmured, relaxing his hold

on her. "You've no idea how badly you're needed."

Jeremy's soft plea crushed Alicen's defenses. She'd longed for his return, and now the strong arms encircling her made her forget all her objections and hurt.

He was sworn to fight, as were all Duke William's men. As a sworn healer, her loyalty lay with those who needed her skills the most. Unfortunately, she knew the victims of battle —soldier and civilian alike—would require her talents in the coming days.

She drew a shaky breath, then raised her head to look into her knight's anxious eyes. Seeing his love, her tone grew strong. "I'll go. Duty must be served. Yours and mine."

Twenty-one

"Alicen!" Ned hurried toward her as she walked Durham Castle's bailey with Rhea and Liza. "The armies take the field on the morrow."

Alicen exchanged a look with Rhea.

"We've only been here two days," Liza exclaimed.

War makes its own time, Alicen thought morosely.

Scanning the inner bailey, she saw Jeremy, Jason Warrick, and William's other captains leaving the keep. As she watched them move toward her, tumult from the portcullis drew everyone's attention.

"'Tis the eve of war, and battle lust begins, I see." Indicating the portcullis, Jason turned to Jeremy with a grin. "Shall we look to the cause of this disturbance?"

Jeremy shrugged, indifferent. "If you desire to do such."

"Methinks a different kind of lust assails you, man."

Jeremy's gaze had been on Alicen, and he realized Jason knew it. "Your tongue will dig your grave, Warrick, do you not mind it," he snapped.

Before Jason could reply, Jeremy strode toward the main gate and the source of the tumult.

A crowd had gathered at the drawbridge to witness a heated exchange between two archers, both claiming they could leap the span between the gatehouse and the barbican at the outermost gate. Twenty-five feet across the moat.

Jeremy knew there would be trouble when he looked at Jason's glittering eyes. His friend was going to start some mischief.

Jason's next words confirmed Jeremy's thought.

"Would you care to wager, friends?" Warrick asked the bowmen. "I've ten florins that says I can make the leap."

"I am for you," the larger of the two men said.

Jason and the large archer drew straws. Jason drew the long straw and thus would jump second. He ordered that a bed of straw cover the top of the barbican, some twenty feet below the gatehouse. The bowman climbed to the parapet and stepped onto the crenel, steadying himself with a hand on each of the waist-high merlons. From the ground forty feet below, he looked like a piece of gristle caught in a giant's squared-off teeth. With a piercing battle cry, he leaped into space. Instead of landing atop the barbicon, he fell short, caught the edge of a crenel with both hands and hung there a moment before falling into the moat.

His opponent had not even managed to extricate himself from the brackish water before Jason had stripped off sword belt, doublet and tunic, shoved them into Jeremy's arms, and climbed to the parapet. With a blood-curdling war cry, he launched himself at the target.

Jeremy assumed Jason was aiming for the lowest crenel atop the barbican. He hit the merlon beside it instead and fell flat on his back in the mud that edged the moat. Jeremy winced at the sight of his friend hitting inflexible stone, but Jason was not down long.

Muddied, his nose bleeding, Jason scrambled onto solid ground, where he for a time stood doubled over, gasping for breath while good-natured taunts filled the air.

"I almost reached it," he groused when Jeremy approached. "A hand span left." He eyed the guardhouse roof as the second bowman prepared to make his leap.

Jeremy shook his head. "I'll pay you twenty florin *not* to attempt that again."

Grimacing, Jason wiped blood from his nose with the back of his dirty hand. "Mayhap you're right. Let the bastard Harold's men attempt to kill me. I'll not do it for them."

Jeremy started to clap Warrick on the shoulder then thought better of it. "You look fit for the sty." His nose crinkled. "You smell fit for it, too."

Warrick scraped a handful of mud from his chest and raised it in his fist. "Not another word, friend, or I'll—"

Again the crowd roared. Soon, Jeremy had watched a dozen men fail the leap. One broke an arm, another a leg, all bruised themselves. None came closer to success than Jason and the large archer.

Each successive attempt was cheered louder than the previous ones, and Jeremy knew not a noble, retainer or servant within Durham Castle was unaware of what transpired.

"Come, Captain Blaine," Jason said, nudging Jeremy with his elbow. "'Tis certain you could hit the mark."

"No." Just then Jeremy caught sight of Alicen, approaching with Ned, Rhea, Liza and Michael. He froze, unable to calm his racing heart. Ease the ache in his chest. Her gaze met his, and she smiled slightly, weaving her way through the assembled throng to gain his side.

"Good day ladies, Ned, Michael," he greeted the group, never looking away from Alicen. "Have you come to see grown men make fools of themselves?"

She shook her head. "Truth be told, we'd heard there were injuries and thought mayhap we could help."

They were in time to see the latest contestant's foot slip just as he began his leap. He fell headfirst into the moat.

"Dickie can't swim," one man cried when the soldier remained submerged.

Three men immediately leaped into the murky water. After frantic searching, they surfaced, two dragging the unconscious victim to solid ground. One thumped his back several times, and with a sputtering heave of his chest, Dickie again began breathing.

Alicen turned shocked eyes to Jeremy. "They do thus for *sport*?"

"They merely ease their worry before battle." He shrugged. "'Tis more agreeable than pillage or ravishment, don't you allow?" When Alicen blushed, he couldn't help grinning.

"He who succeeds at the leap will earn vast wealth," Jason interjected. "A prize of one hundred florins."

Ned gasped. "That's two hundred shillings!"

"Aye, lad. A man could well enjoy himself with such a purse." Jason cocked his thumb at Jeremy. "I strive to coax Captain Blaine to try his hand."

Jeremy waved Jason off. "Leave be, Warrick. I've no need of the winnings. Nor do I wish to soil my clothing." He turned to the others. "Jason still chafes because he failed first."

Warrick's ears reddened. "You'll let Duke William's honor be besmirched to spare your clothes, Jeremy? Or lack you stomach for this?"

Alicen shot Warrick a look of disgust, then clasped Jeremy's arm, pleading quietly, "Don't let him taunt you into this. 'Tis foolish, and you know how happily he makes mischief for his own entertainment."

Sensation radiated through Jeremy at her touch. Suddenly, only the two of them existed. Everyone else faded away as he stared at her, seeing her fear. He knew then the depth of her caring, despite her reluctance to admit such. Cupping her chin in his hand, he smiled and leaned toward her, then realizing they could be overheard, looked up at their assembled companions.

"Pardon us." He clamped her hand in the crook of his elbow and moved a few paces off from the throng.

His tone matched her earlier one when he replied, "He's correct, you know. I cannot abandon my duke's honor."

She scowled. "He seeks to goad you into needless peril."

"Do you care so much for my safety?" Her answer meant the world, and he fixed her with an intense gaze.

She looked away first. "What manner of question is that? You know I cannot abide seeing men hurt."

Her actions gave him his answer. Joy sang in him, and he was overwhelmed with need. "A wager, Mistress Kent?" He crooked a brow. "Since I mean to attempt what all others have failed, why not give me a sweeter prize to win?"

She eyed him warily. "I have little coin. And I'll not risk a farthing on such a foolish enterprise."

Bending his head closer, he whispered, "Then venture the one commodity I've longed for, lo, these many weeks." At her dubious look, he stated honestly, "Your pleasurable company in my bed this night would be a prize worth dying for."

Gasping, Alicen pressed her fingers to his lips. "Speak not so lightly of death. 'Tis ill fortune."

He kissed her hand, then ran his fingers up her arm. "Will you wager? We both know well the delight that will be ours should I succeed."

She trembled at his touch. "Jeremy, don't risk injury—"

"In the morn we ride into battle. 'Eat, drink and be merry, for tomorrow we—'"

"Cease this!" Alicen tried to pull away, but he tightened his fingers into a gentle shackle, effectively preventing escape.

"I want you, Alicen," he whispered hoarsely. "I've felt thus for so long, I cannot remember ever not wanting you."

Her mouth opened and closed twice before she managed to say, "Must you take this foolish dare?"

He grinned, leaning closer. "Danger makes life rich."

"Reasoned with a soldier's logic." With a sigh, she briefly dropped her forehead to his shoulder. "I'll take your wager. But I'll not bind your head when you crack it for pride."

Jeremy laughed, quickly kissed her mouth, then dashed back to the others. He handed his sword to Warrick, spurned removing his tunic, and strode to the watchtower.

Knees wobbling, Alicen stood where he'd left her. An inner chill swept her as she watched him poised atop the merlon. The chill turned to ice in her veins when he emitted a fierce battle cry and launched himself off the parapet.

She closed her eyes for a tense moment, heard a deafening roar, and looked to see him standing squarely in the middle of the barbican, a smile threatening to split his face in twain. Unaware of doing so, she ran toward his perch.

Jeremy descended, fighting through the crush of giddy spectators to find his friends. Noting Alicen's expression contained equal dismay and relief, he paused. He'd forced her into a decision she perhaps regretted. What would happen next?

Jason's grin was as broad as his congratulatory embrace. Arm draped over Jeremy's shoulders, he turned to the others with a laugh.

"The man's invincible," he roared. "Why, I once saw him make a similar leap in a full suit of armor."

At this declaration, Alicen froze, eyes locking with

Jeremy's.

The pain of betrayal he saw there scorched him, but before he could speak, her expression changed to fury.

"More the fools we for doubting him," she said coldly. "Or doubting the lengths he'll go to win a wager." She spun on her heel and fled through the crowd.

Silently cursing his stupidity, Jeremy made to follow her, but Rhea stepped closer and touched his hand.

"Stay, Captain," the midwife advised. "She must needs be alone a little to think matters through. Seek her out later."

Torn, Jeremy glanced down at Rhea then back to where Alicen had disappeared in the throng. Once again, he'd callously hurt the woman he loved. He glared at Jason, but knew his own deceit had done him in, not his friend's ill-timed proclamation. Sweet Jesu, why hadn't he told her he could easily leap the span? Base need had driven him to seek a night of pleasure with her.

His cunning may have cost him his heart's desire.

Shoulders sagging, he turned back toward Warrick and was immediately engulfed in a crowd of well-wishers. Burdened by despair, he received their congratulations.

***

Jeremy paced his chamber like a caged animal, fighting his urge to tear Durham apart. Supper had ended over an hour before, and the castle had gradually quieted as its occupants settled in for the night. Alicen had not appeared at the meal. In fact, had not been seen since afternoon.

Jeremy prayed that Ned and Rhea's presence at Durham would prevent Alicen from returning to Landeyda. But he wasn't certain it would.

It seemed he'd thought a hundred times to search for her, but Rhea had warned against pursuit. And the old midwife knew Alicen far better than he. 'Twould be foolishness he could not afford.

And if he pursued and managed to find her, what would he say? That *love* for her had caused him to deceive her? Nay, lust had overturned tender feelings. Now he waited in torment until his heart returned. If she ever did.

At midnight a quiet knock riveted his attention. He

rushed to throw the door wide, expecting Rhea on the threshold.

Alicen stood alone in the dark hallway, the hood of her cloak drawn up over her hair, and gave him a hesitant smile.

"May I enter?" she asked dryly.

His heart reeled before thundering wildly, and he had to force himself not to crush her to him. Instead, he bowed and politely ushered her into the chamber.

"I thought you'd not come," he stated, unable to keep pain from his voice. "Lord knows you have reason enough to stay away."

"We wagered and I lost. I'm here to repay my debt."

Her declaration made it clear that given the choice she'd not be there. His chest felt pinched by blacksmith's tongs. She tensed as he reached for her, and panic seized him.

"Alicen, forgive my baseness! But it has been so long since we..., I mean I..., you seemed so angry when—" Realizing he babbled, he trailed off. He massaged his forehead, then met her gaze, searching her face for a sign of forgiveness. When he spoke again, his choked voice nonetheless was calm. "I'd never expect you to excuse such trickery, but you *must* believe my deep regret." He gave her a tight smile. "You needn't pay the wager."

Alicen's fragile control threatened to crumble beneath his sincerity. In truth, she wished to be there, yet she resented his tactics. This resentment, and knowing she'd come to him on her terms, steadied her. In anticipation of their lovemaking, she'd drunk an herbal potion of rue and savin. Though she'd gladly bear Jeremy's child, she knew not of his desire for a babe. She'd no wish to discover he merely sought temporary pleasure with her.

Nervous, she removed her cloak, draped it over a chair, then smoothed the cowl. Avoiding eye contact, she examined the room. The furnishings were Spartan: one large coffer for clothing, two chairs and a rug before the hearth, a table beside a window embrasure. The large curtained bed. Tapestries depicting the hunt adorned two walls, Jeremy's mail and weapons another. Altogether functional and impersonal.

Feeling the loneliness of the place, she turned and

saw the need in his eyes. Pain twisted inside her. Until then, she'd never been certain that he missed her. Loved her. With quick strides she closed the distance between them and launched herself into his arms.

"Hold me."

He crushed her to him, tangling his hands in her hair, kissing her as if she were water and he dying of thirst.

"Alicen," he groaned.

They embraced with raw intensity—hands, lips, bodies straining to touch as intimately as possible.

Jeremy pulled back long enough to divest her of her dress. His tunic followed. Then he carried her to the bed, there to resume his fevered caresses. He ripped her chemise in his haste to remove it, but he was too lost in emotion to care. She untied his hose, and that quickly he was as naked as she.

They came together in a wild, intense culmination of their reunion, the only sounds moans of pleasure and incoherent love words. Pillows were swept from the bed and sheets tangled in a passion too fervent to be further contained.

Twenty-two

"Noooo!"

Alicen lurched to a half-sitting position, flailing blindly with her fists. Jeremy had all he could do to stop her from striking him as she lashed out against invisible enemies.

"Alicen! Awake." He managed to control her thrashing by holding her close and murmuring soothingly, "Steady, lass. You dreamed, sweetling, 'tis all. There's naught to fear. 'Twas just a phantom of the night."

Green eyes flew wide, the terror he saw there gradually leaving as she recognized her surroundings. Her breathing calmed to a more normal rhythm. Glancing at the hour candle beside the bed, Jeremy saw they'd slept only a short time after their heated lovemaking had exhausted her. She snuggled her head beneath his chin.

"They pursued me." Voice hoarse, she shook with dread. "They caught me in the woods."

"Shhh," he crooned, smoothing her hair back from her face. "You dreamed. Don't be afraid now."

Her eyes were huge. "'Twas so real."

His embrace tightened. "You're safe here."

"Aye, but you are not. In a few hours you'll face battle." Her voice nearly broke, but she mastered it.

"I'll return to you, Alicen." His gaze was intent.

She shuddered. "Would I could believe that. Believe a man who tricked me into his bed."

Her soft tone struck like shards of glass. "I only thought to keep you near," he muttered, miserable. "Little wonder you hate me."

A frown could not hide the soft luminosity of her eyes as she stroked her hand down his jaw. "You, sir, are a cad."

Jeremy swallowed, her touch tugging the corner of his mouth into a slight smile. "To prove my contrition, I'll obey any command you give."

"You'll do aught that I desire?"

Completely serious, he said, "I am your willing servant."

An impish grin lit her face. "Then walk the battlements, clothed as you are."

He started, caught the mirth in her expression, then slowly smiled. "You're a hard woman, Alicen Kent, to send a soldier to die from exposure."

"You gave your word, sir."

"So be it." He paused only a moment before adding, "But I'm bringing you along."

Grabbing her arm, he started to drag her from the bed.

"Stop!" she shrieked, laughing and struggling to break away. "Brute! Leave be!"

"You cut me deeply, woman," he protested with mock affront as he released her, then joined her in bed. "I am dishonored."

She laughed again. "Methinks honor is too important to you," she teased, mimicking his voice to perfection.

An exaggerated sigh whooshed from his chest. "At least send me to my death with a kiss to ease my final hours."

"Oh, very well, but make quick work of this." Closing her eyes tight, Alicen pursed her lips.

With a laugh, Jeremy bent toward her and gently brushed her mouth with his. Her eyes half opened, and to his complete delight, she pressed her lips harder against his, the light kiss quickly flaming. Her arm encircled his neck, drew him down with her as she rolled to her back. Knowing she feared for his safety, for his return, he made gentle love to her, withholding his pleasure until she had reached fulfillment. At last he released his ardor, and when he climaxed, she again gained that peak.

Afterward, Alicen clasped him in a warm embrace, her lips clinging to his mouth.

Joy flooded him, but fearing his weight would discomfit her, he started to withdraw. She locked her hands behind his back, causing his heart to pound so hard he was certain she felt it.

"Do I perceive that you wish me to remain, Mistress?"

A startled look crossed Alicen's face, then she blushed

and tried to push him off.

"What? A sudden change of heart?"

"You're heavy!" she protested, face now ablaze.

Leaning down, he whispered in her ear, "You did not think such a few moments ago." He rolled to his back, bringing her along, still joined to him. "I'll gladly bear your weight, my lady." He grunted as though she were stout, then grinned.

When Alicen's lips thinned and she started to speak, he held his finger to her mouth.

"Shhh! Talk not of gratitude. 'Tis there in your eyes."

"Why, you arrogant—"

Alicen struggled to break free, but Jeremy's muscled arms held her hips tight to his. Embarrassed that he could so accurately assess her feelings and then tease about them, she doubled up her fist and hit him square on the chest. She swung again, but he caught her hand before the blow fell and pulled her arm behind her back, laughing deep in his chest as she strained against him.

She knew the futility of resistance, yet continued, even when he stymied all her efforts. Finally, growling in frustration, she bared her teeth and nipped him on the chest.

"Ouch," he yelped. "Bloodthirsty minx!"

He rubbed the spot where her teeth had caught him, and Alicen lurched away, forcing him to give up his massage to grab her with both hands. They laughed as they tumbled about the bed, Jeremy trying to kiss her, she doing her best to avoid his kisses.

He was nearly ready to cry stalemate when arousal returned in full measure, and he again filled her. Alicen stilled, eyes widening. Masculine pride brought a grin to his face, and he lifted his hips against her, watching her eyes close from the sensation.

"I am insatiable with you, my lady," Jeremy declared, raising his head to gently kiss her. Seeing ardor burning in her gaze, he dared to hope. He smiled and brushed a tumbled lock from her cheek, whispering, "Kiss me, dear minx. But this time, no teeth."

Alicen slowly lowered her mouth to his. He lay still beneath her hands. She caressed the muscled planes of his chest and abdomen, then kissed his throat, watching his muscles tighten at her touch. Her deft physician's hands soon had him moaning with pleasure.

When she touched the scar on his arm from the wound she had tended months before, she paused, gripped in sadness.

"You've borne so much pain."

"'Tis of no import when I'm with you." His fingers traced the line of her jaw, then trailed down to her breast. He stopped his caress, watching her intently.

She gently pushed his hand away then stretched full length atop him, rubbing skin to skin. "Let me please you."

His breathing quickened as she slid slowly down to cover his chest with kisses. She knew what he caused in her—pleasure so intense she thought mayhap she dreamed it—and she wished to return the favor. When her mouth closed over one of his small nipples, his delighted groan made her smile.

She suckled him as he had her, enjoying her power to pleasure him. A strong yet gentle man—she thrilled to the feel of him beneath her lips, between her thighs. She took his other nipple carefully in her teeth, running her tongue over it while Jeremy shuddered and grew even harder within her.

"Alicen," he gasped, pulling her face up to his. "Sweetling, how you please me!"

He claimed her mouth as his hips began to thrust upward against her, and she soon matched his rhythm. Then he showed her yet another manner of achieving ecstasy, and she met his raging desire with emotions equalling his own.

Much later, she held Jeremy as he slept, biting her lip to keep from weeping. She brushed a lock of hair from his forehead and softly kissed his temple. When he rode out to battle at first light, her courage would equal his, and not even he would know of the fear threatening to bring her to her knees. But now, in the dark of night, dread permeated her soul. She fought that dread, fought the tug of sleep. If this was to be the last night she'd ever lie with Jeremy, then she would not waste it in slumber or fruitless worry. Instead, she would spend the remaining time with him recalling and committing to memory every moment they had shared.

And she would pray that God would safely return to her the man who owned her heart.

***

"They're charging, Captain!"

Jeremy moved Charon into line as fifteen of Harold's knights rode down on his seventeen. Thick woods edged the crossroads on all sides, reducing the benefit of superior numbers and limiting all but frontal assault.

"Our foe is desperate," he called to his men. "They grow reckless."

His orders were to keep Harold's troops from gaining refuge at Escomb or retreating to Harold's keep at Raby, and so he and his men guarded the road to the enemy camp.

The sound of helmet visors slamming into place mixed with the building crescendo of destriers in full charge stirred Jeremy's blood. Yet he calmly adjusted his shield and positioned his lance. A glance down the line to each side told him every man had done likewise.

"I'm for the lead rider," he shouted. "Mark the griffin upon his shield."

As coolly as could be expected in the face of the oncoming phalanx, the others called their marks. Then they started forward in a controlled trot, eighteen abreast. When the enemy had closed to twenty rods, Jeremy signaled the charge.

"On! On!"

The two lines met at a dead run, the impact shaking the ground. Jeremy's lance shivered in his hand, splintering with a resounding crack against his foe's shield. Yet he failed to unhorse his foe, so drawing sword, Jeremy closed in.

All around them men and horses fell. The smell of blood filled the air, but Jeremy ignored that and the sounds of clanging blades and dying men and destriers, concentrating completely on his enemy.

His shield warded off the enemy's blows as Jeremy's sword pounded back. They battered each other for several frenzied moments, until Jeremy managed a particularly vicious strike which dropped his opponent's guard. That slight opening was all he needed. With one clean thrust, he pierced the knight's throat. The man died before he fell from his saddle.

Sweat blurred Jeremy's vision as he fought in the melee's center, wheeling Charon again and again to meet new attackers. Undaunted, he hacked at the hazy images before him, unhorsing an opponent. But when he pulled Charon around, his saddle girth broke, dumping him cursing at the man's feet. Landing flat on his back cleared his sight.

He saw death awaiting him in the form of a mail-clad enemy with sword upraised.

Quick reflexes kept his head attached to his body as the blow arced downward. He rolled, avoiding the blade, bringing his own sword up in the move. His enemy's momentum followed the path of his swing, and he impaled himself on Jeremy's weapon. The man collapsed dead on the ground.

At once unbelievably weary, Jeremy rose on shaky legs. Planting his foot on the dead knight's chest, he freed his sword and wiped the blood off on the grass. It took a moment before he realized the fight had ended. Those of Harold's men still living had fled, pursued by William's retainers. He stood alone—every warrior at his feet a corpse. Too numb to notice the carnage, he removed his helmet and pulled his coif back, then wiped sweat from his face with the hem of his tunic. He drew several deep breaths and assessed his injuries.

Though every joint and muscle ached, he was fit. But his damaged equipment forced him to concede the field. He sheathed his sword and tossed the broken saddle onto Charon's back. From the equipage strewn about, he chose the largest destrier still standing, two stout shields and a serviceable sword. He secured these weapons on his useless saddle, mounted the new horse and led Charon back to the camp.

And, as had happened every rare quiet moment during the last month, his thoughts turned to Alicen. Only memories of their night of ecstasy kept him from despair. He'd not seen her since the fighting began, but news of her reached him from Durham. Casualties had mounted with each battle, and the cold weather made living conditions in the field miserable. By the score, the wounded and ill were taken in carts to the castle.

Alicen and Antonio Saldi, William's physician, had made one guardroom a ward for the critical cases. A second, run by York's physicians, held less seriously wounded. Rumor held that Saldi, the venerable Italian healer, even studied Alicen's techniques. Jeremy smiled at that thought. Pride in her skill assuaged his guilt.

But only for a few moments. He remembered the reason she presently resided at Durham—to heal injuries he and his fellow warriors caused. Because of him, she slaved to knit broken bodies back into men. He'd fought for a month without two consecutive days of rest, yet he'd wager all he owned that Alicen had worked harder, most likely long into every night as well as through each day. How could he subject her to such torment? He'd promised her protection.

He'd given her a view of hell.

By the time he arrived in camp, the afternoon weather had turned bleak. A cold rain drove men inside as the horses huddled together for warmth. Jeremy stopped at William's tent to report his troop's activities.

Wearily rubbing his forehead, the duke nodded at Jeremy's account. Afterward, he studied his captain. "Return to Durham for a week. You need rest."

"But my lord—"

William raised a brow. "You've fought dawn to dusk for a month." He produced vellum, quill and ink, writing hastily as he spoke. "Go to Durham this very day and remain until Wednesday next. Deliver this requisition to the seneschal." He read aloud: "Threescore of herrings, a score of sheep, ten salted pigs, five stone bags each of figs, rice, raisins, oats, and rye, five hogsheads of wine. Have I omitted aught of import?"

"I think not."

William rolled the vellum into a scroll and handed it over. "'Tis too cold to fight."

Jeremy thought to protest his removal from the field, but didn't. He could see Alicen! His dark mood suddenly lifting, he nodded assent, then bowed slightly.

"I'll change saddles and mounts immediately and depart."

William cocked his head. "For once you barely resist

my will. Have I witnessed a miracle?"

"Aye, my lord." Jeremy smiled. "You're far wiser than I. I must admit."

"Truly a miracle." William indicated the scroll in Jeremy's hand. "Deliver that posthaste. We've need of many supplies."

As he left the tent, supply list tucked inside his tunic, Jeremy thought of his chosen lady. 'Twould be heaven to see her. Hold her. Make love with her.

This last image brought him up short. He'd told no one of his congress with her, though some knew of his regard. Would she refuse his bed? Although they would be discreet, such activity approached a public declaration of being lovers. Mayhap she'd not wish for such an arrangement.

She had every right to spurn him, considering his duplicity. Chagrined, he relived the eve of battle and the trick he'd used to draw her to his bed. Recalled their incredible passion. He would die without her love, but had he destroyed the bond between them?

Could she love him if she distrusted him?

***

He arrived at Durham too late to do aught but order a hot bath and a cold meal and retire. Though he longed to see Alicen, he was not at his best, so thought to seek her out after he'd rested. After he'd had time to plan another apology for tricking her. Too weary to think, he chose sleep.

Mid-morning the next day he entered the infirmary. Locating her proved easy. Chestnut hair tied back from her face, she sat beside a soldier's pallet. As Jeremy stared, pride and love filled his heart. He felt the most fortunate of souls for having found this incredible woman.

However, when she raised her head and he saw her exhaustion, his breath caught. Quietly, he approached from behind as she bent over the patient, resalving wounds and changing bandages.

"When was the last time you ate a hearty meal and slept a full night?" he asked without preamble.

She started then stiffened, turning to send him an ominous look. "Captain, I know myself. Your concern is unwarranted."

Planting fists on hips, he glared down at her. "Dammit, woman, cease being mulish. You're working yourself into the charnel house. I'll not allow it!"

"You'll not *allow* it?" She abruptly stood, fire flickering in her tired eyes. "Jeremy Blaine, you've no voice where I'm concerned. I take no orders from you."

"You'd be a damned sight better off if you did. You're ready to drop."

"I'm perfectly fit," she stated too adamantly to sound convincing. "If you haven't observed, all labor hard here."

Jeremy started to reach for her, then dropped his hand to his side and uttered in a deep, tender tone, "You hardest of all, lass. You're played out. Seek your rest."

Alicen resisted the comfort his words stirred in her, the joy evoked by seeing him safe before her.

"Leave me in peace, sir," she replied in a voice too weary to be commanding.

She turned away, but her dismissal of him ended almost immediately when she caught one foot on a nearby pallet and stumbled to her hands and knees. She scrambled to regain her feet only to fall back to her knees, unable to rise.

Jeremy swiftly knelt at her side to lift her into his arms. "Enough of your headstrong folly. You're going to rest. Now."

"Put me down this instant! I'm needed in the ward." Alicen struggled feebly, strength ebbing like a tide.

Her effort merely saw her held more closely.

"The wounded will do without you for a little. Otherwise, you'll die at this pace. Then where would we soldiers be?"

Dizziness scattered her thoughts and sapped her anger. Thus, she had to endure him carrying her across the courtyard to the keep. He stopped only after entering his own room and laying her on the bed. He had claimed her for all to see, and she was too exhausted to attempt resistance.

"Jeremy—" She struggled to rise. "I cannot stay here."

"Lie still." His voice was firm as he carefully pushed her back down. "You're not leaving this bed until morn."

"But 'tis not yet past midday!" Difficulty focusing her eyes forced Alicen to remain prone. Knowing she couldn't fight blind, she concentrated on controlling her whirling senses.

Jeremy ignored her protests, stripping her of slippers and hose, the apron covering her frock, and the frock itself. Alicen grew steadily more tense as each article of clothing came off. He knew that, regardless of her fatigue, he'd have a battle on his hands if he hesitated a moment before divesting her of her chemise and adding it to the pile of soiled apparel at his feet.

"This garment needs a good washing," he muttered gruffly, removing it so deftly she had no time to say him nay. Just as deftly, he covered her with a sheet and blanket, then strode to the chamber door. "Page!"

When a youngster in Durham's livery appeared, Jeremy ordered him to bring more water, another basin and clean cloths. The youth's jaw dropped wide when he saw the woman in the bed.

"Mistress Kent!" He shot Jeremy an anxious look.

"She's merely exhausted, not ill. Now, fetch what I bade you get."

Jeremy returned to Alicen's side. Her forehead felt warm but not feverish, and though dark circles smudged her lovely eyes, her color was good. He hoped she only needed rest. If she was truly ill...He could not bear to think of it.

"This is unnecessary," she complained weakly when he held his hand to her forehead.

"I'm giving the orders now," he whispered. He smoothed her hair back from her face. "Lie still."

When the page returned with the requested items, Jeremy dipped a folded cloth into the cool water, wrung it out, then placed it on Alicen's brow. Her eyes flickered open, then closed.

"You cannot force me to remain here against my will," she murmured, eyes still shut.

"Aye, I can." He stroked her cheek with his knuckles. "And I will, if I must tie you to the bed to do so."

"You are cruel, Jeremy."

His hand froze against her face. "You think me cruel for preventing your death?"

Eyes glazed with fatigue fixed on him, and she squinted before speaking, as if to focus her thoughts.

"You force me to do what I wish not to. Make me feel what I wish not to."

"Exhaustion fashions babble," he chided gruffly, swallowing around the lump lodged in his throat. "Hush now. Sleep." He pressed a soft kiss to her lips. "We'll talk in the morn. For now, you must rest." He kissed her again. "Rest, my love."

Jeremy steadfastly guarded her for the rest of the day, shielding her from all who would disturb her. He spoke to Rhea and Liza, assuaging their fears. Ned's concern made the lad restive, so Jeremy sent him to gather William's supplies. The boy need not sit at Alicen's bedside and worry. 'Twas better he be kept occupied, since Jeremy worried enough for all.

At dusk Jason arrived with Saldi and a missive from William. The kindly physician confirmed Jeremy's belief that Alicen needed sleep more than aught else.

"Keep her resting quietly until the morrow." Saldi handed Jeremy a packet of medicine. "If she stirs, mix this in her wine, and she'll slumber through the night. I'll examine her more thoroughly in the morn."

Jeremy extended his hand to the old physician. "My thanks to you, Antonio, for your regard."

A broad smile creased a hundred wrinkles in Saldi's face. "She is an astounding healer," he replied with genuine affection. "We must not allow such talent to destroy itself. You were wise to make her rest, Captain."

"'Twas more I appeared when she collapsed than from any of my doing," Jeremy replied dryly. "She couldn't very well refuse me when she couldn't remain standing."

Both Jason and Antonio voiced agreement to that observation.

"Send word should you need aught," Warrick said. "Does the weather turn favorable, we'll lay siege to Harold's stronghold by week's end. You'd be wise to rest, as William intended." He slapped Jeremy on the back then left with Saldi.

Jeremy saw them to the door before returning to stand over the bed, gazing down at the woman who occupied it and his heart. He studied Alicen's comely features—the straight nose, generous mouth, and strong chin that comprised an unforgettable visage. She was not classically beautiful like many women he'd met, but her inner beauty would last long after time weathered any outward attractiveness.

He recalled vividly the feel of her—each curve and soft spot—the way she moved against him, her cries when she found her pleasure. Desire tightened his groin, but he ignored it. He'd never deceive her again. Instead, he'd lure her to him for life.

Yet would she love him—marry him—when this war ended? Could he win her heart? Hours slipped by as he worried these questions like a hound worrying a bone.

Close to midnight, Alicen stirred. She started to sit up, but even in her sleep-drunken state, realized her lack of attire and gave up the attempt.

"'Tis late," she said quietly when she spotted Jeremy sitting nearby.

"Aye." The love in his eyes shone in his tender look.

"You've remained beside me all this time?" At his nod, she stared up at the canopy over the bed and ran a hand through her hair. "You thought I'd awaken and leave." She spoke softly, but heard the note of accusation in her own voice.

"Nay." His reply was soft as well. "I sought to keep you undisturbed, naught else." He glanced to the wine on the stand beside the bed. "Saldi left a draught should you be unable to sleep." He grasped her hand and brushed it with his lips. "Will you require such?"

She stifled a yawn. "Nay."

Releasing her hand, he gently massaged her temples and forehead. "Return to your slumber, lass. You've need of it yet," he whispered as he continued the massage.

Jeremy had hardly finished speaking before noticing she again slept. Succumbing to his own fatigue, he disrobed and joined her in the bed. Pillowing her head against his shoulder, he held her close, sighing at the feel of her warm beside him.

"I love you, Alicen," he said softly. "Heaven knows I've tried not to, but I cannot help myself. I love you."

Closing his eyes, he fell into the first contented sleep he'd enjoyed since the fighting started.

***

"Will you tell him of the child?" Antonio Saldi asked

as he finished examining Alicen before his morning rounds the next day.

Blushing, she shook her head. "I've only been certain of it myself these few days past." At seeing Saldi's expression, she firmly added, "He must concern himself with the siege, naught else. Distraction could be calamitous, and learning of a babe might cause him more harm than good."

"I know him well. You must not keep this from him."

"I must for now." Alicen reached to touch the healer's arm. "Please believe me when I say 'tis for Jeremy's good."

Saldi shrugged then smiled. "Who am I to contradict your belief? I am happy for the babe within you. The miracle of life. I wish you to be happy, also."

Her smile was more poignant than joyous. "I am, dear friend. Yet, 'tis fear I feel crowding in against the joy. Fear that Jeremy may not live to see his child grow to manhood."

Wordlessly, Saldi grasped her shoulder and gently squeezed. "No one knows God's will. But we must greet each new day with hope. Hope remains always."

He rose quietly from the stool beside the bed and left her.

His words heartened Alicen.

Life grows within you despite your attempt to prevent it, her mother's voice said softly in Alicen's mind. *Such events happen for a reason.*

Should ill befall Jeremy—though she refused to believe it would—the child would be evidence of the love that filled her soul.

The opening door startled Alicen from her contemplations. Jeremy entered, burdened with a tray of food, and she felt herself suddenly quivering at sight of him.

"Where are my clothes?" she demanded, stifling her desire to invite him into bed for a long, passionate greeting.

"Somewhere you can't find them," he replied casually, a slight smile tugging the corners of his mouth.

"I wish to have them now."

"Haste is unnecessary." He set the tray down on the table. "You'll not leave until you've eaten."

New-found energy lent acid to her voice. "Captain,

you cannot order me about. I intend to go to the infirmary at once."

"The men will doubtless enjoy their angel of mercy clad much like Eden's inhabitants before the Fall." When Alicen drew the blanket closer around herself, Jeremy grinned. She'd regained her spirit, he decided happily.

"Dishonorable cad," she fumed. "'Tis always your wretched way to practice stratagems."

"I'll return your garments after you eat. They are cleaned and dry."

"I demand my clothes now!" Alicen balled her fists in temper.

He bent to the tray, then set it on her lap. "Food first."

"But the wounded need me."

Her beseeching tone pulled his gaze to hers. "Antonio is with them. They'll endure until you've taken nourishment." He sighed. "Think, Alicen. Die, and your skills die with you. By resting when you require it, you'll treat a far greater number of patients."

"What of last night? While I slept, grievously injured men needed attention."

"They were tended. You've trained your workers well—unless the case is grave, they can function without aid. Be proud of their skills and take some much earned respite." He sat on the stool. "Will you feed yourself, or must I?"

She glared at him before looking to the repast he'd brought. "The devil take you, Captain."

Jeremy chuckled. "Of a certain, you feel much better."

And looked very appealing in her state of undress. Mayhap he could convince her to allow him—

A soft knocking stayed his lusty thoughts. Stifling a sigh, he rose to open the door. 'Twas Rhea, carrying Alicen's clothes. He ushered the white-haired midwife inside.

"I've informed her she must eat before dressing," he told Rhea in a whisper calculated to carry to Alicen's ears. He knew it had when she sniffed in affront. "I'll leave you to see that she carries out my command."

"That won't be necessary, Captain," Alicen retorted icily. "I'll yield to your tyranny, if for no other reason than to be rid of your tormenting manner."

Jeremy bowed and gave her his most charming smile. "Then I'll trust you to see to your own needs before returning to your duties." He nodded to the midwife. "I must needs speak to the armorer this morn. Enjoy your meal, Mistress Kent."

He could feel Alicen's burning gaze as he left the chamber, but her animosity warmed rather than angered him. He'd forced her to attend to herself before anything serious befell her, and this heartening fact pleased him. If he could not prevent the reality of Durham's desperate need of her skills, he could at least keep her fit to perform them.

"'Tis good to see you rested," Rhea commented as the door closed after Jeremy. A smile squeezed her face's myriad wrinkles into lines of joy. "Your Captain Blaine is so gallant to you."

Alicen flushed. "The man is intolerably arrogant. And he's not *my* captain. His heart and soul belong to William."

"He loves you deeply."

Alicen hid in a show of anger the hope those words brought. "He forced me to stay here, then had the gall to confine me until I ate. Is there no end to his treachery?"

"Treachery?" Rhea asked, bemused. "The captain knew you to be overtaxed. We all saw it, but he acted to keep you from harm. Knowing you'd not stop until you sickened—as you very nearly did—he intervened."

"Interfered, you mean."

Rhea shook her head as she sat down beside the bed. "The two of you love each other. Can you not admit such truth? Why deny what your heart knows?"

Alicen bowed her head. "Rhea, I'm so afraid for him."

The hoarse statement hung in the air as she subdued her raw feelings by attending to the meal. Mouth-watering smells lured her despite her distress, and she set about eating. After all, she'd given her word that she would. Spiced wine washed down fresh bread, eggs, hot cakes and thick slices of ham. In between bites, she motioned to the tray.

"Have you broken your fast?"

Rhea nodded. "At dawn. I've just come for a short while. Ned is on tenterhooks to see you. I told him I'd return to the wards within the hour."

Alicen smiled. "Tell Ned I'll meet him in the infirmary, and we can talk while I work."

"Captain Blaine would do well to chain you to this bed."

Alicen flushed but kept her own counsel. Truth to tell, Jeremy had only to ask and she would spend every night beside him. But he hadn't asked. He'd tricked her into a night of passion, then taken advantage of her physical condition to keep her with him last night. Although he'd likely saved her from illness by making her rest, his methods angered her.

"Why must he be so overbearing?"

"Mayhap since you rarely listen to quiet advice." A gentle smile lit Rhea's face.

Blushing fiercely, Alicen drained the dregs of the wine and put the tray aside. "I need my clothes, Rhea." *If I'm not dressed and out of this bed before Jeremy returns, I may not let him leave this chamber all day.*

Twenty-three

Jeremy crumpled William's urgent missive in his fist. Harold had escaped to Escomb, taking refuge in his fortress, and William planned to lay siege to it by week's end, regardless of the weather. His promised week's rest would be only three days. He and Jason Warrick had orders to report to camp in the morning.

That was, if Jason lived to ride on the morrow, Jeremy pondered darkly as he caught sight of his confederate entering the hall with Alicen on his arm. The pair laughed and talked as if fast friends.

That thought stabbed. As he strode across the hall toward them, Jeremy saw Jason help Alicen from her wet cloak, giving it and his own to a servant before again offering her his arm. She flashed Jason a smile and tucked her hand into the crook of his elbow. It took all Jeremy's self-control not to bellow for them to cease being so...so...familiar. He'd worked himself into a near rage by the time he intercepted them.

"Warrick, I need a word with you," he stated harshly. Shooting Alicen a glare, he added, "Alone."

Jason turned to Alicen with a surprised look that melted into a captivating grin. "Leave it to Blaine to deprive me of your company, Mistress, but I feel this has the smell of import about it." He covered the hand she rested on his elbow with his free one. "Please allow me the first dance with you this eventide?"

Alicen laughed. "Well you know there'll be no dancing tonight."

"A pity, that," Warrick said, "as Christmas is but two days off. I grow tired of just the yule log burning in the great hearth. We must needs have dancing."

Alicen glanced at Jeremy before saying, "'Tis grim business we've all been about for so long. It bleeds the soul of happiness."

"There's truth to that," Jeremy growled. "But until this war ends, there'll be little of consequence to celebrate." He crooked a brow at Warrick. "If you will?" Turning, he walked out, with Jason Warrick right behind him.

Alicen watched the two soldiers stride off. She appreciated Jason's humor. Although he often didn't consider the consequences of his actions beforehand, his heart was merry, and he made her laugh. Also, she enjoyed being treated as his friend.

And though Jason turned most every woman's head, he was not as handsome in Alicen's opinion as her heart's desire. Both men stood the same height, but Jeremy's massive shoulders were nearly a handsbreadth wider than Jason's broad ones. Jason carried his size well, yet Jeremy's fluid grace made Warrick look almost awkward.

Alicen's throat constricted. She loved Jeremy with all her heart, but terror in thinking of him possibly dying in combat clutched her vitals, made her weak with dread. Made her deny her love to protect her soul should something happen to him. Sweet Jesu, what a coil this was! Thinking of the babe that grew within her calmed her somewhat. She would have to be brave for their child.

***

As soon as they were out of sight and hearing of those in the great hall, Jeremy rounded on Warrick.

"What were you about just now with the healer?" he snarled.

Jason blinked. "Naught of import, man. We met by chance at the gate."

"And I surmise you gallantly escort—on your arm—any and all you meet at the gate?"

"She said she'd been in the village," Warrick stated with a shrug. "I'd been riding patrol. We returned the same time. So, we rode to the stable, the rain caught us in the courtyard, and we had to run for the keep. Naught else."

"Warrick, I'm warning you, stay away from Alicen Kent."

"To what do you refer?" Warrick's tone had hardened.

"I witnessed your entrance into the hall just now. You made untoward advances."

Jason's face flushed. "I shared a jest with the woman! Where's the harm in that?"

"I know your whoring ways, Warrick. But be advised—do not play this lady false."

"Play false?" Sudden realization lit Jason's eyes. "You stubborn ass. I've no designs upon your lady."

"You'll stop at very little to lure a woman to your bed. But give Alicen a wide path."

"She is capable of deciding for herself. What claim do you have to her?"

Jeremy felt the color drain from his face, and he dropped his voice to a threatening rumble. "If you misuse her, I'll kill you."

Warrick started to laugh, but sobered instantly. "So that's where the wind sits. Still, you o'erreach yourself to say I've poached on a private sanctuary." He raised a deprecating brow. "I enjoy Mistress Kent's company. She's a pleasant, learned woman, quite unlike the courtiers you and I have tupped in the past. I've no wish to fight you over a wench, nor is my intent to seduce the healer. If, however, she finds she also enjoys my company, I'll do naught to discourage her."

He started to smile, but Jeremy's fisted blow wiped that expression from his face and stretched him out on his back on the flagstones. He stared up stupidly at Jeremy.

"Heed me well, villain! Slake your lust with Alicen, and you'll die by my hand. I swear it." Jeremy held himself rigid to quell the urge to beat Jason senseless. Several labored breaths calmed him further before he said, "William has ordered us to ride at dawn. The siege of Escomb begins at week's end."

He said no more, but stepped over Jason's inert body and strode back to the hall.

***

Alicen rose from her seat as Jeremy neared the high table, yet her question died unasked when she saw his look. Something was terribly wrong. He did not speak to her or even glance her way, but crossed the hall in stony silence to sit with Michael Taft, who'd arrived from William's camp just before dusk.

"The captain looks furious." Rhea sat beside Ned and Liza on Alicen's right. "What mishap sparked such venom?"

"I know not. He stormed up, demanded a private word with Captain Warrick, and left with him." Alicen paused, then her eyes widened. "Where is Warrick? I fear the two have come to blows."

"They would never fight," Ned insisted. "They're friends."

"Friends or no, intuition tells me that is what happened." She gently touched Ned's shoulder. "I'll return anon."

Alicen found Jason sitting propped against the passage wall, cradling his head in his hands.

"Captain, what befell you?" She knelt. "Are you badly hurt?"

Jason raised his gaze with an effort and stared bleary-eyed at her.

"I fell and hit my head," he muttered, recoiling from the touch of her hand. "'Tis naught to concern you, Mistress."

From the purplish mark spreading across his jaw, Alicen doubted the truth of his statement, but she had no desire to have her suspicions confirmed. "Can you stand?"

"If you assist me."

She helped him gain his feet, then saw he'd be unable to walk alone and leaned him back against the wall. "Stay here. I must get some men to aid you."

She hurried back to the hall and enlisted the services of the two nearest soldiers, leading them to where Jason swayed on wobbly legs, and giving instructions for them to put him to bed.

"I'll see to him in the morning," she added.

"Gone on the morrow," he muttered. "Leave for Escomb."

"What?" Alicen's voice was sharper than she realized.

"We ride at dawn," he stated with a bit more clarity.

His words sent ice through her blood. Jeremy would return to the field on the morrow. Chills assailed her at the thought. She tried to force her fears back into the cell in her heart where she'd locked them, but failed. He'd be fighting, perhaps bleeding or—.

Suddenly, she realized she stood alone in the passageway. The soldiers had already helped Captain

Warrick to his bed.

***

Jeremy, glaring at the small group from Sherford, watched as Alicen quickly departed. His anger deepened. Her concern for Warrick prompted her to search for the blackguard. Jeremy clenched his flagon of ale so tightly his knuckles whitened.

Why should I be angered, he told himself. *The woman has never responded in kind to my declarations of love. She keeps me always at bay with her sharp tongue and quick wit.*

He swallowed the drink without tasting it, observing Alicen's return. When she again left, this time with two soldiers, he followed, arriving in time to overhear Warrick tell her of the siege. Was her obvious pallor caused by concern for Jason? Or for him?

"Are you lost, Mistress?"

The sudden sound of Jeremy's voice behind her made Alicen jump. She whirled to face him. "Do you enjoy startling people, Captain?" she snapped. Her anger surprised her, especially since her fear for him had her near collapse.

His brow raised mockingly. "I merely asked if you were lost. What is so startling about such a question?"

Not knowing how to answer, she blurted out, "I didn't expect to find you here."

"Did you expect to find Jason Warrick?"

His cold tone momentarily numbed her, then her temper rose. "If you must know, I came to see what befell him." She glared. "He'd been stunned...He said from falling and striking his head. I had two men-at-arms help him to his room." She wanted to accuse Jeremy of striking Jason, but her anger died as she saw unfathomed sadness in Jeremy's eyes. What was amiss with him?

"I seem capable of naught else but convincing you I'm a villain," he said bitterly, avoiding her look. "Have I been so cruel that you cannot abide my presence? You share a jest with Warrick, yet hiss like a wet cat when I'm near."

His pained expression wrenched her heart. "Jeremy, that's untrue, I—"

"Am I such a monster you must protect yourself from

me?" he asked hoarsely. "Am I, Alicen?"

Reaching out, she touched his arm and felt the coiled tension of hard muscles beneath her fingertips. He seemed ready to fly asunder. How could she explain that his presence made her go weak inside, that she feared only her reaction to him, not anything he would do to her? Her mouth went dry.

"I protect myself from fear you'll not return," she stated with quiet anguish. She felt him start, saw his gaze swing to hers. "I fear for your safety. And I fear you may not desire me enough to come back for me."

Groaning, he enveloped her in a fierce embrace, holding her so close she thought she'd melt into his body. His heart pounded against her breast, his heated breath brushed her cheek. She wished more than anything to stay in his embrace.

"I swore I'd return," he stated, face buried in her hair. "What more do you wish?"

"For you to keep your promise."

In response, his lips swooped down on hers in a heated, passionate kiss that shook her to her soul. Then he was lifting her in his arms and bearing her swiftly to his chamber.

***

A fortnight later, Alicen awoke before dawn from the grip of a terrifying dream. Wiping sweat from her face, she rose and dressed, then went to pace the battlements. A foreboding sky greeted her as she gazed toward Escomb, and she knew with certainty something terrible would soon occur.

Mother, I've had a premonition. Can you tell me what it means? There was no answer, and Alicen concentrated harder, sending her urgent thoughts toward Landeyda, where she assumed her mother's spirit would be. Still, Kaitlyn's voice remained silent. Did this mean her premonition would come true?

Too anxious to eat, Alicen forced herself to return to the hall for a draught of mulled wine. The warm drink did little to assuage the cold fear engulfing her.

The siege of Harold's stronghold had commenced as planned, and already William's troops anticipated victory. Led by Jason Warrick, a group of knights had managed to poison Escomb's water supply. The weather then turned dry, and the inhabitants of the castle were now severely short of potable liquids. Casualties had dropped considerably since then, allowing Alicen time to venture into Durham village to treat the townspeople. Common maladies kept her mind focused on matters other than military strategy.

But not entirely. When she thought of the deaths Escomb's inhabitants would suffer if they chose not to surrender, her skin grew clammy with horror. Pray God Harold would not hold out against William until such an atrocity occurred. But Harold was a warrior, Alicen reflected grimly. Warriors fought to their last gasp. Duty, honor and courage meant more to them than life.

The morning passed with excruciating slowness, and she felt the entire time as if a vice crushed her chest. Certain Jeremy was about to suffer some misfortune made awaiting word of the troops more agonizing by the moment. She paced and fretted, unable to lose herself in her work or ease a stifling anxiety. Her actions more than once drew Antonio's questioning look. But by keeping her own council she avoided articulating any of her fears. Since no comforting words would soothe the dread enveloping her, she remained silent.

Until midday.

Alicen stood leaning against a window embrasure in Durham's south tower, staring fixedly at the countryside. She snapped to attention when a sudden chill breeze engulfed her.

Go, Alicen. You are needed.

"Mother? Why didn't you speak of this earlier?"

Go to him.

Indecision vanished with her mother's command, and Alicen raced into the hall, seeking Rhea. The midwife sat at a table with Pearl and Liza as the latter nursed her baby.

"Where is Ned?" Alicen asked breathlessly.

Rhea gave her a curious look. "In his chamber, fetching the babe a poppet he fashioned. He'll return anon." Looking up, she added, "Ah, here he is."

The boy grinned when he saw Alicen, but the expression faded as he looked at her. "Is aught amiss?"

"Sit here," she indicated a spot on the bench beside Rhea. "I have much to speak of and little time."

Her friends listened silently as Alicen outlined her plan, and no one spoke for a long moment after she finished.

"I'm going with you," Ned finally stated resolutely.

"And I," Rhea added. "Such a trip is too dangerous to attempt alone."

Alicen shook her head. "Nay, I cannot put either of you in jeopardy. I must go to Escomb, but I'll not risk you as well."

"But how will you survive without protection?" Liza asked, eyes huge with fear. "There are armies in the field!"

"I'll dress in man's attire and hope none challenge me," she replied simply. "And I'll not stop long enough to encourage trouble." She looked around at the circle of stricken faces, not daring to tell them she feared her mother's silence that morning had been to protect Alicen from some terrible event. "I must go. Here, I cannot attend my duties properly, especially not knowing if Jeremy..." Her voice trailed off as she held back her thoughts. Speaking them could bring disaster.

"Let me go with you," Ned begged. "I could help you, even protect you. Brigands are less apt to attack two travellers. Besides, you may need my assistance at the battlefield."

"Nay, lad, 'tis too dangerous for you."

"But not for you?" The boy's mouth set in a grim line.

Alicen saw stubborn determination suddenly light Ned's eyes, and she sighed. Some of her headstrong ways had doubtless been conveyed to her apprentice. There'd be no keeping him at Durham now he knew her plans. "Come with me if you will, but we must leave now. Every moment counts, and we have a hard ride ahead."

"How may we help?" Rhea asked.

Alicen bit her lip in thought. "Mayhap one of the wounded will say where William's army is located, if the question is couched properly. We need to know so we don't run afoul of the enemy. Meet me in the infirmary when you have the information. I need to assemble my instruments and supplies." With a nod, Rhea rose and Alicen looked to Liza, who'd been hanging on every word of the conversation. "Could you see to some food for us?"

"Aye," the young mother answered, handing the boy to Pearl. "I'll pack enough for several days. Who knows what the troops are eating in the field?" She bustled off toward the kitchens.

"Ned, saddle our horses and bring them 'round to the side gate. If anyone asks, say we're off to the village to deliver a babe and will not return for some time."

The apprentice could barely contain his excitement. "I'll be ready in a quarter hour."

"Good. That will provide me enough time to pack clothes and supplies." Alicen stared moodily after the departing boy.

Did she endanger him? Ned wanted so to please, to learn her craft. That he could be injured in the process chilled her. Yet, she'd said he could accompany her, and her word was her bond. She laid a gentle hand on Pearl's shoulder. "You've the most crucial task of all, sweet lass." When the girl's blue eyes turned on her in wonder, Alicen said, "You must keep Liza, Rhea and the babe safe until Ned and I return."

Pearl nodded, an awed look on her face at the responsibility heaped upon her frail shoulders.

***

A shouted challenge forced Alicen and Ned to rein their lathered mounts to a halt. They had ridden hard the entire six leagues to Escomb. In truth, she doubted she could have pushed Hercules much further at the pace she'd kept. Ned's horse nearly staggered with fatigue. Yet their grueling ride put them at William's first outpost at mid-afternoon. A good sign.

She pulled back the hood of her cloak. Recognizing her immediately, the sentinel waved both riders on toward the encampment. They had no difficulty finding William's tent. The Duke of Tynan's scarlet banner hung at the entrance, and two armed guards flanked the opening. William, clad in battle armor, was just leaving his quarters.

"Alicen!" He could not mask his surprise, but this promptly became elation. "And Ned! What brings the two of you here?"

Suddenly embarrassed by her impulsive deed, she

flushed. Were she not still mounted and looking down on her lord, she'd have felt only as tall as his knee. How to explain to him what had prompted this misadventure? William forestalled her reply by offering his hand to dismount, but once she stood beside him, she could no longer avoid telling her fears. She hoped that no real reason existed for such terror.

She caught a deep breath, then said hesitantly, "We, that is, I, feared something dreadful had occurred, and we—"

Tumult on the road from Escomb drew everyone's attention. Alicen turned to look over her shoulder in the direction of the din. What she saw made her heart quaver. The troops of York and Tynan were returning from battle—fatigued, sullied, bloodied.

But a single image arrested her attention, causing her to nearly swoon. Charon, trappings and caparison covered with blood, was being led by a grim-faced Michael Taft.

The charger's saddle was empty.

With an anguished cry, she rushed headlong into the crush of troops, heedless of the massed soldiers, horses, and equipment of war. In a few painful moments she stood at Taft's stirrup.

"Lieutenant?" Her expression completed the question.

He looked astonished at her presence but managed to gesture toward the wagons of casualties. "He's badly wounded, Mistress. We had to put him on a litter."

Without reply, she hurried toward the injured men. It took just moments to locate Jeremy. Then, she had to fight a wave of nausea that threatened to debilitate her completely.

The sight of him blood-soaked from neck to left hip brought a panic subdued only by forcing herself to assess his injury as a healer would. Seeing him only as a patient, not as the man she loved, steadied her. She'd treated more grievous wounds, but would need a clear head to save this life. Emotion could not interfere in her decisions.

He lay semi-conscious, a crossbow bolt protruding from just beneath his left collarbone. Blood trickled from under a rag bound over his temple. Someone had removed his breastplate, and Alicen observed that his chain mail had prevented the bolt from penetrating through his body. Most likely, pieces of metal were embedded in the wound, but the greatest danger was loss of blood. He could ill afford to lose more of such a precious commodity.

"I didn't remove the quarrel," Taft said from beside her. "I feared he'd bleed to death before we got him here."

The strain in Taft's voice only echoed Alicen's dread. If, as she suspected, the point had struck an artery, Jeremy could be dead within minutes.

"Good thinking, Lieutenant," she responded with outward calm. "Let's get him to his tent. Ned?"

The boy, too, was at her shoulder, pale but showing a brave front. "Shall I fetch a brazier?"

"Aye, lad. We must cauterize the wound immediately."

Her apprentice had brought her bag of instruments. Taking it, she followed the men bearing Jeremy. Once they had him on his pallet, she set to work carefully packing wads of bandages around the quarrel and holding them tight to Jeremy's flesh.

"Lieutenant, remove his mail while I control the bleeding. Roll it up like cloth, then lift it over the bolt. The shaft mustn't penetrate any deeper." She glanced at her apprentice. "Are the instruments ready?"

"Anon."

She nodded to Taft, and he swiftly but carefully rolled the thigh-length mail up his captain's body. Although the wadding she held to the wound was soaked with blood, it was flowing steadily, not pulsing. Praise to God.

"Ned, come hold this bandage in place." She exchanged the boy's hands on the cloth for hers, then readied her irons. "Michael, we'll need two or three more men to hold him steady."

Taft's shout brought Malcolm Fish and two others. They each seized one of Jeremy's healthy limbs while Taft pinned Jeremy's body to the pallet and Alicen removed the quarrel.

Jeremy's cry voiced the agony of the damned when she cauterized his wound, but the men kept him supine, and she quickly had the bleeding stopped. The wound wasn't as severe as she'd feared, but he'd lost a tremendous amount of blood on the return from Escomb. She shuddered to think what would have happened if

Ned and she hadn't arrived when they did.

Thank you, Mother, she silently voiced.

She applied ointment to the wound and left it unbandaged to monitor possible bleeding. It took only moments to stitch closed Jeremy's scalp laceration and bind it with a clean cloth. His blood-soaked shirt had been tossed to the tent floor. She would leave his hose for Robert, his squire, to remove later.

Bending down from the small stool on which she sat, Alicen lifted the ruined shirt to hand to Robert. An object fell atop Jeremy's hauberk. His dagger. She bent to pick it up, then examined it with a start.

All color drained from her face. Her eyes betrayed her! Embedded in the dagger's hilt were the same stones set in the same pattern as those in the amulet which never left her neck...She gasped. Then a breeze ruffled her hair, and her mother's voice spoke.

You were fated to be together, Daughter. But you must convince him you can love a soldier. That he does, indeed, hold your heart.

"Oh, Jeremy," she whispered, choked with emotion. Then, realizing there were others present, she slid the dagger into her sleeve, rose and turned to the gathered soldiers. "Thank you all for your assistance." Her voice shook from anxiety and wonder. "If he lives, you have yourselves to credit."

The men voiced protests at her claim, but she waved them from the tent with the admonition that they had, indeed, saved their captain's life. Then she returned to the pallet. Reaching into her sleeve, she withdrew the dagger and squeezed the scabbard tight in her hand. *Love me enough to live, Jeremy.*

Twenty-Four

Pain penetrated Jeremy's dulled mind and pulled him to cognizance as Alicen sat down at his side. Weak and disoriented, he made no meaning of the fact that she was in his tent near the battlefield. A grim smile touched his lips.

"Did I not keep my promise to return?" he asked rasped. "Harold's man was not much of a bowman, for I still live."

Alicen blanched, and abruptly clasped her hands in her lap. "Please, don't speak thus." Her voice was husky. "You could have been killed."

He blinked several times, then said slowly, "Should I die, you may return to Landeyda and your own life. Without such soldiers as I to plague you, your current miseries will cease." He turned his head to stare at the tent wall. "Leave me to die, Alicen. Return to your home."

"Nay!" Alicen grasped Jeremy's chin and swung his face toward her, then caressed his cheek. "Why do you speak thus?"

His eyes were clouded by physical and emotional pain. "You endure hell...slaving in this infirmary...My fault...responsible for your suffering."

"Suffering? I don't—"

His gaze momentarily cleared. "No lies, Alicen. Truth. You'll fare better with me gone."

She bit her lip and blinked back tears. "Would I treat your wounds if I did not seek your recovery?"

"Healers can do naught else."

He was too disoriented to understand his words, or hers. Seizing his hand, she held it over her heart. "I would feel no differently were I not what I am."

Alicen carefully folded the blanket back away from his injury. She brushed dark, tumbled hair from his forehead, her heart swelling as she gazed down at his pale features.

"I love you, Jeremy Blaine," she murmured. "You'll

never drive me away."

As much as she wished to stay beside her fallen knight, others needed her. Ned was eager to sit with the captain, and Robert, Jeremy's squire, stood ready to report on any change in condition.

She returned to the tent only after darkness prevented her from adequately treating anyone else. Ned had fallen asleep on the floor, so Alicen made a pallet of cloaks, coaxed him onto them, and covered him with a mantle. Robert slept in a corner.

Removing only her boots, she slid under Jeremy's blanket and curled up against his side. Her arm carefully wrapped about his waist, she used her body's warmth to alleviate his chills. She kissed his temple, whispered an affirmation of her love, then gave over to sleep.

At dawn, Alicen rose to find the tent's other occupants still asleep. She hurried to the stream for her morning ablutions and went to find food. Cooks were already preparing the morning's fare in large kettles. Nodding to them, she filled two wooden bowls with porridge and carried them to the tent.

Ned was just stirring when she arrived, and her waving the bowl of warm food beneath his nose served to bring him wide awake. His brown eyes snapped open.

"How is the captain?" he asked immediately, gaze shifting to the pallet where Jeremy lay.

"He spent a quiet night. Most likely he'll sleep the sun around. Will you tend him again?"

Ned nodded assent as he ate. Finishing the porridge, he wiped his mouth on the back of his sleeve. "I'll send for you if aught should go amiss."

***

Night had again fallen, and Alicen was carrying bowls of stew to Ned and Robert when her apprentice burst from Jeremy's tent. Pausing only long enough to locate her, he rushed forward, dark eyes burning with urgency.

"Come quickly! 'Tis Captain Blaine. He and Warrick fight!"

"Fight?" Jeremy was wounded, why would Warrick fight with him?

Ned grasped her arm, causing her to spill some of their supper. "Hurry! You must stop them!"

Still confounded, she nonetheless dropped both bowls of stew and followed Ned at a run. Upon entering the tent, the sight before her made her breath stop entirely.

Jeremy, naked but for his bandages and the sling supporting his left arm, was being wrestled to the floor by Warrick. Taft and another soldier stood by as if ready to help subdue Jeremy. Outraged that they treated their injured comrade so callously, Alicen fairly flew across the tent toward the melee.

"Merciful Jesus, what are you doing?" she cried. "Release him this instant!" She bent swiftly to examine Jeremy, then glared up at the others. "The wound has reopened. What were you thinking?"

Her sharp tone chastened the men, and they dropped their gazes to the ground.

"He insisted upon going to find you," Jason muttered miserably. "But I didn't think he should be up and about—"

"He's out of his head with delirium," she cut in acidly. "All he required was a draught to make him sleep. Now, could you please assist him back to his pallet?"

"No," Jeremy protested, struggling weakly as they lifted him. "I'll not lie down." Shaking off the men's hands, he stood swaying, then grabbed Alicen's arm for support. The bulging vein at his temple gave evidence of his agitation. "You must leave," he said, gasping. "Too dangerous here. I'm responsible. Return to Durham...Landeyda."

She knew his strong will was all that kept him standing.

"Hush." Placing her hand flat against his broad chest, she kept her eyes on his face. "We'll discuss this when you lie down so I may see to your injuries." Gently, she guided him toward his pallet.

He resisted but couldn't break from her grasp. "You mustn't remain. I'll not let you. Durham is safe...must return now—"

"I'll be here as long as I'm of use, Captain. You cannot force me to leave." She eased him down, pulled the blanket up to his waist, and began assessing the damage caused by his struggle.

Alicen's sincerity penetrated Jeremy's lethargic mind,

made him hope she truly cared. But darkness beckoned. There was much he must say, yet speech eluded a tongue that grew more unwieldy by the moment. He closed his eyes, attempting to concentrate his strength, and caught her elbow with his hand. "So many hurt...need attention...your care. I don't want you..." his voice faltered, and his chest heaved with the effort to speak.

"All the wounded at Durham are being tended," she softly assured him. Over her shoulder, she said to Ned, "I'll need my instruments. And bring the captain some wine."

Catching her look, Ned went to fill a chalice, then poured in an ample measure of Alicen's sleeping draught.

"Drink this," she instructed Jeremy when the boy returned. "'Twill ease your discomfort." Supporting his head, she helped him drain the dregs, then laid him back onto the pillow. "Now sleep."

He kept his grasp on her. "Promise to leave before you're injured," he pleaded. "Dangerous here. You cannot stay. Promise me."

"You've no choice in whether I tend you, and I'll not leave 'til your recovery's certain. If you wish to argue this, we'll do so on the morrow. For now, gather your wits and rest."

"Promise..."

He slept. Alicen had Taft restrain Jeremy on the chance he would flinch as she began to probe his wound. To her relief, she saw that the artery she'd cauterized still held. Blood seeped only from small vessels. Wondering at the cause of the bleeding, she took her thinnest blade and carefully probed for the source. Several shards of steel left in his wound from his chain mail were the cause.

Alicen felt her mouth go dry. Had those tiny pieces of metal remained in his body, Jeremy could very well have died of infection. Her concern for him had nearly cost his life, as her haste to cauterize the main vessel had likely made her careless in finding and removing debris from the wound. She thanked God and Jason Warrick for their intervention. Had Jeremy and Jason not fought, chances were good she'd never have re-examined his wound. That would have proven fatal. Now, so long as the cauterization held, Jeremy stood an excellent chance of recovering.

Taft left as she finished closing the original wound with two stitches. After covering Jeremy with a blanket, she caressed the rough stubble on his cheek. Just looking at him brought a slow fire in her belly that spread languidly throughout her body.

He wanted her to return to Landeyda. But she could not imagine life there without him, even with their child to remind her of their love. Once, she had indulged herself in the dream of putting war's carnage behind and returning to her quiet life at home. Now a future there alone loomed bleak. Could she bind this heartsick warrior to her side for life? She meant to try.

When she rose from Jeremy's pallet, she saw Jason Warrick standing at the tent's entrance, expression stricken. He straightened at her approach.

"Mistress Kent, please accept my apology—"

Her hand on his arm stopped him. "Nay, Captain, 'tis I who should apologize." Despite her fatigue, she smiled. "I had no cause to so abuse your concern. Forgive my sharpness. It has been a hellish day, and I fear I'm near exhaustion."

"Jeremy will recover, will he not?"

"With good fortune, he should be abed a week at most."

Jason's relief burst through in a huge grin before he sobered. "I could not have lived with myself had I injured him more severely."

"I'm certain he'll suffer no major setback." She paused. "Thank you for intervening today." At Jason's incredulous look, she added, "Had he not begun bleeding again, those pieces of mail I missed at first would have caused a dangerous, likely fatal, infection." She smiled. "Your fight with him probably saved his life."

Jason shook his head in amazement, then crooked his arm to her. "May I see you to Duke William's tent?"

"Thank you, but I'd prefer to stay here, close to Jeremy."

"God give ye rest." Poised to leave, he hesitated, turning to her once again. "Mere gratitude palls at all you've done for us. There must needs be a more fitting reward for your services."

"I need no reward," she replied with a shrug. "Healing is my calling, and a patient's recovery truly is ample payment."

Jason raised her hand to his lips and kissed her knuckles. "You're remarkable."

Blushing, she looked away. "Nay, not at all."

"Jeremy spoke true when he said we'll not see your like again." Alicen started in surprise at his words, but he didn't seem to notice. "To my mind, the man loves you more than life, though he may not have told you such. Since his previous misfortunes with women he loved, he has kept his heart well-guarded."

He has pledged his devotion to me, Captain, Alicen thought bleakly. *'Tis I who've been unable to speak my thoughts to him.*

"Seek your own rest, Mistress Kent." Jason gave her shoulder a quick squeeze, then opened the tent flap. "Good night. Again my thanks to you. You're an angel of mercy."

"I prize your faith in me," she returned with a slight smile. *And especially Jeremy's faith.* "Sleep well, Captain."

"And you, Mistress."

She tied the tent flap closed, then froze, powerless to move as Jason's words rang in her head—*He loves you more than life.*

Could a soldier love a woman above duty and combat? Above living? She shuddered at the realization that, though she'd loved Jeremy for some time, she'd not told him such. Fear of abandonment prevented her from risking her heart. Yet, he'd risked reopening his wounds to see to her safety.

'Twas time to put aside her fears for a chance at happiness. Her mother's words rang in her head: "You are destined to be together." The dagger and amulet proved that. If Jeremy died knowing naught of her love, she would live with that horror always. If he lived yet left, at the least he would leave knowing she cared for him.

And their child?

Nay, she'd not use the babe to bind him to her if he was of a mind to go. If he found another woman to love and take to wife, Alicen would raise their child alone. But not in secret. Once Jeremy had regained his lands and settled in, he would know of their offspring. Alicen would never deny him as much opportunity to be part of the child's life as he wished.

She sighed softly and sat down on the pallet to remove her boots. At the first opportunity, she would declare her feelings. Then, let fate do what it might, he would know her heart was his for the asking.

***

"This is madness!"

The emerald fire in Alicen's eyes threatened to turn all in Jeremy's tent to cinder. No one could meet the intensity of her stare, and five grown men—hardened warriors all—avoided eye contact with the enraged woman who paced before them.

With a resigned sigh, Jeremy caught her by the shoulders and stopped her agitated movement. When she lowered her head and refused to look at him, he gave her a gentle shake.

"Be reasonable, lass," he said calmly.

Her head shot up and she glared at him. "You ride into combat little more than a week after suffering grievous wounds, yet question *my* reason?" Pushing his hands away, she stepped back. "How dare you accuse me of being unreasonable!"

"You removed my stitches yesterday," he countered. "And said I heal quickly."

"I didn't say you'd healed enough to return to battle. Should that wound reopen, you could bleed to death in moments."

"Aye, and I could bleed to death from your sharp tongue even as I stand here."

Alicen chose to ignore that set down, but her chin raised a fraction. Then, noting the stubborn tilt of Jeremy's jaw and his determination to see this challenge through, she turned angrily on the others in the tent. Her look fell first upon William.

"My lord duke, you'll stand by and let an injured man defend your honor?" Her quiet tone only served to emphasize her ire. "You've no healthy knight to ride in his place?"

William's face flamed, but his voice was firm when he replied, "Harold's challenge was champion against champion. Sir Jeremy is my man."

Alicen nodded slowly, as if absorbing a new and unique bit of information. "And the Duke of York has no champion to ride for his banner?" She slanted her gaze at the young man standing beside William.

"I do, but my knight has never defeated Sir Jeremy," Duke Richard stated gravely. "Even though they once fought when Captain Blaine was injured."

The other men muttered their confirmation of this fact.

Alicen shook her head. "Why dare I think warriors would heed a physician's counsel? 'Tis unconscionable to send a weakened man to fight, yet you'll do so in a wink. And all for honor." She felt tears burn the backs of her eyes, and abruptly wished only to escape.

But before she could move, Jeremy encircled her waist with his arms and gathered her close. "Leave us," he quietly told the others.

"Release me!" she ordered, struggling to break free.

Her actions only served to see her held tighter. Jeremy's strong chest pressed against her back, and the firm yet still gentle tightening of his embrace warned she'd not escape without using a weapon. And she had none to use, were she inclined to do so. Still refusing to acquiesce to his superior strength, she made an attempt to twist away. Her efforts failed.

"Be still, minx," he ordered, his mouth so close to her ear his breath teased her. "You and I must needs talk."

Shoulders slumped in dejection, she said in a choked voice, "I have spoken my piece, and you've not listened. I've naught left to say."

"I've heard every word you've uttered—"

"And yet you'll ride out to fight." She choked back a sob, hating her weakness, hating his seeing her so vulnerable.

Leaning down, he placed a soft kiss on her temple. "That is my duty," he stated simply. "Yet 'twill never change my love for you."

"Love!" Summoning all her strength, she wrenched from his arms and spun on him, enraged. "How dare you say you love me, then put yourself in such danger?" Trembling uncontrollably, she stepped away when he reached for her. "Don't touch me! You declare your love, yet won't consider what will happen to me or even to Ned should you die in battle." Tears blurred her vision and choked her voice, but she managed to add, "I'll not remain to watch you fight, Jeremy. Ride against Harold's champion, and I'll be gone when you return."

Anger mixed with pain hit Jeremy like a fist to his chest. "So that's the lay of things. I implored you to leave for safety's sake, but you'd not. Now, you're more than happy to."

"I stayed because you needed me. Now, all you need is your glory."

She buried her face in her hands in a vain attempt to stem her tears. This time, when Jeremy enfolded her in his arms, she made no effort to free herself. Instead, she laid her head on his chest and sobbed.

He rubbed her back and shoulders, whispering soothing words, easing the tension in her body.

"Ah, my sweet, stubborn minx," he crooned, continuing his ministrations. "How can I make you understand what duty compels me to do?"

Lifting her head from his chest, she fixed him with glistening eyes. "You cannot make me grasp such reasoning. Does duty compel you to die, Jeremy?"

He shook his head, then brushed away her tears with gentle fingers. "Nay, sweetling. But I must fight. Single combat will spare men's lives, not to mention the women and children who now suffer inside Escomb's walls."

Alicen's mind returned to a similar scene in which he had fought another to spare more casualties, and abruptly pride in his selflessness warred with her fear for his life.

"Too much strain could reopen your wound," came her fierce whisper. "If such should happen..." She lowered her head back to his chest, trembling. "I cannot bear the agony of witnessing this. I intend to leave this place of death as swiftly as Hercules will carry me."

Jeremy's body tensed at her words. "Am I naught to you but a faceless victim who requires tending?" he grated out. "Do you feel for me as for any man with guts in hands, pleading that you make him whole again?"

"Nay." Her arms slid around his slim waist to lock behind his back. "I've given myself to you. None other.

Does that not tell you of my regard?"

He held her closer. "You've never spoken of such feelings, lass. What am I to think?"

"You've stolen my heart, Sir Jeremy Blaine. And now you make sport with it by risking your life unnecessarily."

His hand beneath her chin lifted her face to his. "I do not sport with what I hold dear," he said, then brushed her lips with a kiss. "Just as I do not sport with my life by entering into combat. Do not demand that out of love for you I withdraw from the field. I'll do so if you ask. Yet this is the swiftest way to end the war and regain all. All I want to share with you."

Her heartbeat accelerated alarmingly at his declaration. But caution made her ask, "You mean to share your bed with me as your mistress?"

"I mean to share that and far more with you as my *wife*."

"I, marry a soldier?" she mocked, trying to make light of her sudden yearning to do that very thing. "Duke William would have me wed a Sherford merchant. You must be mad."

Jeremy shook his head. "Mad, indeed, to think I could truly win your stubborn heart. Know you not that I would gladly die for you?"

"I want no man to lay down his life for mine."

Only the look that briefly flashed in Alicen's eyes kept Jeremy from despair. He'd seen a spark of hope and love shining there for him, and understood that fear he'd be killed kept her from openly committing her heart. He sighed. His headstrong, self-reliant healer would require proof before she accepted that he'd return to live out his days with her.

"I'll not allow you to leave," he stated grimly. "During the challenge, Harold may attempt escape. The roads will not be safe to travel."

"I won't remain here while you fight." Alicen raised her fists and shoved against his chest until he released her. She backed farther away.

He started after her but halted, arrested by her look of pure anguish. Holding both hands toward her in supplication, he said quietly, "Alicen, I need you—"

She jerked as if he'd struck her. "Nay, you do not.

You need your horse and your weapons and your duty, not me." Face bleak, she added, "And I don't need you."

He looked at her with all the tenderness in his heart. "You're wrong, lass. I need you as all living things need food and water." Two steps closed the gap between them, then he reached out both hands to capture her face. "I'll die if we're separated. Those weeks you were at Landeyda and I at Tynan, I was mad with longing. All who approached me risked their lives to do so. And it was all for want of you."

When he caressed the line of her jaw with his long fingers, Alicen's eyelids closed. But her eyes brimmed with tears when she opened them again.

"I've been so long alone, I dare not believe I could be part of someone's life," she said, voice husky. "Should that wish not come true, I'll never recover."

He dropped his hands from her face and gently grasped her shoulders.

"Alicen, look at me," he commanded softly. He waited until her gaze met his before saying, "Today I fight not for William but for you. I hold my duty most dear, and that duty is to see you safe, happily wed to me, and the mother of my children."

His words struck a chord so deep in her she thought she'd collapse from the sensation of it. But before she could respond and tell him of the child she carried, Michael Taft shook the tent flap to gain their attention.

TWENTY-FIVE

Taft peered inside the tent just long enough to say, "Time grows short, Jeremy. We must get you armed."

Jeremy nodded. "Michael, send in Fish, Naismith, Burke and Weed."

He held Alicen close, regretting what he had to do. He'd not risk losing her. Yet, would her affection die from his latest plot? He told himself to have faith, to trust her strong nature. But doubts nagged him.

The soldiers entered.

"Take Mistress Kent and confine her in Duke William's tent 'til my return," he succinctly ordered his men. He ignored Alicen's indignant gasp and her furious expression. He shifted his gaze from the men to the woman in his arms. "You know her to be cleverly resourceful and thus realize you must not be lax in your duties. Know now that, should she escape you, I'll execute you to a man."

"How dare you!" Alicen cried, twisting in his grasp. She sought to strike him, but quickly found her arms pinned behind her. Muttering dark oaths, she thrashed against him until his embrace immobilized her in a crushing hold. "You'll not keep me here against my will," she ground out through clenched teeth. "I'll not stay to see you die."

"Nay, you'll not," he agreed huskily. "You'll stay to see me return in triumph." Burying his face in her hair, he whispered, "Trust me, my lady. Naught of this Earth will keep me from your side." His hold gentled, and she felt him shaking. "Forgive me, love. I'll fight poorly if I fret over you. Confined, you'll be safe, not abroad endangering yourself."

Alicen lifted defiant eyes to him, then straightened in his hold. When he released her, she turned proudly on her heel and left the tent, her escort surrounding her.

Heart leaden, Jeremy called for Taft and Robert, and they immediately set about their battle preparations. As

Michael and the squire helped him into his mail and armor, he flexed his sore shoulder, recalling Alicen's fears. He'd often borne serious injuries into battle—'twas a warrior's way. She saw only danger and pain, not ultimate victory. And this victory would be most sweet—his lands and a life far from war's carnage.

He fervently prayed she'd be part of that life.

"Do you think this will hold?" Taft asked again, this time coupling the question with a shove to Jeremy's sound shoulder. "Cease your woolgathering, man! 'Tis time to fight."

Jeremy's eyes refocused from the future to the present. "What say you, Michael?"

"Will this extra gusset of mail hold in place?"

Glancing down at his left shoulder, Jeremy nodded. "'Tis secured to the arming doublet. I see no reason why it won't."

"The bulk will make your armor fit more tightly," Taft warned. "Will you be able to maneuver with it?"

"Aye. It won't hinder me."

Jeremy rarely bothered protecting an injury. But his promise to provide for Alicen prompted him to add reinforcement. A regretful grimace twisted his lips. Mayhap he'd not have a woman to return to after this day's work. She of a certain resented his callous treatment. But did she resent it enough to refuse his suit?

"Woolgathering again?" Taft cut in caustically. "'Tis no time for aught but the task at hand." He dropped Jeremy's hauberk over his head and buckled his cuirass into place. "Purge the woman from your mind, or you'll not keep your head on your shoulders long enough to think of her ever more."

Jeremy shot his friend an annoyed look. "Don't presume to tutor me, Michael," he growled. "Just get this damned armor secured."

In a few moments more the task was completed. Jeremy strapped his sword to his waist, then took his helmet from Robert.

"Your shield and mace are on your saddle, Sir Jeremy," the young man said respectfully. "Do you require aught else?"

"Just a moment alone, lad."

Taft and the squire had moved to the tent opening when Ned burst in. Jeremy knew he gaped in surprise at this intrusion even as Ned skidded to a halt before him.

"Captain Blaine, thank Jesu you're still here," Ned gasped, breathless from haste. "I was asked to deliver this to you."

Brow raised, Jeremy accepted a leather pouch from the boy's trembling hand. He tousled Ned's blond hair. "Thank you, lad. I—"

"You're not to open it 'til you're alone," Ned broke in when Jeremy's hands moved to the pouch's string. "Please, sir."

Jeremy nodded, then glanced around. "I was just about to be so, Ned. You arrived in the nick of time."

With youthful impetuosity, Ned threw his arms around Jeremy's waist and hugged him, even though unyielding armor kept the man from feeling the embrace.

"Have a care, sir," he intoned softly. "Don't let that evil man hurt you."

Jeremy returned the boy's hug and muttered gruffly, "I've no intention of that happening, lad. Put your mind at rest." Brown eyes full of admiration turned up to his, warming him. "Go to your mistress now. She needs you beside her."

An uncommon dampness teased Jeremy's eyes as he watched Ned depart with the others. He loved the boy like a son. Perhaps he could adopt him. At least foster him. Would Alicen approve? The lump he swallowed turned to a cinder lodged in his heart. Even if she loved him, would they ever wed? She saw a soldier, not a man worthy of her devotion. Mayhap he was a fool to think he could convince her otherwise.

Dismayed, he knelt in front of the small crucifix sitting on the only table in his tent. It was then he remembered the pouch in his hands. Almost absentmindedly, he opened it and reached in to pull out the contents.

His fingers closed around metal, and curious, he drew the object out to examine closely. It was his dagger. He'd not even noticed its absence, must have dropped it during his latest convalescence. But what arrested his sight was wound around the cross-guard.

Alicen's amulet.

His breath caught in his chest as he realized why it had looked familiar to him so many weeks before. It was the exact duplicate of the pattern on his dagger's hilt.

"Christ be praised!" he whispered fervently.

Tears of joy filled his eyes as he bent his head, thanking God for this token of Alicen's love. He'd not thought to see such a thing, especially this day. His prayer done, he put the amulet around his neck and tucked it safely beneath his arming doublet, against his skin. Then he rose and strapped his dagger to his side. He knew her heart was in that amulet, and he would defend it with his life.

The hair on his nape raised suddenly, but the sensation was curiously comforting rather than startling. *Best keep your promise to her, Captain,* whispered Kaitlyn O'Rourke. *She's waiting for you.*

"My word on it," he answered firmly, eyes raised to heaven.

***

Perspiration clung like a caul to Alicen's skin. How long had she awaited word of the combat? It seemed her pacing would wear a path in William's fine Persian rug. Her guards remained outside the tent, one posted at each corner.

Ned had been so excited about the trial of arms that Alicen had allowed him to go to the field. His enthusiasm only made her more keenly aware that her view of such activities differed vastly from others'. And why should it not? After all, it fell to her to mend the results of such folly.

And suffer a terrible loss should Jeremy fail to triumph.

All manner of fears played through her head like the notes of a funeral dirge. She contemplated escaping, but immediately abandoned the idea. Her success would mean death to four innocent men. Jeremy had given his word to execute them, and he'd see it through. No, she had to remain confined until such time as he came to fetch her.

Or returned to her on a bier.

Have faith, Daughter.

"How can I, Mother," Alicen cried in a fierce whisper.

"Father died in battle. You lost your life at a soldier's hands. Soldiers fight and die. Why should I believe Jeremy will live?"

He has your amulet and the power of love to protect him.

"And no other soldier ever died in battle while carrying another's love with him?"

I'll not deny that. But Jeremy has your amulet and his dagger. A potent combination that will protect him this day. You are fated to be together, and no power in the mortal world will interfere with that destiny.

"But how?"

Centuries ago, a Druid high priest had the pieces made for himself from stones considered sacred to the order. The arrangement of those stones in both the dagger and the amulet create a formidable protective force, especially when the two pieces are together.

Intrigued despite her fears for Jeremy, Alicen asked, "How did they come to be separated?"

The legends aren't specific, but some time after the high priest died, the two pieces disappeared. The amulet was found in a cairn in Ireland by your great-great-great-great grandmother, and passed down to her daughter, and thus through our female line to you. I've no idea how Jeremy acquired the dagger, but the legends say the pieces are destined to be together. That's how he came to be at Landeyda.

Alicen shook her head in wonder, barely able to comprehend the import of her mother's words. She struggled with her rampant emotions, paced and prayed, pressed cold fingers to her temples and rubbed chilled arms with icy hands. Naught alleviated her torment.

***

Jeremy stared down at the man sprawled at his feet. Sword tip pressed against the throat exposed beneath the knight's helmet, he asked again, "Do you yield?"

"Aye," came the faintly muffled voice behind the visor.

Jeremy stooped and retrieved his opponent's sword before stepping back to allow him to sit upright. "Then show yourself."

When the plumed helm was removed, the surprised gasp from William's camp carried far in the still air.

"Harold," Jeremy stated quietly, quirking a brow.

"Aye, Blaine," Harold of Stanhope sneered, black eyes glittering hatred. "Who else to fight you? Those dolts I hired are as worthless as tits on a boar."

"A man fights best when he defends his own," Jeremy said on a shrug. "Hirelings have little to lose but their lives. That oft makes living more dear than their lord's ill-gotten lands."

"A warrior philosopher." Harold's contempt revealed itself in his curled lip. "What an accomplished man you are."

"Not nearly as skilled in butchery as you, it seems."

The vanquished knight spewed bloody spittle onto the ground at his conqueror's feet. "You've bested me, Blaine, now finish what you undertook to do."

Jeremy took another step back. "Nay. I've enough blood on my hands without adding yours. You'll find your reckoning in London." He nodded toward the usurper's horse. "But I'll take your steed, and this fine sword." Then he smiled as he added, "And the lands you stole from William that are now rightfully mine."

"If you'd stayed in France another year, I'd have owned all of Tynan." Harold yanked his gauntlets from his hands and threw them to the ground.

"Do you truly believe you'd have kept it?" Having sheathed his own sword, Jeremy gestured with Harold's. "Rise, knave. The dukes of Tynan and York crave a word with you."

Harold rose unsteadily, stood swaying a moment, then straightened. A haughty stare filled his eyes when he spoke. "I'll rot in hell before I let you haul me to London in irons."

Before anyone could move, the conquered knight unsheathed his dagger and drew it across his own throat. A gout of blood issued forth as he collapsed face first on the ground.

"Sweet Jesus," Jeremy cried, dropping Harold's sword and kneeling beside the stricken man. In pure reflex, he shouted, "Fetch Alicen, quickly! Bid her bring her instruments."

A rider was already thundering off toward camp when Jeremy saw that Harold of Stanhope was dead.

***

The sound of hoofbeats reached Alicen's ears, the rumble ending in a scrabbling flurry outside the tent. She was nearly to the opening when she heard a breathless voice cry, "Mistress Kent, come quickly! And bring your medicaments."

She rushed outside, only to find her legs had turned to water. She stumbled toward a rider whose face had become too blurred to recognize, and started to fall. Vaguely, she felt herself being lifted onto a destrier, her medicament satchel slung over her shoulder. She clung blindly to the rider, able to think only that Jeremy was dying. Or dead.

And that her life would end with his.

Her mind was blessedly numb by the time her escort reined in beside the bloody form of a prostrate knight. She slid from the destrier's back, felt herself beginning to swoon, and started to pitch headlong to the ground.

Strong arms caught her and pulled her up against a chest encased in steel. Although she knew she could not stand on her own, she was nonetheless still upright in this man's arms.

"My apologies, kind sir," she muttered, not lifting her head. "I seem to have lost my balance."

Jeremy's embrace tightened and his smile widened, though Alicen could not see it with her face pressed to his shoulder.

"I told you to stay in the tent," he grumbled. He kissed her temple, then with a slight gesture, indicated to a pair of soldiers to remove Harold's body. In the meantime, he blocked Alicen's view of the corpse.

Jeremy's pleasure at holding her was lost on Alicen, but the sound of his voice registered. That alone rent the dam that had held her emotions in check. He was alive! And he had frightened her half to death. She wept uncontrollably, heart-wrenching sobs of agonized relief that unnerved every man on the field.

Jeremy, at a loss to comfort her, responded in the only way certain to gain her reaction. Leaning down, he said in her ear, "Are you so despondent I yet live, Mistress, that you cry thus?"

His words struck with such force that she gasped,

choked back her tears, and glared up at him. Then she pushed back from him as far as his embrace would allow. "I thought you were *dying*, you lout! Why else would I be so hastily summoned?"

"And you wept that your talents were not needed?" He cocked a brow, venturing a wry smile. The sparks in her eyes encouraged him. Lips twitching, he fought a grin. "I should have known such a willful, stubborn woman would disobey my orders."

"Better willful and stubborn than foolishly heroic," Alicen countered acidly, too weak with relief at her love's good health to actually break from his arms. Abrupt concern darkened her eyes, and she looked anxiously at him. "Are you injured?"

"Nay, not in the slightest."

That did it. With a snort of disgust, she pushed free and stepped back, scowling. "Why did your man not tell me you were safe?" she shouted. "I nearly swooned with fear!"

"Fear for my life?" Jeremy asked drolly. Widened eyes added to his amazed expression. "Do you admit to caring for me?"

Alicen clenched her jaw. "Certainly not. Do I appear so foolish?"

Jeremy could not contain his smile. It threatened to crack his face with its breadth. He removed his helmet, tucked it beneath one arm, and pulled his coif off his head. Then he swept her an elegant bow. In his richest tone he declared, "Mistress Kent, I wish to wed you. As well you know, I'm oft in need of a skilled physician, and I am brainsick enough to bind myself to one as headstrong as you."

Alicen was momentarily silent, then she sniffed haughtily. "I care not for the ravings of a lunatic, sir knight. Mayhap a stronger blow from your enemy would have cleared your thinking. Though 'tis doubtful."

He chuckled, but quickly donned his sternest mien. Before she could react, he'd encircled her with an arm and drawn her close. "If I rave, lady, then all the world is mad. For I do want you as my wife."

"And what if I am not of like distemper to wish you as my husband?"

"Then, I'll marry you against your will." The pained look his comment brought made him laugh aloud. "You see, you've little choice in the matter."

"I can highly recommend *Lord* Jeremy Blaine, Mistress," William called from where he sat his palfry at his champion's back. "He brings to this union the largest holding in my duchy—Sherford. And Whitecomb to the north. Though that estate is in need of repair, rest assured the young lord has ample funds to see it done properly."

Jeremy shot William a startled glance. Whitecomb was indeed the gem of Tynan's properties. Abandoned for several years, if run efficiently, it would provide the protection Sherford currently lacked. The thought of such a great estate being his made his heart leap.

William paused only a moment before adding, "He'll truly need a worthy wife to help manage such a holding."

The woman Jeremy held more than deserved the comforts of being lady to such a manor. If he could only convince her of such.

"Best you consent to marry me, Alicen," he growled, squeezing her gently. "No other man among these assembled would take you to wife."

At this, Jason Warrick grunted. "'Tis well known you'd kill any one of us who dared attempt to wed her."

Alicen laughed along with the troops at Warrick's remark, yet refrained from comment on Jeremy's proposal. He offered her his hand, his look that of a boy who sought a gift too wonderful to ever obtain. In that blue gaze she saw the depths of his heart, and hers soared to join it.

But pride demanded reprisal in kind to his barbed offer. Assuming an expression of strained patience, she sighed in mock despair as she laid her palm against his. "I suppose I must needs take you, for, in truth, 'tis no more than my duty to womankind."

Jeremy's black brows drew together. "How so, Mistress?"

"'Tis my burden to save them from your cunning ways," she replied tartly. "Therefore, I'll make sacrifice of myself on the marriage altar, thus ridding the world of one of its plagues."

While the men cheered, Jeremy drew Alicen closer

for a deep kiss. Her arms wound around his neck, then her hand crept to his hair to ruffle it with trembling fingers. Unmindful of their audience, she kissed him soundly.

As the cheering escalated, he broke off the kiss, still clasping Alicen close, and bent his head. "No elixir you could devise would ever cure me of my love for you, lass," he whispered for her ears only.

Alicen felt her eyes fill with tears at his statement. She gently ran her fingers down his cheek and across his lips. "No battle you could fight would ever quell my love for you, sir," she murmured in reply.

Jeremy caught his breath when the meaning of her declaration became clear, saw in her expression her deep regard, and lifted her off her feet to twirl around and around in a giddy dance of adoration.

"Stop," she cried finally, laughter bubbling from her throat. "Put me down, churl."

When he set her again on her feet, to the raucous huzzahs of every soldier, she clung to him to remain upright. Taking advantage of her disorientation, he brushed her lips with a kiss.

"Lord help us," Taft exclaimed. "If we don't separate those two, they'll never pause for breath long enough to endure the nuptials."

Laughing as loudly as anyone else, Jeremy firmly set Alicen away from him and turned to the assemblage.

"Let it not be said that I bore my duty with ill grace," he proclaimed, voice dripping irony. "I'll save this woman from her ill-tempered ways and myself from a life of untended wounds."

"I'll cause many of those wounds, if you don't temper your loutish manner," Alicen pronounced, cuffing him on the arm.

"What? Mend my ways and lose my favorite jousting partner?" He rubbed the spot where she'd struck his armor. "Nay, I look forward to your sharp tongue and your tender care of my hurts."

Abruptly solemn, she whispered, "May my sharp tongue be all that cuts you for ever more."

"I intend it to be," Jeremy replied, kissing her yet again.

When he broke the embrace, Alicen's eyes held only

concern. "You're certain you've not been injured."

"Aye, but you could ascertain for yourself." He winked. "In my tent. After all, even a physician of your skills cannot detect wounds hidden beneath armor."

His heated look sent ripples through Alicen's belly. "Then best we see to your needs anon," she murmured, breathless.

***

Escomb's walls were silhouetted by blazing sunset as Alicen and Jeremy sat atop a rise overlooking William's camp. Cook fires held back the encroaching dusk, and the laughter and songs of the victorious troops carried on a breeze to the lovers' lookout.

Jeremy leaned back against the oak on the crest and beckoned Alicen into his arms. "It grows cold, lass. Let me warm you."

She needed no second invitation, but moved onto his lap to wrap her arms about his waist as he enveloped her with his cloak.

Reaching beneath his doublet, he pulled out the amulet, removed it from his neck and put it around hers. "I thank you for the lending of this, but it belongs to you," he said quietly as he kissed her forehead.

"It kept you safe in battle."

He nodded. "And now I wish it to once again protect you." After a short pause, he asked, "When did you discover its likeness to my dagger?"

"After you were injured at Escomb." She related the history of the two tokens.

"Remarkable."

"Indeed. But there's more." When he quirked a brow in question, she continued. "I had a premonition that a man would change my life. The moment I saw you, I knew you were that man."

"Your mother brought us together, you know." At Alicen's startled look, Jeremy stated, "After the first battle. We were in Sherford to seek a physician, and I heard a voice say the area's finest healer lived at Landeyda. Later, when I questioned my men about who had directed us to you, no one knew what I spoke of. They'd heard nothing." He smiled. "She's remarkably persistent."

"That she is," Alicen said with a laugh. Looking into

his deep blue eyes, she saw his heart. "I love you, Jeremy," she whispered, just before laying her head on his shoulder.

"How came you to such a conclusion?" he asked, voice as quiet as hers.

Lifting her head, she leaned back to see his features. "I listened to my heart. My mind refused to accept your goodness, but my heart carried the day." Pausing briefly, she added, "Much as my body carries your child."

Jeremy went rigid, his arms tightening around her. "When?"

"The night before the attack on Escomb." At his sharp intake of breath, she captured his face in her hands. "I know what you believe, Sir Jeremy Blaine, yet you are mistaken. I came to you because I wished to. No other reason." She chuckled ruefully. "I even tried to prevent conception, but 'tis evident I failed." Her statement met with no response, and at Jeremy's continued silence, apprehension seized her. "Don't you desire this babe?" she finally managed to ask.

Jeremy's heart lurched at her vulnerable tone. "Don't you?" he countered softly.

"So much so it frightens me."

Gently, he drew her closer and kissed her forehead. "How long have you known?"

"I was certain a few days before you returned to Durham from the field."

"Yet you kept this secret."

Now Alicen grew tense. "I feared the news would distract you." She swallowed hard before adding, "And I wished you to love me for myself, not for a child I carried."

"I love you more than aught else," Jeremy vowed, burying his face in her hair. "Our babe will have a place in my heart, but the greater portion belongs to you alone."

Alicen felt her throat tighten as she stated, "If my love for you dies, I'll die with it. I will never stop loving you."

"Kiss me, minx."

A sudden breeze whirled around them.

'Twas destiny. Kaitlyn O'Rourke's voice filled both their minds. *You've each other now, and no need to fear the ghosts of the past. And you've love enough to defeat*

any foe.

"Well said, Mistress O'Rourke," Jeremy declared before he lowered his lips to Alicen's.

ABOUT THE AUTHOR

Laurie Carroll's first novel, *A War of Hearts*, was a Romance Writers of America Golden Heart finalist. She has been a member of RWA since 1988, but has been writing practically since she could hold a pencil.

A high school English teacher in West Michigan for twenty-one years, Laurie holds both a Bachelors degree in English and a Masters degree in telecommunications from Michigan State University.

She speaks to writers groups across the Midwest, often on her two favorite subjects—grammar and swearing, and has even spoken in New Zealand on American English.

Laurie is the primary line editor for ImaJinn Books and lists photography and travel as some of her hobbies.

She loves to hear from her readers. Write her at this address:

>Laurie Carroll
>P.O. Box 557
>Ada, MI 49301

Tired of mundane romance?

Dare to ImaJinn

Vampires, ghosts, shapeshifters, sorcerers, time-travelers, aliens, and more.

Somtimes Scary. Always Sexy!

Find ImaJinn books online at
www.imajinnbooks.com

For a free catalog, fill out the order form on the next page.

Please send me a free ImaJinn Books catalog.

Name_____

Address_____

_____

City_____

State and Zip Code_____

Mail to: ImaJinn Books
           P.O. Box 162
           Hickory Corners, MI 49060-0162

Or request a catalog by:

E-mail: catalog@imajinnbooks.com

Phone: 1-877-625-3592